Dave Tucker turned away from his sons' beds intending to return to his own. It was then that he saw the shape emerge from the shadows in the corner of the room. The shape of a man. Holding a gun.

"Hey, wha—"

"Shh," said the man. "If you make any noise, I'll kill you."

"W-who are you?" Dave Tucker whispered.

"You know me," said the man quietly. "You've known me all your life, ever since you were a child. Don't you recognize me?"

Dave Tucker shook his head.

"I'm the Boogeyman," the intruder said, and at that moment, D___ T___ ___s certain he w__

Another Fawcett Gold Medal title
By B. W. Battin

ANGEL OF THE NIGHT

The Boogey Man

B. W. Battin

FAWCETT GOLD MEDAL • NEW YORK

A Fawcett Gold Medal Book
Published by Ballantine Books

Copyright © 1984 by B.W. Battin

Library of Congress Catalog Card Number: 83-91250

ISBN 0-449-12411-8

Manufactured in the United States of America

First Ballantine Books Edition: April 1984

Prologue

The sight of the house terrified him. Tucked into a small grassy valley, it had never seemed threatening to him before. The white house was his home, a warm, friendly place where he could be snug on cold winter days, where he played with his dog, Bullet, planted his own small bed of vegetables each year, opened Christmas presents, hunted Easter eggs with his younger sister. But today home was a very scary place.

The reason was the sealed envelope in his pocket, a note from Mrs. Bagley, his sixth-grade teacher. A message he had been ordered to deliver to his parents, who had to sign it to prove he had shown it to them.

The walk from the school-bus stop was maybe half a mile. Usually he had Bobby Davis for company, but today Bobby had been sick. Playing sick, more likely. Bobby didn't like school very much, and his mother usually fell for it when he pretended to feel ill in the mornings. Mrs. Davis didn't seem to notice that Bobby always felt okay on the weekends and during the summers.

The house was still a quarter of a mile away or so. As Johnny Evans neared it, he found himself walking slower and slower. He had a pretty good idea what was in the note from Mrs. Bagley. It probably mentioned the black eye he'd given Freddy Grant. The dirty word he'd carved on his desk. The damage done to his science book when Ralph Hopewell had taken it away from him, thrown it into a mud puddle, and stomped on it. Johnny had tried to explain, but Mrs. Bagley had said it was his fault, because he was responsible for the book. Johnny had just been glad it was the book getting stomped and not him. Ralph Hopewell was *big*.

The boy sighed. It probably mentioned classwork too. He was always staring out the window instead of paying attention to

1

Mrs. Bagley. Well, Johnny thought, the stuff Old Lady Bagley talks about just isn't that interesting. She never talks about Pac-Man or *Star Wars* or anything like that. She talks about things like history, stuff that's not even happening anymore. Or about English, and nothing could be dumber than studying English when all the kids in the class already speak it perfectly.

An old yellow pickup was coming toward him. It was old Tom Wilson, who did yard work and stuff for the Davises. Wearing his customary battered straw hat, Tom honked and waved as he passed by, the old truck rattling as it made its way along the narrow paved road.

It was a pleasant November day, the weather still mild and not yet wintry. Directly ahead of him were the Rocky Mountains. They were really miles away, Johnny knew, but they looked close, as if he'd get there with just a few minutes of walking. It was nice out here, much nicer than living in the city, even if his dad did have a long drive to Denver and back each day. Johnny's family had moved here three years ago, when he was eight. When he'd lived in Denver, his dream had been to have a motorcycle someday; now it was to have a horse.

At this moment the thought of a horse depressed him. After his parents saw the note, there would be no horse, no motorcycle, no anything. He'd be lucky if he could still watch TV. He considered opening the note and signing it himself but immediately dismissed the idea. If he got caught, as he most likely would, he'd be in even bigger trouble than he was now.

In an effort to think about something else—anything else—he recalled that this was election day. His mother would have already voted; his dad would stop at the polls on his way home from work. But then Johnny's thoughts returned to the note in his pocket. He didn't care about the election. No matter who won, *his* life would be the same: bad.

Johnny ran his fingers through his thick brown hair. A thin boy, he was tall for an eleven-year-old, blue-eyed, fair-skinned. His mom kept telling him that he was handsome, that girls would really go for him someday. He worried that she'd say it when his friends were there and embarrass him. Why did mothers always have to say stuff like that?

Suddenly the answer to that question seemed very unimportant, because he'd just stepped into his driveway, its gravel crunching under his feet. He was home.

Feeling very small, insignificant, helpless, Johnny Evans moved steadily toward the big white house. To his right was the barn, also white. Although the place had a lot of land around it, it wasn't a farm and, according to Johnny's mother, had never been one. Johnny thought she was wrong; any place that came with a barn had to have been a farm at some time or another.

From within the structure came the sound of a dog barking. It was Bullet, apparently locked inside. Although Johnny's first impulse was to let him out, he checked himself. The dog had probably been put in there for bothering Mrs. Crawford's chickens again. If Bullet was being punished and Johnny let him out, it would just make things worse. With a sigh he headed for the front door.

Carefully closing the gate behind him, he stepped into the small picket-fence-enclosed front yard. The grass, receiving no water this late in the year, had turned brown; the flowers planted with such loving care in the spring were now withered stalks. Stepping onto the porch, he stopped in front of the door, suddenly feeling like a stranger here, as if he should knock. Johnny shook off the feeling, steeled himself, and stepped inside.

"It's me, Mom," he called, having decided to give her the note immediately and get it over with.

Receiving no answer, he called out again. Still no reply. Neither his mom nor his sister was here. He felt disappointed; he'd worked up the courage to do what had to be done, and now there was no one here to give the note to.

For a moment he stood in the middle of the living room, uncertain what to do. Finally he pulled off his coat and tossed it onto the couch. Immediately retrieving the garment, he looked around to make sure his mom wasn't standing behind him somewhere, watching. She always got mad when he left his coat in the living room, and this was no time to make her mad.

Where was she, anyway? It was unusual for her to be gone at this time of day; ordinarily she'd be in the kitchen, cooking. Had she gone somewhere and taken Michelle with her?

Empty, the house seemed kind of spooky. He could hear the muffled sounds of Bullet's barking. Poor dog wanted out of the barn. Feeling strangely ill at ease, Johnny began moving through the living room, heading toward the hall that led to his bedroom. Suddenly he stopped, convinced he'd heard a noise, like somebody breathing. He listened intently, hearing nothing, not even Bullet's barking. When he started moving again, the floor creaked under his weight, the noise seeming unnaturally loud in the stillness of the house.

And then he heard it again, more clearly this time. It sounded like a soft sob. And it had come from the kitchen. Suddenly he was mad.

"Come on, Michelle. Don't play stupid games. You can't fool me, anyway. You know that."

When there was no response, he dropped his coat on a chair and headed for the kitchen, determined to give his sister a piece of his mind. He had enough to worry about today without having his dumb kid sister playing stupid games with him. She usually got home ahead of him, because her school was closer than his. Their attending different schools had something to do with integration or segregation or whatever it was called.

"All right," he said angrily as he entered the large, modern kitchen, "what are you trying to prove, Michelle?"

His sister stood beside the dishwasher, staring up at him.

"Well," he demanded. And then he noticed how pale she looked, the tears running down her cheeks. She was trembling.

"It's okay, Michelle. I didn't mean to get mad. Honest."

The little girl just stared at him, shaking. She was eight, with Johnny's blue eyes and brown hair that was perhaps a shade lighter than his.

"Hey, Michelle, it's okay. Really. Stop crying."

He resisted the impulse to take her in his arms and comfort her. Such behavior was suitable for mothers, not older brothers. From behind him he heard the rustle of cloth. It had to be his mother, and now she'd find Michelle crying because he got mad at her. It would be just that much worse when he gave her the note from Mrs. Bagley.

As he turned to face his mother, he caught a glimpse of Michelle's eyes, which were riveted on something behind him. There was something in that look, something his mind didn't get a chance to assimilate because he found himself staring at a man he'd never seen before.

"Who are you?" He turned to Michelle. "What's this guy doing here?" And then, facing the man again, he saw the shotgun.

The note in his pocket forgotten, Johnny stared at the man, uncertain what was happening, what to do. Outside, Bullet barked, then fell silent. From behind him came his sister's voice, the words whispered so softly that Johnny could barely hear them:

"He . . . killed . . . Mommy."

1

Oh, Lord, Melissa James thought, what have I done? She was staring at the vote totals a young woman was marking on the blackboard. In yellow chalk, under the race for county sheriff, the figures read:

JAMES 11,634

RAINES 5,651

Cheers came from the other side of the room as some new vote totals were posted there. The room had been used as the party's county campaign office. For tonight most of the desks had been removed to make room for the milling party workers and candidates. At one end of the room, a microphone and podium had been installed; a bar occupied the other.

Again Melissa studied the vote totals. They hadn't changed in the last few seconds. No one had rushed to the board to erase the error, nor had a sudden surge of votes come in for the incumbent sheriff. It wasn't supposed to have worked out like this.

"Hey," a voice said behind her, "how does it feel to be the new sheriff of Ramsey County?"

Melissa turned to find herself facing Priscilla Stern, the person largely responsible for getting her into this mess. Like Melissa, she was in her mid-thirties, tall, and fairly slender. Unlike Melissa, she was a blond, who kept her hair very short. Melissa's was dark and shoulder length.

"Priscilla, I don't want to be the sheriff."

"I'm sure there'll be nothing to it." She smiled.

"Nothing to it? Priscilla, I know absolutely nothing about law enforcement. How can I be sheriff?"

"Certainly you know something about law enforcement. You organized that neighbrhood crime watch when you lived in Denver, didn't you?"

"That hardly qualifies me to be sheriff."

Glancing around the room, Priscilla was obviously looking for an excuse to end the conversation. For her, things had to be positive, upbeat; when they weren't, Priscilla disappeared.

"Don't be such a worrywart," she said, putting her hand on Melissa's shoulder. "Being sheriff is just a political job. You know, you handle public relations and things like that. They have professionals to actually catch the crooks."

"You promised there would be no chance I'd actually get elected."

Priscilla frowned. "Well, how was I to know there would be such a scandal right before the election? Until now Raines has always been unbeatable; you know that."

Why, Melissa wondered, couldn't the grand jury have waited until *after* the election to find out Raines was a crook?

Dropping her hand from Melissa's shoulder, Priscilla again glanced behind her. "Oh, there's Al Crenshaw. I've got to catch him before he leaves. Now, don't be upset about anything, Melissa. You won; it should make you happy. Enjoy your victory." She disappeared into the crowd.

Melissa once more turned her attention to the vote totals, which were unchanged from the last time she'd checked them. She had neither an interest in politics nor the need of a job. A widow, she and her two children had been living quietly and comfortably on the money left by her late husband. Jim's insurance policies had paid off the house and even provided her with a monthly income. So how did I get into this mess? she wondered. And then she recalled. It had begun over a card game.

She, Priscilla, Joyce, and Sheila had been playing their weekly game of bridge. Priscilla and Joyce, who were politically active, were complaining about their party's lack of a sheriff candidate in the upcoming election. No one would run, because Raines was unbeatable. He'd be unopposed; their party would be represented by a blank on the ballot in the sheriff's contest. It was Joyce who'd come up with the idea. Why not use Melissa? Of course, Priscilla had said, delighted with the suggestion. You wouldn't even have to campaign. Just lend us your name. That's not too much to ask, is it?

Reluctantly, Melissa had agreed. It seemed a small favor, just her name on the ballot. And she hadn't campaigned. She hadn't made a single speech. She had no campaign committee to raise funds. She hadn't even planned to go to the polls today, although she did, as it turned out. So she could vote for Raines.

When the scandal broke, everything changed. The Denver newspapers and TV stations, usually unconcerned with the affairs of suburban Ramsey County, had come in droves. Within a week after Raines's indictment, Melissa had been on the newscasts of three Denver TV stations and quoted by the city's two major papers. She hadn't really said anything; she'd just expressed her dismay that such a thing could happen. And she'd worried. A sheriff who'd just been indicted for a number of offenses, including taking bribes, was no longer unbeatable.

She recalled the neighborhood crime watch she'd organized. It had been before the kids were born, before Jim began to rise in the company. They'd been living in the city then, in a fairly typical middle-class neighborhood that was suffering more than its share of burglaries. Although Melissa's house was never broken into, most of the neighbors' had been. The problem was so bad that you couldn't leave your home without worrying about how many of your belongings might be missing when you returned. Residents of the area complained about the permissiveness of society and the overly lenient courts. Some armed themselves, and that was what prompted Melissa to take action, the fear that her neighbors would start shooting pets, children, and one another.

With the cooperation of the Denver Police Department, she set out to organize a neighborhood crime watch. She had handbills printed and sent news releases to the Denver media. Within a month two people were patrolling the neighborhood by car twenty-four hours a day. Armed with a walkie-talkie, they were in contact with a third volunteer, who would phone the police should the two on patrol spot anything suspicious. It wasn't the job of the crime-watch volunteers to apprehend suspects, merely to watch and report.

In addition to coordinating the effort, Melissa had spent many hours on patrol, often filling in when no one else was available. She'd learned what to look for—how to recognize a burglary in progress or a situation that was an open invitation to criminals—and she'd learned some things about the law, in part through the periodic lectures given her group by the Denver Police Department's community relations office.

The program had been a tremendous success. The number of burglaries in the neighborhood dropped off sharply, transforming the area into one of the most crime-free sections of the city. The police chief had given Melissa an official-looking certificate of appreciation.

Melissa sighed. It had been an interesting, rewarding experience. And it was woefully inadequate training for a sheriff.

"Melissa! Where's Melissa?"

She turned to find Steve Menton hurrying toward her. A bald man, he was about forty, a hardware store owner, and the party's county chairman. He was grinning.

"Raines has conceded," Menton said breathlessly.

Melissa nodded.

"Come on," Menton said, taking her arm. "You're the first confirmed victory of the evening. We've got to announce it."

Melissa allowed herself to be led to the podium. Menton switched on the microphone, then tapped it and blew into it, only to discover it wasn't working. Finally he just shouted.

"Hey, everybody, listen up! Sheriff Raines has conceded!"

The announcement was greeted with cheers and applause.

"I give you Melissa James, sheriff-elect of Ramsey County!"

After the clapping and shouting died down, Melissa waved and smiled, then left the podium. She had absolutely nothing to say. She wanted to go home.

As she usually did, Melissa awoke groggy, sleep giving up its hold on her reluctantly. She rolled over, reaching for Jim, and only after finding nothing but the smooth coolness of the sheets did she realize that he couldn't be here. He'd been dead for more than three years.

She was over it now and had been for quite some time. Her grief having spent itself, she'd done what all well-adjusted people do: She'd gotten back to the business of living. The vice-president of a company that made computer chips, he'd been under constant pressure. Too much pressure, apparently. The heart attack had come when he was forty-one.

A tear trickled down her cheek, and she wiped it away. It still hurt only when she awoke like this, her mind befogged by sleep, and reached for the familiar body that was no longer there.

Flipping the covers aside, she dropped her legs over the edge of the bed. As she sat there, staring sleepily at her feet, a new realization came over her. She was the sheriff-elect of Ramsey County. It had not been a bad dream. She was about to become the chief of a law enforcement agency of . . . of how many officers? Melissa had no idea. Nor did she know what the department's budget was, what equipment it needed, what training its personnel required. Please, God, she thought. Let it be a mistake. I don't want to be sheriff.

She rose, slipping on her robe, and went to wake the children. "Rise and shine!" she called, sticking her head into her son's room.

The lump under the covers didn't budge. Billy was like his mother, definitely not a morning person.

"Hey, Billy James! Up! Now!"

The lump stirred and emitted a groan.

"If you don't hit it in three seconds, I'm coming over there and tickling you awake."

The threat did it. The eight-year-old was instantly sitting up, his feet on the floor, staring sleepily at the blue carpet. Dark-haired and a little on the chubby side, Billy had his father's round face and the same cheerful smile. In fact the only trait he clearly got from his mother was his dislike of mornings.

Leaving him to get moving at his own pace, Melissa crossed the hall to Sarah's room and opened the door. Fully dressed, the girl was sitting on the bed, putting on her shoes.

"Mother!" she said with exaggerated exasperation. "I wish you'd knock."

At eleven Sarah had reached the age at which privacy, even from her mother, was becoming important. She was tall and slender like her mother and had Melissa's turned-up nose. As was the rest of the clan, Sarah was dark-haired. She was most like her father in her ability to wake up instantly, all traces of sleep gone—a trait certainly not shared with her mother or brother.

"Want to help with breakfast?" Melissa asked.

"Sure. What do you want me to do?"

"Instead of cereal, let's have bacon and eggs this morning. You cook one, and I'll cook the other."

"I'll take the eggs."

"You've got 'em. Let's go."

As they started down the hall, Sarah stopped her. "Mother," she said, again sounding exasperated, "you never told me."

"Told you what?"

"About last night. Linda Sue made us go to bed before any of the election results were in." Linda Sue Jennings was her regular baby-sitter, a teenage girl who lived down the block.

Melissa sighed. "I won."

Sarah's eyes widened. "You mean . . . you mean you're the sheriff?"

"I'm the sheriff-elect. I don't actually become sheriff until sometime in January, I think."

Her daughter simply stared at her in disbelief. "*You're* the sheriff?"

"Me. I'm the sheriff."

"Wow!"

As they walked toward the kitchen, Melissa's daughter was silent, although her mind was obviously working furiously, apparently trying to figure out just what impact this would have on their lives. Melissa realized her election would have to be at least somewhat of a surprise to the children. They'd known she was running, of course, but she'd made it clear that her winning the election was quite unlikely, that she was really a candidate in name only. Then, when the scandal broke, she hadn't said much about the sudden change in her chances for victory, feeling, she supposed, that to speak of the unthinkable would somehow give it credibility, make it more likely to happen.

In the kitchen Melissa started the coffee perking and the bacon frying while Sarah set the table. The kitchen was large and modern, with all the latest appliances and a no-wax floor that looked like Mexican ceramic tile but wasn't. Though only one story, the house was large: four bedrooms, a den, a two-car garage, a big patio out back. It shared the block with similar houses, brick-faced modern homes belonging to corporate vice-presidents, doctors, and the like, people who were well-off but not wealthy. Melissa had always liked this house. It had a pleasant, relaxed atmosphere about it. It was warm, cozy, a home.

She was turning the bacon when Billy walked in. Sarah, realizing this was her cue, got the eggs from the refrigerator.

"How do you want yours?" Sarah asked her brother, who had just seated himself at the big wooden breakfast table.

"My what?" he asked, sleepily staring at his place mat.

Sarah sighed, giving her brother an exaggerated look of disgust. "Your eggs, of course."

"Scrambled," he replied without looking up.

"Well, I'm having mine poached on toast." When Billy showed no interest in how his sister ate her eggs, she turned to Melissa. "How about you, Mom?"

"Poached on toast would be nice."

Sarah looked at her triumphantly, as if Melissa had just taken her side in some truly earthshaking matter. Setting the eggs on the counter, she got the poacher from the cabinet below the built-in stove.

Turning down the burner under the bacon, Melissa took a pitcher of orange juice from the refrigerator and filled three glasses. Billy simply stared at his.

"Did you tell him?" Sarah asked as she carefully broke an egg into one of the poacher's cups.

"Tell me what?" Billy demanded, suddenly coming to life.

"Mom won."

The boy frowned, traces of sleep still lingering in his expression. "Won what?"

"What do you think, noodlehead?"

"She means," Melissa said, "that I was elected."

"Oh, boy!" Billy exclaimed, excitement spreading across his face. "When can I go for a ride in a police car—I mean a sheriff's car?"

"I don't know, honey." Hell, Melissa thought, I'm not even sure what color they are. She tried to picture one and couldn't.

"Will you wear a uniform? Will you have a gun? Boy, I sure hope you can take me to school in a sheriff's car."

"I don't take you to school now. Why would I start just because I'm the sheriff?"

Billy looked crestfallen. "But Mom, you'd have to! Boy, if Ronnie Jones could only see me come rollin' up in a sheriff's car. You've got to. At least once, Mom."

Melissa was rescued by the ringing of the phone. Sarah, who was closest to the wall-mounted Trimline, answered it. "Oh, okay. How are you? Uh-huh. Just a sec." Stretching the cord, she handed the receiver to her mother. "It's Keith."

Keith Adamson was the man Melissa had been going out with the past few months. An attorney, he was forty-five and like Melissa had suffered through the loss of a spouse, his wife having died of cancer a few years ago. Lately the relationship had been getting serious. Although no firm commitments had been made, the subject of marriage had come up more than once.

"Hi," Melissa said, taking the phone from her daughter. She tucked it between her ear and shoulder and began laying the bacon on a paper towel to drain.

"I heard what happened," he said solemnly. "What are you going to do?"

"I've been thinking about skipping town. Is there a law against flight to avoid assuming public office?"

Keith laughed. "I don't think you'll have to go that far. Just let the people who know what they're doing run things. If you just put in an appearance from time to time, you'll probably be doing all that's required of you."

That was probably good advice. Still, something in Keith's words irked her. It was as if she were being told: Stay home, little housewife; it's the real world out there, too tough for the likes of you. "That's not what I was elected to do, Keith. I was elected to be the sheriff. I at least have to try, don't I?"

"Listen," Keith said gently, "I don't want you to be hurt by this, but you've got to remember that people really weren't voting for you; they were ousting a crook, getting rid of a jerk who didn't deserve the office. No matter who ran against him, the result probably would have been the same."

"That's true," Melissa admitted. "I'll certainly never convince anyone I was elected because of my stunning qualifications. Even so, I am the sheriff—or at least I will be—and I'm going to have to figure out how to handle this thing."

"The senior officer down there is Captain Pruitt. I think he's got close to thirty years in law enforcement, most of it with Ramsey County. Why don't you drop by and see him? I'm sure he'll be glad to show you around and tell you a lot of what you'll need to know."

"How do I know he wasn't one of the crooks?"

"Chuck Pruitt? I've known him for years. He's entirely honest. Besides, as far as the grand jury could determine, Raines was acting alone; no one else in the department knew what he was doing."

Fully aware of just how unprepared she was to step in and clean up a corrupt police force, Melissa hoped the grand jury was right.

"I'm sorry I couldn't be with you last night," Keith said, "but I really did need to finish preparing for trial in federal court this morning. And speaking of court this morning, I have to go or I'll be running late. If you get a chance, stop by and see Chuck Pruitt."

Melissa said she would. When she hung up, Sarah had everyone's eggs ready. Melissa added bacon to the plates; then the two cooks joined Billy at the breakfast table.

"Who was that?" the boy asked.

"Who do you think it was?" Sarah asked, her tone making it clear she thought Billy was pretty dumb if he didn't know who his mother had been speaking to.

"It was Keith, Billy," Melissa said.

"I said it was him when I answered the phone," Sarah told her brother. "You were sitting right here."

Billy ignored her. "When's he going to take me to see the Broncos again?"

"I don't know," Melissa replied. "You'll have to ask him."

Studying her two children as they ate, Melissa wondered how they'd react if she and Keith decided to get married. So far, at least, they hadn't seemed to resent him. But then going out together wasn't marriage. Billy would adapt all right, she decided. Ever since Keith had taken him to that football game, the boy had been ready to adopt him. If there was going to be a problem, it would be Sarah, who was older, remembered her father better.

Still, if anyone could pull it off, it would be Keith, who seemed to have a real way with kids. Because his wife had been incapable of conceiving and unwilling to adopt, he had none of his own, which had been one of the major disappointments in his life. That he'd make a good father for Billy and Sarah was unquestionable.

But did they really need a father? She and the kids seemed to be getting along just fine as a threesome. Introducing a fourth person could just complicate things. Sarah, it seemed, would gain very little from it. Melissa watched her daughter take a bite of poached egg. The girl's dark hair was straight and thick, cut fairly short. The freckles she'd had in abundance as a toddler were nearly all gone now, and her face, though still clearly that of a child, was changing. Soon would come menstruation, breast development, and then the rapid transformation into womanhood. These were not the sort of things a father could help with; these were mother-daughter things.

But then there was Billy, bigger-boned than his sister, a little athlete who loved all kinds of sports. He played baseball, basketball, football, soccer, volleyball, and no doubt others of which Melissa was unaware. When it came to athletics, Melissa could be no help. The only sport she'd ever liked enough to play was softball, and she hadn't done that since she was a teenager. Nor was she likely to take Billy to see the Broncos play, since she considered sitting through a football game a thoroughly unrewarding way to spend a Sunday afternoon.

It would be nice if Billy had a father, she decided. But not necessary. The boy could play all the games he cared to now. The only thing he lacked was someone to take him to the professional sports events in Denver from time to time. Surely other people in the neighborhood attended games in Denver; she could arrange for Billy to go with them. But that wasn't really the same thing as having a father, was it?

Of course, she was overlooking one extremely important aspect of all this. How did *she* feel about marrying Keith? Before Melissa could deal with that question, the phone rang. Reaching around Billy, she answered it.

"Melissa, it's me, Steve Menton," said the county chairman of her party. "I have some news that will surprise you. Raines has resigned as sheriff."

"That's probably just as well."

"Don't you know what it means?"

"The county's rid of a crooked sheriff two months sooner than expected."

"Don't you know who becomes sheriff?"

"You mean who finishes out his term? No, who?"

"According to the laws of the county, if an incumbent resigns after losing an election, the sheriff-elect takes over immediately."

Stunned, Melissa said: "You mean I'm it? Now? Today?" Billy and Sarah were staring at her.

"You're the sheriff. Well, there's the matter of having you sworn in. I called Judge Hawthorne at home, and he'll do it this morning at ten in his chambers."

"I . . ." She didn't know what to say.

"Be there at ten, okay? And congratulations. After ten o'clock, you'll be Sheriff Melissa James. How does that sound?"

"Uh, well, I think it will take a little getting used to."

When she hung up, she found her children looking at her expectantly. "Everything okay, Mom?" Sarah asked.

Still in somewhat of a daze, Melissa said: "I have to start being sheriff a little sooner than expected. They're swearing me in this morning."

"Oh, boy!" Billy exclaimed. "Will you come home in a sheriff's car? One with red lights on top?"

"I don't know, Billy. I haven't been a sheriff before. Now,

15

you hurry up and brush your teeth and get ready for school. I don't want you to miss the bus.''

The boy quickly left the table.

''You too, Sarah.''

''We've got some time,'' the girl replied. ''You want me to do the dishes?''

''No, I'll do them, but thank you for the offer. Go on and get ready.'' Sarah, too, left the kitchen.

While Melissa had been on the phone, her breakfast had gotten cold. She pushed the half-eaten meal away from her, feeling weak and afraid.

2

Trying to concentrate on where she was going and not what would happen when she got there, Melissa drove her compact station wagon along the wide divided street. Once, this had been rolling ranchland, but the cattle had long since been replaced by suburbia. Homes and more homes, trees, lawns, backyard barbecues, dogs, tricycles, plastic swimming pools.

She was headed for Rockland, the county seat, a small town that was indistinguishable from the surrounding urban sprawl. Melissa presumed it had been a separate little community at one time, before metropolitan Denver swallowed it up.

It was a mild day for early November, sunny and pleasant. She came to a spot where neighborhood streets paralleled the one on which she was driving, a chain link fence separating them from the thoroughfare. Ahead were some three- and four-story apartment buildings. She was getting closer to the city.

After stopping at a red light, she turned left, passing more homes and a small shopping center. Driving slowly, she looked for a building that appeared governmental. Melissa had never been to the Ramsey County Courthouse before; she'd had to look up its address in the phone book. On her right was an unimposing white building that appeared to be what she sought. It had a flagpole from which the U.S. and Colorado flags were flying.

Unable to spot a parking place, she turned the corner. Across the street was a house that had been converted into the office of a bail bondsman. The side entrance to the courthouse had a sign above it that said Sheriff. A number of patrol cars—white with gold stars on their doors—were parked in a small paved lot adjacent to the building. At least she knew what they looked like now.

And then a sign attached to the wall of the courthouse caught her attention. It said:

RESERVED

SHERIFF

Why not, Melissa decided as she pulled into the lot and headed for the vacant parking space. I'm certainly entitled.

Not wanting to enter through the sheriff's department, she walked around to the front of the building. The courthouse's interior turned out to be as utilitarian as its white stucco exterior. The small lobby had beige painted walls and a tile floor that would have been at home in a supermarket. The directory informed her that Judge Thomas Hawthorne's chambers were on the second floor. She took the elevator.

On the second floor Melissa followed a hallway that led her past a courtroom in which a trial was obviously in progress. As the door opened and a man stepped out, she heard someone within saying something about a defendant. The people sitting on the wooden benches that lined both sides of the corridor watched as she approached. On one side of the hallway was a fat woman with pimples on her face; on the other were two unsavory-looking men in rumpled clothes, one of whom took in every inch of Melissa as she walked by. She was sure that in the few moments it took to pass him, she had been undressed, fondled, and maybe even raped in the man's mind. It made her want to grab something and strike him with it. She walked faster, hoping to get out of his sight as quickly as possible.

Ahead the hallway turned to the right. As soon as she rounded the corner, she saw a sign saying Judge Thomas Hawthorne, District Court. In the outer office Melissa found a young woman busily typing.

"Yes?" the woman said, looking up from her typewriter. She was blond, attractive, in her mid-twenties.

"I'm Melissa James. Judge Hawthorne's expecting me."

"Right," the woman said, appraising Melissa more carefully now. "The swearing-in ceremony. How does it feel to be the new sheriff of Ramsey County?"

"Scary," Melissa said truthfully.

The woman smiled. "I'm sure it won't be as bad as you think. The anticipation of something is usually worse than the event itself."

Fine, Melissa thought. You be sheriff.

The woman picked up her phone. "Mrs. James is here, Judge." Replacing the receiver, she said: "He'll be right out."

The judge appeared a moment later. Dressed in his judicial robes, he was a short man with gray hair and stern blue eyes. Smiling, he extended his hand. "Mrs. James, I'm Judge Hawthorne. Congratulations for winning the election."

"Thank you," Melissa said, accepting the judge's hand.

He stepped to a door in the side wall of the office. "If you'll come in here, we'll get you sworn in."

Following the judge, Melissa found herself in a courtroom. Media people occupied the front row of seats. Having suddenly become newsworthy when the incumbent sheriff was indicted, she had met quite a few news people. The familiar faces included a photographer from channel seven, a reporter from channel nine, another from the *Denver Post*.

Logically she understood the presence of the reporters. The unexpected resignation of the discredited sheriff would be news; so would the hastily arranged swearing-in of his successor. Still, the whole thing seemed unreal. The media covered *other* people. There was something inherently wrong with her being *on* the six o'clock news, *in* the *Rocky Mountain News* or *Denver Post*. In the natural order of things, she read and watched the news, listened to it on the radio, but she didn't participate in it.

The judge led her to a position in front of the bench, and then everything seemed to happen at once. A woman joined them, holding a Bible in front of Melissa.

"Put your hand on the Bible, please," the judge said. As Melissa did so, the TV lights came on; from the corner of her eye, she saw a man with a camera on his shoulder move into position.

"Repeat after me," the judge said. "I, Melissa James . . ." As cameras clicked and TV photographers moved to get the scene from different angles, Melissa promised to uphold the laws of Ramsey County and the State of Colorado, to defend the Constitution of the United States, and to execute the duties of her office to the best of her abilities.

"Congratulations," Judge Hawthorne said when the oath had been concluded. He took her hand, shaking it a little longer than was customary, apparently for the benefit of the photographers.

"Good luck," the judge said warmly. With that, he turned and headed for his chambers. The woman with the Bible had vanished. The TV lights were switched off, and the crews began packing away their gear.

"Do you have any major changes in mind?" a voice beside her asked.

Melissa turned to find herself facing the reporter from the *Denver Post*, a tall woman with cascading light-brown hair. She was unable to recall the reporter's name.

"I've only been sheriff about a minute," Melissa said. "I won't know what I'm going to do until I've had a chance to familiarize myself with things."

"Do you have any plans for eliminating corruption in the department?" The woman held a notebook and pen, ready to record whatever was said.

Melissa hesitated, trying to sort out her thoughts. Finally she said: "Uh, the grand jury didn't indicate any widespread corruption in the department. It just named Sheriff Raines, as an individual. Of course, we always have to be on our guard, to . . . uh, to make sure our professional and ethical standards are the highest."

Melissa studied the reporter's face, hoping for some indication of how well she'd answered the question. Revealing nothing, the woman closed her notebook and smiled politely. "Thanks," she said.

Melissa wanted to faint. She started toward the door, hoping no other reporters were interested in talking to her. A man in a khaki uniform intercepted her.

"Mrs. James?" He was about fifty, tall and wiry, with thin gray hair.

"Yes."

"Hi, I'm Captain Pruitt. If you're ready, I'll take you downstairs and show you around."

Melissa felt relief flooding over her. At least she wouldn't have to walk alone into the sheriff's office and try to explain who she was. "Thank you, Captain," she said. "Thank you very much."

The sheriff's department occupied a fairly large chunk of the first floor. Pruitt led her down a long hallway lined with offices, pointing out things like the detective division and property room and shift commander's office.

"Actually, I'm the shift commander on day shift," he explained, "so no one uses that office except on swing and graveyard shifts."

Melissa nodded. The walls throughout this part of the building were a light green; the floors were covered with supermarket-type tiles similar to those in the rest of the courthouse.

"This is my office here," Pruitt said, indicating a closed door to the right. "Across the hall here is yours." He pushed open the door and ushered Melissa inside.

Though hardly plush, it was clearly the boss's office. It was larger than any of the others she'd seen and had a big wooden desk instead of the usual gray metal one. Behind the desk were the U.S. flag and the blue and white Colorado banner with its red *C* and gold ball. The walls were bare; whatever Sheriff Raines had hung there had been removed. The place had been stripped of those little touches that made it her predecessor's; now it was ready for the things that would make it hers.

"This is for you," the captain said, opening the middle desk drawer. He handed her a black ID holder, which she recognized from having seen numerous cop shows on TV.

Melissa opened it, finding a gold star-shaped badge pinned on one side and a card on the other. It said that the person to whom it had been issued was a sworn officer of the law in Ramsey County, Colorado, and identified her as Melissa James, sheriff.

"I'll have to get a photograph of you and fill in your height, weight, date of birth, and that sort of thing." He gave her an apologetic look. "We can take a Polaroid at the booking desk, get this laminated, and it'll be ready by noon."

"Thank you," she said, handing it back to him.

"If you want a uniform or a gun, you'll have to provide them yourself," the captain said. "It's that way for all the officers. The department pays a side arm and uniform allowance. The only weapons we provide are shotguns and sniper rifles. Uh, if you do decide to carry a weapon, department regulations specify a thirty-eight."

Melissa had no intention of wearing a uniform or carrying a gun. She wondered whether regulations concerning things like firearms were at the discretion of the sheriff, but didn't ask.

The next stop on the tour was the booking desk, where Pruitt took her photo. Although no number hung from her neck, Melissa thought the tense, unsmiling face in the picture could easily be that of a just-apprehended felon. She considered asking the captain to take another but, afraid of appearing vain, discarded the idea.

"This," Pruitt said, indicating a large cage made of chain link fencing, "is just for temporary holding. If we bring in, say, three or four prisoners at one time, we need somewhere to put the ones waiting for processing. Once they're printed, photographed, and the paperwork's done, they go upstairs to the county jail."

As they walked on, Melissa asked: "Where is everyone? I've only seen about three people since you brought me down here."

"Well, they're all out, doing their jobs. We're too small to have a whole lot of support personnel. We don't have a lab or an accident-investigation unit or a public relations department or anything like that."

As they started down another hallway, a door opened, and a khaki-uniformed officer stepped out. "Morning, Captain," he said as he approached. "Just took a prisoner up. Stopped him on a traffic violation, and he came back a hit on the computer check. Two warrants for signal fives out in Rocky View Estates.''

The officer was in his thirties, chunky, with thick blond hair. His eyes found Melissa's, then returned to Pruitt's, apparently asking an unspoken question.

"Uh, this is Mrs. James, the new sheriff," the captain said. "Mrs. James, this is Sergeant Nelson."

For a moment the sergeant eyed her with undisguised contempt. Then he nodded once and strode off toward the booking desk.

The hint of a frown appeared on Pruitt's face, quickly replaced by a reassuring smile. "Come on," he said. "I'll show you the communications center."

Arriving there, Melissa decided the term communications center was a little grandiose. It was a small room with maps of metro Denver and Ramsey County on the wall, what looked like a small computer, and a young woman wearing a headset. She sat at a small table that held a call director and what Melissa assumed was a two-way radio.

"Ten-four, three-Edward," she said. "The highway department's been notified." She wrote something on a large pad.

"Put it on speaker," the captain said. Glancing over her shoulder, the woman flipped a switch on the radio. Dressed in a khaki uniform, she had short red hair and freckles.

"Three-Edward to control," said a man's voice over the speaker.

"Go ahead, three-Edward," said the red-haired woman.

"Advise the highway department that they better get out here quick. Drivers don't see this thing until the last second, and then they swerve into the other lane to miss it. There's going to be a forty-five here if it isn't fixed."

"Ten-four, three-Edward."

"What's that about?" Melissa asked as the captain reached over and flipped the switch that cut off the speaker.

"Sounds like there's a big pothole somewhere, and we're trying to get a highway repair crew out there to fix it. That's the sort of thing we spend most of our time doing. That and having cars towed when they're blocking driveways." He smiled.

Though still using her headset, the red-haired woman was now

22

obviously talking over the phone, presumably to someone at the highway department.

"What's a forty-five?" Melissa asked.

"That's an accident with injuries. The officer was saying that he was afraid there would be a serious accident, that somebody might get hurt."

"Is that a computer?" Melissa asked, pointing at a machine that looked like a typewriter keyboard with a TV screen mounted above it.

"That's just a terminal. The computer's in Denver. You can put, say, a name or license plate number or the serial number of a gun into the machine, and it will tell you if the person's wanted, the gun's been reported stolen, whatever. It's tied in with Denver PD and other law enforcement agencies in the area.

"A lot of important things happen in this room," the captain went on. "Every time an officer is given a call, arrives at the scene, gets out of his car or back into it, it's logged. That way if a man leaves his car for any reason and then we don't hear from him for a while, we know that he might be in trouble and where to look for him. If you've ever phoned us to report an accident or a crime, this is where your call came in."

Pruitt guided her out of the radio room and down a hallway. Almost immediately she was back in her office. The captain stopped at the doorway.

"Well, I'm going to leave you to get things in order here in your office or whatever else you might need to do," he said. "If you need anything, either stick your head out the door and holler or dial extension twenty-seven. If neither of those works, call radio and see if I'm logged out somewhere." He grinned.

"Thank you for showing me around. And for meeting me in the courtroom. I really do appreciate it."

"It's the least I could do. Besides, Keith Adamson called me this morning and asked me to do what I could to help you out. Of course, at the time we didn't know you'd be sworn in as sheriff quite this soon."

Pruitt left her, and Melissa sat down behind her desk. She'd been a little surprised to learn that Keith had called the captain. Somehow it seemed only a step or two removed from having your mother call the principal, asking that little Johnny be given special attention.

Of course, that *was* her situation. It was like the first day of school. She was like a little girl in need of someone to take her by the hand and lead her around. But then in school the children weren't alone; they were a group. You were part of a collective in which you could hide, become just another face among the many. And your status was strictly subordinate. The teachers made all the decisions, told you what to do.

But now there was no group in which to hide. And there was no one to tell her what to do, for she was in charge; she was the teacher.

Sitting here at the sheriff's desk, she felt like a trespasser, the subordinate who, even though fearful of getting caught, tries the boss's chair just to see what it's like. But the desk was hers, as was the office with its U.S. and Colorado flags, its bare walls awaiting her personal touches. Regardless of their reasons, the voters had put her here, in charge, her authority established by law.

Hearing footsteps in the hallway, she tensed. A khaki-clad man walked past her open doorway, glancing in her direction and then quickly looking away before their eyes could meet. What would I do, she wondered, if someone came in and asked me to make a decision about something important? The thought terrified her.

Just before noon a young woman in civilian clothes brought Melissa her newly laminated ID card, saying Captain Pruitt had asked her to deliver it as soon as it was ready.

After the woman had left, Melissa resumed what she'd been doing since Captain Pruitt showed her around: sitting at her desk, wondering what to do next. Looking in the desk, she had found some keys, official stationery, and a pair of handcuffs. Behind her on a small table was a monitor that allowed her to hear the department's radio traffic. After listening to it for a few minutes, she'd switched it off, bewildered. Officers were ten-eight or ten-nineteen, or looking into a signal five or a signal seven or a ten-forty-four. She had no idea what it all meant.

It was lunchtime, and Melissa had no idea what she was

supposed to do. Did she check out with someone, leave word where she could be reached? Or did she just leave? It certainly seemed unlikely that she'd be missed.

The phone rang, startling her. She stared at it dumbly for a moment, as if uncertain whether to answer someone else's telephone; then she realized that the phone was hers, that everyone in the department must know who was occupying this office, that the call had to be for her. She lifted the receiver.

"Sheriff James, this is Marla in radio. Sergeant Nelson is requesting your assistance on a signal one." She gave an address, which Melissa copied down.

"Uh, all right. Tell him I'm on my way."

"Ten-four," Marla replied, quickly breaking the connection.

Grabbing her purse, Melissa started for the door, wishing she'd asked the woman what a signal one was. Suddenly she realized that she had no idea how she was supposed to get there. Did she take a patrol car? Uncertain whether she could even drive one, she shuddered at the thought. Still, she didn't want to appear any more ignorant than she had to. If there was a special car she was supposed to use, one for the sheriff, then she should take it.

On the verge of panic, Melissa hurried across the hall and into Captain Pruitt's office, which was empty. All right, she thought, he said radio would know where he was. But Melissa had no idea what radio's extension was. Returning to the hallway, she realized that she wasn't even sure *where* radio was. She'd become turned around during her tour of the building and doubted she could find anything she'd seen without hunting for it.

Come on, she told herself, forget all this nonsense about what car you're supposed to use. You can find your way out of the building and you can find your own car. For the moment, that's all you have to do. She hurried down the hallway.

Slowing her compact station wagon, Melissa looked for the turnoff. Both city and country people lived here, the spot being on the outer fringes of Denver's urban area. The homes were large and far apart, sometimes with small farms separating them. People living out here and working in the city spent a lot of time driving each day. Ahead was her turnoff. When she reached it, Melissa turned right, in the direction of the mountains.

She had driven about half a mile when she spotted the patrol cars, parked in front of a large white house. Turning into the drive, she noticed the big white barn and wondered whether the place might have been a farm at one time. As she pulled to a stop, an officer wearing sheriff's department khaki stepped briskly up to her car.

"May I ask what you're doing here, ma'am?" He was blond with blue eyes, in his early twenties.

"I was called," she said, feeling intimidated by the uniform and unable to accept that she was this man's boss.

"Called?" He frowned.

"Sergeant Nelson called me. I'm the . . . wait a minute." As she reached for her purse, the young deputy tensed, his hand moving closer to his holster. "I'm just going to show you my identification," she said quickly, noticing for the first time just how tense the young man seemed to be. Her own anxiety deepened. What's going on here? she wondered.

Melissa handed the deputy her identification. When he examined it, the surprise on his face was obvious. "I'm sorry, ma'am, but I didn't know who you were. I've never seen you before." He stepped away from the car so she'd have room to open the door.

Melissa told him not to worry, noting that this was the first person who'd shown her any deference because of her position. Finding the front door of the house ajar, she pushed it open and stepped into a large living room furnished mainly with antiques. From another part of the house, she heard voices. To her left was a stairway. They were coming from up there. Gripping the banister, she headed toward the voices.

"Where is everybody?" she called as she reached the top step.

Captain Pruitt appeared from a door to her right, making no effort to conceal his surprise at finding her here. "We've got things under control," he said. "There was really no need for you to come to the scene."

"I was asked to come," Melissa replied. Through the open

doorway behind the captain, she could see an antique dresser, the corner of a brass bed.

"I asked her to come," Sergeant Nelson said, stepping out of the room. "Something this big requires the sheriff's personal attention. At least," he added, "it always before."

Again that hint of a frown appeared on Captain Pruitt's face.

"There's two in here and two downstairs in the kitchen," Nelson said. "Goldman's dusting down there now."

Melissa nodded, uncertain what she was supposed to do. She recalled the look of contempt Nelson had given her when they first met. Now his expression seemed vaguely cocky. She decided she disliked this man.

"In here," the sergeant said, stepping into the bedroom.

Captain Pruitt, looking resigned, stepped back from the doorway. Unsure what she would find, Melissa entered the room. Instantly her eyes were drawn to the bed, fixing on the horror she saw there. Though she wanted desperately to look away, she seemed unable to turn her head.

The center of the bed was a bloody mess, and part of that gore was two lumps, the bodies of two adult human beings, a man and a woman. At least Melissa thought it was a man and a woman; their features had been obliterated.

"Used a shotgun," Nelson said. "Pretty much blew their faces away."

His voice seemed to be coming from a long way off. The room was swirling. Suddenly Melissa realized she was about to collapse or get sick, or maybe both. She couldn't let herself do that, not in front of these men. Especially not in front of Sergeant Nelson, whose motives in summoning her here were becoming clear. Fighting nausea and dizziness, she turned, faced the sergeant, met his gaze, and held it.

"Do you have any idea who did it?" she asked calmly.

The sergeant studied her a moment, a little of the cockiness gone from his expression. "No suspects at this time. But the killer left us a message. It's in the kitchen."

Realizing she had more to face, Melissa walked out of the room and headed down the stairs, only willpower keeping her stomach under control. Unable to be a true leader, to tell the captain to handle this, the sergeant to get that, she could at least retain her dignity. She would not fall apart; she would not be reduced to the helpless female. Especially when she realized that's exactly what Nelson was hoping she'd do.

At the bottom of the stairs, Melissa hesitated, looking for the kitchen. She spotted its entrance off the dining room and headed for it. She had to suppress a gasp when she saw what was on the kitchen floor.

Though less grisly than what she'd seen upstairs, this was even more horrible. The two children lay side by side, their faces untouched, the shotgun blasts having been directed at their midsections. A boy and a girl. Melissa thought of her own son and daughter.

A man in civilian clothes was dusting the refrigerator for fingerprints. "Hey!" he snapped. "Don't touch anything."

Melissa realized she'd placed a hand against the counter to steady herself. She quickly withdrew it.

"How did you get in here?" the man demanded. A thickset fellow with dark curly hair, he was about thirty-five and had a reddish complexion.

Melissa didn't answer him. Those poor children, she thought. Those poor children. In her mind she could see not the faces of the boy and girl on the floor but those of Sarah and Billy. The room swirled.

"This is our new sheriff," Nelson's voice said from behind her. The mockery in it penetrated her daze, brought her back to reality.

"Oh," the man replied, sounding at least partially mollified. To Melissa he said: "I'm Roger Goldman, the closest thing the department has to a fingerprint expert."

"I'm Melissa James."

"Glad to meet you," he said, although Melissa thought she detected a distinct note of insincerity in the words.

She turned to face Nelson and said: "Give me the basics."

Again the sergeant studied her a moment before answering. "Friend of the family found the bodies. When she arrived, the dog was locked in the barn, barking. The front door was open a crack, but it appeared there was no one home. The friend decided to come in and investigate. You see what she found.

"It happened sometime between the time the family came

home from work and school yesterday and this morning, when the bodies were discovered. The victims are all members of the same family. The husband's name is Edward Evans. The wife was Anne. The kids were named John and Michelle, ages eight and eleven.''

Hearing the ages of the dead children stunned Melissa. Her kids were eight and eleven. She had the urge to run to a phone and call their school, make sure they were all right. Instead, she stood there, staring at Sergeant Nelson, her thoughts a confusion of horrors. Oh, God, she thought. Oh, God. Oh, God.

"We're still waiting for the medical examiner," Nelson continued, "but as far as we can tell, none of the victims was sexually molested or anything like that. Nothing in the house appears to have been vandalized, nothing taken. Whoever did it was only interested in killing.''

Melissa forced herself to function. "You said the killer left a message. Where is it?''

"Turn around.''

Melissa did so. On the cabinet doors below the counter, neatly written in purple crayon, were the words:

THE BOOGEYMAN WAS HERE

3

Walking along the mall, he stared absently into the display windows as he passed them. As he often did, he had come to the shopping center just to kill time, to watch people. At a sporting goods store, he stopped to admire the guns in the window, then turned and crossed to the other side of the mall. Checking his watch, he discovered that he had an hour to kill yet before heading home to get ready for work.

As one would expect on a Wednesday afternoon, the mall was

uncrowded. Two middle-aged women carrying bags containing their purchases passed him, then a man with a newly purchased snow shovel. Despite the mild weather, winter was coming. Halloween and election day had come and gone. Soon it would be Thanksgiving. The man shuddered.

He recalled how his father had thrown the turkey leg on the floor, then grabbed his mother's hair, pulled it until she screamed, the cranberry sauce sliding off the table. He remembered his terrified shrieks as his father put the carving knife to Mother's throat, threatening to kill her for . . . for what? He had no idea. There had never seemed to be any reasons. Just violence. Constant violence.

I hate Thanksgiving, he thought, stopping to look at a pair of boots in the window of a western-wear store. He wished days like Thanksgiving and Christmas—especially Christmas—could be done away with, stricken from the calendar. He'd learned very early in life that holidays meant not cheerfulness and celebrating but violence and cruelty.

He recalled a picture he had drawn in crayon as a child. Santa Claus with claws instead of hands. That was how he thought of Santa, as Santa *Claws*. Pushing these thoughts aside, he continued his stroll through the shopping center. He got like this every year at this time, but November and December would pass, and in January he'd feel better.

A woman wheeled a toddler in a stroller past the man. The child scowled at him.

Entering a large department store, he went to the hardware section and spent a few minutes examining hand tools. As he made his way toward the exit, he came upon a woman scolding a boy.

"Don't you ever do that again," she said, angrily shaking him. The boy looked at the floor, refusing to meet her eyes.

The man moved on, unconcerned. At a drugstore he bought a sports magazine, then settled down on one of the mall's benches to read the cover story, which concerned this year's race for the Super Bowl. From time to time he looked up to survey the passing shoppers, his eyes always returning to the magazine a moment later.

Suddenly he found himself staring intently at the man and two boys coming toward him. All three were laughing and giggling. The man was giving one boy a ride on his shoulders while the other skipped along beside them. Dark-haired and thin, the man was in his twenties. The boys were young, preschoolers probably. The man on the bench suddenly felt hot. The rage was coming.

The man with the children stopped a few feet away, taking one boy off his shoulders and lifting up the other one, both kids giggling wildly.

"Hey! I can see far, Daddy," said the boy now getting the elevated ride.

"Hang on tight," the father warned.

"Are you scared, Danny?" asked the boy on the ground.

"No," replied the other boy. "I'm not a sissy."

The father chuckled, and the threesome continued on its way.

How dare they? the man on the bench thought. How dare they carry on like that in public? It's shameful, disgusting. The heat seemed concentrated in his face now, as if his nose, his ears, his cheeks were all too hot to touch. He was trembling. The family would have to be punished for its behavior.

That was his job: to watch families and discipline those that needed it, those that angered him. He'd known for some time that he was really the Boogeyman. But not until last night did he finally act on that knowledge, punishing the Evans family for its behavior.

It was at this very shopping center that he'd become aware of the Evans family. The mother and the girl had come here. Watching them as they walked slowly along, holding hands and chatting happily, he'd felt the anger stirring, growing. He had followed them home, watched them, learned more about them. And then he had shown them—shown the world—what happened to those who offended the Boogeyman.

Quickly he headed in the direction in which the man and boys had gone. They had been moving at a leisurely pace; he should have no trouble catching up to them.

Sitting at her desk, Melissa checked her watch. It was four o'clock. Her children were home from school. She had called home and was reassured by Sarah that all was well. Still, Melissa could not leave them there alone; she had to go home.

Not that there was any point in remaining here. Since she had returned from the terrible scene in the big white house, no one had set foot in her office; the phone had not rung once. Melissa had spent the afternoon sitting here, trying not to see the bodies without faces and the lifeless forms of the children. She'd dashed for the door once, gagging, but she'd managed to get control of her stomach at the last moment. If she'd run to the bathroom to throw up, everyone in the department would have undoubtedly known about it.

Taking her purse from the bottom drawer of her desk, Melissa looked up to see someone standing in her doorway, a woman in a khaki uniform.

"Can I see you a moment?" the deputy asked hesitantly. It was the woman Melissa had seen in the radio room.

"Sure. Come in."

"My shift just ended," the woman explained as she entered the office, "and I thought I'd stop by and welcome you, since we're the only two women in the department—the only ones who are sworn officers, anyway." She smiled.

"Thank you," Melissa replied. "Sit down."

The officer did so. For the first time, Melissa realized how attractive the deputy was. Her red hair was full of sheen and highlights, and she had a pleasant smile, large blue eyes.

"I'm Marla Clark," she said. "I just wanted to let you know that if there's anything I can do to help, all you have to do is dial extension eighteen and holler."

"Thank you. I'm probably going to need all the help I can get."

The deputy hesitated, as if uncertain whether to speak her mind, then said: "Be prepared for a battle. This department is populated by two types of people: sexists and extreme sexists."

Melissa nodded. She'd already figured out that being unqualified was only one strike against her; being female was another.

"I'm the first woman officer the department ever had," Clark continued. "I was hired because of pressure from women's groups. When they got no satisfaction from Sheriff Raines, they turned to the county commission. The commissioners can't tell an elected sheriff what to do, but they do control the department's funding. They convinced the sheriff he needed some women on the force, so he hired one—me—stuck me in radio as soon as I'd finished training, and forgot about me. To the commissioner he said: 'I've hired one woman officer; now let's see how that works out before hiring any more.' He was still seeing how it worked out two years later, when he lost the election.'' She rolled her eyes.

"I'll look into it," Melissa promised. "If you've been held back because of your sex—"

Clark held up a hand. "No, please, I'm not here asking for any special favors. Honest, I'm not. I just wanted you to know how women stood around here so you'd know what you were up against."

"I believe you. But I'm still going to look into it." Not that it will do any good, she thought. The chances of her actually making any significant changes in the way things were done in the Ramsey County Sheriff's Department seemed slim. She had been put here to be a caretaker, to keep the chair warm until a qualified honest sheriff could be elected.

Melissa asked: "What's the feeling out there about Sheriff Raines?"

Clark frowned. "You realize, of course, that I'm not the best person to ask, because, being locked away in radio all day, I rarely get the chance to talk shop. And things being the way they are around here, when I do chitchat, it's usually with the secretaries, not the other deputies. Anyway, now that I've said that, I think it's safe to say that except for a few people who were in Raines's inner circle, no one around here misses him all that much. He was a competent police officer, but not much of a leader of the troops. He did all kinds of things—like changing work schedules or assignments or days off—without ever considering what effect these moves might have on morale. So, as you can imagine, morale was pretty low a lot of the time."

"Who were these members of Raines's inner circle?"

"Sergeant Nelson and some of his friends." Although Clark's expression and tone of voice remained neutral, Melissa got the distinct impression that Sergeant Nelson and his friends were not among the deputy's favorite people.

"Where does Captain Pruitt fit in?"

"As far as I know, he's an honest, competent police officer.

33

But let's face it, the only thing I can say with certainty is that he almost always uses correct radio procedure.'' She shrugged. ''Have the reporters started hounding you yet?''

''What reporters?''

''The reporters from just about every radio station, TV station, and newspaper in Denver. As soon as they learn what happened here today, they'll be all over the place. The only reason they weren't here hours ago is that they can't read our radio transmissions too well in the city. They can hear me okay, but they have trouble with the cars, so they're usually getting just one side of a conversation, and that's not always enough to figure out what's going on.''

Until this moment Melissa hadn't even been aware that the media monitored the radio traffic of law enforcement agencies. It made sense, though. How else did they find out what was happening so quickly?

This was the first time the mass killing had come up in the conversation. Melissa didn't want to talk about it. She didn't want to think about it.

Apparently sensing that Melissa wanted to end the conversation, Clark rose, saying she was late. Melissa, too, stood, her eyes meeting the deputy's.

''Thanks,'' Melissa said, meaning it. ''Come back.''

The officer smiled. ''I will.''

As soon as Clark was gone, Melissa quickly slipped her purse strap over her shoulder and headed for her car. In the hallway outside her office, she hesitated, wondering whether she should tell the captain she was leaving and finally deciding it would be pointless. No one cared whether she came or went.

In the parking area she hurried toward the spot where she'd left her car, seeing a number of white sheriff's cruisers but no small brown station wagon. The patrol cars, she noted absently, had large black numerals painted on their roofs, presumably so they could be identified from the air. Where was her car? She stopped to examine her surroundings. Had she come out the wrong exit? Was she in the wrong lot?

Oh, damn, she thought, why did I have to get lost now? I have to get home and take care of my kids. Some way will have to be found to work this out. I can't neglect Billy and Sarah like this.

Now, calm down, she told herself. Get your bearings. There's the street you used, and the entrance to the lot . . . and there's your parking space, with a white patrol car in it, number fourteen painted on its roof. She rushed back inside.

"My car's been stolen," Melissa said flatly. She stood in front of Captain Pruitt's desk, looking down at him.

"Stolen from where?" he asked, looking confused.

"Outside, in the parking lot. It was in the space marked sheriff. Now there's a white car there, and mine's gone."

"A white car?"

"A patrol car."

He frowned. "What's its number?"

"Fourteen."

"But fourteen *is* your car."

"Captain, what are you talking about?"

"Fourteen is the sheriff's car. It's yours. After we got it back from Raines, it was sent out to be cleaned and tuned up. It just came back a little while ago."

Melissa sighed. "Well, I came here in a brown station wagon. Where is it?"

"I don't know, but I have my suspicions. Hang on." He flipped open a small book of phone numbers, ran his finger down the page, then picked up his telephone and dialed. "Al, this is Captain Pruitt over at the sheriff's office. Did you tow a brown station wagon from here today?" He stared at something on his desk while he listened. "Uh-huh. Who called for the tow?" He frowned. "I see. Okay, thanks, Al."

Replacing the receiver, he said: "One of our officers had your car towed by mistake. It was in the sheriff's parking space, and the man had never seen it before. It's standard practice to immediately tow away any cars that get into the reserved parking spaces out there."

"But in this case someone was trying to prove a point, wasn't he? Who was the officer who had my car towed? Was it Sergeant Nelson?"

"No, it wasn't Sergeant Nelson. I know the officer, and I can assure you he's not the type to get involved in any funny business. I intend to check with him, but I'm sure, knowing the officer as I do, that it was an honest mistake."

"So where is my car?" Melissa asked tiredly.

"At Al's Towing and Wrecking."

Thoroughly exasperated now, Melissa slapped her car keys down on the desk. "Captain, my car was wrongfully removed. I expect it to be delivered to my home tonight, washed, vacuumed, and with a full tank of gas. And since I'm the offended party here, I do *not* expect to be charged for any of this. Please arrange it."

She turned, strode angrily to the door, then stopped. "Captain," she said softly, "where do I find the keys to car number fourteen?"

"Hanging on the keyboard in the squad room."

"Where's the squad room?"

"Come on. I'll show you."

"Wow!" Billy exclaimed for the umpteenth time. "A real patrol car! Is it hard to drive?" He sat at the kitchen table, where he'd stationed himself after at least half a dozen trips outside to examine the sheriff's cruiser.

"No," Melissa replied. "It's got an automatic transmission just like our car does." She didn't tell him how relieved she'd been when she discovered she could actually drive the thing.

Melissa stood at the stove, waiting for the water to boil in the big pot she used for cooking spaghetti. Sarah, who did not share her brother's love of police cars, was in the living room, watching TV.

"It has two antennas on it," Billy said excitedly. "Do all the cars have two, or just the sheriff's car?"

"I don't know, Billy. I haven't looked at the other cars that closely."

"When are you going to show me how the red lights and siren work?"

He would probably disown her if she admitted that she had no idea how to turn on the emergency equipment, so she said: "I'm sorry, but you're not supposed to use those things unless you're actually on a call."

Though obviously disappointed, the boy nodded sagely. Things like red lights and sirens were serious business.

Melissa reduced the heat under the bubbling spaghetti sauce. Although she usually made it from scratch using fresh basil she grew in a big flowerpot hanging in one of the kitchen's windows, this sauce had come from a bottle. I'm neglecting my family, she thought.

Still, she realized that lots of working mothers had to spend time away from their children and eat prepared foods. In a way, Melissa supposed, she and her family were being called upon to make a few sacrifices for the good of the community. Had Raines been unopposed, he'd most likely still be sheriff, despite the scandal.

The water was boiling now, and Melissa dropped in the spaghetti. "Hey, Sarah," she called into the living room. "We need some help in here."

"What, Mom?" the girl asked a moment later as she entered the kitchen.

"I need three of your special salads. You've got about eight minutes to make them."

"Okay," Sarah replied, heading for the refrigerator.

I must have done something right, Melissa decided. How many eleven-year-olds will instantly leave the TV set to help out in the kitchen without so much as a single word of protest?

Billy watched as his sister assembled the lettuce, green peppers, and other ingredients on the counter. Making a face, he said: "Ugh! Salad!"

When Sarah ignored him, he turned his attention to Melissa. "What kind of stuff did you do today? Did you catch any crooks?"

"I spent most of the day in the office," she replied. And she recalled the one time she left that office, the bloody bed, the faces without features, the two little bodies on the kitchen floor. For just a moment she had to hold on to the counter to steady herself.

Certain she would be unable to keep it down, Melissa had skipped lunch. Now she wasn't too sure about dinner.

"When are you going out and catch crooks?" Billy asked.

"I think the deputies will do most of that."

"Oh," her son said, once more clearly disappointed.

*   *   *

The kids were watching TV in the den, so Melissa and Keith Adamson had the living room to themselves. They sat on the couch, Melissa leaning forward while Keith massaged her shoulders.

"Ummm," she murmured. "Don't stop."

"I wonder whether this constitutes unethical stroking of a law enforcement officer."

"Don't worry. It'll be our secret."

They were silent for a few moments; then Keith said: "I was certainly surprised to hear Raines resigned. I figured he'd hold on to his office until they dragged him from the courthouse, kicking and screaming."

Melissa didn't respond. She had no desire to discuss Raines or anything else pertaining to her new job.

"Hey," Keith said, dropping his hands from her shoulders and gently pulling her back beside him, "this has to be one of the biggest things that's ever happened to you, yet you won't talk about it. How come?"

She sighed. "One reason is that I was ignored all day. Whether I was there or not was of practically no consequence to anyone."

For a moment Keith studied her in silence. He was a tall man with just a touch of gray in his dark hair, a trim body. Frowning, he said:

"Melissa, you're not qualified to run that department. You know nothing at all about law enforcement. The voters simply used you to get rid of a crooked sheriff. All they expect you to do now is to hold on to the office until the next election."

"Maybe, but I just don't feel right about it."

"If it makes you feel better, donate the salary to charity. You don't need it."

Melissa shook her head. "It's not that I'm taking the money under false pretenses. I never pretended to be anything other than what I am."

"Then what's your problem?"

"My problem is that I *am* the sheriff—even if the department can run itself just fine without me. I'm the only person in the county who's designated by law to carry out certain duties. I can't just ignore that. I can't." She fixed her eyes on his, driving home the point.

He gave her one of those tender looks a parent reserves for a child who's just said something silly. "Look, honey, you don't even know what those duties are. How are you going to perform them?"

"Keith, I can find out what they are."

He sighed. "Captain Pruitt's a competent, professional lawman. You should let him handle things."

She searched his face, finding nothing there except a sincere desire to help. Melissa had to admit that what he said made sense. And yet, even though she hadn't wanted it, the voters had given her a sacred trust. What happened in the sheriff's department was her responsibility, and she couldn't rid herself of that burden simply by handing it over to Captain Pruitt.

"Listen, Keith, try to understand. If a deputy kills some innocent people, it's my fault." She held up a hand to silence him before he could speak. "Ultimately, it is. It's my fault. If some of the officers are taking bribes, it's the same thing. Sure, I can wash my hands of the whole mess and hand everything over to Captain Pruitt, but I can't give him the ultimate responsibility. As long as I hold the office of sheriff, I'm the one the reporters or grand jury or investigators will call to ask why things went wrong."

"Melissa—"

"Really," she continued, cutting him off, "what am I supposed to say in a situation like that? That I'm not accountable because I'm just a figurehead? The law says I'm responsible, period."

"Melissa—" He was interrupted again, this time by the doorbell. Rising, Melissa went to see who was here. When she opened the door, she found a middle-aged man wearing greasy coveralls and a battered blue cap.

"Hi," he said around the cigar jammed in the corner of his mouth. "You Mrs. James, the sheriff lady?"

Melissa nodded. At the curb was a car with its lights on and its engine running, parked behind Keith's Buick.

"Pleased ta meetcha," he said, starting to offer a greasy hand, then quickly withdrawing it when he noticed its condition. "Pretty nice night for November. Can't stay this way much longer."

"Can I do something for you?" Melissa asked, confused.

From his pocket, the man produced a set of car keys and handed them to her. "I'm Al," he said. "I'm the one who towed your car. It's in the driveway. It's been gassed up, washed, and vacuumed."

"Thank you," Melissa said, trying not to think about what the man's greasy coveralls might have done to her upholstery.

Al smiled. "There's no charge." Jerking a thumb toward the car waiting at the curb, he added: "I've already got a ride." He nodded politely, turned, and was gone.

Stepping onto the stoop, Melissa peered around the bushy evergreen tree that grew next to the house and spotted her station wagon behind the sheriff's cruiser. The windows appeared to be rolled up; she'd check it later to make sure it was locked.

"Who was that?" Keith asked as Melissa returned to the couch.

She told him the story of her missing car. "Despite what Captain Pruitt says, I think it was an effort to make a point, to let me know I'm not wanted."

Keith slipped an arm around her. "I was wondering where your station wagon was when I saw the patrol car. I was going to ask, but you seemed so reluctant to discuss anything that happened to you today." He squeezed her a little more tightly. "I think I'm just beginning to get the idea. It might make you feel better if you told me everything. What have they been doing to you down there?"

Melissa saw the two little bodies on the kitchen floor and tried to push the image away, only to have it replaced by the bloody scene in the bedroom. Why, she wondered, why blow the parents' faces away but not the children's? Why do any of it? What kind of a lunatic was loose out there?

"Honey . . ." Keith was looking at her, concerned.

"I haven't told you the worst. It'll be on the news before long, I guess, so you might as well hear it from me. There was a . . . a killing today." She stopped, surprised to discover a tear rolling down her cheek.

"A killing? What killing?"

"A . . . a whole family. The parents and two children." And

40

then the tears came in earnest. "Oh, God, Keith," she sobbed, "it was awful."

While Keith held her, Melissa told him about the mass murder. And let out all the emotions she'd kept pent up since witnessing the grisly scene, feelings a sheriff could not display in front of her deputies, or a mother in front of her children. When her tears finally stopped, they sat there in silence, Keith's arm around her, her head resting on his shoulder.

Am I strong enough to undertake this thing? she asked herself. She knew Keith's answer to that. At least he wasn't using her emotional outburst to prove that she had no business trying to run the sheriff's department. But then he wouldn't. He'd made his point; it wasn't his nature to hound you.

"Hey, Keith," Billy said, rushing into the room, "when are we gonna see the Broncos again?"

Keith studied the boy for a moment, then said: "How do you know I'm going again this season? I might not, you know."

The boy looked worried. "Why not?"

"Well, I've got other things to do."

"Aw, come on. Going to the game's a lot more fun than doing mushy stuff with Mom."

Removing his arms from Melissa, Keith cocked his head. "Ummm, I don't know. Doing mushy stuff with your mother's a lot of fun for me."

"As much fun as football?" Billy asked, obviously not ready to believe anything as foolish as that.

Suddenly Keith sprang from the couch, grabbed Billy, and lifted him in the air, the boy giggling and squealing.

"Say uncle," Keith said.

"No," Billy replied between giggles.

"Say uncle."

"No. If I say uncle, you'll put me down."

Keith lowered the boy to the floor. Billy looked at him curiously for a moment; then realization spread across his face.

"Oh, no! I *did* say uncle."

"You sure did, pardner. But I'll tell you what. If it's okay with your mother, I'll take you to see the Broncos again sometime before Christmas. Okay?" He again sat down on the couch.

Billy began jumping up and down. "Oh, boy. Oh, boy."

Sarah, who had just entered the living room, watched her brother's antics, the look on her face indicating that such behavior was very much beneath her dignity.

Spotting the girl, Keith said: "Sarah, you can come, too, if you wish."

"To a football game?" She looked shocked.

"Sure, to see the Broncos play."

"No, thank you," she replied icily and headed for the kitchen.

Melissa was uncertain whether the coolness in the girl's reply had been directed solely at the notion of attending a sporting event—Sarah disdained all athletics—or whether some of it might have been meant for Keith himself. One of these days, she decided, I'll have to have a heart-to-heart talk with my daughter and see what I can learn.

"How about you, Mom? Are you going to go?" Billy asked, his expression making it clear he'd just as soon she didn't.

Melissa shook her head. "You and Keith have a good time."

Billy grinned.

Trembling and drenched with sweat, the Boogeyman lay in bed, trying to force the memories of the nightmare from his head. Though his dreams never recurred identically, were never instant replays of each other, they always told the same story. There were the familiar drunken shouts, the sound of a blow delivered by a fist followed by another, then another. His nightmares were punctuated with those blows. When as a boy he heard the sounds coming through the wall at night, he would cringe each time he heard the fist smack into flesh. And then, lying in bed, he'd slowly curl into the fetal position.

Once, when his father stormed into the room, the boy had wet himself, even though the violence was rarely directed at him. His father had demanded to know whether there had been any men hanging around the house while he was at work. The boy had said no; the man had left the room, closing the door behind him.

Then the horrible noises again, a blow being delivered, a body falling. As the boy had so many years ago, the Boogeyman winced.

Horrible though they were, these images were not what had awakened him, trembling and terrified. They were merely a prelude to it. No, no, he thought, don't think about that. He quickly sat up, dropping his legs over the edge of the bed. The glowing red numerals on his digital clock informed him that it was 3:41 A.M.

Think, he told himself, think about something else, about the family the Boogeyman must punish. Yes, yes, that was a good thing to consider. He had followed the man with the two boys to a small apartment building, where they entered number six. It was a neighborhood of houses and apartments, middle-class, moderately priced, children piloting tricycles down the sidewalks. The mailboxes were clustered at one side of the apartment building; the one for number six bore the name Tucker.

Though close to Denver, the building was in Ramsey County, which fact was important, for the Boogeyman could not punish anyone outside his own territory. It would be impossible for a single boogeyman to handle the entire world, so there were numerous boogeymen, each with a specific geographic area to cover. His turf was Ramsey County. In Denver, with so many people, there were undoubtedly numerous boogeymen, although how many he didn't know, since boogeymen made no effort to communicate with each other.

The Tucker family. Although he hadn't seen her, he presumed there was a Mrs. Tucker. There could also be more children than the two he'd seen. These were things the Boogeyman would have to learn, because no member of a family that had to be disciplined could be spared. All who had partaken in making the punishment necessary would have to share as well when it was meted out.

Funny, he thought, how people seemed to associate the Boogeyman strictly with children, for he cared about Mommy and Daddy, too. He cared very much about Mommy and Daddy.

In a few hours he would learn more about the Tuckers. Punishment, once decided upon, had to be carried out as swiftly as possible.

4

"Bye, Mommy," the two voices called in unison.

Looking back toward her apartment, Kathy Tucker viewed a sight that brought tears of happiness to her eyes. Her husband, David, stood in the doorway, a child on either side of him, all three waving good-bye. Resisting the impulse to run back and hug them, she blew them a kiss, then hurried past the doors to other ground-floor apartments, heading for the street, where she'd be picked up by her car pool.

The apartment house was small, especially compared to some of the monsters in Denver, but it suited them. There was off-street parking in the graveled lot adjacent to the building, and traffic in the neighborhood wasn't too bad, which was important when you had children. Someday, she knew, they would out-grow the small two bedroom apartment. But not soon. Certainly not until the construction business picked up and Dave was called back to work. A carpenter, he'd been laid off for months. Soon the unemployment would run out. Then what? Welfare? She didn't know and hoped she wouldn't have to find out.

For now they were getting by. Her job as a bookkeeper paid fairly well. Combined with Dave's unemployment, it was enough. Barely. Oh, hell, she thought as she reached the curb, why do I worry about these things? I've got two marvelous sons, a wonderful husband, and we're all healthy. As long as we've got that, we've got everything that really matters, don't we?

Suddenly having the feeling of being watched, she shivered. Her eyes scanning the area, she took in the brick houses across the street, parked cars, a tricycle left out all night in a front yard, the two-story building in which she and her husband rented a ground-floor apartment. There was no one in sight.

Taking a deep breath, Kathy Tucker slowly let it out. Though sunny, it was a chilly morning, a hint of the winter to come. She was just cold; that was all. Tomorrow she would abandon the light jacket she wore, in favor of a heavier one.

A slender twenty-six-year-old blond, Kathy was accustomed to being watched. Although as a teenager she had enjoyed the attention of the boys in her high school, she was an adult now, and the stares of men seemed less innocent than they once had, more menacing. Whenever she stood for any reason at the office, she could feel the eyes of the males in the room. It wasn't paranoia; she'd caught them doing it. Still, that the same feeling should come over her out here at seven in the morning *was* paranoid.

At the end of the block, Janice's red car appeared. Kathy waved; Janice honked. And the feeling of being watched persisted.

The Boogeyman waited until the red sedan passed, then sat up in the front seat of his car. Parked partway down the block and across the street from the building in which the Tuckers lived, he'd had a clear view of blond, shapely Kathy Tucker as she'd waited for the red car to arrive. He'd learned her name simply by looking up Tucker in the phone book before leaving home this morning. As did many couples these days, the Tuckers had both their names listed.

In addition to discovering that Kathy Tucker was blond and pretty, which was unimportant, he had learned that she left for work at seven in the morning. If her job was in Denver and she worked full-time, she'd probably return home about six. He still needed to find out about David Tucker. And about the children. He really didn't need to learn too much, just enough to know when all the members of the family would be alone and vulnerable.

Stretching, he shifted his weight, trying to find a more comfortable position. His thoughts wandering absently, he considered his role as the Boogeyman. He knew neither what power chose boogeymen nor how the appointees were selected. When you became one, you just knew; that you were the Boogeyman was undeniable. That there were other boogeymen, each, like you, with his own turf, was also undeniable.

The only part of all this he'd been unable to reason out was whether he was a supernatural being. It seemed that as the

Boogeyman, he should be an evil spirit or something like that. A bullet should pass harmlessly through his body. And yet he was uncertain about this. Although it seemed reasonable that the Boogeyman would be immortal, he wasn't about to leap in front of any speeding cars just to test the notion. Hot pans still burned his hand; the razor still cut his face; his eyes still ached after a sleepless night. Perhaps the transformation to a supernatural state didn't occur all at once but came gradually.

A car emerged from the parking lot serving the building in which the Tuckers lived. It was a full-sized sedan. The car he'd followed here from the shopping center yesterday was a yellow compact.

Again the Boogeyman stretched. That's the answer, he decided. I'm not fully supernatural yet, but I will be eventually. These things take time.

He yawned.

Down the block from the green car, fourteen-year-old Melanie Bascom stood on the sidewalk, a new 35-millimeter camera in her hands. An avid photographer, she had received the camera yesterday for her birthday. It was what she'd wanted more than anything, and now that she had it, she could shoot close-ups, vary her f-stops and shutter speeds, all the things she'd been unable to do with her old box camera.

A tall, thin girl with sandy hair, she had just reached the stage at which skinny and bony were being transformed into something else, although she was uncertain exactly what the end result would be. All she knew for sure was that the same boys who'd once dubbed her Skinny Legs now looked at her in a totally different way than they ever had before. Her mother said she was becoming quite slender and shapely, but then mothers always said things like that. Sure, she knew about sex appeal and all that, but it was something you said about other people. The thought that she might have it—ever—had simply not occurred to her.

Looking around her, Melanie tried to spot something that might make a good picture. She wasn't going to be too particular. There were only two exposures left on the roll, and she simply wanted to use them up so she could drop the film off for processing on her way home from school. Her dad had promised to help her convert a storage closet in the garage into a darkroom, but for now she had to have her film developed commercially.

Darn, she thought, still having found nothing on which to use her last two exposures. She knew the sort of picture she'd like to take, something similar to the example in one of her photography books. It showed a spiderweb, the morning dew on its strands reflecting the gold of sunrise, and in its center the waiting spider. It was a marvelous photograph, certainly way beyond anything she'd been able to do with a box camera. Although she'd have to forget about spiderwebs until spring, there were undoubtedly numerous photographic possibilities to be found on a cool and sunny November morning in Colorado. The trouble was that none of them was apparent right now on the block where she lived, and she didn't have time to look elsewhere. Sighing, she put her eye to the viewfinder and took a shot looking down the street to the north, then turned and took one looking south.

Having dismissed the two shots as basically wasted, Melanie barely noticed the green car in her viewfinder as she clicked off the last exposure on the roll. She hurried into her house.

It was about ten minutes before eight when Melissa strode down the hallway toward Captain Pruitt's office. The media knew about the killings now. About nine last night, reporters had begun calling her at home. Having no idea how to respond to their questions, she'd referred them to Captain Pruitt, saying he was in charge. The story in this morning's *Denver Post* said a Detective Lieutenant Castle was in charge. The Denver news media was now aware that the sheriff of Ramsey County had no idea who was in charge of what was undoubtedly the biggest case the department had ever handled. Melissa resolved not to let anything like that happen again.

The door to Captain Pruitt's office was closed. Without knocking, she pushed it open and stepped purposefully into the room. It was empty. Returning to the hallway, she saw a man in a deputy's uniform coming toward her.

"Have you seen Captain Pruitt?" she asked.

The officer was young, with light-brown hair. He eyed her curiously. "He might be in the briefing room."

"Where's the briefing room?"

"Around the corner, second door on your right," the deputy replied with perhaps just a trace of smugness in his voice.

"Thank you," Melissa said, briskly stepping past him.

Rounding the corner, she stopped at the appropriate door, discovering that *briefing room* was just another name for the squad room. As she reached for the knob, she heard laughter and a voice within saying:

"Yeah, she's got a pretty cute ass and her tits aren't too bad, but how are you going to feel when she decides to paint the patrol cars pink?"

The question, apparently less humorous than what had been said previously, was followed by a few chuckles. Girding herself, Melissa opened the door and stepped into the room.

Standing at a desk, Sergeant Nelson faced a group of about half a dozen seated officers. All eyes were on Melissa; no one spoke.

"I'm looking for Captain Pruitt," she said.

Momentarily taken aback by her unexpected arrival, Nelson had regained his composure. He grinned. "Last time I saw him, he was in his office," he said, pointedly letting his eyes roam over Melissa's body.

"He's not there now," she said flatly. I will not let this jerk get to me, she thought. I won't.

"I'm afraid I don't know where he is, then."

"Continue with what you were doing," Melissa said, taking the chair beside the desk. The other men in the room, who were seated in metal folding chairs, watched the sergeant and her intently.

Again Nelson grinned. It was he who had made the comments about Melissa's physical attributes; she recognized his voice. "All right," he said to the assembled men, "as I was saying, we have no idea who we're looking for in this mass killing, so we need all the help we can get. The captain wants us to report anything we get wind of. Someone tries to coax a kid into a car. Someone sees a prowler in the neighborhood where the murders occurred. Report anything, anything at all." He turned to Melissa. "Anything you'd like to add, ma'am—uh, I mean sheriff?"

"No. Carry on."

With a wave of his hand, Nelson dismissed the men. They stood, gathering up their nightsticks and other gear, and quietly filed out the exit at the rear of the room. As the door closed, Melissa heard a muffled conversation begin. It grew fainter as the men moved away from the door. She was unable to make out the words.

Still grinning at her, Sergeant Nelson said: "Are you planning to attend all the briefings, ma'am?"

"From time to time," she replied coolly.

He hesitated, as if searching for something to say, his grin fading. Finally he said: "If you'll excuse me, I have to go to work. The patrol sergeant spends his day out there with the men, not in the office."

Melissa watched as he stepped through the same door the other men had used. She had never met a person she disliked quite as much as Sergeant Nelson. But then she was sure Sergeant Nelson wouldn't have it any other way.

Back in the hallway, she headed for Captain Pruitt's office. When she reached it, Melissa found the captain talking to a man in civilian clothes. Stepping through the open door, she joined them without waiting for an invitation. Both men started to rise; she waved them back down.

"Where do I find Lieutenant Castle?"

"I'm Lieutenant Castle," the man in civilian clothes said, again rising. He was a big man, tall, with thinning dark hair.

Accepting his proffered hand, Melissa introduced herself, then said: "Lieutenant, I want a complete briefing on the murders yesterday. I want one every day, and I want to be informed whenever there are any significant developments in the case."

Towering over her, the man stood there looking at her curiously. Suddenly Melissa realized that, thanks to some facet of his male upbringing, he wasn't going to sit down until she did. Melissa lowered herself into a chair. So did Lieutenant Castle.

"Uh, just what is it you want to know?" he asked.

"I want a briefing, just like the briefing you'd give the captain here."

The lieutenant glanced at Pruitt, who was poker-faced. Melissa could see intelligence in the big man's eyes. And wariness.

Dealing with an inexperienced woman sheriff was unfamiliar territory, and he was going to feel his way cautiously.

"We've checked with the Evanses' neighbors," he said. "No one saw anything that would help us—at least no one we've spoken with so far did. We've also been checking friends and family and people at the place where Mr. Evans worked. So far no leads there either. No trace of the shotgun the killer used. We found five sets of fingerprints that we can't identify, that don't belong to the victims or someone else associated with the house. They probably won't be much help unless we get a suspect so we can make a comparison. We've sifted through the fireplace, the trash, the ashtrays. We vacuumed the entire house and sent the contents of the bag to the lab in Denver for analysis. We should hear from them today."

"What do you plan to do now?" Melissa asked.

"We're going to continue interviewing people. Right now there's nothing else we can do. We don't have a single lead."

He studied her a moment, apparently waiting to see whether she had any further questions. When she didn't ask one, he stood up. "If you'll excuse me, I need to get back to work. There's no chance at all I'll ever solve the case by sitting in the captain's office."

"Thank you, Lieutenant."

At the door the big man stopped and turned. "One thing I forgot to mention is the crayon, the purple crayon used to write the Boogeyman message. There were crayons in the house, but none that color, so the killer must have taken it with him. Maybe he found it there. Maybe he brought it with him. Also, the color of the crayon is something that hasn't been released to the media. You always keep a couple of things to yourself—to trip up people who give false confessions and things like that."

"Lieutenant," Melissa said, "what do you think it meant, the message?"

He frowned. "My feeling is that it was written for one of two reasons. First, it could have been someone killing for a rational purpose, just using the message to throw us off, to make us think it was a psycho. Second, the killer is truly crazy and the words contain some message that only makes sense to the fruitcake who wrote them."

"Which do you think is the most likely?"

"My gut feeling?"

"Yes."

"My gut feeling says it's a psycho, but I hope to hell I'm wrong."

"Why?"

"Because," he answered, fixing his eyes on hers, "if he's a psycho, he's probably going to do it again."

After Castle had left, Melissa and Captain Pruitt eyed each other in silence for a moment, the lieutenant's words seeming to hang in the air: *If he's a psycho, he's probably going to do it again.*

Finally Melissa spoke. "He seems competent."

"He is."

"How many detectives does the department have?"

"Five. Lieutenant Castle is in charge of the division."

"How many of them are working on the Evans murders?"

"All of them."

"Why wasn't he at the scene yesterday?"

"He was. He arrived after you left. He was on another case, and we had trouble reaching him."

Melissa nodded. The captain, she noticed, seemed less friendly today than he had yesterday. Perhaps it was just that he had problems enough right now without her adding to them. Well, she thought, I'm here; you'd best start getting used to me.

"Captain," she said slowly, "how many female officers are on the force?"

He studied her a moment before answering; then he said simply: "One."

"Why aren't there any more?"

"Sheriff Raines didn't believe women had any place in the department."

"I see. Is Marla Clark a competent officer?"

"I don't know. No one's ever been out in the field with her."

"Is she qualified to do the same work the other deputies do?"

"She's had the same training the men get."

"Then let's give her a chance. I want her transferred out of the radio room and assigned to regular patrol duties."

The captain wrinkled his brow. "There's no one else who's

trained to handle the computer and to do some other things that job involves.''

"Hire someone. Let Marla train the new person."

"There's no money in the budget for any additional personnel."

"Captain, you're not trying to help. Transfer Marla Clark out and someone else in."

"Who?"

"Whoever you pick."

"You don't—" He stopped himself from completing the sentence, and when he spoke again, his manner was almost fatherly. "Look, this isn't going to work very well. There are a lot of the deputies who will really resent it. There's going to be a lot of unhappiness."

"Captain, this isn't the first police force to accept women as officers. The men's egos will recover."

He sighed. "All I can do is advise against it. I think you'll be making a lot of unnecessary problems both for yourself and the department."

"Your advice is noted, Captain. I'm sorry I have to go against it."

Pruitt nodded. He looked resigned.

"Also," Melissa continued, "I want the department to begin actively seeking qualified women applicants whenever there's a vacancy to fill. And I want to have final approval before anyone's actually hired."

"You already have that. Only the sheriff can commission someone to act as an officer of the law." He hesitated, then went on. "You really don't have to do this, you know. I mean, if you'd prefer, you can spend your time with your family just like you've been doing. The other senior officers and I can run things here. I mean that you don't have to try to run the department just because . . ."

He trailed off, a mixture of acquiescence and frustration on his face. Melissa thought he was eyeing her as a parent might look upon an errant child who simply would not listen to the voice of experience and wisdom. She pushed the thought aside.

"I see your point, Captain. I only hope you understand why I can't do things that way."

Pruitt nodded, although there was nothing in the gesture that indicated he understood.

"Uh, excuse me," the Boogeyman said to the woman who had opened the door. "I'm looking for a J. Tucker. Do you know if there's anyone by that name living in the building?"

"There's a Dave Tucker two doors down," she said, pushing a strand of dark hair out of her face. She was about twenty-two, thin, dressed in a western shirt and jeans.

"This was J. Tucker. Uh, he has three kids and works at Sears." He smiled politely, the harmless man innocently trying to locate someone.

She shook her head. "No, they only have two kids and Dave's a construction worker, a carpenter. At least he is when he's working. He's been laid off." Then, apparently to explain how she knew all this, she added: "My husband and I play cards with them a lot."

"Well, I've apparently found the wrong Tuckers. You don't know anyone else by that name, do you?"

"Not in this building."

"Thank you for your help," he said, turning to leave.

"Dave's probably there, if you want to talk to him. Maybe he knows the people you're looking for."

"No, I'm afraid that's not too likely. Thank you again."

As the Boogeyman walked toward his green sedan, which he'd parked across the street from the apartment building, he mulled over what he knew about the Tuckers and decided he knew enough. It was time to administer the punishment.

That afternoon Melissa sat at her desk, staring at the clock on the wall. It was nearly four, and since her meeting with Captain Pruitt and Lieutenant Castle, she had remained in her office, undisturbed, with nothing to do. At noon she had interrupted her boredom by going out for lunch. I'm still being ignored, she thought.

In front of her was the *Denver Post* she'd bought while she was out, the same edition she had at home. The banner headline read: FAMILY OF FOUR SLAIN. Melissa had picked up the paper so she could check out the situations-wanted ads. She was thinking about hiring a housekeeper, someone to clean the place up and fix a hot evening meal for the kids. She would definitely need someone like that during the summer, when the kids were out of school, and with her sheriff's salary added to her income, paying for it should be no problem.

The situations-wanted ads had been no help. If there were any housekeepers out there looking for work, they weren't advertising the fact. Melissa decided to check with her friends to see whether any of them knew of someone. If that failed, she could try the state employment service.

Shifting her gaze away from the clock, she noticed someone standing in the hall looking in at her through the open door. A uniformed deputy.

"Can I have a word with you?" he asked politely.

"Sure. Come in."

The man remained standing when he reached her desk. About thirty, he was tall and athletic-looking, with dark, wavy hair and eyes that were nearly black.

"My name's Bob Sanchez," he said. "I came to apologize."

"Apologize for what?"

"I'm the one who had your car towed."

Uncertain what to say, Melissa remained silent.

"It was an honest mistake," he continued. "I saw the station wagon there, and it's always been a standing order that anytime there's a car in that space that's not the sheriff's, it's supposed to be removed immediately." He gave her an embarrassed smile. "It just never occurred to me that the station wagon might belong to the *new* sheriff."

"Your apology's accepted."

"You mean you're not going to assign me to life on graveyard shift, or even worse, put me permanently on warrants?"

Melissa shook her head. "I don't even know what that means, putting you on warrants."

"Oh. Well, when you're on warrants, you take a stack of outstanding arrest warrants and go out to serve them, to bring in the people. Usually you have to do this about five in the morning, because the people you're after are almost certain to be home at that time and because it's the best time to catch them unawares."

54

"I can understand why you wouldn't like going to work at five in the morning," Melissa said.

"That's only part of the problem. The rest is that the people you're trying to serve the warrants on usually aren't too anxious to go. So you wind up having to physically subdue some of them—and there are always a few that are twice your size. You also end up having to chase some of them. There are always a couple who will peek out and see it's a cop, then head for the back door as fast as they can go." He shook his head. "I spent two hours chasing a woman through a cornfield once. She ran out of the house wearing just her bra and panties. It was at one of those—what do you call them?—communes. That's it; it was a commune. Everybody in the place got up to watch, and they all cheered for the girl every time she got away from me."

Melissa laughed. "What was she wanted for?"

"Speeding."

"Speeding? All that for a speeding ticket?"

He shrugged. "Sometimes the warrants say murder, sometimes failure to appear on a traffic citation. They've all got to be served. This particular girl was from a wealthy family. Before she joined the commune, she used to speed around in her expensive sports car getting tickets, which she never paid. She had over a thousand dollars' worth."

"Amazing," Melissa said.

"Oh, you'd be surprised how many people don't pay their traffic tickets. And for some reason they're always so surprised when they get arrested. It even says right on the citation what will happen to them." He shrugged. "Well, I don't want to take any more of your time. I just came in to say how sorry I am about your car. They didn't charge you for it, did they?"

"No. And stop apologizing. As you said, it was an honest mistake."

"Thank you," he said and started to leave. Reaching the door, he stopped and turned. "Oh, I almost forgot. Welcome to the sheriff's department. If there's anything I can ever do to help you out, just ask. And remember, I owe you one because of your car." He disappeared into the hallway without giving Melissa a chance to respond.

She leaned back in her desk chair. She had met two people

now who appeared willing to give her a chance. Marla Clark and Bob Sanchez. At least not everyone here was politely efficient and yet somehow patronizing, like Captain Pruitt, or openly hostile, like Sergeant Nelson. And where there were two, there might be more. Though not exactly bubbling with self-confidence, Melissa felt more optimistic than she had. A lot more.

That evening Melissa and Keith sat at a booth in a small Mexican restaurant not far from her house. She studied Keith's face, his features illuminated by the flickering orange light from the candle on the table. As he put a bite of enchilada into his mouth, their eyes met briefly; then his returned to his plate. Shortly, Melissa presumed, he would be ready to discuss whatever was on his mind.

Dining together at the small Mexican restaurant had been a last-minute thing. Keith had called, asking her to have dinner with him. She'd started to say no, because it was so unexpected and because a dinner at Maria's hardly seemed worth cooking a hurried meal for the kids and arranging for a baby-sitter. But then she'd begun to realize that this was more than an impromptu invitation, that there were things on Keith's mind.

"I was lucky to get Linda Sue on such short notice," Melissa said, referring to her baby-sitter.

Keith nodded, and Melissa let her eyes wander around the restaurant. The place was nothing fancy, just a few booths and tables, one waitress for the handful of patrons who'd showed up on a Thursday night. Despite the ordinary decor and light mid-week business, this was one of Melissa's favorite restaurants. It served the best chili rellenos in metro Denver.

"Starting tomorrow," Melissa said, "I'm going to regularly attend the briefings for both day and swing shifts. Also, I'm going to start spending some time each day in the field with the officers investigating the Evans murders. It's the biggest case the department's had in quite a while, and I want to know what's happening with the investigation."

"What about Billy and Sarah?" Keith asked as he sprinkled some salt on his refried beans. Melissa's own plate was empty; Keith was a slow eater.

"I've been thinking about that. I've just about decided to hire a housekeeper, someone to clean the place up, cook dinner for the kids, and keep an eye on them until I get home.''

"They'd be better off if their mother was there," Keith said softly.

"Keith, all across the country women who work have to leave their children in the care of others.''

"Yes, but most of them *have* to work, Melissa. You don't.''

"Many of them *want* to work. Not have to, Keith, want to. Besides, I do have to. I'm the sheriff of this county, and the responsibilities of that office can't be given away; they're mine. But then we've been through all that.''

Putting down his fork, Keith reached across the table and took her hand. "Look, I really don't think you've thought this thing through. If you start going along with the investigating officers when they go out, you're going to be in the way. You're going to mess things up. These men can't be bothered with an inexperienced person. What they're doing is just too important.''

"Thanks for the vote of confidence," Melissa said, withdrawing her hand from his. "I didn't ask for this job, you know. Hell, I was so anxious not to get elected that I voted for Raines. The only reason I was even on the ballot was as a favor to Priscilla. But dammit, I did get elected, and I'm stuck with it. I just can't ignore the fact that I'm the sheriff here.''

"It's not just me," Keith said. "I mean, I'm not the only one who's concerned about the effect you might have on the functioning of the department if you involve yourself too deeply in things you don't really know anything about. Captain Pruitt called me today to—''

"Captain Pruitt! What is this, some kind of a conspiracy? Do all you men have to get together to make sure the fool woman doesn't mess anything up?''

"Hey," Keith said, "keep your voice down. Everyone in the place can hear us.''

Melissa felt tears of anger and frustration welling up. Not wanting to let Keith see her cry at this particular moment, she rose and strode from the restaurant. She stopped in the graveled parking area, still fighting to hold back the tears. I'm acting like a child, she thought.

Behind her she heard footsteps approaching in the gravel, and then Keith was there. "Melissa, I—"

"Just take me home."

Putting a hand on each of her shoulders, he studied her face. "Come on, honey. We're adults. I have to tell you what I think. In similar circumstances, wouldn't you tell me?"

She looked into his eyes for a long moment before answering. "Yes, I suppose I would. But I wouldn't join in a conspiracy against you."

He sighed. "Chuck Pruitt's a friend. He has what he perceives to be a problem, so he called and asked me to help if I could. That's not exactly a conspiracy."

It sure comes close, Melissa thought, but she remained silent.

"Honey, if this is what you feel you have to do, then you have to do it. I told you what I think; you considered it and disagreed. That's that. I admire you for your determination and principles. And you have my complete support from here on out."

"Are you saying that just to placate me?"

"You know me better than that, Melissa."

She nodded. And then the tears came.

Keith took her in his arms. "It's going to be rough."

"I know," she said between sobs. "I know."

He squeezed her tightly.

It was about four in the morning when Dave Tucker heard a noise that awakened him. Ordinarily, the thunk of something falling in the boys' room wouldn't have aroused him, but he was too excited to sleep well. Slipping his feet into his slippers, he stood up. The noise hadn't disturbed Kathy. She was sound asleep on her side of the bed, a motionless lump in the shadows.

Moving slowly through the dark apartment, Dave Tucker headed toward the room where his sons slept. The reason he'd been unable to sleep was because the call he'd been waiting for and waiting for had finally come. He had a job. Despite the sorry state of the housing industry, the Denver area was growing, and all those new arrivals had to live somewhere, even if doing so used up nearly all their income. A builder Dave had worked for previously had come up with enough money to build thirty new homes. For the next few months Dave would be employed.

Just the thought of it made him smile. Sure it would be cold out there framing houses this winter, but it meant he had his pride back. Although he didn't really mind being with the boys all day—or the cleaning or the cooking, for that matter—it was embarrassing as hell when he had to tell someone what he was doing. Somehow the terms house-husband or out of work or laid off always ended up meaning unemployed. No job. No respect. A failure. These notions made no sense; he knew that. He and Kathy should be proud of the way they were raising the boys and making their life together, and yet knowing that his lack of self-esteem was illogical did nothing to ease the feeling. Only a job could do that.

Slipping quietly into the boys' room, he studied the two lumps under the covers. Nothing in the room seemed out of order, although he was unable to see much, because the only illumination was from the moonlight coming through the window. Well, boys, he thought, week after next you'll be staying with Grandma and Grandpa during the day, just like before. You going to miss having your dad around all the time?

After watching his sons for a moment, a very contented Dave Tucker turned away from their bed, intending to return to his own. It was then that he saw the shape emerge from the shadows in the corner of the room. The shape of a man. Holding a gun.

"Hey, wha—"

"Shhh," said the man. "If you make any noise, I'll kill you."

"W-who are you?" Dave whispered, positioning himself between the man and his sons. "What do you want?"

"You know me," the man said quietly. "You've known me all your life, ever since you were a child."

Trembling, Dave Tucker said nothing.

As the intruder stepped into the weak light coming through the window, the silencer on his gun became visible. "Don't you recognize me?" the man asked softly.

Dave Tucker shook his head.

"I'm the Boogeyman," the intruder said, and at that moment Dave Tucker was certain he was about to die.

5

All conversation came to an abrupt halt when Melissa stepped into the squad room. The men of the patrol day shift stared silently at her, some eyeing her curiously, a few with open hostility on their faces. Their eyes followed her as she moved to a chair near the desk and sat down facing them. Neither Sergeant Nelson nor Captain Pruitt was present at the moment.

"I hope all this silence isn't on my account," Melissa said with a nonchalance she didn't feel.

The half-dozen or so men exchanged uncertain glances. Some sat in the folding metal chairs; others stood. They were mainly young, in their twenties, except for one paunchy officer who appeared to be in his forties.

"Uh, well, you see," the paunchy one said, "we're not used to having women in here, so we don't usually watch what we say." He gave her an embarrassed grin.

"I'm afraid I don't understand," Melissa said. She did, but she didn't see any reason to make it easy for him.

"Well, you know how men are. We swear a lot, say things you're not supposed to say in front of a woman."

"Think of me as the sheriff, not as a woman."

The chubby deputy was beginning to look quite uncomfortable. "Ma'am, I'm afraid there's no way I could not think of you as a woman."

Subdued chuckles from the other men.

"Shit," Melissa said.

The snickering stopped instantly, and the deputy to whom she'd been speaking nearly blushed.

"Okay," Melissa said, "let's not have any more of this nonsense. If you stop talking when I come around, then it's because you don't want me to hear what you're saying, not because you're being profane. I assure you I can swear with the best of you."

"Ma'am," the pudgy deputy said, "I'm afraid I just wasn't raised that way. My daddy'd turn over in his grave if I ever talked dirty in front of a woman."

Melissa sighed. "As I said, think of me as the sheriff, the person you have to oblige if you want to get along here."

Am I going too far? she wondered. Am I getting in over my head? Before the discussion could go any further, the door opened and Captain Pruitt stepped in, accompanied by Sergeant Nelson. When he spotted her, that hint of a frown appeared on Pruitt's face. Nelson strode past her without giving the slightest indication that he was aware of her presence. A snub, she decided, since the sergeant could hardly have failed to notice her.

Glancing at the clipboard in his hand, the captain said: "District one-Adam. Gas Company's going to be tearing up the eight-thousand block of Fenton Street. It'll be reduced to one lane of traffic for the rest of the week. In district three-Baker we had a signal eight arising from a signal fifteen last night. If the assailant bails out, he may come back to the house, and there'll be more trouble. Here's the report from graveyard." He held out a sheet of paper, which one of the deputies took from him.

"Okay," Pruitt went on. "We still need all the help we can get on the Evans murders. If you run into anything that might have any connection at all, let us know. No matter how thin it might seem, give us what you've got immediately. Any questions?" When no one spoke, the captain said: "Sergeant Nelson has today's hot sheets."

The sergeant handed a sheet of paper to each deputy, leaving the extras on the desk, and then followed the others out the door at the rear of the room. Melissa picked up one of the papers the sergeant had left behind. At the top it said HOT SHEET and gave the day's date. Before she could read further, the captain said: "It's a list of motor vehicles that were stolen or used in a crime. The officers are supposed to familiarize themselves with it and keep an eye out for any of the cars. The reports come from throughout the metro area."

Putting down the hot sheets, Melissa nodded. "Captain, have you found anyone to replace Marla Clark in radio yet?"

He studied her a moment before answering. As you can see, Melissa thought, Keith was not able to talk me out of it. "I haven't picked anyone yet," he said.

"I'd like someone to be in there with her by Monday."

"All right," he replied evenly. "Anything else?"

"Yes. I'm going to spend some time in the field with Lieutenant Castle each day until we catch whoever killed the Evans family. If I'm not in my office, that's where I'll be."

Although Melissa had watched for that hint of a frown to appear on Pruitt's face, it hadn't been there. He seemed to have adopted a *que-será-será* attitude toward her: If the fool woman messes it up, she messes it up; it's not my fault.

Leaving the captain to go about his business, Melissa headed for her office. As soon as she sat down at her desk, Marla Clark hurried in.

"Here," she said, handing Melissa a sheet of paper. "It's a complete list of all the radio codes. I thought you might need it."

"Thank you. I do need one. I was going to ask Captain Pruitt to get me something like this."

"I've got to run," Marla said. "I've got about thirty seconds to make it to the radio room."

"Wait, one question before you go. How long would it take you to train someone to take over your job?"

Marla, who had been halfway out the door, turned, a smile appearing on her face. "You mean you're going to—"

"I hope to have your replacement in there with you on Monday. How long will it take to train him or her?"

Marla frowned. "Oh, no more than a few days, as long as it's someone who can type."

Melissa made a mental note to tell Captain Pruitt to make sure the trainee he selected could type.

"Who's it going to be?" Marla asked.

"I don't know yet. Captain Pruitt's going to choose someone. Apparently there's no money in the budget for hiring anyone, so it'll have to be someone who's already here."

Again, Marla frowned. "That's going to be sticky, you know."

"I know."

"Thank you," Marla said, glancing at her watch. "And now I'm definitely late." She hurried out of the room.

Melissa leaned back in her desk chair. Am I really doing this for the principles involved? she wondered. Or am I just angry and vengeful? That she'd been treated poorly since becoming sheriff was undeniable, although what bothered her the most wasn't the hostility of Sergeant Nelson but the way Keith and Captain Pruitt had treated her like a child, as if they were the grown-ups arranging things behind the little girl's back, all in the kid's best interest, of course. Damn, she thought. Damn.

And yet she couldn't totally dismiss the idea that they were right. Was she behaving like an angry little girl? Was she striking back at the grown-ups? Pushing these questions from her mind, she turned her thoughts to her own children.

Although Sarah and Billy seemed to be getting along just fine with a working mother, she still needed to find a housekeeper. When she found someone, through either friends or the state employment office, she would have to check the person out thoroughly. You couldn't be too careful when you were trusting someone with your kids.

Both Sarah and Billy—especially Billy—had been full of questions about the murders. Whenever the topic came up, Melissa tried to steer the conversation elsewhere. At least neither of the Evans children had gone to the same school her kids attended, so to Sarah and Billy the dead boy and girl were strangers. Like the people killed in those auto crashes you saw on TV. They were always just names, not real people.

Melissa scanned the list of radio codes Marla had given her. It began with the ten codes, many of which had to do with communicating over the radio. Ten-nine meant repeat the last. Ten-five meant relay another officer's transmission. There were also ten codes for traffic accidents and things like that, but the real heavy stuff was listed under the signals. Signal one meant homicide, the one code she'd already learned. *Sergeant Nelson is requesting your assistance on a signal one*, Marla had said, apparently not realizing that Melissa had no idea what a signal one was. Well, I know now, Melissa thought. I doubt I'll ever forget.

She recalled what Captain Pruitt had said at the morning briefing. A signal eight arising from a signal fifteen. Checking the sheet of paper before her, Melissa translated the captain's words: shooting arising from a family fight. These numbers, Melissa realized, were the secret jargon of the department, the way of communicating that only members of the club could understand, and she resolved to memorize them.

"Are you ready for your briefing?" Lieutenant Castle asked as he stepped up to her desk.

"Are you on your way out as soon as you finish with me?"

The lieutenant nodded.

Picking up her purse, Melissa rose. "Then you can brief me in the car. I'm coming with you."

"Let's go," Castle replied, giving no indication of how he felt about having her company.

Bathed in perspiration, his breath coming in short gasps, the Boogeyman lay in bed, trying to push the nightmare back into his unconscious. In the dream, a boy again, he had come home as he had that day. Although the house was different—a small brick place rather than the white frame home in which he'd lived—he was certain the Horrible Thing awaited him inside. No matter how hard he tried to turn away from that brick house, his feet had refused to change direction. He'd moved steadily forward, toward the white door, toward the Horrible Thing.

He guessed it was about eight or nine in the morning, but he didn't bother to look at the clock to see whether he was right. After punishing the Tuckers, he'd come straight home, gone to bed, fallen almost immediately into a deep sleep that had lasted until the nightmare awakened him. Closing his eyes, he tried to drift again into sleep. He had plenty of time before he had to go to work; the alarm would wake him.

Again his thoughts took him back to his childhood. He was in a park, walking with a dark-haired woman whose face he was unable to make out, yet whose presence made him feel warm and protected.

"Look, Mommy!" he exclaimed. "Look at the kite."

"It's very pretty."

"Can I have a kite?"

The warm, protective presence with the indistinct face hesitated, then said: "We'd better check with your father."

A chill ran through him. And then he looked up at the face he was unable to see and discovered the features were becoming clearer. It was a pretty face, framed by dark curls, but it had an ugly blue spot. Suddenly the face was changing, turning red. Oh, no, no, no! the boy pleaded. No, no, please. The face was all red now. And dripping.

Instantly it was gone, and the boy was approaching a door again, a green one on a stucco home. Once more he was unable to turn away. The change in the appearance of the house was just an attempt to fool him, but he wouldn't fall for it. He knew what lay beyond that closed door. Despite his efforts to resist, he saw his hand reaching for the knob, turning it.

The Boogeyman sat bolt upright in bed, trembling. The nightmare would not go away. The Horrible Thing had once again climbed out of his unconscious and into a sleeping mind that was unable to resist it. The Boogeyman longed for the day when he would become entirely supernatural, for then he would no longer have to endure these human sufferings. Then the nightmares would be gone, the human memories of no consequence. His yearning for that time was so strong it was almost agonizing.

Someday, he thought. Someday. And then he closed his eyes, and the loving presence with the blurred face came again. Stay with me, he pleaded; stay with me. Don't let the nightmares come again.

"We don't really know any more today than we did yesterday," Lieutenant Castle said as he turned onto the narrow country road where the Evans family had lived. He and Melissa were the only occupants of the detective's unmarked car.

"The lab in Denver found some fibers that don't appear to have come from anything in the house, but there's no reason to believe they came from the killer. Could have been left by the Avon lady, could have been on the husband's clothes when he came home from work, could have been dragged in by the dog." He shrugged.

"What do you do now?" Melissa asked.

Glancing at her, he replied: "We keep on plugging away and hoping."

Melissa was beginning to like Castle. Although he didn't go out of his way to be nice to her, he didn't appear to have anything against her either. He simply went about his job as one would expect a competent professional to go about it. Back-stabbing, bickering, personality conflicts, and the like seemed beneath his dignity.

They drove past the large white house with the white barn, the place where four people had been slain by . . . by what? A mentally ill individual in dire need of help? Or a monster? They're not mutually exclusive, Melissa decided. A crazed killer was no less a crazed killer for being a psychotic, nor were his deeds any less odious. And his victims were certainly no less dead.

Castle turned left into a gravel driveway that curved up a hill to a large Spanish-style house surrounded by big shade trees. In the summertime, when the trees had their leaves, it would be beautifully shady and cool here, Melissa decided. As she and the lieutenant got out of the car, Melissa noticed how chilly the morning had become. The sun, which had been shining when they left the courthouse, was hidden by clouds now, and the darkening sky had a wintry look about it. The Indian summer that Coloradans had been enjoying appeared to be at an end.

"There he is," Castle said, indicating a man in a straw hat who was packing some kind of shredded material around a rosebush. Castle had already interviewed the Davises, who owned the place; he and Melissa were here to see the part-time gardener and handyman.

The house was huge, white with a Spanish-tile roof. A long terrace faced a lawn that was green even this late in the season. The rosebushes that the man was tending, nothing but thorny stalks now, ran along the terrace.

"You Tom Wilson?" the lieutenant asked as he and Melissa stepped up behind the man.

"That's me," the man said, rising and wiping his hands on his khaki work pants. Tall and thin, he appeared to be in his late sixties or early seventies. Clear blue eyes regarded Castle and Melissa from beneath the brim of the straw hat.

"We're from the sheriff's office," Castle replied, showing his ID. "I'm Lieutenant Castle and this is Sheriff James."

The gardener-handyman studied her a moment, then said: "I heard about you on TV."

Melissa smiled politely.

"Mr. Wilson," the lieutenant continued, "we're investigating the murder of the Evans family. I understand that you often drive by their place, and—"

"I saw the boy that day," Wilson said, interrupting. "It was in the afternoon. Johnny was walking home from the highway, where the school bus leaves him off. Usually Bobby Davis walks with him, but Bobby was here that day. He stayed home sick."

"Did you see anything out of the ordinary, Mr. Wilson?"

The old man frowned. "No," he replied slowly, "not that I can recollect. Johnny waved at me, and I waved back, like always."

"What time was that?"

"Ummm, about three-thirty, I guess."

"Did you notice anything unusual at the Evans house? Was anyone there, a strange car in the driveway maybe?"

The gardener shook his head. "It's sad, you know, a thing like this. Johnny was a nice boy. The whole family was nice."

"Do you know of anyone who might have a grudge against any member of the Evans family? Has anyone ever threatened them to your knowledge?"

Again Tom Wilson shook his head.

Castle handed him a card. "If you should think of anything that might help, please give us a call."

Pushing his straw hat farther back on his head, Wilson studied the card. "I sure will," he said. "You can count on it."

As Melissa and the lieutenant turned to leave, the gardener said: "I don't know whether it will help you any, but I did see a car parked across the road from the Evans place. It was the day before they were killed or maybe the day before that." He stopped, apparently waiting to see whether Castle was interested.

"Go on," the lieutenant said.

"It was a blond guy. Had his car jacked up, and he was changing a tire. I wouldn't have thought anything about it except that he was still there changing the same tire when I came back going the other direction about half an hour later.''

"Can you describe the man?"

"Like I said, he was blond. He was in his thirties, I guess. Beyond that, I can't say much. I only saw him for a moment, and he was squatting beside the tire he was working on. The second time I passed, the only look I got at the man himself was in the rearview mirror.''

Castle, who'd been taking notes throughout the interview, quickly jotted something in his notebook. "How about the car?"

"It was green. I'm not sure about the make. Nowadays they all look alike. Used to be that you could tell—''

"Was it full-sized or a compact?"

"It was a big one—I mean a full-sized one. It was big like a large Chevy or Ford, not like a Cadillac or anything like that.''

"Is there anything else you can tell us about the man or the car that might help us?"

The gardener looked off into the distance, thinking. "No," he said finally, "I don't think there is.''

"Do you think you could come up with a sketch of the man if I put you together with a police artist?''

"I'm sorry," Wilson said, "but I'm afraid I wouldn't recognize the guy if he walked up and introduced himself. I just didn't get that good a look at him.'' Readjusting his straw hat, the gardener looked at Castle and Melissa apologetically.

After thanking Wilson for his help, they headed for the home of Abigail Thornton, one of the Evanses' neighbors who hadn't been in the first time officers stopped by.

"Control to three-oh-one," Marla's voice said over the two-way radio.

Castle grabbed the microphone. "Go ahead, control.''

"Give me a ten-twenty-one, ten-three.''

"Ten-four," the lieutenant said, quickly replacing the mike in its holder on the dash.

While Melissa tried to recall what those numbers meant, Castle spun the car around and headed back toward the Davises' house. Apparently realizing she didn't know the codes, he said: "Control wants me to call in. Ten-three means it's an emergency.''

"What could it be?" Melissa asked, sensing the tension in the air.

"I'll know in a moment."

They were back at the Davises' house now. Castle stopped the car and climbed out. Through the windshield, Melissa saw him speak to Wilson, who motioned toward a door at one end of the terrace. Castle stepped inside without knocking. The Davises aren't home, Melissa concluded; the gardener gave him permission to enter the house.

Returning to the car a few moments later, the lieutenant allowed his eyes to meet Melissa's and linger there a moment. Then he started the car. "There's been another one," he said.

"Another what?" But Melissa was fairly certain she knew the answer. An iciness seemed to spread through her body.

"Another murder. Another family of four."

Reaching the road, he rolled down the window, then took the red light that had been resting between them in the seat and placed it on the roof of the car. He flipped a switch on the dash.

"You'd think it would fall off of there, but it doesn't," he said, as if searching for something to say that didn't relate to the four bodies awaiting them. "They stay up there real good."

Melissa, her thoughts swirling, said nothing.

Melissa's knees felt weak as she looked down at the two boys, their bodies violated by the bullets some lunatic had fired into them. They lay side by side in the double bed. Beside the bed, on the floor was their father, David Tucker, a bullet hole in his head. In the bedroom lay his wife, Kathy, also with a single bullet hole in the head.

Kathy hadn't ridden to work with the other members of her car pool this morning. Concerned, one of the women had phoned several times, getting no answer. Finally she called the apartment manager and asked him to check. He did.

"Looks like the woman and kids were shot while they slept," Castle said. "The husband must have gotten up for some reason. Maybe he heard the prowler and decided to investigate."

Melissa nodded. The man who stood beside her was treating her as an equal, discussing the investigation with her. She had to reply, to say something intelligent, and yet she was afraid that if she tried to speak, the words would freeze in her throat. As long as you've got this damn job, she told herself, you're a professional, and you have to act like one. You have to deal with things like this. You have no choice.

"How did the killer get in?" she asked, grateful that her voice hadn't wavered.

"I don't know. There are no signs of forced entry."

"It's probably safe to say they didn't let him in," Melissa said, ignoring that part of her that wanted desperately to run from the building, to be outside, where death didn't hang so heavily in the air.

"No," Castle said thoughtfully, "he sure as hell wasn't invited."

They turned from the scene in the bedroom and stepped into the hall. Melissa was relieved; death was out of her sight now.

The two-bedroom apartment looked like one of those places young couples sought but rarely found. Though clean and well maintained, it was probably moderately priced, because it was out of the city and because it wasn't one of those big modern complexes with all the luxuries. Who were the Tuckers, Melissa wondered, before they became bodies, statistics, names in the newspaper? They had jobs, friends; they shared happiness and pain. And it all just ended, instantly. Now there's nothing.

In the kitchen was the same fingerprint man Melissa had met at the previous killing. Squatting beside the black case in which he carried his supplies, Roger Goldman was dusting the wall near the refrigerator. Just above his head in purple crayon were the words:

BE WARNED

THE BOOGEYMAN WATCHES

THE BOOGEYMAN PUNISHES

Punishes, Melissa thought. What could these people have done that resulted in the sudden end of their lives? What did they do that caused some lunatic to destroy them?

"Why do you think the killer used a different kind of gun and left a different message this time?'' Melissa asked Castle, who was standing beside her, watching Goldman.

"The message isn't different," Castle said. "Only the words are. The meaning's the same. He's telling us that he's the one that did it and that he calls himself the Boogeyman. If he keeps on killing, the messages may become his means of letting us know why he's doing it. Maybe he's already trying to let us know and we just can't see it." He rubbed his cheek. "I say *he*, by the way, because this kind of killing is usually the work of a male. I haven't ruled out a woman.

"As for the different weapons, that's easy. A shotgun's okay out in the country, like at the Evans place, but it makes too much noise to use in an apartment building like this. Here you'd want a handgun, preferably with a silencer."

Glancing up from his dusting, Goldman gave her a smile that was at least part smug smirk. Stupid woman, it seemed to say.

"Come on," Castle said to Melissa. "Let's get some fresh air."

Captain Pruitt had been here when they arrived, but after conferring with Castle, he'd left. There had been no sign of Sergeant Nelson, much to Melissa's relief. Outside they found a thin black man with close-cropped hair who'd apparently just arrived. Castle introduced him as Randy Wright, the county medical examiner.

"Eight people, he's killed now," Wright said, dropping his cigarette butt in the gravel and grinding it out with his shoe. "Just what we need, a psycho running around loose."

"You want the particulars before you go in for a look?" Castle asked, pulling out his notebook.

"Yeah," Wright said, taking out one of his own.

"Victims are Kathleen Sue Tucker, age twenty-six; David Monroe Tucker, twenty-seven; and their two boys, Daniel, three, and Dean, four."

Oh, God, Melissa thought, taking a couple of steps backward so she could brace herself against a patrol car. Hearing the names of the two boys had been like twin stabs in the chest. No longer were they hapless strangers; now they had names. Now they were real people. She struggled to hold back her tears. The sheriff did not cry in front of the medical examiner and her subordinates. The sheriff had to be tough.

The parking area was full of official-looking vehicles—patrol cars, the ambulance waiting to haul away the dead. Deputies were strategically placed to keep the curious away. Technically I'm in charge of all this, Melissa thought. I'm the one who's supposed to see that the lunatic killing these people is stopped. She shuddered. Organizing a neighborhood crime watch had certainly not prepared her for anything like this.

If Melissa could have been granted one wish at that moment, it would have been to go back to Tuesday and have Sheriff Raines win the election.

6

"He was muscular . . . you know, athletic-looking," the young woman said. Her name was Claudia Baca, and she sat in a small chair facing Melissa and Castle, who sat on her living room couch. She was describing the man who had come to her door looking for someone named J. Tucker.

"His hair was blond, not too long, but thick. Real thick."

"How about his eyes?" Castle asked.

"Brown. Dark brown." Her own dark-brown eyes displayed a mixture of confusion and fear. She had obviously been jolted when she learned what happened to the Tuckers and even more shocked when she realized that she might have spoken to the killer. Shifting her eyes away from Castle, she pushed a few strands of dark hair out of her face and crossed herself, her lips moving silently. It was the third time she'd done so.

"How old was he?"

Her eyes returned to Castle, and she frowned. ";It's hard to say. In his twenties or thirties, I guess."

Melissa surveyed the room. The apartments here were rented

furnished, apparently. This one had the same kind of furnishings the Tuckers' had: modern, cheap, the sort of stuff one found in a motel room.

"Do you think you could pick him out of a mug book?" Castle asked.

"I'll know him if I see him," Claudia Baca said. "I'll never forget him, now that I know what he did."

"There's no proof that he's the killer," Castle cautioned. "The man's a suspect at this time, nothing more."

Claudia Baca nodded, but her eyes said the man was the killer as far as she was concerned and nothing was likely to change her mind.

"Why?" she asked, searching Castle's face. "Why would someone kill all those people like that?"

Castle shook his head. "I don't know. Even if we catch him, we may never know."

"The man, the one who was here, he seemed so . . . so cheerful, so polite. He was just a nice, friendly guy. How could he . . . ?" Again the young woman searched Castle's face, looking for an answer he was unable to give her.

There is no explanation, Melissa thought. Something inside the killer's head has broken down, the equivalent of a severed wire or a blown fuse or a short circuit. But we don't understand the human brain; when it breaks, we don't know what's wrong, we can't fix it. All we can do is try to find the man with the broken brain before he can hurt anyone else.

Castle made arrangements for Baca to come in and look at mug shots later that day; then he and Melissa left the apartment. Outside they found a detective who'd been checking the second-floor apartments. In his forties, he was tall and thin, and his name was Lester Hanson.

"Brown and Walczak are checking the places on the other side of the street," he said. "Upstairs I only found one person who saw anything." He flipped open a small notebook. "Uh, a woman named Ramona Lane. She says she saw a guy parked across the street yesterday morning, and it looked as if he might have been watching this building. She didn't get a very good look at him, but she says he was blond, about thirty."

"What about the car?" Castle asked.

"She says it was a green Chevy, full-sized, about two years old."

Melissa and Castle exchanged glances.

That afternoon Melissa waited in her office while Claudia Baca looked at mug files in another part of the building. Instead of sitting here at her desk waiting, Melissa would much rather have been with Baca so she could be on hand when the young woman looked up and excitedly exclaimed: *It's him! This is the one!* But Lieutenant Castle had led her from the room, saying the woman would do much better without someone constantly peering over her shoulder.

To pass the time—and to keep her mind from presenting her with grisly instant replays of what she'd seen this morning—Melissa had switched on the monitor behind her and used her list of codes to follow what was happening. So far it all seemed fairly routine. An officer was dispatched to deal with a shoplifter at a mall, another was sent to direct traffic at the scene of a small fire, and another took a report on a minor accident. They took coffee breaks, arrived at the scene, left the scene, came in to the courthouse for one reason or another, and there were codes for all of it, a never-ending stream of numbers. It was a whole language, with numerals used for nouns, verbs, adjectives. Over the radio a woman would never be raped; she'd be signal-twoed. If the rapist was arrested, he became not a prisoner but a ten-sixteen, and the unit bringing him in would report that it was ten-eight—back in service—and on a ten-nineteen—coming in to the courthouse. It went on and on.

Although listening to the monitor helped keep her mind occupied, there were too many occasions when the radio was silent, when neither the dispatcher nor the officers in the cars had anything to communicate. And during those periods of quiet, Melissa would find herself picturing the two little bodies lying together in what had turned out to be their deathbed, their dead father lying a few feet away on the floor. When that happened, she would look away from her list of codes and try to recite them from memory. So far, at least, it had worked. And she was learning the radio codes. She knew all the signals and the ten codes through ten-thirteen, which had to do with weather and road conditions.

And tonight? she wondered. What will happen when I lie down in bed and close my eyes? Will there come a point at which I'm too tired to recite radio codes, too tired to keep out the image of what I saw in that room? Certain that's what would happen, she shuddered.

And then she jumped, startled by the telephone. She stared at it a moment, trying to decide whether to say Sheriff James or just James or maybe even just Sheriff. Finally she grabbed the receiver and said: "Hello."

"Melissa, that you?"

Melissa said it was.

"It's me. Priscilla. Where are you?"

Melissa was confused. "What do you mean? You know where I am. You just called me."

"No, no, no," Priscilla said, irked. "I mean, why aren't you here? It's Friday afternoon."

"Priscilla, what are you talking about?"

"It's Friday afternoon. We play bridge on Friday afternoons, remember?"

"Priscilla—"

"The three of us have been sitting here for an hour waiting for you. We've been playing hearts, to kill time."

"Priscilla," Melissa said more angrily than she'd intended, "I have a job now. I'm sheriff of this county, and I can't just run out and play cards whenever I feel like it. You're the one who got me into this, you know. If it costs you a fourth for bridge, I guess that's what happens when you start asking your friends to run for office. I'm sorry, but those are the breaks."

"Melissa . . . I mean, well, nobody ever thought you'd win. And . . ." Though Priscilla didn't finish the sentence, Melissa was fairly sure she knew what her friend had been on the verge of saying: that no one expected Melissa to *really* be the sheriff, that it would be just fine if she played cards because that *was* what everyone expected.

And then Melissa wondered why she'd restrained her anger. Why didn't I just tell her? she wondered. Why don't I just tell her that there's a madman out there who's slain two families and that somehow playing cards doesn't seem very important when you've seen eight bodies in the last three days and when you don't know how many more you might see before the killer is stopped?

Inwardly Melissa sighed, knowing she wouldn't say these things, because she might start crying halfway through the words. And because she doubted Priscilla would understand.

"You'll have to get along without me for the next few years," Melissa said with all the cheerfulness she could muster. "Why don't you try Alexandra Curtis?"

"Oh, Melissa, if you'd ever played with her, you'd never even suggest it. She bids so timidly that—"

"Priscilla, I'm sorry, but I have to go. Something's just come up." Lieutenant Castle had just stepped into her office.

As soon as she ended the conversation and hung up, he said: "Claudia Baca didn't find him in the mug files."

"Oh," Melissa said, disappointed.

"I really didn't expect her to. The guy's a psycho, not a crook. Still, it's something you have to do."

"What now?"

"I'm sending Claudia Baca into the city to spend some time with Denver PD's artist. If they come up with a good sketch, I'll give it to the papers and TV stations. Maybe somebody out there will recognize him."

"I hope someone does," Melissa said softly. "He's got to be stopped."

"He will be. The question isn't whether we'll get him, but how long it will take."

Melissa's eyes met his. "What you're really saying is that you don't know how many more people will die." She studied the big man's face a moment; then she asked: "Do you have any kids, Lieutenant?"

"Three. They're mostly grown now, of course. How about you?"

"I have two, a boy and a girl, eight and eleven."

Castle nodded, his eyes saying he realized these were the ages of the Evans kids, that he understood how hard it was for her to look at the bodies of the slain children. He said: "There'll be a meeting in the detective division office in a few minutes to discuss the case. You might want to sit in on it.''

"Thank you," Melissa replied. "I do."

The detective division office was barely big enough to hold the half-dozen or so gray metal desks that had been crammed into it. The four men sitting at them watched Melissa in silence as she sat down on a wooden chair near the blackboard, at which Lieutenant Castle stood. She knew the names of all these men now. Walczak and Brown occupied the two closest desks; behind them were Hanson and Roger Goldman, the fingerprint man. Goldman eyed her for a moment with an expression that was close to a sneer, then looked away; the others eyed her suspiciously.

"The word's out that there's been another killing," Castle said. "Two reporters called me just a few minutes ago, so you can figure they'll be here in force before long. Remember, all questions get referred to me." He paused, allowing his eyes to drive home the point.

"Okay," he continued, "let's talk about this thing. First, for the benefit of any of you who don't already know, Claudia Baca couldn't pick anyone out of the mug files, and she's in Denver right now with a sketch artist." He turned to the blackboard and wrote SUSPECT in the upper left corner. Beneath that he wrote *blond, athletic build, about thirty, green Chevy.*

"What else do we know about him?" the lieutenant asked.

"That he calls himself the Boogeyman and leaves messages in purple crayon." It was Walczak who'd spoken, a slender man in his thirties with thick dark hair.

"What does that tell us?" Castle asked.

"The only thing it tells us for sure," Lester Hanson said, "is that the guy's a psycho."

Castle wrote the word on the board. "What about the purple crayon? Does that tell us anything?" When no one responded, Castle said: "Okay, let's look at the victims, then."

This time it was Brown who spoke up. He was a bald man with a shiny head, about forty, on the chubby side. "Both times it's been a family of four, but I'm not sure the number means anything. It's pretty clear that he's attacking families. I don't think the size of the family matters. Next time it could be six or eight. Or ten.''

"Okay," Walczak said slowly, "here's one for you. If you can believe the second Boogeyman message, then he's punishing these people. So who's he punishing, the kids or the parents or both? And what's he punishing them for?"

"The families didn't have much in common," Hanson said. "One was pretty well-off, and the other was just barely keeping off welfare. One lived in a big house in the country, the other in a small apartment. They didn't go the same places or know any of the same people, and as far as we can tell, they never met. How'd they end up being killed by the same guy? What's the connection?"

When it became clear no one was going to offer an answer for that question, Goldman said: "There were no fingerprints in the Tucker place that matched any I lifted from the Evans house. Our killer's either lucky or careful. I'd say careful."

"Even though the guy switched weapons," Walczak said, "he still used a gun both times. Another thing is that—so far, anyway—he's shot the parents in the head but not necessarily the kids. With the Tucker kids, he shot one in the head, like the parents, and the other in the chest. Maybe that means something, maybe not." He shrugged.

The room fell silent.

Having worked up her courage, Melissa said: "There were no signs of forced entry at the scene of either killing. The medical examiner says the Evans family died late in the afternoon. Their doors were probably unlocked, since the place is in the country and the kids would have been going in and out. But not at the Tuckers' apartment, especially not in the middle of the night."

The men at the desks stared at her. Since she had come into the room, her role had changed from that of a curiosity to a nonentity. No one had expected her to speak.

"What are you suggesting?" Castle asked.

"That he knows how to pick a lock."

"You're assuming too much," Goldman said quickly. "The Tuckers could have forgotten to lock the door. Or even a window."

"You know it wasn't a window," Castle said. "You were

there. All the windows were latched, and all the screens were in place.''

"I'm just pointing out things I don't think she considered,'' Goldman replied sourly.

"From talking to the neighbors,'' Castle said, "I'd say the Tuckers weren't the type to leave the door unlocked. I'd say she has a good point.''

Goldman nodded sullenly.

The meeting went on for another half hour. When it ended, the only conclusion Melissa could draw was that unless they got very lucky, they were a long way from catching the Boogeyman.

Back in the office she was getting ready to sit in on the swing-shift briefing when the reporter from the *Denver Post* showed up. "Got a moment, Sheriff?'' the woman asked.

"If it's about the murders, Lieutenant Castle's in charge of the investigation, and I'm referring all questions to him.''

"I'll save everything substantive for him, but I still have a couple of questions I think you can answer.''

Motioning for the woman to sit down, Melissa said: "I'll listen to them, but I don't promise to answer them.''

"Good enough,'' the reporter said, taking a seat. Her expression suddenly became quite serious. "It's terrible to realize there are people out there who can do something like this, isn't it?''

Melissa nodded, trying not to picture the two small lumps under the covers or the two little bodies on the kitchen floor.

"I suppose the department's going all out to catch the killer.''

"Every detective we've got is on the case full-time, and in one way or another I think the entire department's involved.''

The reporter, who'd withdrawn a notebook and pen from her purse, said: "How do you—someone with no experience with anything like this—how do you cope with it?''

"Fortunately, the department has competent officers like Lieutenant Castle to head up the investigation.''

"No, I mean how do you cope with it emotionally? Less than a week ago you were a full-time homemaker, and now you have to deal with a killer who's wiped out two entire families in less than three days.''

Melissa hesitated. This statement would be for public consumption, and she wanted to choose her words carefully. "I deal with it by keeping one thought foremost in mind: There's a very dangerous psychopath out there who absolutely must be stopped."

And then she wondered whether she'd said too much. She had been careful not to reveal any sensitive information about the investigation, but she didn't want to say anything that might prejudice the case either. It was time to end the interview.

"That's about as much as I can say," Melissa told the reporter. "If you want to know anything else, I think you'd better check with Lieutenant Castle."

Shoving the notebook and pen back into her purse, the reporter rose. "Thank you for your time, Sheriff," the woman said, and then she was gone.

Melissa checked her watch, discovering it was too late to attend the four o'clock briefing. Suddenly feeling very tired, she decided to call it a day.

The Boogeyman sat in his kitchen the next morning leisurely eating ham and eggs with hashbrowns, the potatoes having come frozen from the grocery store. Manufactured in the 1950s probably, the breakfast table had metal legs and a blue Formica top. Actually the whole house looked like something from the 1950s, but the Boogeyman really didn't care. He rented it; he didn't own it.

Once, he had owned his own place. It was so long ago that it seemed like something from another life. He considered that a moment. Maybe it hadn't been that long ago; perhaps his mind was just playing tricks on him. Maybe he simply wanted it to be long ago. So he could forget.

The marriage had lasted about two years, ending in divorce. It had produced one child, a boy named Teddy. A boy who'd never seen his first birthday. SIDS, they'd called it, sudden infant death syndrome. The baby had just plain died. No reason. He was just dead. The wife had picked him up first thing in the morning and screamed because he wasn't warm anymore. He was room temperature.

And he'd never be warm again.

The Boogeyman was uncertain whether he blamed his wife for the infant's death. Would Teddy be alive right now if she'd checked on him to make sure everything was all right?

Maybe, maybe not. But whether she was at fault wasn't the most troubling question concerning his former wife. It was that he couldn't remember her name.

There was forgetting, and there was forgetting. If her name had been pushed from his memory because it was painful, that would have been okay. But it seemed to him that he'd never known it. Even going back in his mind to the wedding was no help. In his memory, the minister would say: *Do you take this man . . . ?* No names. Just *you*.

He pushed these thoughts aside. Her name really wasn't that important, he supposed. Being unable to recall it was just a minor irritation, something that wasn't quite right.

Beside his plate was the morning paper. He'd deliberately put off reading it so he could savor the prospect. The banner headline would be about him, about the Boogeyman. Having finished his breakfast, he got up and poured another cup of coffee from the pot on the stove, then returned to his seat and unfolded the paper. The banner read:

SECOND FAMILY SLAIN IN RAMSEY COUNTY

As he read the story, he noted with satisfaction that the paper was referring to him as the Boogeyman now. The *Post* was the leader; soon all the media would call him that.

The story jumped to A-11, and he hurriedly found the new page so he could continue reading. Toward the end of the piece, the new woman sheriff was quoted as saying the entire department was involved in the search for the killer. Suddenly the Boogeyman found himself gripping the paper so fiercely he was tearing it. Muttering curses under his breath, he read the words again, then hurled the paper at the wall.

A dangerous psychopath, she'd called him. Furious, he grabbed the plate that held his breakfast and stepped to the sink, where he stood staring into it, trying to slow the angry churning of his thoughts so he could think clearly. And then he slammed the dish into the sink, shattering the plate and a glass from which he'd drunk orange juice. A dangerous psychopath. How dare she call me that? he thought. He slammed his fist down on the counter, making the dishes in the drain rattle. With a swing of his arm, he knocked the drain and its contents onto the floor. China shattered.

How dare she call me that? he demanded furiously. How dare she?

Later he sat on a bench in a small park. The day was sunny but cool; in the distance a box kite hung in the air, kept aloft by a nippy breeze that penetrated your clothing, reminding you that January was the month after next. He was the only one here, the only one willing to waste Saturday morning sitting in a chilly park that could offer nothing but brown grass and dormant trees.

When his rage had subsided, he'd cleaned up the broken glass. He was calm now. It was time to think. Melissa James's words could not go unpunished; he knew that. What he didn't know was how to go about it, for these circumstances were entirely different from those that had led to the disciplining of the Evans and Tucker families. This should be a special punishment, one that would make others think twice before mocking the Boogeyman.

He leaned back and closed his eyes, trying to empty his mind. After a few moments he sat erect once more, his eyes drifting to the spot where the box kite had been. It was gone.

I need a way, he thought, a way to punish the woman sheriff. Two hours later he still didn't have one.

Sitting in the front seat of Keith's Buick, Melissa watched as the traffic thinned and the lights became fewer. They'd be at her house in a few minutes.

It had been a nice night. Dinner in one of Denver's better restaurants. Then a play. And finally they'd parked in the foothills of the Rockies at a place from which you could look down on the lights of Denver. They'd talked of inconsequential things, made out like teenagers. It was late. Linda Sue's mother was probably wondering where she was; Melissa would have to give the baby-sitter a few extra dollars to square things.

Inwardly Melissa sighed in contentment. Not once this evening had she thought about Sergeant Nelson or Captain Pruitt or the murders. These concerns would be back, she knew, but for a while, at least, she'd put them aside. You had to be able to do that, she realized. It was the only way you could cope.

Glancing at Keith, she found him looking at her. Their eyes met for a second before his returned to the road. Neither of them spoke; the mood was too fragile and too special to risk breaking it. Good to his word, Keith had said nothing to discourage her from being a full-time sheriff. Before leaving her house, he'd asked about the progress of the case, wished her luck in apprehending the killer, and that was that, subject closed for the evening. Their relationship had changed; they understood each other better now. We're closer, Melissa thought. We found out some things about each other, and now we're closer.

Unwilling to leave her children unattended on the weekend, Melissa had decided not to go to the office today. She'd called in, got a progress report from Lieutenant Castle, told him she could be reached at home. She'd felt guilty. The dedicated lieutenant and the officers under his command were working, aware that days off were unimportant when there was a mass killer to be dealt with. Meanwhile, the sheriff stayed home.

Had she gone to work, however, she'd have felt guilty about abandoning her kids. And her presence would probably have not hastened the apprehension of the killer by so much as a second.

Quickly she pushed all this from her mind. These were things to be dealt with on Monday, not now. This was the time for recharging, for regaining her sanity.

Watching Keith as he piloted the Buick through the darkness, Melissa felt that within the car they were insulated from the rest of the world, that in here it was just the two of them in their own private cocoon, safe and snug. She wished she could slide over next to him, but the car's bucket seats and floor-mounted shift lever wouldn't permit it.

"Thanks," she said softly. "For such a nice evening."

Without speaking, he reached over and squeezed her hand.

A few moments later they turned onto Melissa's street, passing the darkened homes of the upper middle-class. Ahead was her white patrol car, which now had the driveway to itself because she'd put the now little-used station wagon in the garage. She finally felt comfortable enough driving the cruiser to agree to give Billy his long-awaited ride. On Monday she would drop him and Sarah off at school on her way to the courthouse. Suddenly she realized there was another white patrol car at her house, one parked at the curb. As they pulled into the driveway, an officer climbed out and hurried toward them.

"What is it?" Melissa asked as she climbed out of the Buick. Somewhere inside, she felt hope starting to stir. Maybe they'd caught the Boogeyman. Maybe the horror was over.

"Lieutenant Castle sent me to get you," the deputy said. It was Bob Sanchez, the officer who'd mistakenly had her car towed.

"Why?" Melissa asked, the hope still very much alive. Maybe, just maybe.

"There's been another one."

"Another what?" she asked, confused.

"Another murder. The Boogeyman. He's done it again."

7

The house was about ten miles away, in a neighborhood much like Melissa's. Bob Sanchez parked the cruiser behind two ordinary-looking sedans that Melissa recognized as unmarked detectives' cars. One was Lieutenant Castle's.

The house was a large two-story frame home. As they stepped onto the cement porch, Walczak opened the front door. "In the kitchen," he said, pointing in the appropriate direction.

Melissa and the uniformed deputy passed through a dining room in which stood a massive wood table, and then stepped into a large modern kitchen where they found Lieutenant Castle standing beside a distressed-looking man of about fifty. Near the refrigerator was the bloody body of a middle-aged woman, lying facedown on the floor.

Melissa was surprised at her reaction. The twinge of shock and revulsion she should have experienced wasn't there. Instead she simply felt empty, drained. This was the ninth body she'd seen in less than a week. Was that how it worked? After a while you just accepted it as a thing that happened, another example of how rotten the world really was? Oh, God, she thought. Feeling like this is worse than the shock and revulsion.

Letting her eyes explore the room, she saw the message on the wall near the back door. In what looked like green felt-tip, it read:

THE BOOGEYMAN STRIKES AGAIN

Her gaze met Castle's, and he said: "Good evening, Sheriff."

"Good evening," she replied, and she saw in the lieutenant's eyes that he too thought something was wrong here. "How many victims?" she asked.

"Just one. Sheriff, this is Melvin Peters. The victim's his wife. Mr. Peters, do you think you can tell the sheriff what you told me?"

Peters nodded. He was a good-looking man with just a trace of gray in his thick dark hair and a trim body. In his eyes was a mixture of terror and bewilderment.

"Why don't we step in here?" Melissa said, indicating the dining room.

The man, who seemed unaware of his wife's body on the floor, complied mechanically, almost lethargically. When they sat down facing each other across the dining table, Melissa said: "Tell me what happened, Mr. Peters."

His hands were folded in front of him on the table. He stared at them a moment or two, then looked up and began. "I was downstairs . . . uh, in the basement recreation room. There's a pool table down there, and a Ping-Pong table. I was shooting pool by myself, just passing time, when I heard a boom from upstairs . . . a shotgun blast. I ran upstairs, and just as I opened the door, I saw the front door closing, so I ran to the window, and I saw a man running across the front yard. I . . . I called for my wife, and when she didn't answer, I started looking through the house. I finally found her in the kitchen, and I saw the writing on the wall, and I knew what happened." He stared at her as if he really didn't see her.

"Did you and your wife live here alone?" Melissa asked.

He nodded. "We have two daughters, but one's married with kids of her own and the other's away in college." Taking a deep breath, he added: "They don't know yet. I have to tell them."

"The man you saw, can you describe him?"

"No. I just saw a silhouette."

"Do you have any idea why he killed your wife but not you?"

"He must not have known I was here. The door to the basement stairs was closed. It looks like a closet."

Melissa noticed that Lieutenant Castle was standing in the kitchen doorway watching impassively. Asking Melvin Peters to remain where he was, she stepped into the kitchen, where Bob Sanchez and Detective Walczak were waiting. Castle joined them.

"Well," the lieutenant said to Melissa, "do you believe him?"

"No."

"I don't either. Before we disturb anything in here, Goldman will have to dust and shoot pictures, but I'm going to start searching the rest of the house now. He didn't have time to get rid of the weapon because the neighbors heard the shotgun blast. One of them called at about the same time Peters did. Brown's checking around the neighborhood now, but I'll bet you nobody saw anyone running from this house."

"I know something else we can do," Melissa said, hoping her suggestion wouldn't earn her contemptuous looks from these men. "Let's have someone go downstairs and shoot some pool while I talk to Mr. Peters again."

Castle nodded. "It's worth a try."

"I'll go downstairs and practice a few shots," Bob Sanchez said, grinning.

Walczak, looking confused, said nothing.

Taking her seat across the table from Peters again, Melissa waited until the three men had gone into the living room, then said: "How long were you shooting pool?"

"Oh, for an hour or so, I guess. Why?" He stared at his hands while he spoke.

"I'm just trying to establish some things. Uh, were you at the pool table all the time you were down there, or did you do other things?''

Frowning, he studied her a moment before answering. ''As well as I can remember, I was shooting pool the whole time. That's really all there is to do down there by yourself.''

''Do you have any idea how the intruder got in?''

''The front door wasn't locked. He probably walked in.''

''Do you always leave the door unlocked at night?''

''Uh . . .'' He trailed off, looking confused. ''Well, Terry didn't always lock it during the day, because she liked to go out that way to work in the yard sometimes, and she didn't want to worry about locking herself out. Then, when she came back in, she'd forget to set the lock again. I think she'd been raking leaves today. We'd been putting it off.''

Melissa wondered how he could speak so matter-of-factly about his wife when she'd just been brutally murdered. He seemed dazed. She supposed the real impact of what had happened here hadn't hit him yet. Even if he was his wife's murderer, the shock of it had to be waiting out there like an emotional sledgehammer.

''Let's get back to the basement, Mr. Peters. You said you were—'' She stopped because she'd just heard the sound of someone shooting pool. Peters showed no reaction; it hadn't dawned on him yet.

''Anyway, Mr. Peters, you said that the killer didn't know that you were here.''

''Yes,'' he replied cautiously, his eyes searching hers.

''Because you were in the basement, shooting pool.''

''Yes.''

''Then the killer must have been deaf, Mr. Peters.''

As the realization hit him, his eyes widened. ''The door . . . it must be open.''

''It's closed,'' Lieutenant Castle said, stepping in from the living room. In the silence that followed, the clicking of pool balls seemed as loud as shotgun blasts.

Peters's jaw dropped, and his lower lip began quivering. ''Well, uh, maybe the guy only wanted to kill Terry. He's crazy, isn't he? You can't know what a crazy person will do.''

''We're searching the house,'' Castle said to Melissa. ''I had

Sanchez start in the basement, since he was there already, and Walczak's upstairs.''

"You can't do that," Peters said, rising. "You don't have a warrant."

"This is the scene of a felony, Mr. Peters. I don't need a warrant."

"I . . ." Standing beside his chair, Peters shifted his eyes from Castle to Melissa, then back to the lieutenant. "Do I need a lawyer?"

"That's up to you, Mr. Peters. You're not under arrest at this time, but you're certainly entitled to have a lawyer present if you wish."

Looking excited, Bob Sanchez hurried in from the living room. "Could I see you out here, please," he said to Melissa and the lieutenant.

They accompanied him into the living room, where in hushed tones he said: "I found it. Inside the pool table. There's a panel underneath that comes off, and there's a shotgun in there."

"Good work," Castle said. "If Goldman ever gets here, we'll have him dust it, and—"

"That's not all, Lieutenant," Sanchez said, interrupting him. "There was one other thing in there. A felt-tip, a green one."

Castle nodded. "Okay, good. Go upstairs and tell Walczak."

Peters was still standing in the same spot when Melissa and Castle returned to the dining room.

"Mr. Peters," the lieutenant said, "now I do think you'd better get in touch with a lawyer."

The man simply stood there, staring at him.

"We found the gun and the green marker, Mr. Peters. Inside the pool table."

The man slowly sank into his chair. "I . . . I didn't plan to do it. She wouldn't give me a divorce. I—"

"Mr. Peters," Castle said quickly, "before you say any more, I have to inform you that you're under arrest. You have the right to remain silent. Anything you say . . ."

While being informed of his rights, Peters stared at his hands. When Castle had finished, the man said: "It's an old story, Lieutenant. I'm in love with a younger woman. My wife wouldn't give me a divorce, so we argued. I . . . I went berserk."

"Mr. Peters, do you understand that you don't have to say any of this? And that you're entitled to a lawyer—and that the court will appoint one if you can't afford it?"

"Sure, and just what do I want with a lawyer, Lieutenant? Will having an attorney bring Terry back to life? Will it make Julie wait until I'm out of prison so she can marry a murderer? Will it convince the corporation I work for that it would be just fine to have a killer as its executive vice-president? I'll have to get a lawyer, Lieutenant. I know that. But there's really no rush, is there?"

"Would you stand up, please, Mr. Peters?"

As the man did so, Castle produced a pair of handcuffs and stepped around the table.

"That was a good idea," Sanchez said, "having someone go down and shoot pool." He slowed his patrol car at an intersection, then turned left. Behind them the Peters house disappeared from sight.

"It really didn't accomplish very much," Melissa replied. "The gun and felt-tip would have been found anyway."

"Even so, you handled yourself real well in there for someone who's only been in law enforcement a few days." He glanced at her and grinned, his features dimly illuminated by the dash panel lights. "I know Walczak was impressed. He told me so."

"I've still got a lot to learn."

"It's not that hard. It's like anything else you do. Mostly it's just a matter of common sense."

It was an oversimplification, but Melissa was feeling too pleased with herself to care. After pausing at a stop sign, Sanchez turned onto a thoroughfare. While he drove, Melissa studied his profile. His was the kind of face girls tore out of movie magazines and taped onto their walls. It was ruggedly masculine and at the same time gentle, with smooth skin and dark eyes that sparkled with a warmth that seemed to come from somewhere deep inside. The word *doll* came to mind, but that was entirely too adolescent. Hell, she decided, the man's downright *sexy*.

Chuckling inwardly, she pushed these thoughts from her mind. She was thinking like a teenager, and at thirty-five she was too old for that sort of thing. And then a sobering realization hit her.

I just saw the victim of a murder, she thought. How can I be so cheerful when a woman's life has been brutally ended? Terry Peters was alive; she had aspirations, fears; she laughed and she cried. Don't I care?

And then she realized what all police officers must realize. Sure you care; you wouldn't be human if you didn't. But you see so many horrors that you have no choice but to remain emotionally detached, for to do otherwise would render you unable to function. Not to mention what it might do to your sanity.

Apparently she had learned a valuable lesson. You neither ignored the horrors nor allowed yourself to be overwhelmed by them; you learned to manage them. And as long as the system worked, you learned not to question yourself too closely about it.

"Do police officers have an unusually high burn-out rate?" she asked Sanchez.

"A what?"

"Burn-out is when you can't handle it anymore, and you either opt out or flip out or maybe both."

"I've never heard anyone cite any figures, but I know we're overworked, underpaid, and underloved, so I guess we wouldn't be surprised to learn we were burned out as well."

"How long have you had this job?"

"Eight years. Started when I was twenty-one. First real job I got after college."

"Do you plan to make it your permanent career?"

"Oh, I don't know. I like it, or I wouldn't have stayed. But permanent career just sounds so . . . so damned unalterable. I'd hate to think that I'm locked into one job and that's all I'll ever do. I'm not even thirty yet, not for another eight months anyway, and I guess I like to think I'm still young enough that I've got all my options."

"Are you close to making sergeant?"

He laughed. "Well, I'm eligible, but so's about half the force. The trouble is that there aren't any openings. And there won't be until one of the present sergeants leaves for some reason. Last time that happened was three years ago, when Sergeant Walker retired."

Sanchez signaled for a turn, then eased the patrol car onto the access ramp for an expressway. For a few minutes neither spoke; then Sanchez broke the silence.

"You're learning how to handle it, aren't you?"

Uncertain what he meant, Melissa hesitated, then replied: "You mean how to deal with the death, the violence?"

"Yes."

"If a week ago anyone had told me I could harden myself to it this quickly, I'd have told them they were crazy."

"It doesn't take very long," Sanchez said. "I guess you never know how quickly you can adjust to things until you have to. The first couple of times, I just about threw up. But I got over it. And then it frightened me a little to discover I could look at someone like that woman back there and not feel what I was supposed to feel. It was like maybe there was something wrong with me. But after a while, I got over that, too."

"That's pretty much how I felt tonight," Melissa said, surprised to hear the deputy echoing her thoughts so exactly. "I was learning to deal with it, and one part of me felt relieved, while another part felt guilty." She wondered why she was telling this to someone she hardly knew, who was her subordinate. But then the answer was obvious. She was telling him because he was willing to listen and because he understood.

"Look behind us," Sanchez said. "They all came roaring up, saw the patrol car, and suddenly decided it was time to start obeying the speed limit."

Melissa looked. There were at least a dozen pairs of headlights behind them. "I'll bet they'll be glad when you pull off the freeway."

The deputy chuckled. Again they drove on in silence for a few moments; then Sanchez said:

"The way I finally got over the guilt was by telling myself that I had nothing to do with what caused those people to get killed or injured or beat up or whatever happened to them. They'd have been in exactly the same condition if I was there or not. I had to control my feelings to do the job, and because I was doing the job, maybe over time two or three people didn't get hurt or killed—just because I was out there. Maybe one of those drivers back there right now will be alive just because he saw this car and had to slow down. I'll never know for sure, but

I'll bet there are some people out there right now who are alive because of me. It makes me feel good. It makes me glad I learned to control my feelings so I could keep on doing this job.''

He glanced at her, and Melissa thought she saw just a trace of embarrassment on his face. "Maybe I didn't say it too well," he said. "But I think you know what I mean."

"I think you said it very well," Melissa replied.

A few moments later the deputy let her off at her house, and she hurried inside, finding Keith asleep on the living-room couch.

"I'm back," she said softly.

For a moment he lay there on his stomach, his face pressed into the crack between the cushion and the couch's back; then, just as she was about to speak again, he rolled over, slowly opening his eyes.

"Hi," he said, sleepily. After a long moment, during which he seemed to be trying to determine just where he was and how he got there, he sat up. "Were more people killed?" he asked.

"A woman was murdered, but it wasn't the work of the Boogeyman. Her husband did it, then wrote a Boogeyman message on the wall, hoping to throw us off the track. We found where he hid the shotgun he used on his wife and the marker he used to write the message."

"Where'd he hide them?"

"In the pool table."

"Oh." He shook his head as if to dislodge any remaining bits of sleep that were dulling his brain. "The kids are in bed. I paid off Linda Sue and sent her home."

"What do I owe you?"

He dismissed the matter of repayment with a wave of his hand.

"I've got to reimburse you," Melissa said. "Someday you may defend a client my department has arrested."

"Your scrupulous honesty is noted, Sheriff James. However, I should point out two things to you. First, I'm not a criminal lawyer, and second, I've never handled a single case that was tried in Ramsey County."

"What," she teased, "are we too small potatoes for a big-time lawyer like you?"

"I'm the firm's specialist in federal matters; you know that. You also know that the federal courthouse is in Denver, which is not in Ramsey County." He yawned.

"Come on," she said. "I've got to get some coffee in you. If I let you drive home like this, it would be worse than letting you drive home drunk. Drunks may not drive too well, but at least they usually stay awake while they try."

In the kitchen she made them each a cup of instant coffee, which they drank at the breakfast table. After forcing him to take the money for the baby-sitter, she kissed him good night and sent him on his way. Then she sat down on the couch to think.

Changing from Bob Sanchez's company to Keith's had been something like walking out of a room in which a rock concert had been in progress and into one in which chamber music was being played. Well, she thought, I may be a thirty-five–year–old widow, but I haven't forgotten what it's like to respond to a man's sexuality. She realized with a little bit of a start that under almost any other circumstances, she would most likely be in bed with Sanchez at this moment had he made even the slightest effort to get her there. The attractiveness of the man was almost dizzying.

Knowing what she'd see, Melissa resisted the impulse to go and look at herself in the mirror. Her face, though no longer that of a twenty-year-old, was smooth-skinned and attractive, her hair thick and dark. She was tall and slender, with firm breasts and long legs. Though not in the same league as Marla Clark, she wasn't bad. And why am I considering this? she asked herself. She had no answer for that question, at least none she could allow herself to accept.

Although she and Keith occasionally made love, their relationship was hardly a sexual one. Mainly, she supposed, because the kids were always around, which meant they could only make love at Keith's place, with the kids at home under the supervision of Linda Sue Jennings. And when she'd met Keith, she hadn't been looking for a sexual relationship. She'd been seeking someone reliable, someone who was good with kids. Had she unknowingly been looking for a husband? That was another question for which she had no answer.

Pushing all these thoughts from her mind, she stood up and headed for the bedroom. It was time to get some sleep.

The Boogeyman sat on the same park bench he'd occupied yesterday. It was a bleak Sunday morning, gray and overcast. A breeze even frostier than yesterday's blew candy wrappers and dried leaves along the concrete sidewalk in front of him. Once more he had the park to himself.

He'd had the dream again last night. This time, being chased by armed men, he'd run along what seemed to be some sort of a pier. Ahead had been a parked car, his car, a means of escape. And yet, as he neared it, he realized that the Horrible Thing was within, waiting for him. Although he was unable to see through the windows, which were all mirrors, he knew what was inside.

But the men were still coming, deputies led by the woman sheriff, all of them with guns except the woman, who held a rope, one end of which had been made into a hangman's noose. *He's a dangerous psychopath!* she yelled. *We have to lynch him!*

The men cheered.

The car was his only hope. Trembling, he reached for the door handle. Unable to touch it, he started to withdraw his hand, and suddenly, very close now, came the shouts: *Lynch him! Lynch the psycho!* He shoved his hand forward, grabbed the handle, and yanked the door open. He caught one brief glimpse of the Horrible Thing and slammed the door closed again.

Quickly he ran to the edge of the pier, stared at the cold gray liquid below. Unable to enter the car with the Horrible Thing inside and facing certain death at the hands of the woman sheriff, he jumped. It was only then that he remembered that the gray liquid was acid.

Shaking and dripping wet, he'd sat up in bed, the sound of his scream still lingering in the room.

Just thinking about the dream made him shiver. How, he wondered, how am I going to punish this woman sheriff? As he'd done the day before, he sat on the cold bench, thinking, trying to come up with a workable plan.

He was ready to leave the park when he saw a man coming toward him, a tall fellow with a black hat and a heavy coat. The

Boogeyman remained on the bench, watching the approaching figure.

"Nippy day," the man said as he passed the Boogeyman's bench.

"Yes," the Boogeyman replied. "I don't think I'll stay out here much longer."

The man nodded politely and continued along his way. Because of the man's heavy coat, the Boogeyman hadn't spotted the Roman collar until the priest was just a few feet away. Seeing the clergyman reminded the Boogeyman of something he should have recalled before now, something that might just solve the problem of how to deal with the woman sheriff.

The Boogeyman rose and began walking toward the street. He would have to do some checking to make sure everything was still as it had been. He would have to wait a few hours, until church services were over. Even so, unable to stop himself, he began hurrying.

It was a little after one o'clock when the Boogeyman parked his green car in the street and strolled up the concrete walk toward the main entrance to the church. About fifteen years old, the two-story brick structure was simply styled, without a steeple or the traditional, churchy doors and windows. A ten-foot-high cross was incorporated into the brickwork on the building's face.

The man he sought here was A. J. Sebastian, the caretaker. Before moving to his present address, a couple of years ago, the Boogeyman had rented a small apartment in a duplex. The other half of the structure had been occupied by A. J. Both men were alone—the old caretaker was a widower and the Boogeyman divorced—so a friendship of sorts had developed. Many evenings had been spent over a checkerboard, A. J. sipping whiskey until he couldn't even come close to winning a game, at which point they'd call it a night.

And then one evening the old man had abruptly stopped playing and announced that he'd discovered something at the church, something he'd been totally unaware of for the ten years he'd been working there. Something no one else knew about, not even Reverend Maxwell. A secret the caretaker was going to share only with him, if he'd come to the church and take a look.

The Boogeyman had obliged. At the time he hadn't been all that interested in what A. J. had shown him. But then, in those days, he hadn't known he was the Boogeyman. Or that he would have to find a way to punish a woman sheriff.

Seeing no sign of the caretaker, the Boogeyman headed for the rear of the church, where he found a small parking area and beyond it a small brick house, the rectory, the home of Reverend Maxwell.

Although the church was in a developed area—upper-middle-class homes mainly—vacant land abutted its landscaped property on each side, the neatly trimmed hedges, flowerbeds, and lawn abruptly giving way to scrub brush and weeds. Of course, this time of year the transition was less of a visual shock than it would be during the summer, when the flowers were in bloom, the grass green, the hedges more than a collection of leafless twigs.

"Well, I'll be damned," a familiar voice said behind him. "What are you doing here?"

The Boogeyman turned to find A. J. standing in the doorway of a small rear entrance to the church. Tall and thin and wearing rumpled work clothes, the old man hadn't changed a bit. Joining him on the stoop, the Boogeyman shook his hand.

"I was in the neighborhood," the Boogeyman said. "Thought I'd stop by and see what you were up to."

Releasing his hand, A. J. slapped him on the back. "Well, I'm sure glad you did," he said warmly. "Come in, and I'll fetch you some coffee."

The Boogeyman followed the caretaker into a fairly large kitchen. The old man got two mugs from a cabinet and filled both from the coffee urn on the counter.

"Sit down," he said. "Sit down."

The two men seated themselves at a long wooden table that looked as if it belonged at a picnic area in a national park somewhere. A. J. slid a steaming mug of coffee across the table, and the Boogeyman picked it up.

Producing a flask, the caretaker said: "Fix up your coffee for you?"

"No thanks, A. J."

The old man poured some into his cup, took a swig right from the flask, capped it, and quickly returned it to his pocket.

"You know, don't you," the Boogeyman warned, "that stuff's going to kill you if you don't lay off it?"

"You think that kind of talk can scare a seventy-seven-year-old man?"

"No, I suppose not."

The Boogeyman studied his old friend. The caretaker's nose was permanently red, the result of years of consuming too much booze, but his eyes were bright and clear. In them the Boogeyman could see both warmth and intelligence.

"You oughta stop by the apartment one of these days," A. J. said. "It's been a long time since we played a game of checkers."

"I'm on swing shift now, but maybe I'll get the chance on one of my days off. If not then, I'll for sure come over the next time I work day shift."

The caretaker nodded. "Anytime at all. You just stop by."

The Boogeyman took a sip of coffee. "You remember the last time I was here?"

"Sure do."

"Did you ever tell anyone else about your secret?"

"Nope. Unless you did, the only people know about it are you and me."

"I haven't told anyone," the Boogeyman said.

"Then it's just as secret as ever." The caretaker grinned. Then he shrugged. "Hell, it really wouldn't make that much difference if anyone found out, would it? Just as long as they didn't tell Reverend Maxwell, that is." He chuckled.

It would make a big difference to me, the Boogeyman thought as he smiled at his old friend.

Twenty minutes later he left the church, promising to stop by A. J.'s apartment for a game of checkers in the near future. The Boogeyman knew how he would punish Melissa James now, although one part of what he had to do saddened him.

As he started his car and pulled away from the church, he pushed the unpleasant part from his mind. Some things were unavoidable, and when you were the Boogeyman you had duties that took precedence over personal concerns. In any position of importance and authority, one had to make sacrifices.

When he was a few blocks from the church, he began whistling softly.

8

Sitting down at her desk, Melissa put her purse in the bottom drawer, then checked the clock. It was a few minutes before eight, Monday morning, the start of a new week.

"Good morning," Captain Pruitt said as he stepped into her office. "Have a good weekend?"

"Fine," Melissa replied. "I guess you heard that we had a false alarm on another Boogeyman killing."

The captain nodded. "I know most of the story." Pulling a chair a little closer to Melissa's desk, he sat down. "I've taken care of the change in radio room personnel you wanted. Uh, Officer Clark goes on patrol duties this morning. There was no need to keep her in the radio room to train her replacement, because I'm replacing her with the officer who filled in for her on her days off. A deputy named Dixon. He'll train another officer to fill in for him on his days off."

"Very good, Captain. Thank you." When Pruitt started to get up, she added: "Has the department ever considered using civilians in the radio room so the sworn officers can be kept out on the streets?"

"We have civilians on swing and grave shifts. Used to be one on day shift, too, until Sheriff Raines found himself with a female officer he didn't know what to do with."

"I'd like to go back to the old system."

"I agree. Using sworn officers in the radio room is a waste of manpower. But right now there's no money in the budget for hiring a civilian to do that job. For the moment the only way I can take Clark out is to put another officer in."

"So what happens to Clark now?"

"For the moment I've got her on day shift so we can keep an eye on her while she gets some on-the-job training from an experienced officer. When I think she's ready to be on her own, then she'll have to go to graveyard shift. She's technically a rookie, and that's where rookies have to start." Something in the captain's expression added an unspoken footnote: *Unless* they get special treatment.

He didn't have to worry about that, since the last thing Melissa wanted was for Marla Clark or any other woman the department might hire to get special treatment. All officers were to be treated alike, trained alike, assigned to the same jobs.

"I want you to deal with Clark as you would any other officer," she said.

"That's how it should be," the captain said, rising.

"Uh, one other thing, Captain. I realize that people can be set up, put into situations in which they just about have to fail. Or life can be made so miserable for a certain individual that the person in question quits."

His eyes met hers. "I won't let anything like that happen."

"You wouldn't necessarily know, would you? A lot of things can happen out there when nobody's looking."

"I'd know," he said, his eyes still fixed on hers.

Melissa believed him. "Thank you, Captain. I'll leave it in your hands."

As soon as he was gone, Melissa stood up, intending to go to the morning briefing. Suddenly Sergeant Nelson stormed into her office.

"We're not working with her," he said angrily. "So you might just as well put her back in radio."

Taken aback, Melissa fumbled for the right words. Finally she said: "You don't run this department, Sergeant. I do."

Dismissing her words with a wave of his hand, he said: "Let me try to explain this to you. When we go out there, our lives are on the line. Sometimes the only thing between you and a knife in the back or maybe getting your ribs kicked in is your buddy. You've gotta have people backing you up you can depend on. So how the hell do you expect this woman radio operator to handle a job like that? What's she going to do when she's up against some two-hundred-and-fifty-pound drunk who'd like nothing better than to stomp some cop's ass?''

Melissa sat down. ''Sergeant, in police departments all over the country, women are doing the job perfectly well. What makes the Ramsey County Sheriff's Department any different?''

He glared at her, his face red with rage. ''You didn't answer my question. And believe me, I've got every right to ask it, because it's my life that's on the line. What's she going to do? How's she going to handle this big mean drunk?''

''How would you handle him, Sergeant. He's bigger and stronger than you are, too.''

''I've been trained to—''

''Well, so has she.''

''It's not the same and you know it. I'm not going out there with her, and I'm not asking my men to do it either.''

''Now, let's get this straight, Sergeant. You refuse to go out on patrol as long as Officer Clark is assigned to your shift, is that right?''

''That's right,'' he said, looking at her defiantly, daring her to do something about it.

''Wait right here,'' she said, rising. She walked past him, across the hallway, and into Captain Pruitt's office, stopping in front of his desk. He looked up at her expectantly.

''You heard?'' she asked.

''Most of it.''

''Come with me, please.''

The captain followed her into her office. Sergeant Nelson was still standing before her desk.

Melissa sat down. ''Sergeant Nelson, I'm ordering you to go about your usual duties.''

''Will one of my deputies be Officer Clark?''

''Yes.''

''Then I refuse.''

Captain Pruitt, who'd been standing near the door, stepped up beside Nelson. ''Sergeant—''

''I'm sorry, Captain. I won't do it. It's my life and the lives of my men that are at stake.''

Melissa stared at the two men before her. There was only one thing she could do, but suddenly the fight had gone out of her. She didn't want this. Her heart pounding, she took a deep breath, then spoke the necessary words. "Sergeant, you've been insubordinate, and you've refused a legitimate order from a superior. I have no choice but to fire you."

"Well, that suits me just fine." He turned and strode from the office.

Captain Pruitt stared at her in silence, his poker face revealing not even a hint of how he felt about what had just occurred.

To break the silence, Melissa said: "Now we can hire that civilian radio operator, I suppose." Instantly regretting the apparent crassness of the statement, she said: "I didn't want that to happen. I . . ." Uncertain what else to say, she trailed off.

"It was inevitable," Pruitt said. "He couldn't accept you, and sooner or later you were going to have to do something about him."

Unless I'd left well enough alone, Melissa thought. If I'd stayed home and tended the kids, none of this would have happened. But there was another part of her that didn't regret what had happened at all. That part felt that Nelson was an ass and that the department would be better off without him.

"I'd better see to the morning briefing," the captain said.

"I'll come with you. I'm the one who fired him, so I'm the one who should tell them what happened."

An uneasy silence settled over the squad room when Melissa walked up to the desk and turned to face the officers. Marla Clark sat in the middle of the front row, the two metal chairs on either side of her vacant, an outcast with whom no one wished to be identified. All eyes were on Melissa.

"You should know . . ." Melissa cleared her throat. She'd sounded squeaky, unsure of herself. She felt weak. "You should know that Sergeant Nelson has been fired. I dismissed him just a few minutes ago for insubordination and refusing to fulfill his duties."

The announcement was greeted with absolute silence.

Melissa nodded to Captain Pruitt, who stepped forward and said: "Same situation as before with these murders. Keep your eyes open for anything that might help." He picked up a stack of hot sheets from the desk and handed them to an officer in the first row. The deputy took one and passed the others on.

"That's it," Pruitt said. "Hillman, you'll be acting shift sergeant until further notice. Clark will ride with you."

As the officers moved out of the room, a tall deputy with thick brown hair stepped over to Marla Clark, said something to her, and then the two of them joined the exiting deputies. When all of them were outside, the discussion of what had just happened began. Melissa caught a few meaningless snatches of conversation.

"Bitch!" someone said in a loud voice.

And then somebody thought to close the door, and Melissa could hear no more of what was said.

"Hillman's a good man," Captain Pruitt said. "He'll teach Clark what she needs to know and keep the others off her back. The men respect him, so they'll cooperate with him."

"Someone will have to be promoted," Melissa said, recalling what Bob Sanchez had told her about the slim chance a deputy had of ever making sergeant.

"Let me have a couple of days to think it over, and I'll give you my recommendations."

Melissa said that would be fine, then headed for Lieutenant Castle's office to get updated on the Boogeyman investigation.

"Good morning," Castle said, looking up from the paperwork on his desk. Complying with her wishes, he no longer rose every time Melissa entered his office.

"Anything new on the Boogeyman?" she asked, taking a seat in front of the desk.

"Nothing," he replied glumly.

"What happened with the sketch Claudia Baca was supposed to provide us with? I notice you didn't give it to the papers."

"I've been trying to decide whether I should do that. The Baca woman spent three hours with the artist, but they never were able to come up with a sketch she was happy with. The one she finally settled for is close but not quite right, to use her words. The trouble is she can't decide what's wrong with it."

He handed Melissa a sheet of paper from which a somewhat rounded face with thick blond hair stared at her, its lips slightly parted in what could be the beginning of a smile. And yet there was nothing really human about the drawing; it was lines on paper, cold, emotionless, not a real face at all. Still, the more Melissa looked at it, the more familiar it seemed. It was no one she knew, but . . . but would it be if Claudia Baca had gotten it right? *Do I know the killer?* Melissa wondered. *Have I met him somewhere?* The thought chilled her.

"I'll go ahead and distribute these within the department," Castle said. He frowned. "If I do that, the media will get hold of one sooner or later, so I might as well give them to the reporters, too. I'm holding a news conference in a few minutes. I can do it then." He rubbed his forehead. "I've discovered that if I talk to all the reporters at one time, I don't have one showing up every half hour or so asking the same questions all the others have asked."

"What are you going to do when you're through with that?"

"There's not much to do. We've found just about everybody we needed to find, and we've run down every lead we had—not that we've had anything that I'd really consider a lead. Now we wait, gather whatever little pieces of information we can, and hope.

"I'll give you an example. One of the little pieces of information we have is that the purple crayon used at the Tuckers' and the Evanses' was the same brand and the same shade, maybe even the same crayon, although the lab can't say that for sure. Maybe that, combined with another piece of information, will give us the lead that breaks the case. On the other hand, maybe it will never help us at all."

"I don't suppose it's a rare color or anything like that."

"We should be so lucky. It's the most common purple crayon sold in the United States. Available just about everywhere."

"If anything comes up, let me know. I'll be in my office."

As Melissa got up to leave, Castle said: "Oh, one more thing I should mention is that I've alerted the swing and graveyard patrol shifts to keep an eye on Claudia Baca's place. I don't think the Boogeyman will try anything, but she is the only person who's seen him."

Melissa nodded, then turned to leave. At the door she turned and faced the lieutenant again.

"I guess I should tell you what just happened," she said.

"I've had Marla Clark assigned to patrol duties. This morning Sergeant Nelson refused to go out on patrol with her, and I fired him."

She watched his eyes, hoping they'd betray his true feelings, but they revealed nothing except the redness that comes from too much work and too little sleep.

"Good," Castle said after a moment's silence. "There are a few more of them out there with similar attitudes, and you can fire them, too, as far as I'm concerned."

Returning to her own office, Melissa felt relieved. In the department there were undoubtedly many people whose opinions she would do her best to ignore, but what Castle thought mattered.

After stropping his straight razor until he was satisfied that it was good and sharp, Archibald Jeremy Sebastian looked into the bathroom mirror and began carefully scraping the shaving cream and whiskers from his face, the blade making that soft sandpapery sound as it cut through the stubby hairs.

He used a straight razor because that was what he had always used. He'd bought a safety razor once, after hearing it advertised on a radio broadcast of a world series game, and thrown it away after using it only twice. The infernal thing had nicked him in three places, and he'd missed two patches of whiskers. Electrics were completely out of the question. He'd be damned if he'd shave with anything that buzzed like a bunch of angry bees.

Besides, a bathroom just wasn't a bathroom without a razor strop in it. And a mug with a brush for applying the shaving cream. Okay, he thought as he finished scraping the whiskers from his cheek and moved on to his neck, so I'm set in my ways. I'm seventy-seven years old, and I've got a right to be.

It seemed to A. J. Sebastian that too often things were changed just to make them different, not better. Grabbing a towel, he wiped his razor, then his face. A moment later he was in the bedroom dressing for work.

Although he wore clean pants and shirts each day, chances were no one was aware of it. All his work clothes were khaki and always rumpled, since he neither owned an iron nor saw any need to own one. As far as A. J. was concerned, you'd have to be crazy to iron work clothes. And fancier stuff, slacks and the like, was permanent press. Of course, sometimes the press didn't seem all that permanent in the stuff he bought over at the discount store, but nobody could blame that on him.

Sitting on the bed, he pulled on his high-topped work shoes and began lacing them up. The bedroom was barely big enough to hold the small painted dresser and the double bed. The living room wasn't any larger, the kitchen not much bigger than the bathroom. But then, the rent was low, and so was his income. And just how much room did one person need? Louise had passed away twenty years ago, and he'd never even considered remarrying. The last time he'd had a woman here overnight, he'd been sixty-four, which was thirteen years ago. It wasn't that the urge had diminished—well, maybe a little—but the simple fact of the matter was there were darn few women out there looking to spend the night with a set-in-his-ways caretaker pushing eighty.

Closing his eyes, he tried to remember how it had been with Louise and found he couldn't. Twenty years was just too long. Whatever happened then had been in another life.

Sure, he could recall events, like the time he wrecked the newest pickup he'd ever owned, the time his favorite dog had died, a big old mutt named Happy. And glad times, too, like when Louise gave him that fishing rod he'd always wanted, the wedding of their only child, Nancy, who lived in Kansas City now with her mechanic husband and five children. The trouble was he recollected these things as he might remember who won the Super Bowl two years ago or the name of the previous lieutenant governor. He had no feeling for his memories anymore; time had sapped them of their happiness and their tears, leaving only empty pictures.

In the kitchen he stood before the old Frigidaire, listening to the loud rattling sounds the compressor made. He hoped it would wait as long as possible before going out. Not that it would cost him. The apartment had come furnished; the landlord would have to take care of the broken refrigerator. The rub was how much time and how much effort it was going to take to get the landlord to fix it. He shrugged. Well, for the moment it was running, even if not quietly.

From the cabinet he got a box of dry cereal and a bowl, which he put on the table, along with a spoon. Then, opening the refrigerator, he hesitated. Should he eat the stuff the way it was supposed to be eaten or the way he liked it? Closing the refrigerator, he grabbed the bottle of whiskey from the counter and sat down at the table. Quickly he took a spoonful of cereal, then washed it down with a swallow of booze. Not bad, he concluded. Not bad at all.

It would be better, of course, without the cereal. But he knew that if he ever reached the point where he gave up eating entirely, he would no longer be heading for serious trouble; he'd be in it.

"I like the hell out of you," he said, picking up the bottle, "but I'm still in charge here, not you."

The way A. J. figured it, if after drinking all these years, he was still only a borderline alcoholic, then his chances of making it to the end of his life without surrendering totally to the bottle were pretty good.

A few minutes later, having consumed a bowl of cereal and a good bit of booze, A. J. stepped out of his apartment and locked the front door. The duplex had a driveway on each side, one for each apartment. In the other half of the building lived two women whom he suspected of being lesbians, although he really didn't care, since they never troubled him. Their car was gone. In the other driveway was his pickup, an ancient Dodge, its finish a mixture of faded red paint, rust, and primer. It used oil, rattled, and got about six miles a gallon, but it started most of the time. And it was all he could afford.

Slipping behind the wheel, he slammed the door, pumped the accelerator a few times, and hit the starter. The warm, sunny weather had returned, so the engine caught fairly quickly. It coughed a couple of times, then settled down to business, gray smoke billowing out the exhaust pipe. After backing the pickup out of the dirt drive, he stepped on the gas and let out the clutch. The truck shook as it started forward. The gears made grinding noises as he shifted into second.

Though surrounded by sprawling, affluent suburbs, this was a grubby little neighborhood. The front yards were full of dried weeds, the houses in need of paint. This, A. J. supposed, was what was referred to as a pocket of poverty.

A few minutes later his surroundings had changed considerably. He was on a winding street that made its way past expensive houses, some with grounds more extensive than a medium-sized city park. The homes were big brick places, most of them. He didn't know who lived in them, though he supposed these were the homes of presidents of companies and people like that. He felt funny driving through here, as if someone was about to run out and tell him he didn't belong in this place, tell him he had to use some other road, one reserved for riffraff.

Then he was out of the exclusive neighborhood, driving on a thoroughfare. As he usually did, he felt relieved. He didn't belong back there where people had tennis courts in their backyards, and just being in those surroundings made him uncomfortable.

As he drove along he thought of his old friend who'd occupied the apartment next to his a few years ago. It was nice that his former neighbor had stopped by to visit him. A. J. wondered whether the man really would come by for checkers some evening. He hoped so. A game of checkers would be nice.

Melissa was on the phone with Priscilla when she heard the door to Captain Pruitt's office close and then the muffled sounds of a discussion. Because the captain's office was diagonally across the hall from hers, Melissa was unable to see who had entered it.

Priscilla had called to ask Melissa to be in charge of organizing an old-fashioned charity ball. "You'd be perfect for the job," she said enthusiastically. "Who'd dare refuse to come when the sheriff was in charge?"

"I explained this to you before, Priscilla. I simply don't have time for that sort of thing anymore."

"Oh, come on, Melissa. Don't be such a stick-in-the-mud. You're not married to that office. Take some time off. Do some other things."

"I'm sure the voters would love to have their elected sheriff spending her time arranging social events."

Priscilla was silent for a moment; then she said: "Melissa, it's not as though you were doing something frivolous—like taking dancing classes on company time. This is for charity. It's to help the whole county."

"You'll have to get someone else, Priscilla. I'm sorry."

"Well, if you're sure you can't do it . . ."

"I'm sure."

"Oh, by the way, I've got the word out that you're looking for a housekeeper, but so far I haven't heard of anyone who's available. I'll keep trying."

"Okay, thanks, Priscilla. I appreciate it."

When Melissa hung up, she could again hear the voices coming from Captain Pruitt's office. Although the words were muffled, the passionate tone of the discussion came through. Then the voices grew louder, and some of the words came through as well.

". . . with this shit." A man's voice.

"I told you that I advised her . . ." Captain Pruitt.

"Well, what's going to happen when she has to . . ." A third man's voice.

Fairly certain that the conversation was about her—specifically her transferring Marla Clark to patrol and firing Sergeant Nelson—Melissa listened intently, but the discussion was being conducted at a lower volume now, and she could again hear only the murmur of muted voices.

Suddenly Melissa heard the door to Captain Pruitt's office open, and then two deputies were in her office. Although one rapped lightly on the doorframe as they entered, neither man waited for an invitation before stepping up to her desk.

"We want to talk to you," the man on the right said. He was in his late twenties or early thirties, tall, with light-brown hair. His companion was about the same age and build, but with black hair.

"Go ahead," Melissa said.

"We don't think it's a good idea to put an inexperienced woman on patrol. People's lives are at stake. Not just the officers she has to work with, but civilians as well, the people we're supposed to protect."

"She's been trained, and she's qualified."

"No she isn't," the black-haired man said, speaking for the first time. "This isn't like the city. Out here we have . . . well, cowboys and people like that. Sure, maybe women work out okay in New York or Denver or someplace like that, but this is different. What's going to happen when she tries to break up a fight in some honky-tonk? How's she going to handle a night-club full of drunk cowboys?''

Having no answer these men would accept, Melissa said: ''Most of the night spots of the type you're describing are in Denver, not out here. The bulk of the people living in Ramsey County are prosperous suburbanites.''

The black-haired man shook his head violently. ''No, that's not true. There's a lot more to this county than just the part around Denver. And out there in that other part are a lot of men who would never allow themselves to be arrested by a woman.''

''You're wrong about the bars, too,'' the other officer said. ''I've had to break up a lot of fights at Jake's Watering Hole.''

''The Lariat, too,'' the other deputy added. ''And Freddy's Barn.''

Melissa sighed. ''You might as well get used to the idea. Officer Clark's only the first. There'll be more.''

The two deputies exchanged glances; then the brown-haired one said: ''Why won't you listen to us?''

''I am listening to you. It's just that I think you're wrong in this case. I'm sure these same arguments were made in just about every police force that started using women as patrol officers. The women have worked out fine. I'm sure they will here, too.''

''I think you're wrong,'' the brown-haired deputy said softly.

For a moment the two men stood there in silence; then the black-haired one said: ''Thank you for your time, ma'am.'' With that, the deputies turned and left.

Staring at the empty doorway, Melissa wondered whether she had made the right decision. The two men hadn't been outwardly hostile; they'd come to tell her they felt strongly she was making a serious mistake. And, as they'd pointed out, lives were at stake. Melissa pushed these doubts aside. Female police officers were doing just fine elsewhere; there was no reason they shouldn't work out well here, once the resistance of the men was overcome. Melissa rose and walked across the hall to Captain Pruitt's office.

"Well," she said, taking a seat, "how does the rest of the department feel about things now that the word's spread?"

The captain leaned back in his desk chair. "Oh, I guess the two that were in your office just now were pretty typical—at least if what I hear is any indication. Most of the men don't like the idea of having a woman on patrol."

"How do they feel about Sergeant Nelson?"

"I'd say he's not as big an issue as the women. There are a few that were in Nelson's little group of buddies, and they're mad as hell. There are also a few that think firing Nelson is the best thing the department ever did. Most of them are in the middle, and that group's a little nervous right now. Whenever somebody like a sergeant gets fired, they realize it could happen to them, too."

"Spread the word, will you. I'm not planning to fire anybody else. I wasn't even planning to fire Nelson."

Pruitt nodded. "I will. But it shouldn't be necessary. Once they stop and think about it, they'll realize they've got the county personnel ordinances to protect them. They can only be fired for cause, and they can always appeal to the county personnel board if they think they've been fired for any other reason."

"Do you think Nelson might appeal?" Until this moment the idea that she could be ordered to reinstate him hadn't occurred to her. He'd probably get back wages to boot, his dismissal becoming nothing more than a paid vacation.

"Wouldn't do him any good. He was fired for cause and in front of me, in front of a witness."

Studying his face, Melissa realized how tired the captain looked. The lines that came with age seemed to be etched more deeply into his face than they had been a few days ago; bags had appeared under his eyes. I'm sorry, Melissa thought. I'm sorry that my sudden arrival in your life has been so hard on you.

"How do you feel about things now, Captain?"

Looking at her sadly, he said: "Under the circumstances, you were right to fire Nelson. I guess I wish the whole thing hadn't happened, though."

Me, too, Melissa thought. And she wondered whether if she looked in a mirror right now she would see signs of wear and tear similar to those that had appeared on Pruitt's face. She felt tired. And old. Much older than thirty-five.

On his way home from work that evening, A. J. Sebastian made his customary stop at B & H Liquors. It was a small store, but well stocked, clean and modern. As he usually did, A. J. looked over the selection of beers and wines, none of which he ever bought, then moved on to the good stuff. After checking out the vodka, gin, rum, and the rest of it, he made his usual selection, a bottle of inexpensive bourbon, which he carried to the cash register.

"How are you this evening, A. J.?" the man behind the counter asked, picking up the bottle to check the price. A heavy bald man in his fifties, he was the owner of the place. His name was Bill Zeckner.

"Not bad," A. J. replied. "And you?"

"Pretty good, I reckon. Except for this arthritis." He held up a hand so A. J. could appreciate the swollen knuckles.

"Guess I'm lucky. I've never had that problem. At my age, it's a wonder; I'll tell you that."

Zeckner nodded. "You are in pretty good shape for your age."

"Wanna know my secret?"

Knowing a joke was coming, Zeckner grinned. "Sure. Why not?"

A. J. leaned forward and whispered: "Sex."

"Sex! Why, you old fart, you haven't had any in so long I doubt you still remember where to put it."

A. J. winked and Zeckner laughed. A middle-aged woman entered the store, her presence putting an end to their banter. A. J. paid for his purchase and left, giving Zeckner a parting wink.

Outside he walked through the chilly evening. Although the day had been warm, it was dark out now, and the warmth had vanished with the sun. The liquor store was on a thoroughfare on which there was no parking, so he'd left his truck on a side street.

When he turned the corner, he left the lights of the thoroughfare behind him and stepped into the shadows, the nearest streetlight at the far end of the block. Reaching his pickup, he slipped behind the wheel, pulled the bottle from the paper bag, and started to uncap it. Then he stopped himself. It'll keep until I get home, he decided.

Suddenly the passenger-side door popped open, and a man was climbing into the cab with him. Startled, A. J. raised the bottle to defend himself, but the man made no move toward him. He simply pulled the door closed and sat there like a passenger.

Confused and afraid, A. J. stared at the intruder, uncertain what to do. "What do you want?" A. J. asked, the words barely getting out.

The man was blond, dressed in dark clothes. A. J. had never seen him before. Or had he? There was something familiar about him.

"Don't you recognize me, A. J.?" the man asked.

And then A. J. knew who it was. "What on earth are you doing here? And why are you w—"

"See this?"

The old man saw it all right, even in the dim illumination coming from the distant streetlight. "It's a gun," he said. "But why?"

"Drive where I tell you to," the man's voice said gently. "If you disobey me or do anything stupid, I'll shoot you in the head."

His heart pounding, A. J. Sebastian reached forward with a trembling hand and turned the ignition switch. The truck coughed, then started.

"Drive to the end of the block and turn right."

A. J. put the truck in gear and pulled away from the curb, leaving a trail of thick, oily smoke. Why, he wondered, why was his old friend doing this? Why was he dressed that way? And the question that concerned him most: What's going to happen to me?

As instructed, he turned right at the end of the block.

"Turn right again at the next intersection," the man who had been A. J.'s friend and was now a stranger said.

Again A. J. complied. They drove in silence for a moment, and then the man said: "You're not being punished, A. J. In fact, I need you to help me out. You should feel honored."

"Honored?" A. J. repeated mechanically.

"Yes, honored. Not many people get the chance to help me out. Turn left here."

A. J. did so. They were now on the thoroughfare, headed away from the city.

"You still don't know who I am; do you, A. J.?"

"Sure I know. You're—"

"I mean who I *really* am."

Not having any idea what his passenger was talking about, A. J. drove on, hoping the man would come to his senses. Or maybe just tell him to stop and get out. Hell, he could have the truck.

"You don't know, do you? You don't know who I really am."

"I . . . I don't know what you're talking about," A. J. said. An icy drop of perspiration trickled down his neck.

"I'm the Boogeyman," his passenger said in a calm, matter-of-fact tone that made A. J. shiver. "Are you honored to be helping me do my work?"

His thoughts swirling, A. J. drove the truck. He was only vaguely aware that he had just wet his pants.

9

Sitting at his kitchen table, the Boogeyman felt terrible.

He should be pleased with himself, he knew, because everything was going so smoothly. He'd forced A. J. Sebastian to drive south out of town, then eastward into the plains, where there was land so desolate the Air Force used it for bombing practice. After shooting the old man, he had buried him in a four-foot-deep grave. The body should not be found.

A. J.'s truck he'd left near the spot where he'd abducted the old man, the keys in the ignition. Perhaps it would be stolen; the Boogeyman hoped so.

Another thing that should make him happy this Tuesday morning was the artist's sketch on the front page of today's *Denver Post*. He slid the newspaper over in front of him and studied the image. Of course it looked nothing like him; there was no way it could. And it only vaguely resembled the face of the man who'd inquired about the Tucker family. The blond hair was right, as were the eyes, but most of the other features were off, the lips too thin, the face too wide, the nose too long.

Pushing the paper away, he sighed. The reason he was so miserable was because of the dreams. He'd come home dead tired after burying the old man, ready for a long, hard sleep. But instead of restful slumber, the dreams had come again. He'd seen himself about to enter a garage, a closet in an office building, a mountain cottage. Each time, he'd awakened just before opening the door, discovering the Horrible Thing. Oh, God, he thought, pressing his palms against his forehead, will it ever go away? Will I ever be free of what happened?

And then he wondered why he had asked the question of God, with whom he could have no relationship. The Boogeyman, he was sure, served a different master.

Melissa sat at her desk trying to sort through all that had happened in the week since she'd become sheriff. A mass murderer had struck twice, wiping out two entire families, and he would quite likely kill again if he wasn't stopped. And then, yesterday, she had fired Sergeant Nelson, an experienced police officer who undoubtedly knew more about her job than she did. She'd had second thoughts about what she'd done, but every time she considered the matter, she would eventually conclude that firing him had been the right thing to do.

And the past week had affected her in ways that were still too nebulous to be fully understood. But that the job was changing her was unquestionable. By forcing her to deal with the Boogeyman and with the hostility directed at her from within the department, the job was causing her to discover new things about herself, to discover strengths and abilities she'd been unaware she possessed. No doubt there would be weaknesses, too. The lesson was just beginning.

And her relationship with Keith was changing. She knew

things about him now—and he about her—that would have only come out slowly under normal circumstances, perhaps not until she'd taken the plunge and married him. Were they things that mattered? Yes, she decided, they were things that mattered. But just how they would affect the relationship was uncertain.

Her thoughts were interrupted by the presence of two people in her doorway, a woman and a girl.

"Can I help you with something?" Melissa asked.

"Yes, uh, my name's Jo Lynn Bascom, and this is my daughter Melanie. She has something that might help you with the Boogeyman case."

Melissa asked them to come in and sit down. The woman was about Melissa's age, tall, blond, attractive. The girl had reached the age at which she was no longer a child but not yet an adult. She was part gangly kid and part slender young woman.

When they were seated, the girl's mother said: "Go ahead, Melanie. Tell the sheriff what you've got."

"I took this Thursday morning," Melanie said, holding up a black-and-white photograph. "I, uh, I'm sort of an amateur photographer, and I just wanted to use up the last couple of shots on the roll so I could get the film developed. Anyway, I shot this street scene. It was Thursday morning, uh, the day before that family was killed across the street."

"May I see the picture, please?" Melissa said.

"Oh, sure," the girl replied, looking a little embarrassed at having failed to hand over the photo. She quickly passed it to Melissa.

Just as the girl had indicated, the picture showed a street scene. Homes, cars, trees. And the apartment house in which the Tuckers had lived. Melissa looked at the girl questioningly.

"I heard on the news about the green car," Melanie Bascom explained. "The car in the picture was green, the one closest to me."

Melissa looked at the photo again. Partway down the block from where Melanie had stood with her camera that morning was a car with someone sitting inside, waiting.

"This one?" Melissa asked, holding up the photo and pointing to the car with a human shape visible through the rear window.

The girl nodded.

"Are you sure it was green?"

"Oh, yeah, I'm sure. I didn't pay much attention to it at the time, but I do remember that it was green."

"Is it a car you're familiar with? Have you seen it before?"

The girl shook her head. "I know most of the cars that are usually parked in our block, and I've never seen that one before."

"It looks like there's someone sitting behind the wheel. Did you get a look at the person?"

"No. That's as close to the car as I got."

"Mrs. Bascom, can you add anything?"

"I never even saw the car. I'm sorry."

Melissa examined the photograph again, and then, her body tingling with excitement, she grabbed a magnifying glass from her desk drawer and held it over the photograph. The license number of the car was almost discernible. If the photo were enlarged . . .

"I brought the negative with me," Melanie said. "Just in case you needed it."

"I think that's exactly what we need," Melissa said, picking up the phone. She dialed Lieutenant Castle's office, and when he answered, she said: "Can you come to my office right away? We just got what might be a big break in the Boogeyman investigation."

Melanie Bascom beamed; her mother looked at her admiringly.

In the darkroom of the Denver photo lab that processed film for the sheriff's office, Melissa and Castle watched as a young man with dark hair and a thick mustache adjusted the enlarger, making the image of the car grow bigger and bigger. Except for the light coming from the enlarger, the only illumination in the room was the dim red glow from a small bulb above the counter.

The technician switched off the enlarger and slipped a sheet of print paper in the spot where the image of the car had been. The picture flashed on the paper; then the young man took the sheet and slipped it into a tray of liquid.

"This is developer," he said. "An image should start appearing on the paper any moment now."

It did, darkening until it was distinct. Using wooden tongs, the technician slipped it briefly into another tray of chemical, then into a third. After a few moments he switched on a white light.

"This fuzziness is the grain of the film," he said, holding up the picture.

Melissa saw what he meant. It was sort of like getting up right next to a TV screen; instead of seeing the picture you started to see the lines and dots it was made of. But in the case of the photo, it didn't matter because the license number, though fuzzy, was readable.

Castle copied it down in his notebook. "Try for the guy sitting in the car," he said to the technician.

The young man complied, and a few minutes later they were looking at a grainy enlargement of a head that could have been young or old, male or female.

"We'll never know what he looked like from that," Melissa said.

"We'll know what he looks like pretty damned quick," Castle said. "If this is his license number."

As soon as the lieutenant told the technician what prints he wanted from Melanie's negative, they headed for Ramsey County.

"We might just have him," Castle said as he drove. "We just might have the son of a bitch."

"I hope so," Melissa replied. "I really hope so."

The Boogeyman sat on the couch in his living room admiring the device in front of him on the coffee table. Resembling a pocket calculator, it was a small but very efficient timer, a tiny computer really, another one of those devices made possible by the invention of the silicon chip. All it did was turn things on and off, but you could program it for a year. It would activate or shut off whatever was plugged into it whenever you told it to—8:15 P.M. on November 21, 2:23 A.M. on January 3, and so on. The device would be an invaluable tool in his plan to discipline the woman sheriff, for even if something happened to him, the timer would still be there, making sure the punishment was carried out on schedule.

He smiled, pleased with his scheme for dealing with the woman sheriff. Though complicated, the plan was a good one. It would clearly demonstrate what happened to those who insulted the Boogeyman. Such disrespect could not be tolerated. The Boogeyman had to be feared. That was vital. A Boogeyman no one was afraid of was useless.

Leaning back, the Boogeyman let his thoughts wander for a while. Then he considered the woman and boy he'd seen at the department store where he bought the timer. She'd been in her late twenties, blond, a little heavyset. The boy, thin and dark-haired, had apparently gotten his looks from his father. He and his mother had been looking at toys, trying them out, giggling, grinning. The Boogeyman had wanted to slap them both for their shameful public display.

Suddenly, unbidden, a scene from the past imposed itself on his consciousness. He saw himself as a child standing in a doorway, watching the scene on the sidewalk in front of the building in which he lived. A chubby dark-haired man had a woman by the hair.

"Look, everybody!" the man shouted. "Look and see the dumbest bitch in the world!" Then he yanked her head back and slapped her face. Looking into the woman's eyes, he said: "You'd better straighten out, bitch. You hear me?"

As she always did when he humiliated her, the woman neither spoke nor cried; she just bore the abuse in silence. The man released her, and she sank slowly to the sidewalk. Then he turned and stomped into the building. As he passed the boy, he said: "Go get your mother. She looks like a tramp or a junkie, sitting there on the sidewalk like that." With those words, the boy's father disappeared into the building.

The Boogeyman remembered the place, a cheap apartment house in a run-down section of the city, the kind of neighborhood where people feared the police and would never even consider calling them over something as commonplace as a family fight. His family had moved from there to the house where the Horrible Thing had occurred.

Forcing these thoughts from his mind, the Boogeyman again considered the woman and boy he'd seen in the department store. Nicky, she'd called the child. He'd addressed her as Mommy.

When they'd paid for their purchases with a check, the Boogeyman had been standing behind them, waiting his turn.

The names on the personalized check had been George C. or Patricia Lopez. Their address had been in Ramsey County.

Melissa and Castle sat in the detective's office waiting for the Department of Motor Vehicles to call back with the information on the license number of the car Melanie Bascom had photographed. Some of Castle's initial optimism had worn off. He said:

"On any investigation like this, it's best not to set yourself up for too much success. Most leads, no matter how good they seem, usually fizzle."

Melissa nodded. As best she could, she'd been holding her hopes in abeyance, trying to simply wait, without expectations.

"The car's the right make and color, there's apparently someone sitting in it, and it was there just before the murder," Castle said. "But none of this proves the car was being used by the Boogeyman. There are probably a million innocent reasons why it could have been parked there that morning."

Again Melissa nodded. Picturing the photo, she focused on the shape visible through the car's rear window. Was that the Boogeyman? It was more of a shadow than anything else, a dark spot that disappeared into the grain of the film when you tried to enlarge it. If the shadow could be brought into focus, would she see the person who'd slain eight people, an insane murderer who might kill again and again until he was stopped? Just what does a crazed killer look like? she wondered. If you passed one on the sidewalk, would he have nervous, darting eyes? Would he drool? How would you know?

You wouldn't know, she decided. The killer would look like Castle or Keith or like Marla Clark or Priscilla Stern. It wasn't what was on the outside that made someone a monster, but what seethed within, unseen. Her thoughts were interrupted by the phone. Castle answered it.

"Okay," the lieutenant said, picking up a pencil, "let me have it." His eyes met Melissa's, and he nodded. It was the motor vehicle department.

A few moments later he thanked the caller and hung up. Frowning, he looked at Melissa. "Something's wrong," he said. "The license number is registered to a red Ford Escort."

Picking up the phone again, he asked for a computer check on the license number. "I'll hold," he said.

About a minute passed with Castle holding the phone to his ear, his eyes fixed on the surface of his desk, a minute during which Melissa could feel their promising lead begin to evaporate. Finally Castle said: "Okay. Thanks."

Replacing the receiver, he eyed Melissa glumly for a moment, then said: "Plate's stolen."

Melissa sighed. "Well, you warned me that the best-looking leads usually fizzle."

"But knowing that doesn't make it any easier to take, does it?"

"No," Melissa said softly, "no, it doesn't."

The structure looked like a row of single-car garages. Ed's Self-Storage, the sign said, although the Boogeyman had always considered the term self-storage a misnomer. One stored furniture and the like here, not oneself.

Getting out of the car, he unlocked the storage facility's metal door and slid it upward. Quickly he drove the car inside and closed the door. He had stored no chairs or refrigerators or TV sets here. He rented the space because it provided the privacy he needed to do certain things, such as switching the license plates on his car.

Fifteen minutes after his arrival, having replaced his license plates with the stolen ones and accomplished the other things he'd come here to do, the Boogeyman backed the car out, lowered and locked the metal door, and drove off. It was a sunny Tuesday afternoon, the weather warmer than it had been the past few days. The nightmares were fading now, their last traces washed away by the bright sunshine. He felt confident, alive.

This was his day off, so he had plenty of time. This afternoon he would check out the address at which the Lopez family lived. Then tonight he'd get the rest of the supplies he needed for punishing the woman sheriff. He smiled. After tonight, he'd be ready to put the plan into action. Melissa James would pay the price of her insolence. The Boogeyman would be feared.

* * *

That night Beverly Watson sat in the guard shack at the construction site in the Rocky Mountains. Through the window she could see the shapes of some of the monster machines the contractor was using to bore through the rock. When the project was completed, a tunnel would run through the mountain carrying much-needed water to the people and grass and fields on the Rockies' eastern side.

Checking the clock, she noted that it was 1:45 A.M. In fifteen minutes she'd have to make her rounds, punching the clock with the special keys that hung at various locations around the fenced compound. She picked up the paperback suspense novel she'd been reading, then put it down, deciding that fifteen minutes was too short a period of time to get involved in the book. She'd wait until after her two A.M. rounds.

In her late thirties, Beverly was a solid, big-boned woman. She wasn't overweight; it was just that some women were born thin and shapely and others could knock the thin, shapely ones across the room with a single punch.

She'd had the job as a security guard for almost a year now, having taken it after her husband ran off with one of the thin, shapely ones, leaving Beverly with their five-year-old daughter and no money. Although she would have preferred more normal working hours, she'd been in no position to be choosy. Night work beat welfare. Fortunately her daughter, Judy, could spend her nights at Grandma's.

Stretching, she saw her reflection in the window. Round-faced and dark-haired, she wore a gray uniform, which included the .38 in its black holster. She'd had to buy the gun and uniform. To get the money, she'd sold the TV set. Her sister had offered to lend it to her, but taking money from family wasn't Beverly's way. Your family raised you to adulthood, after which you were on your own. That was how it was. And how it should be.

Again she studied her reflection in the windowpane and felt just a hint of the hurt that dwelled deep within her. Immediately Beverly closed the door on the feeling. She was too tough to permit herself such emotions. And too busy to have time to waste feeling sorry for herself.

Her eyes drifting from the window, she considered the guardhouse. Little more than a wooden shack with a desk, chair, and portable electric heater, it would afford little protection against the winter wind. The interior walls were bare two-by-fours between which you could see the backs of the boards that made up the exterior siding. In January the electric heater would never be up to keeping the place warm. Beverly shivered at the prospect.

She rose, slipping the strap of the punch clock over her shoulder, and stepped out into the night. The construction area was surrounded by a high chain link fence, a handful of lights on wooden poles making dim pools of illumination in the darkness. It was a clear night, the sky alive with stars. In the city the pollution dulled them, but here in the mountains the night sky was breathtaking.

Suddenly Beverly's hand dropped to her .38, her fingers unfastening the holster's safety strap. She'd seen movement to her left. Quickly she moved behind a bulldozer and squatted, staring into the darkness, trying to see whatever was here. It could be an animal, she supposed, although whatever she'd spotted had seemed larger than a raccoon or any of the other small animals that usually invaded the compound. It seemed unlikely that an ordinary thief would come here to steal; it was a long way from the city, over treacherous mountain roads. Vandalism? Maybe environmentalists? Not likely, she decided, since as far as she knew no environmentalists were opposing the project. Still, something was here; she hadn't imagined it.

Then she saw him. A man carrying something had just passed close enough to one of the lights to become dimly visible. Drawing her revolver, she took a moment to steady her nerves, then stepped out from behind the bulldozer, leveling the weapon.

"Freeze!" she shouted.

The man spun around, and suddenly he had dropped into a crouch and there was a gun in his hand. The bullet slammed into the bulldozer an instant before Beverly heard the crack of the shot. She ducked behind the machine, her heart pounding.

Oh, God, she thought. Except for the pistol range, she had never fired the weapon in her hand. She'd really never even considered that she might have to fire it at another human being. Whoever the man was, all he probably wanted was to get away with whatever was in his hand. Logically, she should let him do just that. Certainly this job wasn't worth dying for.

Crouching behind the bulldozer, she held that thought in her mind until it was slowly replaced by another. The son of a bitch shot at me, she thought. He broke in here while I was on duty, and then he shot at me. With both anger and fear competing for control of her emotions, she peeked over the bulldozer's huge metal blade, seeing nothing. Unhooking the flashlight from her gunbelt, Beverly switched it on, aiming it into the shadows. Another shot rang out, the bullet hitting the dozer's metal blade only inches from her face. Beverly drew back, her heart racing, the only sound her rapid breathing.

And then she heard someone running. Instantly she stepped out from behind the dozer, the light in one hand, her .38 in the other. She saw him, a blond man, moving away from her. She fired twice just as he disappeared into the shadows too dark and too distant for the beam of her flashlight to penetrate. She hesitated, debating whether to risk her safety, and then hurried after him.

She found the spot where the chain link fence had been cut, but no sign of the man. In the distance she thought she heard a car start up, but she wasn't sure. Leaving the fence, Beverly began looking for some indication of what the intruder had been after. It took her only a moment to find it. The door to the supply shed was open. The padlock, open but undamaged, had been picked. The building was about the size of a one-car garage. Stepping inside and shining her light around, Beverly immediately saw what the man had been after, and she understood why he'd come all this way to get it.

In the corner was a wooden box, its lid pried off. Stenciled on its side were the words: DANGER EXPLOSIVES. The blond man had come here to steal dynamite.

Beverly hurried back to the guardhouse to call the sheriff.

10

It was late Wednesday afternoon when Captain Pruitt finally left Melissa's office. She and the captain had spent the day going over the paperwork that kept the department running. She'd signed requests for supplemental appropriations, approved expenditures, and dealt with personnel matters. Pruitt had recommended which officer he felt should be promoted to sergeant: Stan Hillman, the deputy who'd been acting sergeant on day shift since she fired Nelson. Although Melissa wondered whether Bob Sanchez had been considered for the promotion, she accepted the captain's choice without making any suggestions of her own.

Leaning back in her desk chair, she let her eyes wander around the room. On the walls were some inexpensive prints she'd picked up, mountain and rural scenes mainly. Also acquired at her own expense were the large potted plants in the two corners that got the most sunlight. Though still basically a drab institutional sort of place, the office seemed at least a little less austere than it had.

A quiet had settled over the department since Melissa fired Sergeant Nelson. But not the sort of calm that indicated tranquility. This was a forced calm, a facade. The real mood of the place was revealed in whispers, in the exchanges of knowing looks. It will pass, Melissa thought, wondering whether she truly believed it.

There had been no further progress in the Boogeyman case. The sketch that had appeared in the papers had prompted a number of phone calls from people who thought they recognized the man. All had been checked out; none had turned up any worthwhile suspects. At least the lunatic hadn't killed again.

"Good afternoon, Sheriff," Bob Sanchez said, stepping into the room and up to her desk. "Do you have a moment?"

124

"What's on your mind?"

"Well . . ." He hesitated, looking uncomfortable. "Uh, I guess you know some of the department's pretty upset about things right now."

"I gathered that."

"Yeah, well, there are some of us that want you to know that we approve of what you did."

"Thank you. That's good to hear."

Looking still more embarrassed, Sanchez went on. "We were talking, some of the other deputies and me, and one of the guys said someone should buy you a steak dinner for getting rid of Nelson. So I decided that instead of just talking about it, someone should really do it, and here I am." He grinned sheepishly.

Melissa laughed. "Is that what you're doing, asking me out to dinner?"

"A steak dinner," he corrected.

"Right, a steak dinner." She felt herself smiling.

"Do you accept?"

"How could I refuse?"

"Great. When's best for you?"

"Ummm, let's see. I'm going to be tied up Saturday night. How about Friday?"

He smiled the sort of grin a little boy could be expected to wear when presented with his first bicycle. "I'll see you Friday then. Seven okay?"

"Seven's fine."

When he left, Melissa found herself staring at the doorway, a gentle tingling sensation traveling throughout her body. The attention of such an attractive man made her feel . . . alive. And yet she had second thoughts. For one thing, she was his boss. And then there were her kids, with whom she'd planned to spend Friday evening. She saw so little of them anymore. Grabbing her purse, she pushed these thoughts from her mind. The way the invitation had been put, there was no way she could have refused it.

When she slipped on her coat and walked out of the courthouse, the tingling feeling was still with her.

*　　*　　*

Thursday and Friday passed uneventfully, with no further leads in the Boogeyman investigation. As soon as she arrived home Friday evening, Melissa began fixing dinner for the kids, both of whom sat at the kitchen table, watching her.

"What are you making?" Billy asked.

"Hamburger steaks," Melissa replied, flattening out a patty with the palm of her hand.

"Why can't we have hamburgers?"

"Because I don't have any buns, for one thing."

"Why don't you get some? Then we could have real hamburgers."

"I don't have time, Billy. I'm going out tonight."

"Does that mean we'll have to spend the night with old pimple-puss Jennings?"

"Billy! Linda Sue's a very nice girl. That's no way to speak about her."

"Well, she is a pimple-puss."

Sarah joined the conversation, saying: "If you had any feelings at all for other people, you wouldn't say things like that. Linda Sue only has a couple of pimples, and when you're a teenager, you'll probably have some, too."

"Not as many as you!"

Sarah glared at him and then looked away, letting the argument die. As far as Melissa could tell, the children were quite close; it just didn't always show.

"Are you any closer to catching the Boogeyman?" Sarah asked.

"I'm afraid not. The investigation's in a lull right now." That had been Castle's word for it, a lull. It meant there was nothing to do but wait, hope for a break in the case that would enable them to stop him before he killed again. Not just hope, she thought. Hope *desperately*.

"You'll get him, won't you, Mom?" Billy asked a little uncertainly.

"We'll get him," Melissa said confidently. She put the hamburger patties into the hot frying pan and watched them sizzle.

After the meal, much to her brother's annoyance, Sarah volunteered Billy and herself as dishwashers. Melissa took a quick shower and was dressed and ready to go when Linda Sue Jennings arrived at six–forty-five.

An attractive girl, the baby-sitter was sixteen and had light brown hair and soft, lightly freckled skin. And two pimples, which Melissa probably wouldn't have noticed at all had it not been for Billy's pimple-puss label.

"What time will you be back?" Linda Sue asked. She and Melissa were standing in the living room.

"I can't give you an exact time, but I don't expect to be late. If anything comes up to change that, I'll try to give you a call."

"No problem," the baby-sitter said cheerfully. "The longer you're gone, the more money I make. I'm saving up."

"To go to college?"

"No," Linda Sue replied, looking a little embarrassed. "For a car."

"Now that I think about it, that's what I wanted when I was your age."

"Did you get one?"

"Not until I finished high school. It was my graduation present."

The sitter looked worried. "Gee, I hope I don't have to wait that long. I don't have much money yet, and saving's kind of slow. I'm hoping my dad will help if I can show him that I've saved some on my own."

"Hi, Linda Sue," Sarah said, joining them.

"Oh, hi, Sarah. Where's Billy?"

"In the den, being unsociable. What's it going to be tonight? Monopoly or cards or something else?"

"We'd better not decide that until we've checked with Billy," Linda Sue replied.

A few moments later, Bob Sanchez arrived. Melissa invited him to meet Linda Sue and the kids. After introducing her daughter and the sitter, Melissa noticed that Billy hadn't appeared even though she'd called him. Sarah went to get him.

"Billy," Melissa said when the boy finally presented himself, "didn't you hear me call you?"

"I was watching TV. It was the best part of the show. I didn't want to miss it."

Melissa sighed. "Billy, this is Bob Sanchez. Bob, this is my son."

127

"Hi, Billy," the deputy said, offering his hand.

Billy shook the outstretched hand uninterestedly. Looking up at Sanchez, who was dressed in slacks and a sports jacket, he said: "I thought you were a cop. How come you're not wearing a uniform and carrying a gun?"

"I'm not working right now. I'm off duty."

The boy frowned. "If I was a deputy, I'd wear my gun all the time. Just in case I had to shoot some crooks or something."

"I only shoot crooks when I'm on duty."

"What if you see the Boogeyman while you're out? You wouldn't be able to arrest him."

Sanchez smiled. "The Boogeyman would never be allowed in the place we're going. Trust me."

"Enough," Melissa said. "Every now and then, even sheriffs and deputies get to think about something other than work. Okay?"

After admonishing the kids to behave themselves and do as Linda Sue directed, Melissa and the deputy left. Twenty minutes later they were seated at a table in a large steak house.

"Tell me," Melissa said, "is what you said true, the part about all the deputies who wanted to buy me dinner?"

He smiled. "Well, I was the one who suggested it, but at least five or six of them said it was a good idea."

"It was a nice thing to do," she said, returning his smile. "Thanks."

Her words seemed to make him both pleased and a little uncomfortable. His eyes met hers, held them a moment; then he looked away.

Melissa had never been in this restaurant before. A spacious place whose patrons tended to dress western, it was crowded. Although there was no waiting line, vacated tables remained unoccupied only long enough for dirty plates and silverware to be cleared.

They ordered, and about fifteen minutes later the waitress brought them two enormous steaks accompanied by potatoes, salad, and Texas toast.

"This is huge," Melissa said, cutting into her hunk of rare sirloin. Pink juices spilled out where the knife had penetrated.

"You can handle it," Sanchez said. No juices at all escaped when the deputy cut into his steak, which he'd ordered well-done. "My dad was a Texan," he explained. "And to a Texan, any meat that's not burned all the way through is raw, so this is how steaks were always served in my family."

"Is that where you're from, Texas?"

He shook his head. "I've got relatives there, but I've never lived there myself. My dad left when he was young, went to New Mexico, where he met my mom. That's where I grew up, in New Mexico."

"Does your family still live there?"

"My parents are both dead. Killed in an auto accident."

"I'm sorry," Melissa said softly.

"Oh, it was a long time ago—years. It doesn't hurt anymore."

They were silent a moment; then Melissa said: "It's surprising how all by itself time can take the pain away from something that's just about tearing you apart and then make you well again. I know, after my husband died . . ." Uncertain why she was telling him these things, Melissa trailed off.

Sanchez nodded. "I knew you were a widow," he said. "From what it said about you in the paper."

They ate in silence for a few moments; then the deputy said: "How about you? Are you from Colorado?"

"I'm one of those rare people who was actually born here."

"Is your family still here?"

"At the moment they're in South America. My father works for a big international construction company, building dams and things like that. Whenever possible, my mother goes with him."

"Did you get to live in all sorts of exotic places while you were growing up?"

"No such luck. I was in my twenties and married when he took that job. All the time I was growing up, we lived right here in the Denver area."

Briefly Sanchez studied her face; then he turned his attention to his dinner. Watching the deputy as he ate, Melissa found herself wondering whether his skin was naturally dark or whether its swarthiness was merely what remained of a fading summer tan. Sanchez, apparently sensing her gaze, looked up, smiled shyly.

For the next half hour or so, they talked about little things: the TV shows they liked, the movies, places they'd been, restaurants they'd tried. And then almost unexpectedly the meal ended, and they were paying the bill, leaving the restaurant.

As Sanchez steered his white Mustang out of the parking lot and onto the street that would take them back toward Melissa's house, she said: "It's been a very nice evening, Bob. Thank you."

Glancing at her, the deputy smiled his boyish grin. The weather continued to be nice, the evening cool but not chilly. Overhead, stars twinkled in a cloudless sky. Melissa found herself studying the deputy's profile. It was a masculine profile, strong and rugged, yet at the same time gentle. Suddenly Melissa heard herself saying:

"It seems a shame to be going home so early on a Friday night."

Although it was what she'd been thinking, she hadn't meant to say it. Instantly feeling a little self-conscious, she fixed her eyes on the road ahead.

"I was just about to say the same thing," Sanchez replied. "I was going to suggest that maybe you might like to go to a . . . I guess you'd call it a get-together. You see, I know this family, the Hernandez family. They live on a farm not far from here, and every year about this time—once everyone's had a chance to rest up from harvest—they have a celebration. I'm invited, along with anyone I care to bring."

"You sure it would be okay for me to go?"

"Oh, absolutely. Besides, Mrs. Hernandez would never let me hear the end of it if I showed up alone. Ever since she found out I'm single . . . well, let's just say Mrs. Hernandez believes in marriage."

"I'd have to call my baby-sitter."

"You could do it as soon as we get there."

"Okay."

"Does that mean: Okay, let's go?"

Melissa hesitated. Am I doing the right thing? she wondered.

But she had no time to weigh the answer to that question, so she said: "Yes, let's go."

"Mrs. Hernandez will be quite impressed when she discovers that I brought the sheriff."

Leaving suburban Denver behind them, they drove into the countryside, the car's headlights periodically illuminating clusters of roadside mailboxes. Why am I doing this? Melissa asked herself, feeling a little bit giddy. Why am I here with a man six years younger than I am, especially one who is my subordinate at work? But she already knew the answer to those questions. She was here because she wanted to be, because the thought of ending the evening and going home left her with an empty, lonely feeling.

Come on, she told herself. You're thirty-five, not fifty. And you're slim, attractive, desirable. There's absolutely no reason why you should react like an infatuated high school girl just because you're receiving the attentions of a man like Bob Sanchez.

As they drove on, another thought struck her. What if all this was nothing more than Sanchez's way of brownnosing the boss? She pushed the question aside. It didn't have to be answered tonight.

About half an hour after they'd left the restaurant, Sanchez slowed, then turned onto a dirt road beside which stood one of those clusters of metal mailboxes. A few minutes later he turned again, crossing a cattle guard, and pulled up to a large stucco house with numerous cars and pickups parked out front. Sanchez slipped his Mustang between a station wagon and a flatbed truck.

As they stepped onto the flagstone porch that ran the length of the building, Melissa stopped to examine the long strings of red chili peppers hanging there. "What are these?" she asked.

"They're called *ristras*. The Hernandezes grow their own chili, and that's how it's dried."

The deputy ushered her through the front door without bothering to knock. Inside were numerous people, most of them dressed in jeans or other casual attire. They stood in groups, although as with any such gathering the participants were constantly moving about, going from one cluster of people to another. The house was more southwestern than what one usually found around Denver. The furniture was simple but sturdy, the floor brick with

Indian throw rugs, and the ceilings were supported by big rough-hewn logs. Suddenly a squat woman with gray hair that still showed traces of black was standing before them, smiling.

"Bobby, how are you?" she asked. "I'm glad you could come." She shifted her eyes to Melissa, obviously awaiting an introduction.

Sanchez said: "Mamma, this is Melissa James. Melissa James, may I present Mamma Hernandez."

As the two women shook hands, Melissa could feel Mrs. Hernandez's dark eyes appraising her. She noted the woman's turquoise necklace and bracelets.

The older woman frowned, thinking. "Where have I heard your name before, Melissa? I'm sure I've heard of you."

"She's the sheriff," Sànchez said.

Mrs. Hernandez's eyes widened. "The sheriff!" she exclaimed, looking at the deputy admiringly. "My goodness."

Melissa smiled politely, wishing that her job hadn't come up. For the next few hours she wanted to enjoy herself, to be a working person out on a Friday night and not a law enforcement officer or a boss or any of the other things she'd become since election day.

Glancing around the room, Mrs. Hernandez said: "I want you to meet Herman, but I don't see him anywhere. You go get something to eat while I find him." She hurried away.

As Sanchez led her toward a doorway across the room, Melissa asked: "Why did you call her Mamma?"

"Everyone does. Maybe it's because she's like a mother. She minds your business for you, lectures you, even gives you orders sometimes, but always so sweetly and with so much concern for you that you don't really mind."

Stepping through the doorway, they entered a large kitchen. Like the living room, it had brick floors, rough-hewn beams supporting the ceiling. To the left was a table of unvarnished, unstained wood large enough to seat a dozen people. On it were assorted liquor bottles and mixes, a bowl of punch, and glasses. Cans of beer protruded from the ice that filled a big metal tub on the floor.

"What would you like to drink?" Sanchez asked.

"Oh, I guess a margarita seems in keeping with the occasion."

"Done." He grabbed two glasses and began adding the ingredients. A few moments later he presented her with a margarita. His own drink appeared to be bourbon and water.

She tried hers. "Ummm. Very good."

"Next stop is over here," he said, moving to the stove, on which sat an enormous cast-iron pot. Grabbing two bowls from the counter, he ladled some of the pot's steaming contents into each, then handed one to Melissa.

Although she was quite fond of Mexican food, this dish was unfamiliar. "What is it?" she asked.

"Some of Mamma's famous posole."

"Some of Mamma's famous what?"

"Posole. It's like hominy. Try it."

Melissa did so. It was a stewlike dish containing chewy white kernels, seasoned with chili and other spices. "This is delicious," she said, meaning it.

Sanchez grinned boyishly and dug into his own bowl of posole.

After a minute or so Melissa asked: "How did you and Mrs. Hernandez come to know each other?"

"Well, about a year ago—no, I guess it was two years ago by now—anyway, the Hernandezes had a burglary, and I got the call. Like most break-ins, there wasn't much I could do except take a report. We got to talking, and I found out she's from New Mexico, a town about thirty miles from where I used to live." He shrugged. "After that, one thing led to another."

"Did you ever find out who broke into the house?"

Sanchez shook his head. "Never caught the burglars or found any of the stuff."

Mrs. Hernandez appeared, looking perplexed. "You haven't seen Herman, have you?"

"No, we haven't, Mamma," Sanchez said.

"Well, I'll find him. Now, don't you two stand here all night. Go into the other room and meet some people." When neither Melissa nor Sanchez moved, the woman put her hands on her hips and stared at them sternly.

Sanchez laughed. "Okay, Mamma, we're going."

Remembering the baby-sitter, Melissa said: "Do you have a phone I could use?"

"Behind you. On the wall." With those words, Mamma Hernandez disappeared through a doorway, presumably to continue searching for her husband.

After Melissa informed Linda Sue that she'd be late, she and Sanchez moved into the living room, where as the evening wore on they talked to farmers and ranchers and truckers, none of whom seemed aware that Melissa was the sheriff, for which she was grateful. Mainly, though, they talked to each other, unaware at times that they were in a room full of people. And when the evening was over, Melissa found herself unable to recall precisely what they had talked about.

"You know," she said as they neared her house in Sanchez's car, "I don't think Mrs. Hernandez ever did find her husband."

The deputy laughed. "I know where he was."

"Where?"

"Did you notice the Winnebago parked out front, by any chance?"

"You mean he was in the Winnebago?"

"Sure. That belongs to a fellow named Silviano, and if I know Silviano, there was a poker game going on inside."

"Why didn't you tell her when she asked—a male conspiracy?"

"I didn't notice the Winnebago until we left."

"Oh."

And then they were in front of Melissa's house. The porch light was on, its bulb illuminating the front yard, the glow being reflected by the gold star on the side of her personal patrol car. The light seemed to say that she was expected here, wanted, and that this was home, and yet it was an unhappy symbol, too, for it meant the evening was over. Sanchez had switched off the engine; they were sitting silently in the dark.

"Would you like to come in for some coffee?" Melissa asked.

"Sounds good."

"First, I'll have to run the baby-sitter home. She just lives down the block, but I don't want her walking even that far when it's this late."

"Why don't I take her, while you make the coffee? Either way, she gets an officer of the law as her personal escort."

Melissa said she thought that was a good idea. Inside, they found Linda Sue watching television in the living room.

"Hi," the girl said, looking away from the screen. "Kids are in bed."

"Any trouble getting them there?" Melissa asked.

The baby-sitter shook her head, her eyes drifting back toward the TV screen. A Japanese monster movie of some sort was on. An enormous reptile was leveling Tokyo.

Calculating what she owed the girl, Melissa pulled her wallet from her purse. "If you don't mind, Linda Sue, I'm going to have Bob here drive you home."

"That'll be fine," the baby-sitter said, her eyes shifting from the TV set to the deputy. A few moments later, the TV set apparently forgotten, she was still looking at Sanchez.

After paying her and watching her leave with the deputy, Melissa checked on Billy and Sarah, finding both snugly tucked into their beds, sound asleep. She lingered at the door to Sarah's room. Watching the motionless lump under the covers, she experienced one of those moments during which she felt the full intensity of the love she had for her son and daughter, and as such moments always did, it brought tears to her eyes. I'm so lucky to have them, she thought. If anything were ever to happen to them . . . She pushed the thought aside. There was no reason to think anything would.

Gently closing the door, she hurried to the kitchen, where she grabbed a kettle and began filling it with water. Sanchez would be back any moment; there was no time for anything other than instant coffee. As soon as the water was heating in the kettle, Melissa, wanting to let Sanchez in before he could ring the bell and wake the children, headed for a living room window from which she could watch for him. Within moments she saw the white car pull up outside, then the deputy coming up the walk.

"Coffee'll be ready in a minute or two," she said, closing the door behind him. "I hope instant's okay."

"That'll be fine."

They moved a few paces into the living room, then stopped, their eyes meeting. Standing a few feet apart, they studied each other, the room seeming to be filled with an electricity of anticipation. Before anything could come of it, the spell was shattered by the screaming of the kettle.

"I, uh, think the cofeee water's ready," Melissa said, a little dazed.

In the kitchen they sat at the breakfast table, drinking their coffee in silence. The electricity of a few moments ago was still in the air, and it seemed to generate a mood in which words were neither necessary nor wanted.

Finishing his coffee, Sanchez broke the silence. "I think I'd better go," he said. "It's pretty late."

Again their eyes met, and Sanchez put his hand on hers, squeezing it gently. "Thank you for coming with me tonight," he said softly. "I had a good time."

They both stood, moving slowly into the living room. Suddenly Sanchez was holding her, their lips meeting, her arms slipping around him. Tentative at first, the kiss soon became passionate. When it ended, Melissa pulled herself tightly against him, shuddering from the sudden intensity of her desire.

And then they were kissing again, his tongue sliding into her mouth, hers reciprocating. And Melissa knew that if she was going to say no, she had to do it now, while she still could. Should she allow herself to make love to a man six years younger than she, a man whose interest in her was unclear? Should the boss allow herself to be seduced by a subordinate? And what about Keith? And what if the children woke up?

Her thoughts swirling, she tried to sort things out. Sanchez had aroused passions in her that had been dormant since Jim died, and despite all the logical reasons for ending this before she was unable to do so, her body was tingling, wanting him desperately, a voice somewhere deep inside crying: *Yes, yes, yes. Oh, God, yes . . .*

Finally, using all the willpower she had, Melissa pushed herself away from him. He searched her face a moment, and then, his own passion subsiding, he nodded in understanding. "I guess I'd better go, huh?"

"I . . . I enjoyed the evening. Thank you." Although part of her was still urging her to grab him while the opportunity was still at hand, she had the situation under control now. There were just too many reasons not to, too many complications.

She walked the deputy to the door. "Good night," she said gently.

"Good night," he replied, hesitating as if uncertain whether to give her a good night kiss. Then he gave her a parting smile, one of his boyish grins, and he was gone.

Closing the door, she leaned against it a moment, then walked slowly into the living room and lowered herself onto the couch.

"Oh, God," she whispered, shaking her head. "Oh, God."

11

Reverend Paul Maxwell sat at his big antique rolltop desk in the rectory's study, thinking. Before him in the desk's pigeonholes were numerous papers he should be attending to and wasn't. The trouble was that he didn't want to be inside on such a beautiful sunny Saturday morning. So because being outside made him feel guilty for neglecting his paperwork, he sat here grumbling, wishing he were out there. It made no sense, he supposed, but such were the workings of the human mind.

Sighing, he removed a handful of papers from their pigeonhole and spread them out before him. They were notes for this month's church bulletin, which would have to be typed, edited, Xeroxed, and mailed within the next few days if it was to go out on time. Maxwell shook his head. Hell, it never went out on time. No one ever noticed. Chances were no one ever read the damn thing.

Thirty-seven years old, he was a meaty fellow who'd been a linebacker on his college football team, although in those days his body had been a lot more solid than it was now. The duties of a minister in suburbia didn't involve much physical activity. Absently smoothing his thin brown hair with his palm, the minister tried to make himself concentrate on the church bulletin.

Another distraction was his concern about the church's elderly caretaker, who'd disappeared a few days ago. Although A. J.

had done this before, his longest previous absence had been three days. This time he'd been gone five. So far.

Maxwell had stopped by the caretaker's apartment yesterday evening; no one had answered his knock. The two women living in the other half of the duplex said they hadn't seen him in a while but hadn't thought much about it. Apparently A. J. rarely communicated with his neighbors.

The caretaker had a drinking problem. No, the clergyman decided, that was only a euphemism. A. J. Sebastian was an alcoholic; he went on binges. And whenever they occurred, Maxwell worried that the old guy might be dead or injured, the victim of a mugging or a traffic accident.

And when drunks like A. J. did have accidents, how many innocent people were hurt? We're all so self-destructive, Paul Maxwell thought sadly, whether individually, like poor old A. J., or collectively, with our tanks and nuclear weapons.

He knew A. J. drank on the job, although he'd never caught him at it. Even if he did catch him, he'd most likely just give the old guy a stern look and let it go at that. If he tried talking to the caretaker about his problem, A. J. would listen politely, then go right on doing exactly as he had been. And there was no way Maxwell could ever fire the old man.

Rising, the minister walked purposefully out of the study and through the rectory's small living room. He opened the front door and stepped out into the sunshine, breathing cool fall air that bore the pleasant odor of decaying leaves. A hundred and fifty feet or so from him was the church, which Maxwell had been cleaning and caring for himself since his caretaker had disappeared. It was only a minor inconvenience, dusting pews mainly, and never having married, he'd become quite adept at cleaning over the years.

Where are you, A. J.? he asked. Are you all right? Five days was a long time, nearly a week. He sighed. Then, standing there in the cool but sunny Colorado autumn, he bowed his head and prayed for A. J. Sebastian.

When he'd completed the prayer, he returned to the study and picked up the phone. The old man had been missing too long to simply assume he'd be back when the binge ended. It was time to notify the police.

While he dialed, Maxwell found himself wondering where A. J. hid the booze he consumed on the job. There had to be a hiding place. Every now and then the caretaker would disappear for an hour or two, and when he showed up again, his breath would smell of whiskey and the mints he used in an attempt to mask the odor. But then at the moment where A. J. stashed his booze was unimportant.

He heard the phone start to ring at the sheriff's office.

Marla Clark drove her patrol car along the two-lane street, passing homes and small businesses. This was the first time she'd been on patrol alone. Sergeant Hillman, with whom she'd been riding, was off today, and Lieutenant Wheeler, who'd conducted the morning briefing, had simply assigned her to a car and sent her on her way. She was unable to decide whether they were beginning to treat her as an equal or whether the lieutenant had simply been avoiding the hassle of finding another male officer willing to ride with her.

Except for the constant cold shoulder, it hadn't been too bad, she supposed. Most of the heavy sneering went on behind her back. She did hear some of the resentment directed at Melissa James, though, although even that tended to be curtailed around her, probably because some of the men considered her a spy. On the issue of the new sheriff, the department seemed divided. Although James had made some enemies by firing Nelson, she'd also won some respect. For whom will it be tougher, she wondered, Melissa James or me? And then she realized the question was pointless, since it wasn't going to be easy for either of them.

Ahead was a small liquor store on a corner, a white building whose only sign was the red neon lettering in the window that said Discount Liquors. She slowed and turned the corner, then drove partway down the block and pulled in behind a battered Dodge pickup. She and Hillman had first noticed the truck on Tuesday. Although it was legally parked, it seemed out of place somehow, as if it had been abandoned here. On Tuesday they hadn't bothered to run a computer check on the truck's license number. She decided it was time to do so.

"Three-Adam to control," she said into the two-way-radio microphone.

"Go ahead, three-Adam," the male dispatcher's voice replied.

"Need a computer check on Colorado license 090-BHA."

"Stand by." A few minutes passed; then the dispatcher said: "Control to three-Adam."

"Go ahead, control."

"Negative on Colorado license 090-BHA.'

"Ten-four. I'm behind that vehicle in the fourteen hundred block of Raintree. I'll be out here a moment."

"Ten-four."

Climbing out of her cruiser, Marla checked over the pickup. It had been red once, though now most of its original paint was faded, replaced by rust, or covered with primer. Looking in through the window, she spotted the keys hanging from the ignition. Why hadn't someone stolen it?

As she continued her inspection of the vehicle, she discovered the answer to that question. The hood was just resting on its latch and not closed tightly. Raising it, she peered into the engine compartment, finding what she'd expected. The battery was missing. The reason the pickup hadn't been stolen was because the first thief to come along hadn't been interested in anything other than the battery.

Returning to her patrol car, Marla grabbed the microphone and requested the name of the truck's owner. A few moments later control called her back.

"Vehicle is registered to an Archibald J. Sebastian, 5418 Creswell Way, apartment two."

"Give Mr. Sebastian a ten–twenty-one, please, and see if he knows where his pickup truck is."

"Stand by." Another few minutes passed, then: "Control to three-Adam."

"Go ahead, control."

"No answer on that ten–twenty-one."

"Ten-four. I'm going to declare this a derelict vehicle and have it towed. Send a ten–forty-six, please."

"Ten-four."

"Three-Adam's ten–eight," she said as she slipped the shift lever to drive and pulled away from the curb. If Archibald Sebastian was concerned about his truck, he'd report it stolen and discover it was at a local towing company. He'd pay the towing and storage charges and get his truck back. On the other hand, the pickup was so old and dilapidated he might not want it back. Either way the matter was no longer her concern.

"Three-Adam," the male dispatcher's voice said through the speaker.

"Go ahead."

"Heston and Newman, a ten–forty-four."

"Ten-four." Using a driveway to turn around, she headed in the opposite direction, toward the scene of a minor traffic accident.

The officer on the desk that Saturday morning at the Ramsey County Sheriff's Department was a thin dark-haired young man named Hank Coffin. He studied the missing-person report that had just been signed by the heavyset preacher. Archibald Jeremy Sebastian, seventy-seven, caretaker at the minister's church, a boozer. Nothing much the sheriff's office could do with this. The old man would either come back when he ran out of money for booze, or they'd find him dead somewhere. Sometimes old drunks like that simply curled up in a doorway and died. He'd found one like that once. Wino had crawled into an alley to sleep it off, and his liver had given out.

He tossed the report into the appropriate basket. Eventually it would get picked up and delivered to wherever it was supposed to go. Coffin had no idea who actually looked at such reports. Someone did, he supposed.

It was the second evening in a row that Melissa had prepared a dinner she wouldn't be eating. She carried two plates of meat loaf, mashed potatoes, and green beans to the table, putting one in front of Billy, the other in Sarah's place. Sarah brought over glasses of milk for her brother and herself and took her seat.

"Looks good, Mom," the girl said, picking up her fork.

Billy scowled at his plate. "How come we can't have french fries instead of yucky old mashed potatoes?"

"There's too much grease in french fries," Sarah said.

Billy ignored her. "How come, Mom?"

"Because mashed potatoes are better for you."

Giving the potatoes a disapproving poke with his fork, he started on his meat loaf.

Melissa filled the sink with soapy water and began scrubbing the pan in which she'd cooked the meat loaf. She was going out with Keith tonight; Linda Sue would be baby-sitting. While she worked on a spot where the meat loaf had stuck to the pan, she recalled last night. Just thinking about it made her tingle. And yet she'd said no, passed up a chance other women might have jumped at. It had seemed the responsible thing to do, the safe thing.

Inwardly she sighed. And what did you get when you always did the prudent thing? You led a routine, uneventful existence. You were boring.

Oh, come on, she told herself. How many other women do you know who were just elected sheriff? And how many others have the ultimate responsibility for stopping a mass murderer? She shuddered. Just thinking about the Boogeyman unnerved her, for if stopping him was her responsibility, then she had to wonder whether it wouldn't—at least in part—be her fault if he killed again. Melissa scrubbed harder at the burned-on meatloaf, telling herself that it couldn't possibly be her fault, that no one could take that much blame for someone else's actions. Especially when the someone else was a psychopath.

And yet lurking somewhere in her mind was that tiny bit of doubt. Would a competent go-getter of a sheriff have captured the Boogeyman? Would he be unable now to hurt anyone else?

An hour later, showered and dressed, Melissa was waiting in the living room when Linda Sue arrived.

"Hi," the girl said, slipping off her coat. "You keep it up with these two-night weekends, and I'll have that car in no time."

"What kind of a car would you like?" Melissa asked.

"I guess the main requirement is that it has to be cheap— unless I want to be in my twenties by the time I get enough money."

The way Linda Sue said it made the twenties seem so ancient that anyone reaching that age would be on the verge of senility. And what does she think about the thirties? Melissa wondered, and then she decided she didn't really want to know.

The doorbell sounded, and Melissa let Keith in. Sarah came out to greet Linda Sue and him, followed a moment later by Billy, who strode purposefully up to Keith and stuck out his hand.

Keith shook it. "How are you this evening, Mr. James?"

At first a little surprised at having been greeted so respectfully, Billy quickly regained his cool. "Just fine. And how are you, Mr. . . ." Obviously trying to recall Keith's last name, the boy screwed up his face. Finally he said: "How are you this evening, Keith?"

"Great!" With that, Keith scooped him up and rode him one time around the room on his shoulders, Billy squealing in delight. When Keith put the boy down, his eyes met Sarah's and he seemed momentarily unsure of himself. "How are you this evening, Sarah?"

"Fine," Sarah replied, her eyes revealing nothing of what she really thought.

He's marvelous with Billy, Melissa thought, but he's uncertain how to deal with girls. If he was to become the father of these kids, would he ignore Sarah simply because he had no idea how to handle her? Having no answer for that, Melissa pushed the question from her mind.

His eyes shifting back to Billy, Keith said: "I bought something yesterday that you might be interested in."

The boy's eyes widened. "What?"

"I'll give you a hint. They're rectangular and there are two of them."

"Ummm . . ." Billy frowned.

"They're tickets."

"To the Broncos?!"

Keith nodded. "For tomorrow's game." He turned to Melissa. "Uh, if it's all right, of course."

"Fine by me."

"Oh, boy!" Billy said, jumping. "Oh, boy; oh, boy; oh, boy."

"Hey," Melissa said sternly. "None of that in the house."

"Come on," Linda Sue said. "Everybody in the den."

"I wanna play Monopoly," Billy said as they disappeared into the hallway.

A minute or so later Melissa was in Keith's Buick, headed for the Sophisticated Suburbanite, a place whose prices pretty much restricted its clientele to the well-heeled—suburbanites or otherwise. Keith, who could be a little extravagant by Melissa's standards, opted to have the valet park his car, then tipped the maître d' to seat them promptly when it appeared there would be a short wait despite their having reservations. The interior decorating was someone's idea of what elegant dining was like around the turn of the century. The furniture was real wood, and along with the plates and glasses and silverware, it was heavy and quite ornate. Chandeliers hung from the ceiling.

"This is costing you an arm and a leg," Melissa said after they'd been seated at a table for two in a corner of the dining room.

Keith shrugged. "I'm a successful lawyer, and being single, I don't have all that much to spend it on."

Was that a hint? Melissa decided to let it go. When the waiter came, she hesitated, then ordered a margarita.

Keith eyed her curiously. "I didn't know you liked those."

"I guess I've only recently discovered them."

Keith was unaware of her date with Bob Sanchez last night. Though unable to think of a logical reason for keeping it to herself, she was reluctant to tell him. Was she afraid he'd be hurt? Or was it guilt—guilt because of what had almost happened last night in her living room? Neither explanation was satisfactory. Keith had no claim on her; she was free to go out with whomever she chose. And the other thing, the thing that had come so close to happening? Well, hell, nothing did happen, and even if it had, she was also free to make love to whomever she chose.

And yet she felt awkward somehow, the child who'd broken something but didn't want to admit it. Oh, damn, she thought. Oh, damn, damn, damn. Her eyes met Keith's and she forced herself to hold his gaze. I won't look away as though I'm ashamed of something, she thought. I won't.

Keith smiled. "You know, I'm kind of proud of you for the way you handled that business with Sergeant What's-His-Name."

"Nelson. And I appreciate the compliment, but there's really nothing to be proud of. I simply did what had to be done. Nelson didn't leave me much choice."

"Still, I'd have to say you're turning out to be a tougher administrator than I had you figured for. Especially considering that the closest thing you have to any experience is that neighborhood crime watch thing you were involved in way back when.''

Uncertain how she should take that, Melissa picked up her menu and said: "We'd better decide what we want.''

"Shall we have an appetizer?" Keith asked, studying his menu.

"Why not? Like you said, you have to spend all that money on something.''

They settled on cracked crab.

Melissa considered suggesting that she pick up the tab for dinner tonight, then dropped the idea, because it was always such a hassle. Keith was of the old school when it came to such things.

Their drinks arrived, and as Melissa sipped hers, she found herself once more considering the kind of life she led. As she'd concluded earlier, hers was hardly a routine and uninteresting existence, and yet she was unable to shake the feeling that something was missing. Romance was as good a word as any, she supposed. Was romance missing from her life?

Until last night, Keith was the only man she'd had anything to do with since her husband's death. She'd chosen him, she supposed, because he was safe. No risks. A reliable man who'd be good with the kids. And certainly that was what at least a part of her wanted, someone dependable who'd be good for Billy and Sarah. But since last night, Melissa had realized there was another part of her that wanted something else, the part that tingled whenever she recalled her brief but passionate moment with Bob Sanchez.

There were no such tingles with Keith. Their relationship was hardly the stuff romance novels were made of. Life with him would be Little League, yearly vacations, PTA meetings. Not that there was anything wrong with that. Until last night, she hadn't realized that such a life lacked anything.

"Have you decided what you'd like besides cracked crab?" Keith asked.

"Uh, no, not yet.''

Although Melissa had been staring at the menu, her eyes hadn't focused on it. While she quickly scanned the entrees, she was aware that Keith was studying her. She felt transparent somehow, as if he could look into her and know what she'd been thinking.

Linda Sue Jennings sat on the floor of the den with Billy and Sarah, the three of them surrounding a Monopoly board. The baby-sitter picked up the dice and rolled a seven. Billy watched excitedly as she moved her plastic race car toward his hotels on the yellow properties. She stopped on Ventnor.

"You owe me . . ." He checked the property card. "You owe me one thousand one hundred and fifty dollars. Pay up or I get all your property."

All her property was mortgaged, and the cash before her totaled less than three hundred dollars. She handed it all to Billy, who accepted it greedily.

"Linda Sue's out!" he exclaimed, gleefully examining the fruits of his victory.

"You have to pay interest on the mortgaged properties," Sarah said.

"I don't either."

"That's what the rules say."

Leaving them to their bickering, Linda Sue headed for the kitchen to get a Coke. Finding no colas of any variety in the refrigerator, she settled for an orange soda, which she decided to drink here in the peace and quiet of the kitchen, rather than return to witness the boisterous conclusion of the Monopoly game.

Leaning against the refrigerator, Linda Sue recalled the deputy who'd driven her home last night. The man was an absolute, total hunk. And he'd had such a fantastic car. A white Mustang. If only she could someday get enough money to buy something like that.

She'd told Betty Lou about both man and machine in great detail. She'd even told her friend that the deputy had kissed her good night, saying he'd like to call her sometime. Which, of course, was a lie, but telling it had been worth it, because of the way Betty Lou's eyes had lighted up.

After drinking about half the orange soda, Linda Sue decided she'd better get back to the den and make sure Billy and Sarah were behaving themselves. As she left the kitchen, the teenager tried to imagine what it would be like to really kiss someone like the deputy. In her mind his strong arms slipped around her, gently but firmly pulling her against his muscular body. . . .

For a single confused moment, Linda Sue was unable to distinguish reality from what she'd been imagining. In the next instant she realized with a horrifying jolt that someone really did have his arms around her.

She opened her mouth to scream, only to have something soft stuffed into it, and then her arms were pulled behind her, the half-full soft drink bottle dropping to the living room floor, orange soda spilling onto the carpet. Terrified, her thoughts swirling, Linda Sue felt her arms being tied behind her, and then she was turned to the left, pushed into the kitchen, shoved against the refrigerator.

"Don't turn around," a male voice whispered.

Linda Sue tried to find some way to indicate that she wouldn't, but before she could do so, a cloth was tied around her face, holding in the gag. Then a paper bag was slipped over her head. He's going to rape me, she thought. Rape me, then kill me. But then, somewhere in that part of her mind that was still able to function, she realized that the bag was to prevent her from seeing whoever was doing this to her, a precaution that would be unnecessary if she were going to die.

Roughly, she was pushed to the floor, and her legs were bound; then the same voice whispered: "Unless you want me to come back, don't even try to free yourself. Just wait until you're found. It won't be that long."

Linda Sue heard him doing something just above her head, something to the refrigerator. "Remember what I told you," he whispered.

And then he left the room. At least Linda Sue thought he had. She sensed an emptiness to the room. And yet the man could be watching her, waiting to be sure she obeyed his instructions. He had nothing to worry about; Linda Sue had no intention of disobeying.

From the living room came the sound of a child crying, then some muffled words and Sarah's voice. "Don't hurt him," she pleaded. "He's just afraid."

There were more muffled words; then the front door opened

and closed, and as far as Linda Sue could tell, she was alone in the house. Confused and frightened, she sat on the floor by the refrigerator, trembling, not understanding what had just happened.

Despite his precautions, she had seen the man who'd done this to her. Just a glimpse when after tying her hands he'd turned her toward the kitchen. Just enough of a look to know he had blond hair.

At that moment the whole world was tan, the color of the bag. When she exhaled, her breath bounced off the paper and hit her face. A tear rolled down her cheek and was absorbed by the brown paper. Then another. Soon there were too many tears for the paper to absorb.

It was about ten o'clock when Keith's Buick pulled up to the curb in front of Melissa's house. Switching off the engine and killing the lights, he reached over and took her hand.

"Is something troubling you?" he asked. "You've been sort of withdrawn all night."

"Just the problems any working stiff has, I guess."

"Want to talk about it?"

"Not really."

"You've got to learn to leave the problems of the office at the office. It's the people who can't do that who have the ulcers and nervous breakdowns."

Not wanting to pursue this topic any further, Melissa said: "Want to come in for a nightcap?"

"Sure."

As they walked toward the house, she said: "Maybe I should make that nightcap coffee."

"Why's that?"

"I'm the sheriff. If you've had too much to drink, I can't let you drive."

"Coffee'll keep me awake. I'll tell you what, Sheriff. If you decide I'm unfit to operate a motor vehicle on the public highways of Ramsey County, I'll spend the night on your couch."

"I wonder what the neighbors would say after your car spent the night in front of the house, and then you left in the morning."

"You could lead me out in handcuffs, and they'd think you were merely detaining a prisoner."

"Uh-huh. They'd most likely think I was into something . . . what's the word? Kinky, that's it. You know, whips and chains, bondage and all that."

Digging in her purse for her keys, Melissa recalled the chemistry between her and the man who'd brought her home last night, chemistry that was absent now. Exciting though it may be, she told herself sternly, physical attraction is not everything. Now, stop carrying on like a pubescent teenager.

As she slipped the key into the lock, she resolved to get all this straightened out in her mind before Monday. She would have to get Bob Sanchez out of her thoughts, and maybe even out of her life except for their professional relationship. She was a widow and a mother who lived quietly in a fairly well-to-do suburban neighborhood. Where had this sudden craving for hot romance come from? She'd been getting along just fine without it before last night.

In the living room Melissa suddenly slipped her arms around Keith and kissed him on the lips.

"What was that for?" he asked.

"Just for being good old reliable you."

After hanging their jackets in the coat closet, Melissa headed for the den to check on the kids and find out whether Billy, as he usually did, had conned Linda Sue into letting him stay up past his bedtime. Normally the baby-sitter came out to greet her when she returned home, so she assumed Linda Sue was unaware that she was here.

No one was in the den. On the floor was a Monopoly game that hadn't been put away, and the lights were on. Feeling the first prickles of concern, Melissa checked Billy's room, finding it empty. Quickly she checked Sarah's room. It, too, was empty, the bed unmussed except for a spot where Sarah must have sat on it to do something or other.

Worried now, she returned to the living room. Keith was sitting on the couch. "I can't find them," she said.

"What do you mean?" he asked, rising.

"The kids. They're not here. Neither's Linda Sue."

They checked again. The den, the bedrooms, even Melissa's room.

Once more standing in the living room, they exchanged puzzled looks. "Where could they have gone?" Melissa asked anxiously. "Keith, where could they be?"

"Maybe they stepped out for something."

"At ten o'clock at night? Where would they go?" She called their names, getting no response. "If you're playing tricks on me, so help me I'll . . ." The words trailed off. Melissa was too frightened to make empty threats.

"Come on," Keith said, "let's check the backyard. Maybe they're out there looking at the stars or something."

Melissa started to say that such behavior would be ridiculous, but then she realized that things like looking at the stars at ten o'clock on a chilly November night made perfect sense to a child. And a sixteen-year-old girl was a pretty lightweight authority figure. Linda Sue could be manipulated if they put their minds to it.

They hurried into the kitchen, headed for the back door. Keith gasped, and Melissa suppressed a scream. On the floor by the refrigerator, tied, a bag over her head, was Linda Sue Jennings.

Keith rushed to the girl, removing the bag from her head and untying her hands. As he removed the gag from her mouth, the teenager began to sob and babble incoherently. And then Melissa saw what was on the refrigerator door. In purple crayon had been written the words:

THOSE WHO INSULT THE BOOGEYMAN MUST BE PUNISHED

Dazed, Melissa stared at the message, uncertain what it meant. Had the Boogeyman taken her children? And then the unthinkable thing that had been hanging at the edge of her consciousness expressed itself. The Boogeyman *killed* children.

No, no, no. She forced the thought away. Maybe they were still here somewhere. She hadn't checked the backyard yet. Maybe they were there. Frantic now, she yanked open the door and rushed outside.

"Sarah! Billy!"

The only sound was the rustling of unraked leaves as they were stirred by the gentle night breeze. Somewhere in the neighborhood a dog barked and then was silent again.

The glow from the doorway behind her illuminated the spot

where she stood, leaving the rest of the yard in shadows. Though a part of her knew how unlikely it was, Melissa tried to convince herself that the children were out here somewhere, safe. Rushing into the shadows, she felt along the back wall, finding nothing. They were here. They had to be. Dashing to another part of the yard, she tried to force her eyes to see into the darkness. They were here. Dropping to her knees, she used her hands to explore the area around her, finding a garden hose she hadn't put away for the winter, a brick the function of which she'd forgotten, a rock, dried leaves. . . .

And then she spotted an area of shadow she hadn't explored yet. Getting to her feet, she ran toward it. Suddenly her foot caught on something, and she fell face-first into the dry leaves. Sitting up, she tried to see what had tripped her. Unable to find it, she started to cry, and through the tears she saw the shape of an approaching figure silhouetted against the lights from the house.

For just a second she thought it must be the Boogeyman, coming to get her, too. And then she realized it was Keith.

"Melissa," he called, "where are you?"

Scrambling to her feet, she ran to him, throwing her arms around him. They stood there a few moments, just holding each other, and then Melissa's mind began to function again.

"I've got to get some help," she said. "I've got to call the office and get someone out here."

"I've already called," he said.

Carried by the breeze, the wail of a distant siren reached them. Somewhere down the block, a dog began howling at it.

12

Feeling drained of everything except the pervasive numbness that had settled over her, Melissa sat at the kitchen table, watching Roger Goldman dust the refrigerator for fingerprints. Linda Sue Jennings also sat at the table, looking dazed. Their eyes met, but no communication passed between them, for both had withdrawn into themselves, into that place where it was always private, always safe.

The back door opened, and Lieutenant Castle came in, carrying a flashlight. "We've checked the whole place, inside and out, and there are no signs of any violence," he said to Melissa. "So as far as we know, they're unharmed."

Melissa nodded. Keith came in from the living room, where Detective Walczak had been taking his statement. He sat down beside her, giving her arm a reassuring squeeze.

Looking at the baby-sitter, Castle said: "If you saw the man again, do you think you'd recognize him?"

Linda Sue stared blankly at him for a moment, then shook her head. "Like I told you, I saw some blond hair, and that was about all."

"Was he a thin man?"

"I think he was pretty big . . . not fat, just big."

"Was he older than I am?"

The teenager frowned, studying Castle. "Younger, I think."

"Could he have been a lot younger—say, younger than twenty?"

Linda Sue closed her eyes, concentrating. "I don't think he was that young, but I'm not sure."

"What color were his eyes?"

"I don't know."

"Was he wearing a jacket?"

Making a gesture of helplessness with her hand, the girl said: "I was so scared that he could have been naked and I don't think I would have noticed." She shuddered. "When he first grabbed me, I thought I was going to die."

The lieutenant quickly scanned the notebook in which he'd been recording the girl's answers. "Just one more question; then I'll let you go home. Were the doors locked?"

"I always keep them locked."

"Did you actually check to make sure?"

"Uh, I think I checked the back one. I know I did."

"When?"

"It was . . ." She wrinkled her brow. "Uh, I guess it was about half an hour after Mrs. James left. I went into the kitchen to see if there were any potato chips or anything like that."

"Did you lock it then, or was it already locked?"

"It was already locked."

"What about the front door?"

"Uh, I didn't check that one, because it locks by itself whenever you close the door."

"Thank you for your help," Castle said, flipping his notebook closed. "I'll get Detective Walczak to give you a ride home."

Linda Sue nodded. "My mom doesn't know what happened yet. I'm almost afraid to tell her. She's going to be real upset."

After Walczak and the girl had left, Castle joined Melissa and Keith at the breakfast table. He stared at his hands a moment, then shifted his eyes to Melissa. "When you came home," he said, "was the front door locked?"

"I used my key," Melissa replied, suddenly realizing how dry her throat felt. "I'm sure it was locked."

"Okay. Now, when you went out into the backyard, do you remember if the door was locked?"

Melissa recalled seeing the words in purple crayon, then running out the door. Had she unlocked it or just twisted the knob and pulled it open? Everything was hazy, confused. Forcing herself not to think about where her children were or what might be happening to them, she said: "It was unlocked. If it hadn't been, it would have slowed me down, and I'd have remembered it."

Castle nodded. "There are no signs of forced entry. It seems pretty likely that the kidnapper picked the lock on your back door."

What difference does all this make? Melissa wondered. How's it going to help get my children back? And then the significance of the lieutenant's words hit her. There had been no break-in at the Tucker or Evans homes either.

"It's really him, isn't it?" she said softly. "It's really the Boogeyman."

Castle hesitated, then said: "We can't be absolutely certain at this point, but it looks like it."

A tear hit the wooden surface of the table. Melissa stared at it a moment before she realized she was crying. "Why," she asked in that squeaky voice people get when they try to speak while crying, "why does some lunatic have to go around hurting children? What's wrong with the world that it lets things like that happen?''

Keith started to pull her to him, and she pulled herself away. She didn't want comforting. She wanted to know how this could be happening; she wanted someone to tell her.

''Why?'' she demanded. ''Why does this man want to hurt my children?''

Wiping away the tears, Melissa forced herself to stop crying. They sat in silence, Melissa glaring at Castle, not because of anything he'd done but because at that moment he seemed to symbolize their helplessness. Finally she lowered her eyes. Emotional outbursts would do nothing to help get her children back.

''I'm sorry,'' she said. ''I . . .''

Castle held up his hand. ''Don't apologize. There's no need.''

''What are you going to do?'' Keith asked the lieutenant.

''The first thing will be to start knocking on the neighbors' doors to find out whether any of them saw anything.''

''When are you going to start?'' Melissa asked.

''As soon as Walczak gets back.''

''I'm coming with you,'' she said. Then, noticing the frown on Keith's face, she put her hand on his arm. ''I'm the sheriff,'' she said, her eyes meeting his. ''I'm still the sheriff.''

In his eyes she saw only confusion and concern. How could she explain to him that the last thing she needed right now was consoling. As long as she was involved with the investigation, she'd have purpose; she could keep her mind on what she was doing and not on what might be happening to Sarah and Billy. If she had nothing to do but think about that, she'd go crazy.

When Walczak returned, both Castle and Melissa stood up.

''Do you want me to wait here for you?'' Keith asked.

''Please,'' Melissa said.

He nodded.

Unnoticed, Roger Goldman had moved from the refrigerator to the back door. He applied dust to the knob, then carefully blew away the excess. Beside him on the floor was the metal case that contained his fingerprint equipment. He looked up, his eyes finding Melissa's, and for the first time, she saw no hostility there. Her status had changed, she realized. From antagonist to victim.

* * *

Confused and afraid, Sarah sat between her brother and the blond man in the front seat of the green car. She watched the houses pass by, their windows yellow rectangles of hope in the darkness, for inside were families doing what normal people did, the moms and dads watching TV, the kids in bed, the cats and dogs doing animal stuff. Protection, warmth, people who'd help her. These things were all right there, so close she could almost touch them, and yet they might as well be in another world, for they were completely unreachable.

Shifting her position, she tried to get more comfortable. As were Billy's, her hands were held behind her with some sort of plastic strap that encircled her wrists. Another plastic strap, a longer one, connected her arm to her brother's. To keep them from trying to escape by running in different directions, Sarah supposed. And to hamper them should they try to jump from the car.

She was worried about Billy, who sat beside her staring straight ahead, lost in a world of his own. Sarah had seen a prairie dog like that once. Cornered by a German shepherd, it simply froze, became too terrified to move. Even after Sarah chased the dog away, the little creature was unable to do anything except stand there and tremble. Of course, there was one difference between her brother's behavior and that of the prairie dog. Billy wasn't trembling. And somewhere in the back of her mind, she wondered whether that might be worse.

The man stopped at a stop sign, then turned right. She glanced at him warily, seeing only his shape in the darkened interior of the car. Out of nowhere he'd appeared in the den, pointing a gun at them, warning them to be quiet and not to move or he'd shoot them. And then, after tying their hands behind their backs with the plastic straps, he'd used the longer strap to fasten her and her brother together like prisoners on their way to work on a chain gang. Leading them toward the front door, he repeated his threat to kill whoever misbehaved.

And then had come a terrifying moment. In the living room Billy had simply stopped, refused to go on. The man had pointed the gun at him, saying he was going to kill the boy if he didn't cooperate. Using the strap connecting them, Sarah had pulled her brother forward, pleading with the man not to hurt him. Sarah believed the man would have done it. The gun had one of those things on its barrel that made it quiet, and she'd reasoned that he might have already killed Linda Sue, who was nowhere to be seen.

That thought brought more tears to Sarah's eyes. Why, she wondered hopelessly, why did this man come into our home, threaten to kill us, kidnap us, and maybe even murder Linda Sue? What does he want with us?

They passed a church, and a few moments later the man turned right. At the next intersection he turned right again. At first Sarah thought he was going around the block, but then he stopped. There were no houses here, no yellow rectangles of hope. She felt surrounded by the night, lost and alone in its blackness.

"Open your mouth," the man said.

Though she considered refusing, she was too afraid to act on the notion. When she complied, he stuffed a cloth into her mouth.

"You, too, boy. Open your mouth."

Billy simply sat there, staring straight ahead. Reaching over Sarah, the man grabbed Billy's jaw, squeezing near the point at which it was hinged. Instantly the boy's mouth opened; the man stuffed a rag into it.

He got out, hurried around the car, and opened the door. "Let's go," he said, grabbing Billy and pulling him and his attached sister from the car.

They moved through the darkness, Sarah and Billy with their hands fastened behind them, the children connected by a short length of plastic that forced them to walk side by side. The man was leading them away from the street. Bushes caught at Sarah's clothing. Uncertain where she was or where the man was taking them, Sarah cautiously put one foot in front of the other. Twice she nearly tripped over a rock. Billy walked into a bush, but it didn't seem to bother him, and he plodded onward.

The night was black, neither moon nor stars in the sky. Occasionally the man would switch on a penlight, but then he'd immediately turn it off again. When he used the light, Sarah caught glimpses of their surroundings. Range grass, scrub brush, rocks. They seemed to be moving downhill.

Suddenly the earth was flat and free of rocks. The surface beneath Sarah's feet became grass and fallen leaves, then changed to pavement. The penlight came on and went out, and they changed direction. A moment later they stopped.

"Don't try anything," the man whispered. "You can't get away, and I'll kill you if you try."

Then the penlight came on again. They were standing in front of a door, an entrance to a brick building. The light went out. The man was doing something in the dark, but she was unsure what. Then she heard the door open.

"Inside," the man whispered.

Sarah and Billy stepped through the doorway, the door closed behind them, and the penlight came on. They were in a church.

"This way," the man said, pushing them forward.

He left the light on now. They were between the altar and the first row of pews, heading toward the far wall. Everything was made of stained wood—the altar, the pews, even the walls. Beneath their feet was a soft red carpet that covered the area in front of the altar and the central aisle. As they neared the wall, Sarah noted that it was made of recessed wood panels, sort of like a huge checkerboard.

Was this the same church she'd seen from the car? Sarah decided the question was unimportant. What mattered was *why* they were here. Billy walked zombielike beside her, his eyes straight ahead, his mind elsewhere. Though she didn't understand it, Sarah realized that her brother, at least in his head, had gone somewhere safe, someplace where the blond man couldn't hurt him. Uncertain whether Billy would ever be able to come back from that place, she stopped when the man told them to stop.

Her brother stared at the wall. Oh, Billy, she thought, what's going to happen to us?

Putting his hands on one of the recessed panels that made up the wall, the man slid it aside. Sarah recalled the rectangles of yellow light from the houses; before her now was a rectangle of blackness. About four feet high, the opening seemed to be waiting for them, and Sarah was afraid that if she ever went in there she'd never come out.

"Move," the man ordered. "In there."

Terrified, Sarah didn't budge. And then the man gave her a shove. She ducked her head, and the three of them were inside the opening. The man slid the panel closed. There was nothing here, just a cramped space and a metal ladder going up.

Suddenly she felt a tug on the plastic band holding her hands, and her arms were free. Then the strap connecting her to Billy was severed. Holding the penlight in his teeth, the man had a pocket knife in his hand. He cut the strap holding Billy's hands. The plastic fell to the floor. Afraid to risk angering the man, Sarah resisted the desire to remove the gag from her mouth.

"Climb the ladder," the man said. "The boy first."

When Billy didn't respond, the man yanked the gag from Sarah's mouth. "I'll give you a chance to make him go up the ladder. If you can't do it, I'll kill him. Understand?"

She nodded. Her mouth was dry and tasted of dust and old cloth. "Billy," she said urgently, "please get up there. You have to do it."

Billy just stared at her, his expression blank.

"Billy!" she shouted, shaking him. "He'll kill you if you don't."

The boy gave no indication that he'd heard her.

Pushing her aside, the man placed the barrel of the gun against Billy's head.

"No!" Sarah screamed, grabbing Billy and shoving him against the ladder. Grabbing his hands, she put them on the rungs. "Billy, you start climbing right now!"

When he still failed to move, Sarah took hold of his belt and heaved him upward. "Climb it!" she commanded.

Oh, please, she thought. Please climb it, Billy, please.

Again, she pulled on his belt, trying to lift him, to get him started. And then he didn't seem so heavy anymore. He was climbing. Slowly, rung by rung, he was going up the ladder.

Sarah went up next, with the man behind her, the beam of his small light wavering as he climbed. Shaking, afraid of falling, she gripped the ladder with all her strength. Finally, uncertain how high she'd climbed, Sarah reached the top.

She found Billy standing in a narrow passageway, maybe two and a half feet wide, which led to a door. Although Sarah realized they were in some little-used place in the upper reaches of the church, she had no idea what its purpose was. The man climbed off the ladder, and they were moving again.

Passing through the narrow door, Sarah found nothing but a continuation of the passageway. Overhead were all sorts of pipes and things like that. Sarah had to crouch to keep from hitting her head. When they reached a spot where a pipe ran up from the floor and joined those above their heads, the man ordered them to sit down.

Still holding the penlight in his teeth, he pulled a silver chain from his jacket pocket. On each end was something like a handcuff. He fastened one of them to the pipe and the other to Billy's leg. Then he produced another chain, attaching one end to the pipe and the other to Sarah's ankle. She briefly considered kicking the man in the face and trying to escape, but he was bigger, stronger, and faster than she was, and she wouldn't get far.

For a moment the man squatted before his two prisoners, studying them. Staring into his eyes, Sarah recalled the German shepherd and the prairie dog. The man's eyes reminded her of the dog's as it closed in, savoring the kill. But there was more than just that in the man's eyes; she saw things there she didn't understand, frightening things. She looked away.

The gag was still in Billy's mouth. A faint smile appeared on their captor's face as he removed the boy's gag and pocketed it. Then, forced by the lack of headroom to move in a crouch, he made his way to the door that led to the metal ladder. Closing it behind him, he shut out the light, leaving his captives in darkness. Sarah waved a hand in front of her face, seeing nothing. The blackness was total.

It pressed in on her, her mind telling her there were things nearby, almost close enough to touch her, invisible in the darkness. She shuddered.

"Billy," she whispered. "Billy."

When he didn't respond, she reached into the blackness until her hands touched him. "Billy," she said again, and again the boy failed to acknowledge her.

Then she saw light, and she realized she was sitting beside a grate in the floor. Leaning over it, she saw wooden pews dimly illuminated by a wavering light. She saw movement that momentarily confused her, but then she realized she was looking through the spinning blades of a fan. Suddenly the weak light was gone, the darkness engulfing her again.

The glow, Sarah realized, had come from the man's penlight as he left the building. Reaching down her leg, she found the chain attached to her ankle and pushed on it. It was not about to come off. Though small, the links of the chain felt cold and hard, like ball bearings. She yanked on it, and the pipe it was attached to clanked.

Beside her Billy stirred, then muttered something unintelligible.

"Billy!" she cried, suddenly hopeful that he was going to be all right.

"Mommy," he said sadly. "I want Mommy."

Then, before Sarah could respond, he let out a wail that hurt her ears, a long, pitiful cry that came from somewhere deep inside a very confused and terrified little boy. Uncertain whether to hug him and console him or shake him to make him stop, Sarah did nothing. Finally the scream died, and Billy began to whimper. She took him in her arms.

"It'll be all right, Billy," she said. "We'll be—" Her sobs choked off the rest of her words. Until this moment she hadn't known that anyone could be this helpless and frightened, this alone.

"Oh, Billy," she sobbed, squeezing him tightly. "Oh, Billy."

Melissa and Castle stood at the front door of a large brick house, waiting for someone to answer the doorbell. As were most of the houses in the neighborhood, this one was dark. Melissa's neighbors went to bed at a reasonable hour, even on Saturday night. At first she'd felt a little awkward about getting people out of bed, but then she'd realized that compared to what she was going through, the loss of a little sleep was inconsequential.

She and Castle were checking the houses on this side of the street while Walczak handled the other. This was the sixth house they'd visited; so far, no one had seen anything that would help.

She was just coasting, she knew, not allowing herself to expect too much to come from knocking on the neighbors' doors. To hope for too much would be to set herself up for disappointment, which she might be unable to handle right now. She was clinging to her composure, but only just. Knocking on doors gave her something to do, something at least superficially constructive, and kept her from thinking about all the horrors she was better off not considering.

A light came on inside the house, then the porch light. A few moments passed, during which Melissa was sure she and Castle were being studied through the optical peephole; then the door opened, and a gray-haired man in a blue bathrobe was standing before them, eyeing them warily. Although Melissa recognized the man, she didn't know his name. He was one of those neighbors who lived three or four houses away from yours, just far enough so you never got to know them.

Castle held up his shield. "We're from the sheriff's department. I apologize for getting you out of bed, but we won't keep you up for more than a minute or so."

The man nodded sleepily, his eyes shifting from the lieutenant to Melissa. "I thought I recognized you," he said. "You're our neighbor, the new sheriff."

"I'm sorry," Melissa said, "but I'm afraid I don't know your name."

"It's Smithers. Edgar Smithers."

Although Castle had been doing the questioning, Melissa had the man's attention, so she asked: "By any chance, did you notice anything unusual happening around my house tonight?"

The man's eyes widened. "At your house? No. Why? What happened?"

"Did you notice anyone unfamiliar around the neighborhood tonight?"

The man frowned. When it looked as though he was about to shake his head, he suddenly snapped his fingers. "I did see someone, now that I think about it. It was about nine o'clock, I think. I'd gone to get some medicine at the drugstore—some pills for my wife's arthritis—and when I came down the street on my way back, I saw a car pulling up in front of your house."

"What kind of a car?" Melissa asked.

"Ummm, seems to me it was green. I don't know what kind it was."

"A big car or a little car."

"Medium-sized, I guess. It wasn't a compact or anything like that."

"Did you see who was in it?"

"Just one person, the driver, a man."

"How old was he?"

"Oh, I'd say probably twenties or thirties. It's hard to say for sure though because it was dark and I wasn't paying much attention."

"What was he wearing?"

"I don't know."

"What color was his hair?"

Rubbing his forehead, the man looked away, searching his memory. "Uh, I think it was blond." He lowered his hand from his forehead, his eyes again focusing on Melissa. "A blond man in a green car. The killer—what's his name?—the Boogeyman. You mean . . . you mean he was there, at your house?"

"He tied up the baby-sitter and abducted my children," Melissa said without emotion.

The man looked stunned. "Oh, my goodness. Oh, my."

As they left the house and headed for the one next door, Melissa pictured Smithers dashing inside to excitedly tell his arthritic wife the news. The latest gossip, Melissa thought bitterly. Would the man think of the well-being of two helpless children? Would he feel anything for them? She made herself stop. If she kept on like this, she'd be crying before she reached the next house.

"How are you holding up?" Castle asked gently as they started up the walk leading to the next residence.

Fighting back the tears that wanted so desperately to come, she said: "I'll make it. I have to."

In this house the lights were on, indicating that they might have at last discovered a night owl. Castle pressed the button that rang the doorbell.

The Boogeyman sat on the edge of his bed, pleased with himself. The taking of the woman sheriff's kids had gone without a hitch. As planned, he had allowed the baby-sitter to get a glimpse of his face, just enough of a look for her to report a few sketchy details. There should be no doubt in Melissa James's mind that it was indeed he who had taken her children.

She would be given a little over a week to suffer, to search frantically for them.

Leaning back on the bed, he closed his eyes. Nothing could stop the punishment now, not even his capture. The sophisticated timer was programmed, placed, and connected to the explosives, details he'd taken care of before snatching the children. The device had a backup battery that would take over in the event of a power failure. The children would die as planned. Nothing could save them.

He let his thoughts drift for a while, wandering anywhere they pleased. He recalled one of his first jobs: helping an old man who owned a lock-and-key shop. He'd learned very quickly how to use the tools of the trade to let people into their houses after they'd locked themselves out.

Then he saw a boy walking along a sidewalk, enjoying the warm summer sunshine. Although he was both the boy and the watcher, there seemed to be no conflict in his dual role. The boy's life wasn't perfect, he knew, but the threatening parts seemed distant at the moment, chased away by the rays of the sun. He felt cozy, protected.

He turned up the walk, heading toward the front door of a cottage. Like the sunshine, the place was yellow, with lots of blooming flowers, big shade trees. Here was contentment, home. Automatically he reached for the doorknob, twisted it.

But then he hesitated. Contentment? Home? The two words didn't belong together. Something was wrong here.

Suddenly the sunshine was gone, the sky full of black swirling clouds. Gone, too, was the warmth, replaced by a cold, cruel breeze that made him shiver. *Go inside*, something told him. *Get out of the cold*. Again he grabbed the knob, and again he hesitated, shivering. *It's cold out here. Go inside, where it's warm*. He turned the knob, pushed the door open.

Instantly he was sitting bolt upright, trembling. The Horrible Thing had been inside, waiting for him. Once more the dream had come, and as it always did, it had tried to trick him. His heart was pounding furiously. He felt cold. So very, very cold.

Though fully clothed, he got his robe from the closet and

slipped it on, immediately feeling much warmer. Moving to the dresser, he picked up his key ring and spent a moment examining the keys to the cuffs with which he'd chained his hostages to the pipe. Also on his dresser was one of the plastic handcuffs he'd used on the children because the restraints were fast, easy to apply, and reliable. A twenty-two-inch piece of clear plastic, the strap had a hole in one end through which the other end was slipped and then pulled tight. Once applied, it would have to be cut off.

But he had only one of them, and there should be two. He'd taken four, plus a longer strap to connect the two hostages. The extras had been taken as a precaution, just in case he'd had to bind his captives' legs for some reason. Which he hadn't. So there should be two plastic straps here. Where was the other one?

He knew it wasn't in the car, because he'd checked it over thoroughly to make sure no trace of the children had been left behind. He'd looked into the cracks of the seats, under the seats, everywhere. Nothing as large as a twenty-two-inch length of plastic could have been overlooked.

So then where had he lost it? In the street? At the church? At the house? After considering all the possibilities, he concluded that the loss of the plastic strap was probably nothing to be concerned about. Even if found at the church, its discovery would not betray the location of the hostages.

Again he sat down on the edge of the bed. He'd been so concerned with the plan for punishing the woman sheriff that he'd been ignoring his other duties. The next family to be punished had been discovered days ago, and yet other than make a preliminary observation of the family's home, he'd done nothing to see that the punishment was administered. The discipline should not be delayed much longer.

He had only one more thing to do in the punishment of Melissa James, and once he'd done it, he would give his full attention to the Lopez family. Of course, he'd have to tend to the James children for the next week, but that wouldn't take more than an hour or so each night.

He yawned. Soon I'll be a supernatural being, he thought. Soon I can forget about working, about nightmares, about all the foolish human concerns. I'll be a shadow, a thing seen from the corner of the eye, only to vanish when one tries to look at it directly.

And I'll have nothing to do but punish.

The Boogeyman smiled.

13

Outside Melissa's house she and Castle stood beside the lieutenant's car. Walczak and Goldman had already left.

"We'll meet in the morning to discuss what we know and where we go from here," Castle said. "There's nothing more we can do tonight."

Although something in Melissa was crying *No, no, don't stop looking for my kids. They're in danger; they're in the hands of a psycho*, she realized that the lieutenant was right. For the moment there was nothing more they could do. Every law enforcement agency in Colorado already had the license number and a description of the green car. By now most of them had probably been informed of the kidnapping as well.

Unlike an ordinary victim, she had the power to mobilize the entire department and immediately put it to work on the case that concerned her. But because she could do it, she saw what most victims probably didn't. Once all the officers were awakened and assembled, she would have no orders to give, no task to which they could be assigned.

"It's as if they were swallowed up by the night," she said softly. "We have no idea where to look for them."

"It may not make you feel any better, but you can be sure that there isn't a cop of any kind out there that isn't keeping a close watch for that green car. This is special; this is an attack on one of our own. As far as our own department goes, you can count on everybody we've got twenty-four hours a day, for as long as it takes."

"Do . . . do you think they're all right?"

"All I can tell you is that if he wanted to harm them, he wouldn't have to abduct them to do it."

Melissa shuddered, realizing how easy it would have been for the Boogeyman to have left two small bodies for her to find. At least this was better than that.

"Why?" she asked, feeling helpless. "What does he want with them? What does he hope to accomplish?"

Castle was silent a moment; then he said: "I think the message in purple crayon pretty much explained it. You're being punished."

They stood there, neither speaking, until Castle broke the silence. "Let's get some sleep," he said gently. "I'll wait here until you're inside."

Almost mechanically, Melissa walked to her front door. As she closed it behind her, she heard Castle's car start. Suddenly Keith was there, taking her in his arms.

As he held her, Melissa realized she was trembling and crying. And then she summed up in a handful of tearful words the nightmare this Saturday night had become:

"There's a monster out there who's killed eight people, and he's . . . oh, God, Keith, he's got my children."

Keith held her shaking body tightly. Apparently realizing there was nothing he could say that would help, he said nothing.

It was about eight o'clock Sunday morning when they gathered in the detective division office. Chairs had been moved up near the blackboard; they were occupied by the department's five detectives, Captain Pruitt, and Melissa.

Stepping into the courthouse this morning, she'd immediately felt the difference. All traces of the hostility that had pervaded the place since her arrival had vanished. Deputies stopped her in the hall to express their concern, pledge any help they could provide. Apparently departmental bickering was put aside when a sheriff's children were kidnapped—any sheriff's.

Keith had spent the night with her, for which she'd been grateful. In bed Melissa had clung to him, desperately in need of his warmth and strength. Neither of them had slept.

"Okay," Castle said, "let's get started. Roger, what have you got for us?"

"The house had just been cleaned yesterday afternoon, which made my job a lot easier." Goldman glanced at Melissa as if thanking her for being a good housekeeper. "The only prints I found—including on the bag that had been put over the baby-sitter's head—were Mrs. James's, the baby-sitter's, Keith Adamson's, and those of the kids."

Melissa recalled Goldman's arrival. The first thing he'd done was fingerprint Keith and Linda Sue.

Castle said: "The stuff used to tie up the baby-sitter is at the lab, but I don't expect it to help us much. The gag looked like a piece of an old bed sheet, and the cord she was tied with looked like the stuff you can pick up in almost any hardware store.

"The lab in Denver also has a sample of the crayon we scraped from the door of Sheriff James's refrigerator. I'm fairly certain it will match the shade of crayon used at the Tucker and Evans houses. I don't think there's any doubt that it's the Boogeyman who abducted the children."

"Why do you think he did it?" Walczak asked.

"The message said: 'Those who insult the Boogeyman must be punished.' I think it means just what it says. Sheriff James did something to offend him, and he's punishing her for it."

"Do we have any idea what she did?" Lester Hanson asked.

"I've thought about that," Melissa said. "The only thing I can think of is a statement I made to a newspaper reporter. I referred to the killer as a dangerous psychopath."

"If that made him angry, then he can't stand to hear the truth," Hanson said. "But then with a psycho, who the hell knows. . . ." As his words trailed off, he shifted his eyes away from Melissa's.

The room fell silent, the men apparently uncertain how to handle things with the hostages' mother present.

Melissa took a deep breath. "Listen, I don't want you to hold back just because I'm here. I'm the mother of the kidnapped children, but I'm also the sheriff, and I have to hear all of it, including the bad parts."

Again the men were silent; then Castle said: "Lester was saying that psychos are unpredictable. What they do makes sense to them but often not to us. For instance, we have an idea what the killer felt he needed to punish you for, but what did the Tuckers and the Evanses do? What set him off?"

The lieutenant rose, found a piece of chalk, and wrote PUN-ISH on the blackboard. "This word has appeared twice now," he said. "He didn't use it the first time he struck, but I'd be willing to bet that's what this is all about. He's punishing people. I don't know why he's doing it, how he picks his victims, why he calls himself the Boogeyman."

"If he's punishing people," Brown said, "then how come up till now he did it by killing everybody in the family, then suddenly changed his approach? If he followed true to form, he'd have killed the entire James family." His eyes met Melissa's, then darted away.

"I'll tell you what I think," Goldman said. "This guy's got some kind of a mission. Whatever it is, it's what prompted him to kill the Evans and Tucker families. That's his brand of punishment, I guess—capital punishment. But with Mrs. James, it was different. He was mad because of what she said; it didn't figure into this mission of his. So to get even, he snatches the kids, figuring that's the best way to make her suffer.

"I'll tell you something else, too. I think the kids are alive and well for the moment. I think he'll keep 'em that way for a while, just to keep Mrs. James suffering."

The implication, Melissa realized, was that he'd kill them eventually. She forced the thought from her mind; if she let herself start to contemplate all the horrible possibilities, she'd go to pieces.

"What you're saying," Walczak said, "is that we might have some time—at least a little."

"Until we know otherwise," Castle said, "we've got to assume they're alive. What we've got to do is find them before any harm comes to them, which means finding them as quickly as possible. Where do we look? Where does a guy go with two kids when every cop in the area is looking for him? He wrote WHERE? on the board and underscored it.

"How about someplace where there are lots of kids," Walczak suggested. "Someplace where two more would just blend right in."

Castle shook his head. "These kids would stand out. They'd be making a fuss."

Inwardly Melissa winced. No, Billy and Sarah would never accompany a stranger, not without being coerced.

"I'd guess he's got the kids stashed somewhere," Brown said. "Someplace in the hills, or maybe even an abandoned building right smack in the middle of Denver. It's gotta be someplace where he can take two kids and nobody will notice."

"In some neighborhoods in the city, he could walk them in in broad daylight and nobody would notice," Goldman said.

Walczak snorted. "Some neighborhoods right here in good old Ramsey County, too."

"He could have taken them home with him, as far as that goes," Captain Pruitt said, speaking for the first time. "He could have forced them into the trunk of his car, then driven into his garage and closed the door before releasing them. Nobody'd know. He could live in a shack or one of the ritziest neighborhoods in the county. As long as he had a garage, it wouldn't matter."

For Melissa, Pruitt's words brought home the helplessness of the situation. Afraid to look into the faces of the men sitting in the room with her, afraid she'd see her worst fears confirmed in their expressions, Melissa stared at the large map of the Denver metro area that hung beside the blackboard. Somewhere in those square miles of city and suburbs and country might be Sarah and Billy. Her eyes traveled from the map to the blackboard, to the spot where Castle had written WHERE? Oh, God, she thought. Oh, God.

"Your point's well taken, Captain," Castle said. "But the wisest thing for him to do would be to take the hostages to an isolated building, some place with no one around, and I think that's where we should start, at least until we get something more to go on."

Pruitt nodded. "It's a long shot that we'll actually find anything, but I don't have any better ideas. How much help do you need from patrol?"

"Mainly we'll need to have the patrol officers talk to the people in their districts and find out where some of these isolated places are. I'm sure the state police and the other law enforcement agencies will help."

The captain rubbed his chin, thinking. "There are two other possibilities we haven't considered, you know. First, the hostages could be in New Mexico or Wyoming or God knows where

by now. We're only assuming they're still in the area. Second
. . . second, we have to allow for the possibility that they're
already dead.''

Castle's eyes flicked toward Melissa to note her reaction but
avoided making contact. Melissa stared blankly at him. To react
at all, even a little, might cost her what little grip on composure
she had.

"If all he wanted was to kill them," Castle said, frowning,
"then there was no reason for the abduction."

"You said he wants Sheriff James to suffer. Well, let's face
it, as long as we don't know they're dead, dead hostages are as
good as live ones, and a hell of a lot less trouble."

No, Melissa thought. No, no, no. I don't want to hear this.
They're alive, and I won't believe otherwise. I won't. I won't.

Castle divided the detectives into three teams, each to check
out isolated buildings in a specific part of the county. Walczak
was paired with Brown, Hanson with Goldman, and the lieutenant with Melissa.

They were eliminating possibilities, nothing more. Melissa
found this frustrating because it seemed they were doing so little,
the chances of success so remote. And yet she had no better
ideas to offer. At least eliminating possibilities was something to
do, and no matter how terrible this ordeal was for her, it would
have to be hundreds of times worse for someone who had
nothing to do but sit home and wait to hear from the authorities.

"The first thing for you and me to do," Castle said to her, "is
go by your house and get some pictures of the children. I want to
get them to the media. The more people who know what those
kids look like, the better."

Why didn't he get the pictures last night? Melissa wondered.
They could have been in this morning's paper. And suddenly she
had doubts about the way the case was being handled. Were
there things they should be doing and weren't? Would Sarah and
Billy be left to the mercy of a psychopath because the agency for
which she was responsible made too many unnecessary mistakes?

And then a truly horrifying thought struck her. What if the
officers who hated her used this as a way to get even? What if
they intentionally conducted a lax investigation? She instantly
pushed the notion from her mind, realizing it had been induced

by confusion and fear, nothing more. Melissa was certain the officers in the department would risk their lives to save a pair of innocent kids, no matter whose kids they were.

As if he'd sensed some of what she'd been thinking, Castle said: "It's too bad we couldn't have gotten the kids' picture in the morning papers, but by the time we finished up last night it was too late. Since this is Sunday, there are no TV newscasts until this evening. We'll get the photo copied and distributed in plenty of time for them."

Relieved by the lieutenant's explanation, Melissa nodded. Castle was a reliable, competent officer; what could be done was being done. She had to hang on to that thought. It was all she had.

Sore from being unable to find a comfortable position on the wood floor of her prison, Sarah peered through the grate and into the chamber below. It was illuminated by daylight now, some of which seeped up through the grate, enabling her to dimly make out her surroundings.

Beside her her brother sat with his back against the pipe to which they were chained, staring into space. He did that a lot, usually speaking only when she asked him a question. But Billy was all right. He was only being quiet because he was so afraid.

Looking down on the pews, Sarah recalled the instant when she'd first realized that below her the blackness was beginning to gray. At first she'd thought her eyes were playing tricks on her, and when she was certain they weren't, she'd cried. For other than being rescued, the thing she'd wanted most had been for the darkness to go away.

Sarah shifted her gaze to her brother, who continued to sit and stare silently; then, looking beyond him, she saw the cardboard carton near the end of the passageway. Beside it were a number of liquor bottles, some lying empty on their sides, others upright, apparently full. Why were they here? Then, having decided the answer was unimportant, she started to look away, and something caught her eye.

"Look, Billy."

"What?" he replied, still staring straight ahead.

"Look over there, at that box. There's a wire that comes from

171

somewhere up by those pipes and goes into the box. There's something electric inside."

Billy looked in the appropriate direction, then shrugged. "So what? We can't reach it."

Neither of them having anything further to say at that moment, they sat in silence, Billy again staring at nothing, Sarah examining the chain that held her leg. Earlier both she and Billy had removed their shoes and tried to force the shackles over their feet, which had proved impossible. The pipe to which they were chained was solid. There was no way for them to get loose.

Apparently the passageway was here so people could get at the pipes. The way Sarah figured it, pipes didn't need fixing very often, so there wasn't much chance anyone would come here and find them.

"How come that man brought us here?" Billy asked.

"I don't know," Sarah said. "I think it might have something to do with Mom's job, but I'm not sure." Looking into her brother's eyes, she saw fear, confusion, and a mixture of other emotions she lacked the experience to identify.

"Will the man come back?"

"I don't know, Billy." And if he did come back, what would he do to them? Sarah decided not to think about that.

Her brother was quiet for a few moments; then very softly he said: "I want to go home."

Sarah reached for him, to hold him and comfort him, but he pushed her away. "No! I don't want you! I want Mommy."

Although the rejection didn't bother Sarah, the total helplessness in her brother's voice did. Especially when she realized there was nothing she could do for him.

Billy was crying now, quietly, forlornly. A moment later tears were rolling down Sarah's cheeks as well.

Dressed in what he referred to as his Sunday preachin' clothes, Reverend Paul Maxwell pulled his keys from the pocket of his suit jacket, unlocked the back door of the church, and entered the building. He walked along a short hallway, passing doors that led to a storeroom, a janitor's closet, the room containing the building's heating and air-conditioning equipment. At the end of the corridor, he pushed open a door and stepped into the kitchen.

It was a large room with built-in oven and range, lots of cabinet and counter space, and a big wooden table. And it was an often-used place. Charity dinners were held at the church, along with pancake suppers, bake sales, and all sorts of meetings—even the Boy Scouts. Of course, when such events took place here, they were held upstairs in the big meeting room, so naturally the building's designers had put the kitchen downstairs.

No, Lord, he thought, I'm not being ungrateful. This is a nice building, and I'm very glad to have it. It's just that like anything designed by humans, it has its faults.

He liked to check on the building at least once a day, just to make sure everything was as it should be. Having noted that the switches on the electric stove and oven were all in the off position, he opened the refrigerator. Inside were a few jars of things like mustard and mayonnaise, nothing that could go bad. Refrigerators in places like churches were a problem, because people were always putting things inside and forgetting about them, leaving them to mold and rot and smell.

Satisfied that everything was in order in the kitchen, he quickly checked the rest of the building, including the meeting rooms and rest rooms upstairs. When he'd finished, the minister made his way to what he considered the main part of the church, the part in which services were conducted. Here he unlocked the main doors at the front of the building and a side door that was primarily an emergency exit. That done, he went to the lectern and laid out his notes for today's sermon.

Its topic would be self-destructiveness, a subject he'd chosen in part, he supposed, because of A. J. Sebastian's disappearance. His concern about the old man had gone beyond worry; now he was steeling himself for what had to be bad news. Paul Maxwell sighed. He had gone to the authorities, and he would continue to pray for the caretaker, but there was nothing else he could do—except hope the old saying about the Lord's looking out for drunks and fools was true.

Looking up from his sermon notes, the minister took in the rows of polished wood pews, the matching walls of recessed wooden squares, the small high windows through which sunlight streamed into the church. The only thing about the scene he didn't like was the rather ordinary plaster ceiling with its vents for the heating and air-conditioning system. Although he hadn't been here at the time, he knew that the plan for the church had been changed midway through the building's construction because the cost of the project had been higher than expected and the available funds skimpier. The ceiling, he presumed, had been part of whatever compromises had to be made.

Checking his watch, the minister decided it was time to take his position at the front door. A few moments later he was greeting the first of the worshipers to arrive.

Billy tried it again. It had to work this time. It had to.

Closing his eyes as hard as he could, he began slowly counting to a hundred. If he did it right, when he opened his eyes Mommy would be coming through the door at the end of the passageway. She'd be here to rescue him.

When he reached ninety-nine, he hesitated, afraid to speak the last number because he'd have to open his eyes and Mommy might not be there. Because counting was his only hope, the only action he could take to help himself. Finally he said it: a hundred. But still he didn't open his eyes, just in case Mommy was on the ladder and hadn't reached the door yet. He wanted to give her plenty of time to get here.

After waiting a few more moments, Billy decided the time was right. If Mommy was coming, she'd be here now. He opened his eyes, seeing only the things he'd seen before—the passageway, the pipes, his sister, the chains around their legs—and he began to quietly cry.

Sure, he knew deep down inside that counting probably wouldn't work, but he'd thought that maybe, just maybe, if he hoped hard enough . . .

Billy had no idea why the man had kidnapped him. He really didn't care why. He only knew that every minute he spent here made it seem that much more likely that he'd never leave, that no one would ever find him.

"The Broncos are playing the Raiders today," he said sadly. "Me and Keith were gonna be at Mile High Stadium to see the game."

"Help!" Sarah shouted suddenly, startling him. "Up here! Help!"

She was looking down through the grate. Filled with a mixture of confusion and hope, Billy scrambled over beside her and looked down through the spinning blades of the fan. The pews weren't empty anymore. People were sitting in them now, all dressed up for church.

"It's Sunday!" Sarah exclaimed happily. "I should have thought of that before. Of course people would be here on Sunday."

"Help!" Billy yelled.

"Hey!" Sarah screamed.

Then they shouted together while Billy beat on the grate with his fists. And he felt his hope begin to fade. Directly below them was a lady in a white hat who sat between two men, one bald and the other with gray hair. None of them looked up or tilted their heads or did anything else that might indicate they'd heard something.

Billy stared at the woman below him. She had brown hair and wore a dark dress. She was old, like a grandmother. Please, lady, he thought, please hear us.

"Hey, lady!" he screamed. "Hey, we're up here!"

"Hey, you stupid woman!" Sarah yelled. "Look up!"

Suddenly Billy swung himself around and began pounding on the grate with his feet, his chain slapping the wooden floor.

"Help us!" Sarah shouted. "Oh, God, please help us!"

For a while anger, fear, and frustration kept Billy pounding on the grate, but eventually he began to tire. When, feeling totally defeated, he stopped, Sarah was looking at him, tears rolling down her cheeks.

"They can't hear us, Billy. We can't hear them, and they can't hear us."

She reached out for him, to take him in her arms, but Billy rolled out of her reach. He didn't want to be held by Sarah; he just wanted to be left alone.

"Billy!" Sarah said urgently. "Do you have anything in your pockets?"

He ignored her.

"Billy, come on, will you. If you have some pennies or

something, we can drop them down on the fan and see what happens.''

Quickly checking his pockets, Billy found thirty-one cents and nothing else. A quarter, a nickle, and a penny. He crawled over to the grate, clutching the coins.

"Show me what you've got," Sarah said.

Billy opened his fist, displaying the three coins.

"Is that everything in your pocket?" Sarah asked.

"Yeah. Don't you have anything?"

His sister shook her head.

"I'll start with the penny," Billy said. "Should I just drop it in the middle?"

"That's what I'd do."

The openings in the grate were about two inches long and three quarters of an inch wide. Billy held the penny over one of them, glanced at Sarah, then released the coin. It hit the spinning blades with a clink and was gone.

"Did it go through?" Billy asked.

Sarah frowned. "I think the fan just knocked it away."

Using a different opening in the grate this time, Billy dropped the nickel. It, too, was slapped by a blade, and this time Billy saw the coin flipped off to the side. Below the blades the woman in the white hat and the men beside her gave no indication of having heard anything.

"It can't get through the fan," Sarah said. "It can't get through."

"Here, you try." Billy handed her the quarter, the last coin.

Holding it in her palm, she studied it a moment, then turning her hand over as she brought it downward, slapped the coin through the grate. It hit the blades and was hurled away, bouncing off something out of their sight. Below them the bald man glanced to the right, then returned his eyes to the front of the church. He'd heard the coin hit whatever the blades had thrown it against, apparently failing to associate the sound with the fan. Still, even that much of a reaction was encouraging.

"Hey!" Billy yelled.

"Up here!" Sarah hollered, joining in.

They screamed until they were hoarse. And then they cried.

14

"We're looking for a green car with a blond man and two kids in it," Castle said, pocketing his ID. Melissa and he stood outside the booth in which the service station employee was enclosed to protect her from robbers.

"I haven't seen anyone like that," the young blond woman said.

Located at the intersection of two county roads, the gas station was one of those self-service places. Pump your own gas; clean your own glass. Cash only, no change for anything bigger than a twenty.

Castle asked: "Do you know of any isolated buildings of any kind around here where a person could do as he pleased without anyone knowing about it?"

The woman frowned. "Ummm, it's hard to say. If you keep on going that way"—she pointed to her right—"it's all ranchland, and it's all pretty desolate. But as far as I know, the only buildings are ranch houses and barns and places like that. I don't think any of them are vacant."

The booth had one of those metal drawers like drive-in banks have. Castle put one of his cards into it. "If you should think of anything or if you should spot a green car with a blond man and two kids in it, I'd appreciate it if you'd give us a call."

"Sure," the woman replied, retracting the drawer and picking up the card. A moment later Melissa and Castle were on the road again in the lieutenant's unmarked car.

It was another one of those cool but sunny fall days. The country here was flat grassland dotted with scrub brush. To the west the Rockies rose so abruptly it seemed one could stand with one foot on the mountain, the other on the western edge of the Great Plains.

It was early afternoon now. Castle had spent the morning on the phone with other law enforcement agencies and the news media. Melissa had provided the requested picture of Sarah and Billy, which was in Denver being copied for distribution to law enforcement personnel and the media.

Looking through her many envelopes stuffed with snapshots, Melissa had been surprised how old most of them were. She'd found baby pictures, toddler pictures, photos of the kids as three- and four- and five-year-olds, but in all the envelopes there had been only one picture recent enough to accurately show how Billy and Sarah looked now. Snapped in the backyard back in August, it showed the kids standing beside each other, staring at the camera with those silly say-cheese grins on their faces. It was one of those corny family photos that accumulated in a drawer somewhere, pictures that taken together provided a record of so much growing and learning and loving, so much life.

Melissa had gone to get the photo while Castle made his calls. Keith had gone home, and the place was empty, for which she'd been glad. When she started going through the pictures, she'd cried, and for that moment, at least, what she'd needed more than anything else was to be alone with her memories and her tears.

Now as Castle drove along the two-lane highway in rural Ramsey County, Melissa resolved that when this was over, when Sarah and Billy were home, she would take many more pictures than she used to. She'd keep the camera out where she could see it and remember to use it. She'd take pictures every week, maybe even every day. She'd . . .

The thought trailed away, because the thing she'd been trying desperately to block from her mind had just freed itself from her unconscious; now it clamored for attention. This episode in her life would not necessarily conclude with the return home of her children. She would take more pictures *if* they came home.

If.

Oh, God, she thought, realizing how nothing could possibly prepare her to deal with the other possible outcome. To force herself to stop thinking the unthinkable, she concentrated on what she was doing now.

Melissa had doubts about the usefulness of their current efforts.

Though Denver was a metropolis, a place of skyscrapers and freeways and shopping malls, you didn't have to go far to be reminded that this was still the West. Once you left the suburbs, prairie dogs and rabbits outnumbered people. To cover all of it, to check every isolated spot where hostages could be held, was a task of such enormity that it might take an army of investigators weeks to accomplish.

"It's always like this at first when you don't have much to go on," Castle said. He pulled around a slow-moving pickup. "In the beginning, you simply have to do what you can, which usually isn't much. As an investigation goes along, it usually generates a momentum of its own after a while. One lead turns up another, that sort of thing. Once we reach that stage, I think you'll feel a little more confident about what's being done."

"When will that be?" Melissa asked.

"Sooner than you think. For one thing, we'll be getting tips from the public pretty soon. The story's been on the radio for hours now. The TV stations will run it tonight, and the papers will have it tomorrow morning. We'll check out every tip, no matter how unreliable it may seem. We'll work on long shots like this only when we've got nothing else to do, which is why we're working on this right now. For the moment there's nothing else to do."

Melissa nodded. And then she tried to empty her mind, for it swirled with so many dreadful possibilities that it was better not to think at all.

Hungry, thirsty, and defeated, Sarah lay on the floor of her prison, staring through the grate. She hated the grate for letting her see the freedom she was unable to attain, and because earlier it had let her look down on a roomful of potential rescuers whom she was unable to summon. The pews below had filled up twice, indicating two separate Sunday morning services. During the second one, she and Billy had watched dejectedly, too hoarse to yell anymore and having nothing else to drop in the fan.

The grate was solidly made; the pounding Billy had given it with his shoes hadn't left a scratch. They'd tried to pull it up, tugging on it until their fingers hurt, but the grate hadn't budged.

Sarah sat up. Out of habit she brushed her jeans with her

hand, trying to wipe away the dust. The effort was wasted; the floor was covered with the stuff, and her clothes had long since gotten filthy. Besides, she thought miserably, it really doesn't matter anyway.

Billy, too, was a mess. He lay a few feet from Sarah, dirt on his face, his clothes filthy and rumpled, part of his shirttail stuffed between his pants and his belt. Suddenly Sarah had an idea.

"Billy, let me have your belt."

"What for?"

"I want to see if it's long enough to reach the fan."

Unbuckling it, he handed it over. The belt was red with a silver buckle. Because it was too large for him, it had a number of extra holes Billy had made by pounding a nail through the leather.

"If it's long enough," Sarah said, lowering the belt through the grate, "the next time we see people down there, we can let the buckle just touch the blades. Maybe it will make enough noise for them to hear it."

But it wasn't long enough. Although it was impossible to see exactly how far below them the fan was, the belt was at least a few inches too short. Disappointed, Sarah withdrew it from the grate.

Billy, who'd crawled over to watch, said: "Use your belt. If we buckle it to mine, it will be long enough."

"I don't have one." Sarah had on a sweat shirt, and when she wore something that covered her waistband, she rarely used a belt. She handed Billy's back to him.

"Wait a minute," she said. "We can just drop it into the fan. It will probably get all tangled up in the blades. It might even make it stop. Somebody would have to hear that."

"When you going to do it, the next time there's somebody down there?"

"Yeah. There's no point in trying to make noise if there's no one around to hear it."

"I sure hope it works," Billy said, putting the belt on the floor beside the grate.

He sat motionless for a few moments, staring at his hands; then he looked at Sarah, a tear trickling down his cheek, and said: "Are we going to die here, Sarah? Are we ever going to see Mommy again? Or our house? Or our friends? Or . . ."

He stopped because he was crying too hard to go on. Sarah moved to him and hugged him.

"We're gonna die here!" he wailed. "No one's ever gonna find us. Ever."

Holding her bawling brother, Sarah tried to think of some comforting words and found she had none to offer, none that would be believable enough to give any hope. What *is* going to happen to us? she wondered. And then Sarah realized that she, too, was crying.

Melissa had given Keith a key to the house, and he met her at the door when she returned home that evening. Taking her coat, he looked at her expectantly, obviously anxious to hear news concerning the kidnapping.

Melissa sank onto the couch. "Nothing much happened. We basically spent the day checking out the boondocks, except there are a hell of a lot of boondocks and not very many of us." She explained how she'd spent the afternoon.

Keith put her coat in the closet, then sat down beside her. "No leads?" he asked.

"No, none. So we spent the day doing stuff that was probably pretty useless, but at least it was better than doing nothing. A few people called to report having seen green cars with kids in them. One caller spotted the car yesterday afternoon, before the kidnapping. Another one reported seeing a green car in this general area, but it was driven by a woman and had three kids in it, not two." She sighed. "I suppose they were trying to help.

"Tomorrow," she added, "the papers will be carrying a picture of the kids. Maybe somebody will recognize them."

Melissa realized she was staring at Keith, waiting for him to say something like *Naturally someone will recognize them.* Which, of course, he couldn't do. The words would be empty, a transparent attempt to ease her pain.

She pushed away some hair that had fallen in her face. "Oh, God, Keith, I felt so bad about coming home tonight, as if I was abandoning Billy and Sarah, as if I only cared enough to look for them during normal working hours. I know there's absolutely nothing I can do right now that will help them, but I keep asking myself how I can just come home, eat, go to bed, and do nothing while my children are in the hands of . . . of a monster. I keep feeling that whatever's happening to them is my fault, that there's something I could be doing and I'm not doing it."

Keith took her in his arms then, and Melissa realized how grateful she was that someone was here for her to lean on. Though her eyes grew moist, she didn't cry. All day she'd striven to keep a cap on her emotions; now that she was in a position to let herself go, she was unable to do so.

"It's natural for you to try to blame yourself," Keith said. "But absolutely none of this is your fault. You're doing everything you can, Melissa, everything."

Suddenly she pushed herself out of his arms. "It *is* my fault, Keith. If I'd listened to you and Captain Pruitt and everybody else, I'd have stayed home and been a full-time parent and homemaker. If I'd done that, if I'd listened to people who had good advice to offer, my kids would be here right now and not in the hands of some lunatic killer."

Keith shook his head. "It was bad advice, Melissa. I was telling you to stay home and be the good little woman, not to meddle in affairs that should be handled by men. I—"

"Well, dammit, if I'd stayed out of men's affairs, I'd have my children. Which is more important?" Melissa realized she was glaring at him, but she was unable to stop herself.

"Come on, Melissa. You're just trying to find ways to blame yourself. There's no way you could have predicted what was going to happen. You were elected the sheriff, and you had to be the sheriff. You couldn't have ignored your responsibilities and still retained your self-respect."

"Wonderful! I traded my children for self-respect."

For a moment Keith appeared ready to say something, but he didn't speak.

"I'm sorry," Melissa said. "I don't mean to take it out on you."

Keith took her hand. "You're taking it out on yourself, not me."

Melissa nodded. He was right; she knew that.

Keith said: "You know that if there's anything I can do to help, all you have to do is ask."

"I know," she said softly, slipping her arms around him.

They were silent for a few moments; then Keith said: "If you smell anything, that's dinner. I've got beef Stroganoff on the stove."

She did smell it, and it smelled good, which made her feel guilty. While she dined on Stroganoff, what would Sarah and Billy be eating? Or were they lying dead somewhere, their little bodies discarded like . . . She pushed the thought away. Torturing herself wouldn't help the kids.

"When will it be ready?" Melissa asked. She had to eat. Starving herself wouldn't help Sarah and Billy either.

"About ten minutes," Keith replied.

"Will you stay with me until this is over?"

He hugged her tightly. "Of course I will."

There were just too many things here that Melissa didn't want to face alone, too many reminders. Things like the kids' belongings, the dual set of pencil marks on the wall in the garage that showed the growth of a little girl and a little boy, the two jars of peanut butter in the fridge because Billy preferred chunky while Sarah liked smooth, the puffed breakfast cereal no one but Billy would eat. . . .

Again she thought about those markings in the garage. Although Sarah's mark was higher than her brother's, Billy was closing the gap. It had always been a guessing game with them, trying to predict when the two marks would be exactly the same height. And then, unable to block the thought from her mind, Melissa wondered whether she would ever know the answer. If anything happens to them, she thought, I'll . . . I'll . . .

Suddenly the wall she'd built around her emotions crumbled. Trembling uncontrollably, she clutched Keith, tears running down her cheeks.

Holding her tightly, he stroked her hair.

"Sarah."

"Yes."

Sarah tried to see her brother but couldn't. The darkness had come again, and with it the fears. Although she knew it wasn't so, a part of her kept insisting there were *things* hiding in the blackness, surrounding her, moving closer. For an instant she was sure she felt hot breath on her neck, and she suppressed a gasp. That same part of her was certain that if she reached out with her hand she'd touch something that wasn't human.

Another part of her urged her to do just that. Because there was nothing there. Not really. And yet if there was, and if she touched it . . .

"Sarah."

"What?"

"I have to go to the bathroom."

After taking a moment to unscramble her thoughts, she said: "Number one or number two?"

"Number one."

"Just get as far away as the chain will let you and do it."

She heard him moving and then the sound of urine hitting their prison's wooden floor. Sarah hadn't experienced that need yet, probably because they had had nothing to drink. Billy had finished; he sat down again.

"Sarah."

"Yes."

"I'm hungry."

"Me too, Billy. But it's probably better if we try not to think about it."

Her brother didn't reply, and the only sound was the never-ceasing hum that she assumed to be the fan—or fans. She really didn't know how many there were. The floor of the passageway had more grates than the one they were chained beside, but unable to reach any of them, she had no idea what was beneath them.

Later—she was uncertain how much later—Sarah realized that Billy was shaking her, urgently whispering her name.

"What, Billy?"

"Shhhh. I hear something."

It took Sarah a moment to realize that she'd been asleep and then another few seconds to figure out where she was. For just an instant, a wonderful instant of fantasy, she had thought that she was in her bed at home, that her brother had dared to enter her sanctuary and shake her awake.

"I don't hear anything," she whispered.

"Listen."

And then she heard it, too. A thump. Suddenly there was light. Someone had just entered their prison through its only door, someone with a flashlight. For a second Sarah thought they'd been rescued. And then she saw the blond hair. The kidnapper had come back.

"I'm going to let you out of here so you can go to the bathroom and eat," he said, moving the beam of his flashlight from Sarah to Billy. "If you try to get away, I'll kill one of you and put the other one up here. And that one will stay up here forever. Do you understand?"

Neither Sarah nor Billy spoke.

"Do you understand?" the man demanded.

"Y-yes," Sarah replied, her voice a dry croak.

"How about you?" he said to Billy.

Billy nodded.

"Speak up. Do you understand what will happen if you try to get away?"

"Yes," Billy said weakly.

"Good."

Pulling some keys from his pocket, he unfastened the chains from the pipe, leaving them attached to his captives' ankles. "Let's go," he said.

The man went down the ladder first, waiting for them at the bottom. Billy went down next, then Sarah, the chain that dangled from her leg clanking against the metal rungs as she descended. When the three of them were standing in the cramped space at the bottom of the ladder, the man slid the panel open, and they stepped into the darkened church.

"This way," the man said. "Pick up your chains so they won't drag behind you."

Lighting the way with his flashlight, he led them toward the main entrance to the church, through a doorway, and then up a flight of stairs. On the second floor they stopped in front of a door that said MEN.

"I'm going to let you go in there and use the toilet," the man said. "Don't wash up and don't try to leave any messages. I'll check the room over before I leave, and if you've disobeyed me, you'll be severely punished.''

"Sarah can't . . ." Billy's words trailed off.

"What?" the man demanded.

"Sarah can't go in that room."

"The stalls in there work as well for women as they do for men. They also provide all the privacy you need. Either you both get in there now or you'll lose the opportunity."

The man reached inside and switched on the light, holding the door open. When Sarah and Billy stepped into the rest room, the door closed behind them, the man remaining in the hallway.

Sarah squinted in the bright light. The place smelled of disinfectant, and along one wall were some white things with flush handles on them. She guessed that men used them to urinate.

Sarah and Billy slipped into separate stalls. Her mind working furiously, Sarah tried to think of some way to get help. The best idea she came up with was unrolling some of the toilet paper, writing a message on it, then rolling the tissue back up. The trouble with the plan was that she had nothing to write the message with. And even if she possessed a pen, Sarah was uncertain whether she'd have the courage to use it. The man said they'd be severely punished, and she believed him.

When Sarah emerged from her stall, she found the blond man leaning against a sink, waiting for them. A second later Billy stepped out of a stall farther down the line, and the man escorted them from the rest room, switching off the lights.

Again using his flashlight, he led them back downstairs, then along a hallway and into a kitchen, where he switched on the lights. There were no windows here, Sarah noted. Nor had there been any in the men's room, which probably explained why the man used the building's lighting at times and used his flashlight at other times.

"Sit down," the man said, indicating the wooden picnic-type table with two benches.

Billy and Sarah complied. Squatting, the man fastened Billy's chain to one of the table's legs. He picked up Sarah's chain, then hesitated.

"No," he said, looking up at her, "I'm going to let you serve us. You won't try to get away when you know I'll kill your brother if you do." He smiled, and Sarah shivered.

Pointing to a paper bag on the counter, he said: "Dinner's in that sack."

Sarah got the bag and returned to the table with it.

"Pass them around," the man said. He was sitting across the table from Billy.

Looking inside the bag, Sarah found hamburgers and fries, which she distributed.

"Drinks are in the refrigerator," the man said.

Sarah got them, three large Cokes in plastic cups with plastic lids. She carried them to the table and sat down next to Billy, giving one of the colas to Billy and sliding the other across the table to their captor.

Removing the paper wrapper from his burger, Billy stared at it. "It's poison," he said. "I won't eat it."

"It's not poison," the man said. "Eat it. You need to eat."

When the boy made no move to comply, the man snatched the burger away from him and took a big bite out of it. "Satisfied?"

Billy looked at Sarah, apparently to see whether she was eating hers. Considering it pretty unlikely that the food had been poisoned, Sarah unwrapped her burger and took a bite. It was cold, but delicious. She began wolfing it down. From the corner of her eye, she saw Billy take a tentative bite of his, then begin devouring it.

When they'd finished eating, the man said: "There's ice cream in the refrigerator. Go get it."

Sarah did as instructed, returning with the bag she found in the freezing compartment. In it were three small containers of ice cream and three plastic spoons.

While the three of them sat at the table and ate ice cream, Sarah tried to reason all this out. Why would a man who kidnapped them, kept them in chains, and threatened to kill them buy them hamburgers and ice cream? She understood that they were prisoners and prisoners had to be fed, but the ice cream confused her. Did prisoners get dessert? Trying to picture what convicts ate, she came up with an image of someone in stripes eating some kind of disgusting slop from a tin plate.

Realizing that what convicts ate had nothing to do with her

and Billy, Sarah pushed the matter from her thoughts. More important questions were who the man was, why he'd kidnapped them, what he planned to do with them.

As inconspicuously as she could, Sarah studied their jailer. A powerful-looking man with thick blond hair and dark eyes, he looked more like the hero of some TV show than a villain. But then this wasn't television; no hero was going to crash through the door and rescue them, because no one knew where they were. If anyone did, the police would have been here by now.

The man looked up as he finished his ice cream, and Sarah quickly shifted her gaze elsewhere, hoping he hadn't noticed that she was watching him.

"Did you want to ask me something?" the man said.

Sarah hesitated, uncertain whether she should say anything. If she spoke, she might say the wrong thing; yet her silence could anger the man as well. Billy was watching her.

"If you have any questions, ask them," the man said. "I'll tell you whatever you want to know."

"Why, uh, why . . ." Sarah searched for the right word. She'd been on the verge of asking why he'd *kidnapped* them, but she was wary of using the term. "Uh, why did you bring us here?"

"Because I'm punishing your mother."

Sarah and Billy exchanged glances. "What did she do?" Sarah asked.

"She insulted me. She called me a dangerous psychopath."

Sarah was confused. What sort of person kidnapped people over an insult?

"I'm not doing this to hurt you or your brother," he explained. "To punish your mother, I've taken you away from her. It's her that's being punished, not you. You should understand that."

Sarah looked into the man's dark eyes, trying to understand. The intensity of what she saw there frightened her. "How long are you going to keep us here?"

"A week. It will all be over on Sunday morning."

"And then can we go home?" Sarah asked hopefully.

"Come on," the man said, rising. "It's time to go back to the crawl space. And don't forget what will happen if you try to get away."

When Sarah and Billy were again chained to the pipe in their prison, the man went to the carton with the electric wire running to it and shined his flashlight inside. After a moment he returned to his captives.

"I'll be back tomorrow night," he said. "If you have to go to the bathroom, try to hold it until then."

He checked their chains, then shined his light around, its beam lingering a moment on the damp spot where Billy had relieved himself, then traveling to the belt, which lay coiled beside the grate. The man picked up the belt, examined it a moment, then put it in his jacket pocket. A moment later, he was gone.

"He took the belt," Billy's voice said in the darkness.

"I know," Sarah replied.

"Did you believe him?"

"About what?"

"What he said about a week."

"I don't know."

"Well, I don't believe him," Billy said angrily. "Being a kidnapper is worse than being a liar, and he's already a kidnapper."

Uncertain whether that made sense, Sarah said nothing. For a few moments the only sound was the hum of the fan. Then she heard Billy crying softly.

Having found nothing in the men's room to indicate the children had used it, the Boogeyman returned to the kitchen, where he began picking up the burger wrappers, napkins, and other debris from their meal. What he had told his captives was true. He had no desire to harm them; he would do what he could to make their stay here as painless as possible. Their lack of culpability in what their mother had done would not save them, of course. They would have to die, because that would be Melissa James's ultimate punishment. She would have to live with the knowledge that she was responsible for their deaths.

And others would die with them. Melissa James would have a lot to answer for.

After stuffing the trash on the table into the bag in which the burgers had come, he took it to the kitchen's green plastic garbage can. Lifting the lid, he hesitated, wondering whether he should take his trash with him. The can was about half-filled, mainly with papers. Making up his mind, he dropped the bag into the container and replaced the lid. Nothing suspicious about garbage in a garbage can, he decided.

The boy's belt he would not throw away—here or elsewhere. He'd taken it in part because that's what jailers did: take away a prisoner's belt. But he'd also put it in his pocket as a precaution, just in case he needed something to prove that he really had the children.

Under the sink he found a rag, which he used to wipe off the table. After rinsing out the cloth and putting it back where he'd found it, the Boogeyman left, satisfied that the punishment of the woman sheriff was going exactly as he had planned it.

15

Melissa sat in her office, the Monday morning *Denver Post* in front of her on the desk. On the front page was the picture of Billy and Sarah. The banner headline read:

KILLER KIDNAPS SHERIFF'S KIDS

She turned the paper over, concealing both the picture and the headline.

A number of calls had come in since the photo appeared in the paper, people reporting that they'd seen two kids who looked like those in the picture. Most of the children thought to be Billy and Sarah had been spotted in stores and other public places, although one caller reported seeing them on a Denver city bus and another claimed to have encountered them on the campus of the University of Colorado in Boulder.

All the calls were being checked out. The aid of law enforcement agencies in Denver and Boulder had been enlisted to check out the reports coming from those communities, because the

You can buy them just about anywhere. School kids have always been fond of them." The mention of school kids made her think about Billy and Sarah, about what might be happening to them right now. . . .

"Let's see what's inside," Castle said. "Got a letter opener?"

Melissa handed him one. Holding the letter down with a pad of paper, he slit the envelope; then, using the opener and the blunt end of a Bic pen, he eased the letter out and unfolded it. In the same stenciled purple letters, the message said:

> *SHERIFF JAMES:*
> *YOUR CHILDREN WILL DIE SUNDAY, NOVEMBER*
> *23. THEY WILL BE BLOWN UP ALONG WITH A LOT*
> *OF OTHER PEOPLE AT 9:45 A.M. THIS IS YOUR*
> *PUNISHMENT.*

THE BOOGEYMAN

Her thoughts swirling, Melissa stared at the message. A lunatic had just informed her that he planned to kill her children six days from now at 9:45 A.M. Afraid she might scream if she opened her mouth, Melissa stared at the letter in silence. From her monitor, the voice of the male dispatcher who'd replaced Marla Clark in the radio room said:

"Ten-four, two-fourteen. Ten-nineteen and see Lieutenant Castle."

"Ten-four," Goldman said. "En route."

His eyes shifting from the monitor to Melissa, Castle said: "As soon as he gets here, we'll have him dust this."

"There won't be any prints," Melissa said, her voice sounding strangely distant.

"Maybe we'll get lucky."

Lucky, Melissa thought. Sure. The Boogeyman hadn't left a fingerprint anywhere yet. Nor did they have a usable sketch of him. They knew he was big, blond, and drove a late-model full-sized green Chevy with stolen license plates. And that was all they knew. They hadn't learned a single new thing about him in days. They didn't have one good lead. The killer might as well be what he claimed to be: the Boogeyman. He seemed as much of a phantom as his namesake.

And then Melissa corrected herself, for she'd been wrong in thinking that was all they knew about the Boogeyman. They also knew that he killed children.

Looking at Castle, Melissa had the urge to grab him and shake him, to scream, cry, let out all the confusion and fear churning inside her. But something, some internal censor, prevented her from doing so, and all she could do was stare helplessly at him.

"Are you going to be all right?" Castle asked, watching her closely. "Can I get you anything?"

"You can get my children back," Melissa said flatly.

Apparently uncertain how to respond, Castle said nothing.

Sleeping soundly, the Boogeyman dreamed. He was a boy playing on a threadbare green carpet. Across the shabby living room his mother sat on the couch, knitting. Looking over to where the boy played with his toy truck, she smiled. And the boy felt his own face break into a grin, because he loved the woman, loved her more than anyone else in the world.

And then, looking at the woman who was his mother, the boy felt his smile fade because he'd just noticed the bruise on her forehead. Although her dark bangs covered part of it, there wasn't enough hair to hide the spot entirely. The boy knew there were other bruises, too, carefully concealed by makeup. He'd heard the old woman next door saying that was how she could tell when another beating had been administered, when the makeup had been thickly applied in an effort to hide the evidence.

If only I were older, the boy thought, I could protect her, maybe take her someplace where my father couldn't find us. Studying his mother, he realized how old and tired she looked for someone so young. She was still the warm, wonderful person he'd always known, but sometimes her hand would shake so badly that she was unable to hold a coffee cup.

He knew why. It was because of *him*. I hate him! the boy thought. Hate him, hate him, hate him! And then he was consumed with guilt, for a son was not allowed to hate his father. No, he thought. No, no. I didn't mean it. I love my parents. I have to love my parents. But there was no way to assuage the guilt, for deep down inside, he knew the truth.

Forgetting about the toy truck, the boy watched his mother as her fingers manipulated the knitting needles. Her shoulder-length dark hair framed her somewhat rounded face. Her eyes were brown, her skin soft, and her face had a look of kindness about it, an expression that seemed to say she was someone who could be depended on, trusted with your most sensitive emotions, someone who cared.

And suddenly, although the boy was uncertain where the man had come from, his father was there. He stood in the center of the room swearing, swaying because he was drunk. Terrified of the big man with the thick curly black hair, the boy began slinking away.

The man stopped him. "Hey, you stay here, boy. I want you to see how I punish your mother."

What was he punishing her for? The boy didn't understand. But then he never understood.

And then the big man grabbed the woman and struck her in the face, and then he did it again. And again.

The boy wanted desperately to get away. If he had to watch another beating, he'd go crazy. And instantly he'd escaped, into adulthood. He was a man now, walking down a long hallway. Slowly he began to realize he was in Las Vegas, at a hotel. He'd come here to play blackjack, to enjoy himself for a few days. Maybe the boy hadn't even been him. The whole incident was fading from his mind.

Stopping in front of the door to his room, the man slipped the key into the lock, and then he hesitated. It was in there; he knew it was. Still his hand turned the key. And the door opened a few inches. Don't go in there, he thought. Don't. Run!

But he was unable to run. Horrified, he watched as his hand, which seemed out of control, reached up and pushed the door open. And then his feet, responding to commands he hadn't given them, stepped into the darkened room. It's just the hotel room, he thought. It's all right. The Horrible Thing's not here.

And then he turned on the light.

He wasn't in a hotel room at all, but the other room, the one with the shabby green carpet. He was a boy again. He'd just come home.

"Mommy," he called, "where are you?"

When she didn't answer, he looked for her in the bedroom, then the bathroom, finding both empty. Then he stepped into the kitchen.

His mother lay on the floor, face down, a reddish smear on the floor tiles.

"Mommy?" he said uncertainly.

And then he grabbed her and began shaking her, screaming for her to acknowledge him. And slowly he began to realize that she would never speak to him again. Her flesh was cool, and her arm flopped lifelessly when he shook her. Using all his strength, he rolled her over. Dried blood covered her face. Her unseeing eyes stared at the ceiling.

Looking away from the bloody, lifeless face that had once seemed so loving, the boy spotted a box of his crayons on the floor. Looking up, he saw the words on the wall. Written in purple crayon, they said:

THE WHORE HAS BEEN PUNISHED

The boy ran from the house, screaming. Suddenly he was caught in something. A net. His father had caught him in a net. He continued screaming, but the cries were in a man's voice now. And the Boogeyman realized he was in bed, tangled up in the covers. But the knowledge didn't stop him from flailing frantically with his arms until he'd freed himself. He sat on the edge of the bed drenched with sweat, his heart pounding.

Always before, he'd woken up before seeing the Horrible Thing. But not this time. Why? What did it mean?

For several minutes he simply sat there, trying to calm himself. His father had never been apprehended. The Boogeyman neither knew nor cared what had happened to him. Raised by an uncle on his mother's side, he'd renounced his father, dissolved the relationship. Although the fear had never left him, fear that the man might come back. And punish him.

But of course this was silliness. No ordinary human could

punish the Boogeyman. Besides, administering punishment was *his* job.

And that made him think about Melissa James. She would have received his message by now, and as the coming week passed, she would realize there was nothing she could do to prevent the death of her children. There was nothing anyone could do. The timer was connected to the dynamite, electronically keeping track of days and hours and minutes. The only other person who'd known about the crawl space was dead. To be sure the children couldn't be heard, he'd put a portable radio in the crawl space, turned the volume up all the way, then gone down into the church. Listening intently, he'd heard nothing, nothing at all.

Thinking about how ruthlessly he dealt with those who offended him made him feel better. He recalled that he had others to punish, a task he'd been putting off because he'd been so involved with the woman sheriff. Now that the punishment of Melissa James was unstoppable and required nothing further of him except to feed the prisoners, which he did out of kindness and not necessity, he had no more reasons for putting off dealing with the Lopez family. He was off today, so he'd have plenty of time to do what had to be done.

He stretched.

It was about eleven that morning when Reverend Paul Maxwell got around to giving the church its daily inspection. Stepping into the kitchen, he surveyed the room, his eyes scanning the knobs on the stove, the sink, the little red light that indicated when the oven was on. Everything seemed to be in order.

He was on his way out of the kitchen when he stepped on something soft and slippery. Squatting to see what it was, he discovered that he'd stepped on a squashed piece of onion. He stared at it, puzzled. The last time anyone had used the kitchen was at the annual Halloween party, an event organized to give children the chance to enjoy themselves without having to risk the dangers of trick-or-treating. But the smashed onion on the floor was fresh, certainly not a remnant from a party held more than two weeks ago.

Convinced there had to be some simple explanation as to how it got here, he picked it up and carried it to the garbage can. But when he lifted the lid, he saw something even more curious: hamburger wrappers, soft-drink cups, straws, all the usual debris from a fast-food meal.

Underneath the wrappers and cups were papers he'd collected upstairs in the room where Sunday school classes met. He'd put them in the can himself, yesterday, after services and Sunday school were over. And then he'd locked the church. How could someone have eaten hamburgers here after he'd locked the building?

Burglars? Vandals? Not likely, he decided. Such intruders wouldn't have stopped to eat, then neatly picked up their trash and put it in the garbage can. Still, he would have to check the rest of the building more carefully than he usually did.

Putting the lid back on the can, he resumed his inspection, finding nothing else that seemed amiss. When he locked up and returned to the rectory, the clergyman pushed the matter from his mind. As did most such puzzles, the mystery would most likely resolve itself in time.

The chairs in the detectives' office had been grouped near the blackboard again. Melissa and four detectives sat facing Castle, who stood at the board.

"Everybody here seen this?" he asked, holding up a copy of the Boogeyman's letter. The men facing him nodded. "Roger, what did you find in the way of prints?"

"Nothing on the letter itself," Goldman said. "On the envelope I found prints belonging to Mrs. James and to Deputy Parker, who delivered the mail this morning. There were some others, smudges mostly, not good enough for an ID. Chances are they were made by postal workers."

"How do we know this letter is really from the Boogeyman?" Brown asked.

"We got no choice but to assume it's real until we find out for sure that it isn't," Walczak said.

"I agree," Castle said. "But in this case, we've got something more. The letter was written in purple."

Could the letter be a hoax, Melissa wondered, the purple pencil a coincidence? Not likely, she decided. Castle had convinced her that in detective work there was rarely such a thing as a coincidence. And Walczak was right when he said any communication that might be from the killer would have to be considered the real thing until proven otherwise.

She hadn't told Keith about the letter yet. Knowing he'd be in federal court all day, she'd made no attempt to contact him. Melissa was grateful that he was staying with her. Spending the night just down the hall from two empty bedrooms was bad enough with Keith there; doing it alone would be unbearable.

"Speaking of things purple," Castle said, "the lab says the crayon we scraped from the sheriff's refrigerator is exactly the same color as the crayon we got from the Tucker and Evans homes. They've also analyzed the stuff we vacuumed up at the sheriff's house, and apparently there's nothing in it that will help us."

The lieutenant paused, apparently giving the other officers a chance to speak. When no one said anything, he continued. "Okay, the note says the children will be blown up along with a number of other people on Sunday morning. Where do you find people on a Sunday morning?"

"Church," Hanson said. "That's about the only thing around here that's open on Sunday morning."

Castle wrote CHURCH on the blackboard. "Okay, that's the obvious thing. What else is there?"

"Lester's right, if you're just talking about Ramsey County," Brown said. "Church is the only thing that happens here on Sunday mornings. But when we include the city, it's different. There are hotels, motels, rescue missions, and all sorts of other places where there'd be people at almost any time—Sunday mornings included."

Castle wrote Brown's suggestions on the board. "What else?"

"Airports and bus stations," Melissa offered.

"How about radio and TV stations?" Walczak suggested. "They've always got people there. Newspapers, too."

"Police stations and firehouses," Melissa said.

"Police stations," Walczak muttered. "Christ, he could be planning to blow *us* up on Sunday morning."

The room fell silent, the only sound the scraping of the chalk as Castle wrote on the blackboard. When he'd written down all the suggestions, he said: "Any other ideas?"

No one offered any, so Castle said: "I'll get what help I can from Denver PD. They've always been extremely cooperative, but let's face it, it isn't their case. They're not going to tear the city apart for us unless we've got something pretty definite to go on. And right now what we've got is ninety percent speculation and ten percent wishful thinking.

"Anyway, what I think we'll do is this: The sheriff and I will handle Ramsey County while the rest of you work with the other police departments in the area. If there's someone there to ride herd on them, they'll get a lot more done."

"Isn't that cutting Ramsey County pretty thin?" Walczak asked.

"What else can we do? We can't just work Ramsey County and forget about the rest of the metro area. We've got churches here and maybe a couple of motels, but it's nothing compared to what's out there in all of metro Denver. What we've got here I think the sheriff and I can handle with the help of patrol division."

Although no one spoke, Melissa sensed that the detectives sitting around her felt Castle was handling things properly.

"I think the place to start," the lieutenant said, "is with the churches. They're fairly easy to break into, and a church would have a large group of people in a relatively small space." He glanced at the things he'd written on the board. "At a hotel or an airport, people are spread out. It would be hard to kill a large number of them unless you had one hell of a bomb. There's only a handful of people at a firehouse at any time, and businesses like TV stations and newspapers only have skeleton crews working on Sundays."

"He didn't say how many people he was planning to kill," Walczak pointed out. "Maybe he was thinking of five or six and not the number of people who'd be in a church."

Lieutenant Castle frowned. "That's possible, but I don't think our man is the type to blow up five or six people when he can blow up a whole church full of them. He says he's doing this to punish Sheriff James, and he probably feels the more people he kills the more he'll be punishing her."

"I . . ." Melissa's voice was a dry whisper; she cleared her throat and started again. "I know this has come up before, but I don't understand why he didn't simply kill me and my children, like he did with the Tuckers and Evanses. Why so complicated? Why stage a kidnapping, then threaten to blow up the hostages plus some other people a week later?''

Castle studied her face a moment, then said: "He wants you to suffer. He wants the next few days to be the worst days of your life."

"Then why not make the Tuckers suffer, and the Evanses?"

"I'm just guessing, but I'd say different punishment for a different offense. You publicly insulted him. The two families did something else."

"Do you think a psychiatrist could tell us anything that would help?"

"I don't have much use for them, to tell you the truth. If we go to a shrink, he'll probably tell us the guy had a troubled childhood and had the hots for his sister or something like that. Nothing that will help us catch the guy. But if you want to give it a try, I'll set it up."

"I think I'd like to do that," Melissa said.

The lieutenant nodded. "Okay, I'll see if I can arrange something for today or tomorrow."

When the meeting ended, Melissa found a TV news crew waiting in the hall. Referring the reporter to Castle, she hurried to her office and closed the door, unwilling to say anything to the media while her kids were in the hands of an unpredictable madman.

Sitting at her desk, she stared at the closed door, painfully aware of how powerless she was to help her children. Like any ordinary citizen, the sheriff could do little except wait and hope. She was at the mercy of events beyond her control.

Resting her head on her desk, Melissa realized she was empty, devoid of tears, devoid of everything except a pervasive numbing misery.

Sitting on his living room couch, the phone in his lap, the Boogeyman dialed the number he'd just found in the Denver phone book.

"Hello," a woman said.

"Is this the Lopez residence?"

"Yes, it is."

"I'm calling for the city directory, and I'd like to get some information from you for our next edition. Uh, let's see, I have you as George C. and Patricia Lopez. Is that correct?"

"Yes."

"Okay, and how many children do you have?"

"One, a boy, age eight."

"And his name is Nicholas?"

"No. Nick, just Nick."

"I see. And what is Mr. Lopez's occupation?"

"He's a surveyor for the state highway department."

"And are you employed, Mrs. Lopez?"

"I've been laid off. Do you want to know what I did before the layoff?"

"No, not if you're not working at the moment. Is there anyone else living permanently in your home?"

"No."

After thanking her for her help, the Boogeyman hung up. He'd learned everything he needed to know except one thing: whether George C. Lopez would be home tonight. A surveyor with the highway department might be working anywhere in the state, able to return home only on weekends.

Well, he decided, removing the phone from his lap and stretching, I'll have to find out, won't I?

16

"This is all there is to it," the preacher said, ushering Melissa and Castle into the small church. It was a small white frame structure at the end of a dirt road, and it belonged to a fundamentalist denomination whose name Melissa had forgotten.

The minister, who didn't live on the premises, had agreed to meet them here. He was a tall, thin middle-aged man, bald, with bloodshot blue eyes and the smell of alcohol on his breath.

Melissa surveyed the room. It was Spartan: painted walls, a few uncomfortable-looking wooden pews. Clearly, there was nowhere to hide any hostages. The preacher and the two police officers walked to the altar, which consisted of a small raised platform and a lectern.

"Is there an attic or a basement?" Castle asked.

"Just this one room," the clergyman replied. He spoke with a Southern accent.

Melissa shifted her weight; the floorboards beneath her feet creaked.

Castle asked: "Is there any place at all on the premises where someone could be hidden?"

"Like I told ya," the preacher said, "there's no trap doors, no secret compartments, nothing."

"This is a wood floor," Melissa said. "There must be some way of getting to the pipes that run beneath it."

The minister nodded. "Sure, you can get under the building. But it's just a crawl space, and there's nothing there except spiders."

"Do you mind if we check it out?" Melissa asked.

"As long as I don't have to go in there with you, I don't mind at all." He smiled.

The preacher led them outside and around the side of the building, where there was a small wooden door in the wall just above ground level. Melissa, realizing it would be dark underneath the building, went to the car and got a flashlight. When she returned, Castle and the minister had the door open. The lieutenant reached for the flashlight.

"I'll do it," Melissa said. If she was ever going to be a sheriff in more than just name, she was going to have to do her share of the dirty work, and now seemed as good a time as any to start. And even more important, it was her kids the lunatic had abducted, her kids whose lives were at stake. She was more than a sheriff; she was a mother.

Covered with cobwebs, the opening was maybe two-and-a-half feet wide, barely big enough to crawl through. Squatting in front of it, Melissa used the flashlight to knock away the cobwebs. The thought of going in there made her flesh crawl. She didn't mind getting her pants suit filthy; it was the bugs that might be in there, especially the spiders. Girding herself, she switched on the light and crawled forward, a piece of cobweb sticking to her forehead.

It's too late in the season, she told herself; the bugs are all dead by now. But somewhere in the back of her mind, she realized that under the building, where it was warm and protected, all sorts of dreadful creepy crawlies could still be very much alive.

Melissa crawled on the loose dirt, pipes and floor joists just inches above her head, cobwebs entangling themselves in her hair. She went in only ten feet or so, far enough so she could shine her light in all the corners. There was no one else here; no one had been here in years.

Certain that a spider would drop down the back of her shirt at any moment, she shuddered, then crawled toward the rectangle of light that meant escape from this place and whatever creatures dwelled here. As she emerged, Castle helped her up. Outside she found the same chilly, overcast day she'd left a few moments ago, but it no longer seemed dreary. Taking a big breath of fresh air, she dusted herself off, secretly inspecting her clothes for any bugs.

"There's certainly no one there at the moment," she reported.

"Now, as I understand this thing," the preacher said, frowning, "there's hostages involved here, and somebody wants to blow them up come Sunday, possibly in a church. That right?"

"Pretty much," Melissa said.

"Well, then, how do you know the hostages would be there now? Maybe the person's got them won't put them in a church—if it is a church—until Sunday morning."

"We don't know," Castle said. "But we still have to check. The lives of two kids are involved."

"Whose kids are they?" the minister asked.

Melissa said: "Don't you read the papers or watch TV?"

"I watch a lot of TV; I just don't watch the news. Actually, I'm on the cable, so I mainly watch the Christian channel. Too much smut and sex on regular TV." He smiled smugly, the grin of one who is absolutely sure in his beliefs.

Castle suggested the preacher put a lock on the door to the crawl space; then they thanked the minister and turned to leave.

"Hey, you never did answer my question," the clergyman said.

"What question?" Melissa asked, turning to face him.

"Who was kidnapped—whose kids?"

Although Melissa felt a wave of anger at this smug man who denounced smut while reeking of alcohol, she tried not to let it show. "No one you'd know," she said.

The preacher looked at her curiously.

Parked behind a stand of juniper and small pine trees, the Boogeyman watched the home of George and Patricia Lopez. He'd found this spot by following a narrow dirt road up a hill. The Lopez house was below him, on the other side of a two-lane highway. This was one of the hillier portions of the county, an area where a finger of the Rockies pushed eastward toward the plains.

Though he called the Lopez place a house, he was uncertain whether that was the correct term. The dwelling was a mobile home set on a permanent foundation. No longer something that would roll along the highway with a wide-load sign attached to it, the home had ceased to be mobile. Was it a mobile home even so? Or had it become a house? But then he was merely playing with words. What he called the place was unimportant.

Fortunately the Lopezes lived in an isolated location. No neighbors for a mile or two in either direction. No one to hear the shots.

The Boogeyman wondered why anyone would live out here like this. There was a chicken coop and what appeared to be a small vegetable garden, but no livestock, no large fields to harvest, nothing that would account for a home's being here. Despite the mountainous terrain, the area wasn't the least bit scenic. It was hills and scrub brush, drab and uninteresting, with no breathtaking views.

It was around six o'clock when the brown pickup came down the highway, slowed, and turned into the dirt drive leading to the Lopezes' mobile home/house. Watching through binoculars, the Boogeyman saw a man dressed in jeans and a western shirt and hat emerge from the truck's cab and then enter the trailer without knocking. It had to be George C. Lopez.

Putting down the field glasses, the Boogeyman started his green Chevy. He had seen all he came to see. He would be back. Tonight.

When Melissa arrived home that evening, she found a note from Keith telling her that he'd gone to his own place to get some clothes and other things he needed. If she got there before he returned, the message said, she was to put two TV dinners in the oven. Melissa did so, then sank onto the couch.

Instantly she was aware of how empty the house was, how cold and lonely the place seemed without the children to give it life, warmth, to make it a home. She'd wanted to keep working, to keep checking out churches, but Castle had pointed out that the searches should be made in the daytime, since it was too easy for weary officers to overlook clues that might be hidden in the shadows. Reluctantly Melissa had agreed.

With no real purpose in mind, Melissa walked into the kitchen. She and Keith had scrubbed the purple crayon from the refrigerator. Its presence would have been unbearable. It wasn't just the absence of the children that made the house seem cold, she realized. Her home, her sanctuary, her private place had been entered, violated. It no longer seemed safe and secure. Suddenly she was filled with hatred, and she wondered whether she'd made the right decision in electing not to carry a gun.

But of course she'd made the correct choice. She was untrained in the use of firearms, she didn't like them, and she had no time to learn how to handle one properly. What would I do, she wondered as she left the kitchen, what would I do if I had a gun in my hand and met the Boogeyman? That she had no answer for that bothered her, for it meant there was at least a chance that she'd pull the trigger.

She found herself standing in the doorway of Sarah's bedroom. Like her brother's, it was simply furnished with plain but durable things. Neither she nor Jim had believed in fairy-tale-scene wallpaper or the like. The room was just as Sarah had left it: the bed made, everything put away, a big stuffed animal that looked something like a moose occupying a chair in a corner. The room, like the rest of the house, seemed lifeless, sterile. Melissa moved down the hall to Billy's room.

Like his sister's, Billy's room reflected the personality of its occupant. The bed was more thrown together than made, just neat enough for Billy to avoid being told to remake it. Dirty clothes were piled on the chair. On the dresser were a couple of yo-yos, marbles, a baseball glove . . . all the things customarily accumulated by a little boy. Hanging from the ceiling on strings were models of spaceships. One Melissa recognized as the U.S.S. *Enterprise*; she thought most of the others were from the movie *Star Wars*, but she wasn't sure.

Henry, she thought as she left her son's room. That was the name of the mooselike stuffed animal in Sarah's room. Sarah had named it that shortly after receiving it as a Christmas present. She'd been three.

Unable to deal with these thoughts, Melissa hurried to the hall closet and got out the vacuum cleaner. Cleaning would give her something to occupy her mind until Keith returned. She rolled the upright vacuum into the den, plugged it in, and switched it on. The games Billy and Sarah had been playing Saturday night were piled on the couch. Melissa tried not to look at them.

Switching off the machine, Melissa pulled the couch out from the wall, then vacuumed behind it. When she pushed it back into position, she found a long piece of clear plastic on the carpet. Curious, she picked it up, discovering that it was a strap of some sort with a slot in one end. She heard the front door open.

"Melissa, I'm back," Keith called from the living room.

"In here."

A moment later he stepped into the den, slipped his arms around her, and gave her a quick kiss. "Any news?" he asked.

She told him about the letter, the effort to check out any place a number of people might be found on Sunday morning.

Squeezing her tightly, he said: "I worried about the kids all day. I'm afraid my client didn't get his money's worth from me. All I wanted to do was get out of the courtroom and phone you to see whether there was any news. When I finally did get to call, you were out."

He released her, his eyes drifting to the object in her hands. "Why'd you bring that home?"

"I didn't. It was under the couch. What is it?"

"Handcuffs."

THE BOOGEYMAN

"Handcuffs? Doesn't look like any handcuffs I ever saw before."

"They're only used when there's a mass arrest. It's a quick way of securing someone's hands. Once one of those has been applied, the only way to get it off is to cut it off. One of the detectives must have dropped it."

Melissa considered that. Although she was unsure why one of her officers would be carrying a device whose primary use was for mass arrests, she had no other explanation for how it could have gotten here. Tossing the plastic strap on the couch, she said:

"Did you get everything you needed?"

Keith nodded. "It's on the bed. I'll put it away later."

Melissa rested her head on his shoulder, and for a few moments neither of them spoke. Finally Melissa said: "I guess we'd better check on our TV dinners."

As they walked toward the kitchen, Melissa realized that she was getting stronger. Yesterday she'd cried when she came home, and tonight she hadn't. She was learning to cope with the situation. But then she had no choice, not if she was to have any chance of saving her children. She could cry her eyes out when this was over.

Over. She turned the word around in her mind. It had to end, didn't it? And there were really only two ways it could be resolved. Either the children would be rescued, or . . . She deliberately left the thought uncompleted.

"The TV dinners smell good," Keith said when they entered the kitchen.

Melissa sat down at the kitchen table. The thought of food was suddenly nauseating.

Patricia Lopez felt her husband stir; then he sat up in their double bed, letting cold air in under the covers. She pulled the blanket back over her as best she could and began drifting off into the sleep from which she'd never really awakened.

"You hear that?" her husband asked.

"Numpf," she replied sleepily.

And then she was sitting up beside him, for something had

just hit the metal roof of their home and rolled off. "Is someone throwing rocks at us?" she asked.

"I don't know," George Lopez said, climbing out of bed. "But I'm going to find out."

"George," she said, fully awake now, "if there's someone out there, maybe you should call the sheriff."

"I'm not sure there's anyone there. Maybe an animal got up on the roof or something."

Although her husband didn't turn on the light, she could see his dark form move to the closet where he kept his gun.

"George . . ."

"Don't worry about it. It's just a precaution."

Patricia heard him break his shotgun, slip the shells into its tubes, and close the weapon.

"I'll be right back," he said, and she heard the front door open, then close.

She lay in bed, not really worried and yet feeling vaguely apprehensive. A small shadow slipped into the room.

"Where'd Daddy go?" Nicky asked sleepily.

"He heard a noise and went to see what it was."

"I heard it, too," Nicky said. He sat down on the bed.

"Did it scare you?"

The boy hesitated, apparently uncertain whether to admit that the sound had frightened him; then he said: "Well, maybe a little."

She wanted to grab him and hug him, but she knew he wouldn't appreciate it. He was eight, by his reckoning too old to allow himself to be hugged by his mommy. Inwardly Patricia Lopez laughed. She thought his behavior was cute, although she would never tell him so; he'd die of embarrassment.

She chuckled, out loud this time.

"What's so funny?" her son asked.

"Oh, nothing."

"What do you think is out there?"

"Your father said it might be an animal. Maybe a vulture's building a nest on the roof or something."

"Do vultures build nests?"

"I don't know. I suppose so."

They fell silent, but the boy, apparently having no intention of leaving until his father returned and reported what he'd found, remained on the bed.

Patricia Lopez considered herself very fortunate. Part of a family of seven, she'd lived in a mobile home while she grew up. A construction worker, her father followed the jobs wherever they took him—as long as they didn't take him too far east of the Rockies, to that region of the country her dad had seen when he was in the army and never planned to see again. Mostly she and her two sisters and two brothers had lived in Colorado, New Mexico, west Texas, and Arizona, although for brief periods they'd stayed in Utah and Idaho as well.

One thing a family of seven living in a trailer didn't need was unnecessary bodies hanging around, so when Patricia turned nineteen, her father told her in so many words to find someone and marry him, preferably before she was twenty. He wouldn't have thrown her out—at least she didn't think he would—but her parents would have nagged her constantly. In any case she took the first offer that came along, which happened to come from George Lopez, a young construction worker on the same project that employed her father.

Without considering whether she wanted to continue moving from job to job as the wife of a migratory construction worker, whether he'd be the type who'd slap her around, whether she really loved him, she'd blithely walked down the aisle as Patricia Davenport and become Patricia Lopez.

Remarkably, it had worked. George adored her, and she soon found that she felt the same way about him. They had a baby and became a happy family of three. Having decided to give up their nomadic way of life, they saved their money, bought the property here, made the mobile home a permanent home. The spot was isolated, but none of them seemed to mind. They had their own well, their own septic tank, and George had a secure job with the state. They were beholden to no one.

Both she and the boy jumped when the shotgun blast shattered the stillness of the night. Nicky went to the window and peered out.

"Do you see anything?"

"No," the boy replied.

All sorts of thoughts tumbled through Patricia's mind. George had shot at an animal. Or at someone. But then George wouldn't shoot at anybody; the shotgun was just a precaution, just because they lived so far away from any neighbors.

But before she could come to any conclusions, the door opened, and she heard George's footsteps, then saw his silhouette in the doorway, holding the shotgun.

"What was it?" she asked.

"Did you shoot something?" Nicky asked excitedly.

For a moment the shadow in the doorway was silent; then he said: "It was nothing, Patricia. Nothing at all."

Slowly the horrifying realization settled over her: The man who'd just spoken, who'd just used her name, was not her husband. "Who . . . who are you?" she asked.

"The Boogeyman."

Though uncertain how he'd got there, Patricia realized Nicky was standing beside her. She pulled him to her; he was trembling. She heard a click. The man had just cocked the shotgun.

Sitting in the darkness beside her brother, the two of them chained to the pipe, Sarah had spent the past several hours trying to figure out some way to make their presence in the church known. Their original idea of dropping things in the fan below the grate no longer seemed to offer much hope. The only chance, she was sure, would be if the man kept his word and continued to let them out of here each night to go to the bathroom and eat. But how to do it? The man watched them every moment, and she was certain he checked the place over thoroughly before leaving the building.

And if she did do something, and the man found it . . . She didn't even want to think about that.

"It hurts," her brother's sad, soft voice said in the darkness.

"What does?"

"My rear."

"Mine does, too, sometimes. You have to move around every now and then, get into another position."

"At least you don't have to sit on a wallet."

"Take it out. You're sure not going to need it up here."

He sighed. It was a sound he made to indicate that something she'd said was pretty dumb.

"It's your ass," Sarah said.

"You're not supposed to use that word."

Unable to stop herself, Sarah was suddenly furious. "Here we are," she snapped, "chained here like this, and you worry about whether it's okay to say ass."

When Billy didn't respond, Sarah's anger drained away as quickly as it had come. Though she didn't fully understand it, she realized that they weren't really mad at each other; they were sort of blindly reaching for ways to deal with a situation nothing in their experience had prepared them to handle.

"I'm sorry I got mad at you," she said.

"That's okay. You just don't understand about wallets. There's lots of important stuff in there. You just can't leave it lying around."

Suddenly Sarah had an idea. "Billy, is there anything in your wallet with your name on it?"

"Sure, lots of stuff."

"Let me have it."

"Why?"

"If the man takes us down to the kitchen again, I'm going to try to leave your wallet where somebody can find it."

"How come you have to be the one?"

"Because the last time, I was the only one of us who could move around. You were chained to the table."

Billy was quiet for a few moments; then he stirred. "Here," he said.

Reaching into the darkness, she found the wallet in Billy's hand.

"Where are you going to put it?" he asked.

"I don't know. It's got to be somewhere that the man won't find it but somebody else might."

Her brother clutched her arm. "Don't put it where *he* can find it, Sarah."

The terror in his voice was contagious. Sarah was trembling. "We might have to take a chance," she said. "It might be the only way we can get out of here."

"What do you think he'd do to us if he found it?"

Sarah still had no desire to consider that. But before she had to, she saw light coming through the grate. Crawling over to it and looking down through the spinning blades, she saw that the pews below her were illuminated by a flickering glow, its source apparently moving. It had to be the man. She quickly stuffed Billy's wallet into her pants.

The procedure was the same as it had been the night before. The man removed the chains from the pipe, leaving them attached to their ankles, and escorted them first to the bathroom, then the kitchen.

"Sit down at the table," the blond man said, turning on the lights and switching off his flashlight. The children obeyed. In the center of the table was a bag from a hamburger place. The man chained Billy to the table but not Sarah.

Sitting down across the table from his hostages, the man slid the paper bag in front of him. "Okay," he said, "I've got a cheeseburger, a roast beef, and a fish sandwich. Who wants what?"

When the children failed to respond, he removed the three sandwiches from the bag and laid them on the table in a row. "Reach over and take something," he said to Billy.

The boy hesitated, then grabbed the cheeseburger.

"Now you," the man said to Sarah.

Sarah was hungry; the smell of food was tantalizing. Even though she loved fish sandwiches, to accept something she especially liked from this man seemed wrong somehow. She took the roast beef. It was a small act of defiance, something Sarah doubted anyone else would understand, but to her it seemed important. The man pushed a packet of fries in front of each of his captives. Billy, more concerned with hunger than with the source of the food, grabbed them eagerly.

"Get the drinks from the refrigerator," he said, looking at Sarah.

Her heart pounding, she rose and walked to the refrigerator. The wallet was stuffed into the front of her jeans, its shape hidden by her shirt, which hung well below her waist. With her back to their captor, she could remove the wallet undetected.

Inside the refrigerator were three drinks from the same hamburger place that had provided the food. And a lot of unused shelf space. There were a few jars, but nothing behind which she could hide the wallet.

It would be in plain view if anyone opened the door. If their abductor checked, he'd find it immediately. And even if he didn't look into the refrigerator, there was no assurance that anyone else would either. The man might come back tomorrow night, put the drinks in to keep cool, and find the wallet waiting for him. Sarah was trying to decide whether she could open the freezing compartment without being noticed when the man said:

"Hey, don't take all day over there. We want our Cokes."

Grabbing the drinks, Sarah pushed the refrigerator door closed with her elbow and returned to the table, uncertain what to do now. As she sat down, her eyes met the man's, and for an instant he seemed vaguely familiar. Then she dismissed the notion. The man was a stranger.

She still had trouble believing he was doing this because of an insult. Sarah recalled some of the spiteful things she and other children had shouted at each other. Sooner or later someone would always shout: *Sticks and stones may break my bones, but names will never hurt me.* The saying was wrong, Sarah realized. For sometimes names could hurt you.

For a second she blamed her mother for getting her and Billy into this. If Mother hadn't insulted the man, if she'd just kept her mouth shut . . .

Quickly Sarah pushed these thoughts from her mind. Her mother had done nothing wrong. The bad guy was sitting across the table from her. He was big and strong and probably crazy.

Glancing at her brother and their captor, Sarah realized that both had nearly finished eating. Shortly it would be time to go back to the little secret passageway where they would spend the next twenty-four hours chained to a pipe. And she still had the wallet. Where can I leave it? she wondered desperately. Where, where, where?

And then she had an idea. She waited until she was sure the man wasn't watching her, then reached for her drink, purposely knocking it over.

"Oh!" she exclaimed, jumping up. "I'll get something to clean it up with."

Without waiting for permission, she picked up the loose end of her chain and hurried to the sink, expecting to get grabbed from behind at any second. But no large hand descended on her shoulder, so she squatted in front of the cabinet below the sink and opened it, looking for something she could use to wipe up the spilled cola. She spotted a rag hanging from the sink's trap. Grabbing it, she hurried back to the table, trying to keep her disappointment from showing as she wiped up the mess. Like the refrigerator, the cabinet was almost empty, with no safe place to leave the wallet. As she wiped the table, the man watched her impassively.

Worried that the man might decide to punish her in some way, Sarah quickly washed out the rag, gave the table another wiping and the rag another rinsing, then put the cloth away beneath the sink. Hurrying back to the table, she avoided the man's eyes as she picked up her sandwich. It was soggy from the spilled cola.

The man watched her silently, his expression revealing nothing. Did he know what she was trying to do? Unable to shake the feeling that her intentions had been totally obvious, she finished her dripping sandwich and started on her fries, which had somehow remained dry.

Finally she convinced herself that the man wasn't going to do anything except chain them to the pipe and leave. Then a feeling of defeat settled over her. The wallet was useless. The one thing they had that could let someone know they were here, and there was nothing she could do with it except leave it in her jeans and take it back to their dark prison. Only the blond man watching her across the table kept her from crying. She wouldn't give him the satisfaction.

As soon as she put the last french fry into her mouth, their abductor said: "Get this stuff off the table and put it in the trash."

Sarah obeyed, mechanically gathering up the napkins and sandwich wrappers and stuffing them into the bag, which she carried to the plastic garbage can. Removing the lid, she found herself staring at the debris from yesterday's meal, and suddenly she knew what to do with the wallet. Quickly slipping it out of her jeans, she dropped it into the garbage can and tossed the bag on top of it, pulling out some of its contents as she did so, concealing the billfold. She replaced the lid.

Sarah hesitated, afraid to turn around, afraid the man would be standing behind her waiting to tell her that he'd seen what she did.

When finally she did turn, the man had his back to her. Secure in the knowledge that she wouldn't run away when her brother would have to suffer the consequences, he was unfastening Billy's chain from the table.

Her eyes darting around the room, she searched for something big and heavy to hit him with, finding nothing. As he stood up, the blond man smiled at her. "Time to go back," he said.

Sarah moved away from the garbage can, wondering whether she'd done the right thing. It seemed unlikely the man would find the billfold, but would *anyone* find it? Or would it simply get thrown away with the rest of the garbage? Suddenly she was sure it would get thrown away. Why would anyone go through the garbage? Realizing she'd just wasted their only chance of getting help, Sarah began to cry, tears silently sliding down her cheeks.

Switching on his flashlight, the man turned off the kitchen light and led them into the dark hallway. Sarah continued to cry.

17

Switching off the engine, Lillian McGinnis climbed out of the big green delivery van, carrying a package addressed to Patricia Lopez. She knocked on the home's metal door and waited. It was an overcast Tuesday morning, breezy and chilly.

A lanky blond woman in her thirties, Lillian had worked for the parcel delivery firm for three years, and she thoroughly enjoyed the job. She got to meet people, travel around the Denver area, and she had no boss constantly breathing down her neck. And though she'd never admit it to any of her coworkers, she got a tremendous charge out of driving around in the big green truck.

Her secret desire was to drive a diesel rig. Maybe not professionally, but just to drive one, just once. She grinned at the image of herself up in the cab of an eighteen-wheeler, twin stacks belching black smoke. . . .

Lillian's husband was a checkout clerk in a grocery store. Although they both made fairly decent salaries, it took two incomes to get by these days, and there had never been any thought of her not working. Besides, they had opted for a childless marriage, and if she had to stay home by herself she'd get a little flaky after a while. A lousy housekeeper, she considered soap operas inane. There would be nothing for her to do.

She knocked again on the door, waited another moment or two, then put down the package and pulled out a pad of official notices that informed a parcel's intended recipient that she'd been here, finding no one home. As she started to fill in the form, the door swung open a few inches.

"Anyone home?" Lillian said loudly.

Apparently the Lopezes had gone off, forgetting to lock up. Well, there was nothing she could do about it. Too bad she couldn't simply shove the parcel inside, but company regulations required that all items be signed for. In town, she'd leave it with a neighbor; out here there were no neighbors.

When she'd completed the form, she slipped it inside the door, picked up the parcel, and returned to the truck. Starting the motor, she shifted into low gear and followed the dirt drive which circled the house. Absently she wondered whether a trailer on a foundation like this would be any more likely to survive a high wind than an ordinary mobile home, concluding it probably depended on how well it was attached to the foundation.

Suddenly she jammed on the brakes, certain she'd seen someone lying in the dry weeds ten feet or so from the drive. Shifting into reverse, Lillian backed the truck up until what she'd spotted came into view. There was someone there, all right, a man; she could see the soles of his boots.

"Hey," she called, "you okay, buddy?"

She cursed herself for her stupidity. Anyone lying motionless on his back in the weeds certainly was not okay. Afraid of what she might find, Lillian got out of the truck and approached the still form in the weeds. Hearing a sound off to her left, she jumped. Then she saw the bird taking flight.

Certain it would do no good yet unwilling to admit that the man was probably dead, she said: "Hey, can you hear me?"

And then she was standing over him, and she gasped. He was dark-haired, about thirty, and a big piece of his chest had been blown away. He was dressed in pajamas, a robe, and cowboy boots. A shotgun lay beside him. Had he pulled on the boots, grabbed the gun, and come out in the middle of the night to investigate something? Turning away from the sight, she fought to control her stomach; then she dashed back to her truck. Reaching it, she stopped, forced herself to muster some composure.

A phone, she thought, I have to find a phone. Looking up, she found the wires running to the house and identified both electric and telephone lines. She hurried to the front door of the trailer.

Inside she found herself in the living room. The place was nice, with carpeting, a big color TV set. The phone, where was the phone? Glancing into the adjacent kitchen, she saw it, mounted on the wall beside the refrigerator. And below it in purple crayon were the words:

THE LOPEZ FAMILY HAS BEEN PUNISHED BY THE BOOGEYMAN

She knew who the Boogeyman was and what he did. Were there more victims back in the other end of the home? Lillian didn't want to know; she only wanted to get out of there. She'd go somewhere else and call. Besides, nothing here should be disturbed.

She dashed to her truck.

"He's angry," the psychiatrist said. A middle-aged man with graying dark hair, Dr. Henry Melton sat behind the expensive-looking desk in his modern office. Melissa and Castle occupied two comfortable swiveling chairs apparently made of some sort of plastic.

"He's most likely suffered a deep hurt," the psychiatrist went on, "and way down inside somewhere, he's still suffering. So he lashes out."

Castle, who'd made it clear what he thought of psychiatrists, had said very little. This was Melissa's show. She said: "What do you think these families might have done to make him want to punish them?''

The doctor frowned. "There's no way of knowing precisely, of course, but I'd guess that whatever hurt him occurred when he was a child, something to do with his family. These families he's attacking could be like his own, thereby reminding him of whatever happened. On the other hand, they could be everything his family wasn't, and he hates them for having what he never could.

"You see, he's a weak individual with extremely low self-esteem, and he's very easily threatened. Which is why he kidnapped your children. Your words were too damaging to his fragile self-esteem, and he had to strike back.''

"Why does he call himself the Boogeyman?''

The doctor rubbed his forehead. "It could be identification with the aggressor.''

"I don't understand," Melissa said. "I thought that was like someone who'd always been bothered by bullies becoming a bully himself. Where does the Boogeyman come in? There is no such thing.''

"The Boogeyman's a symbol. He represents the true aggressor, which could be a single individual, a group of individuals, even a class of individuals—like the bullies you mentioned. Whatever the connection, it was made by a very disturbed mind, and it might not make a great deal of sense to us.''

Melissa tried to transform the doctor's words into an image of the killer and found she was unable to do so. "If I met this person, what would he be like?''

"He could be almost any age, I suppose. But keep in mind that just because I describe him as a weak person with low self-esteem doesn't mean he appears that way. He could very easily be someone who seems strong, intelligent, likable. The captain of the football team. The president of the chamber of commerce. It's a facade, of course, but some people live their entire lives behind such facades, without ever being found out. Fortunately most of them aren't mass murderers.''

"Do you think there's any significance to his use of purple crayons?''

"I believe you said the note was written in purple, too, except in pencil."

"That's right."

The psychiatrist thought for a moment, then said: "It's possible that purple or purple crayons have some connection with the event or events that hurt him. Actually I think that's quite likely, although you've got to keep in mind that everything I'm saying is little more than educated guesswork, since I've never met the individual we're talking about. Let's face it, it's possible this person simply likes the color purple." He shrugged. "My teenage daughter writes everything in green. As far as I can tell, there's no particular significance to her behavior."

"Doctor," Castle said, "is there anything you can tell us about the killer that might help us apprehend him?"

The psychiatrist stared across the room, looking thoughtful. After a moment he said: "No, Lieutenant. I'm sorry."

"One more question, Doctor," Melissa said. "In the note he threatened to kill my children by blowing them up along with some other people. Is there any chance he's doing this just to show me how easily he could hurt me if he wanted to, that he doesn't really plan to carry out the threat?"

When she looked into the psychiatrist's eyes, she knew what he was about to say. The doctor hesitated, apparently choosing his words carefully.

"It's possible," he said. "But . . ."

"But what, Doctor?"

"But this is someone who makes his point by killing. I wouldn't expect him to make an exception this time."

"Do you think he might have already . . ." She was unable to complete the sentence.

"No," he said softly. "I don't think he'd do things that way. I think he wants the children to die exactly when he says they will. He wants to show you how helpless you are, how powerless to stop him. It's important to his fragile self-esteem. He doesn't just want revenge; he wants to destroy you."

Melissa nodded, the familiar numbness settling over her.

They thanked the doctor, and as they were starting to leave, the phone rang. The psychiatrist answered it, then said: "It's for you."

Castle took the receiver from the doctor's outstretched hand, identified himself, then spent the next few moments listening. When he hung up, his expression made it clear that the news had been grave.

"The Boogeyman has struck again," he said. "Another family."

"How . . . how many?" Melissa asked.

"Three. The parents and a little boy. Used a shotgun on them."

Melissa shuddered.

In his dream the Boogeyman was a boy again. He and two other youngsters were sitting on the floor in the front room of an abandoned house not far from where he lived. Through the broken and missing windowpanes, he could see the last remnants of daylight in the sky. Soon it would be dark. He should go home, he knew, but if he was the first to leave, the others would call him a pussy.

"This place ain't haunted," Jerry said. He was a thin boy with light-brown hair. "If there's any ghosts here, I dare them to come out."

"Well, if there are any, we know who they'll get," Julio said. The boy who had not yet become the Boogeyman hoped Julio was referring to Jerry. Julio was short, a little on the chubby side, and had thick black hair.

"Ohoooowhoooo . . . ." the boy who was not yet the Boogeyman went, trying to sound scary as well as show the others that he wasn't afraid. The boys laughed. Outside, the last traces of gray left the sky.

"See," Jerry said. "It's completely dark now, and there's no ghosts. Anyone dumb enough to believe in ghosts would believe in the Boogeyman."

"Hey, man," Julio said, "I *saw* the Boogeyman."

"Oh, sure. I bet he was with Santa Claus and the Easter Bunny."

"No, man," Julio said very seriously. "I was out alone one night, and it had just turned dark like this. I was walking down the street, and up ahead of me I heard a noise, and then there he was. He stepped out from behind some bushes and started coming toward me."

"Probably Old Bill," the boy in the dream muttered. Bill—nobody seemed to know his last name—was the neighborhood wino, who hung around because all the abandoned houses provided so many handy places for him to sleep.

"It wasn't Bill," Julio said. "Bill's solid all the way through, like we are. But this guy wasn't. I could see *through* him."

"Bull," Jerry said.

"Double bull*shit*," the boy in the dream said.

"Hey, man, no lie," Julio insisted. "I'm telling you what I saw. There was a streetlight behind him, and it was shining through him. I couldn't see exactly what he looked like, except that he was big and he seemed to float. He moved about as fast as someone would walk, but his feet didn't move. He saw me, and he said. 'Juuuulio, I've come for you. I'm going to take you with me and punish you.'

"I was really scared, so I ran through a yard and came out in an alley, and then I really hauled ass, man, because I didn't know what would happen if he got me. When I was almost to the end of the alley, there he was again, coming toward me. And he said, 'Juuuulio, you can't get away from the Boogeyman.' "

Suddenly something crashed to the floor in the next room, and the boys jumped.

"W-what was that?" Jerry whispered.

For a moment no one answered; then Julio said: "It's plaster, man. There's pieces of plaster all over this place that have fallen off."

Again they were silent, the only sounds the noises of the night. A rat scurrying somewhere nearby, a dog barking, a car door slamming partway down the block.

Deciding that Julio's story was probably less scary than the silence, the boy in the dream said: "What happened next, Julio?"

"Man, was I scared," Julio said, picking up the tale. "I didn't know what to do. I figured that if I ran the other way he'd just get in front of me again. So I stood there, and he kept coming closer and closer. I thought he was going to get me and take me away, and nobody would ever see me again. And then, all of a sudden, a truck pulled into the alley.

"I guess the Boogeyman couldn't take the light, because he put his hands in front of his eyes. Anyway, when he wasn't looking, I jumped on the truck—it was a stake truck, open in back. When it pulled out of the alley, it turned toward my house, so I just stayed on it. About a block from my house, I jumped off and ran home as fast as I could. When I got to my door, I stopped and listened, and coming from so far away I could barely hear it, a voice was calling, 'Juuuulio! Juuuulio!' ''

Although the boy in the dream was fairly sure Julio had made up the tale, he shivered. For a moment the boys simply sat there on the dirty floor, each lost in his own thoughts; then Jerry suddenly grabbed Julio, saying in as deep a voice as he could manage: "Juuuulio, it's the Boogeyman. Juuulio, I've got you."

And then they all laughed and launched themselves into a three-way wrestling match on the floor. Finally Jerry broke loose from the other two and said: "I'd better be getting home, or my old man's going to give me hell."

"Pussy," Julio said. "You're just leaving because you don't want to be here when the ghosts show up."

"Ghosts don't scare me, Julio. But my old man does."

The boy in the dream also wanted to go, so he stood up before Julio could talk Jerry out of it. "I've gotta go, too," he said.

Julio went along with the majority, and the three of them left the abandoned house, carefully making their way over the dilapidated porch and down the rotting steps. It was almost totally dark. The neighborhood's streetlights were often the targets of vandals. Julio and Jerry had knocked out two of them one night with rocks. Sometimes people shot them out.

When they reached the sidewalk, the youngsters split up, Jerry and Julio going in one direction, the boy in the dream the other.

The boy headed for home, passing more abandoned houses, dark remains of what had once been homes, places with light and life.

"They're going to tear all the houses in this neighborhood down," his mother had said. "They'll build apartments that the people here now can't afford to live in."

"Where will they go?"

His mother had been unable to answer that, so the boy knew only that the people had gone somewhere. At the first intersection he came to, the boy turned right and saw a streetlight ahead. It was in the next block, where the buildings were still inhabited by something other than winos or memories or ghosts. The boy began to walk faster.

Suddenly a figure appeared partway down the block, coming toward him. The man was silhouetted by the streetlight, its glow shining around him.

And through him?

The boy stopped, his eyes fixed on the advancing figure. And then he was certain the light was passing through the man. It was the Boogeyman. He'd stayed out too late, and the Boogeyman had come for him.

The boy dashed through the remains of a hedge that had died from lack of water and into the yard of a derelict house, plunging into the darkness between it and its neighbor. Suddenly his foot hit something unseen in the blackness, and he fell, landing atop what seemed to be a pile of boards and other things from the abandoned dwelling. In the back of his mind, he hoped there were no nails protruding from anything—or pits waiting for him in the darkness—but his greatest fear was of the Boogeyman.

Basically unhurt and too terrified to be aware of any minor cuts and scrapes, he scrambled over the debris and ran into the backyard. Dimly he made out the outline of a garage, and then he was past it. He stopped in the alley behind it, panting, uncertain which way to go. Right would take him away from the Boogeyman, but away from his house, too. He went left, in the direction of home, his mother, safety.

His heart thudding madly, he rushed for the street at the end of the alley. And he recalled Julio's story. When Julio had been almost out of the alley, the Boogeyman had appeared again, cutting off escape. And suddenly the Boogeyman *was* just ahead, but unlike Julio, the boy had no truck to hop onto and ride to freedom. And the Boogeyman called his name.

The voice was familiar.

And then the boy recognized it. It was his father's voice. And at the same moment he realized that his father was the Boogeyman.

"Where the hell have you been?" the father/Boogeyman said crossly. Dazed, the boy felt himself being picked up, shaken. "Don't you know you're supposed to be home before dark?"

"Y-yes, sir." He could smell the liquor on the man's breath.

"I've got enough trouble with your mother, always whoring

around like she does. Then, when you didn't show up, she whined and whined until I came out to look for you.''

"I won't do it again," he heard himself say, his voice strangely distant.

"If you do, I'll lock the door and you can never come in again. Understand?''

"Yes, sir.''

And then the Boogeyman took him home, to the place where the three of them lived. The boy. His mother. And the Boogeyman. And somehow all this made sense to the boy. That the Boogeyman lived with them explained so much.

And then he was home, the Boogeyman/father accompanying him to the door. Suddenly he realized that the Boogeyman was no longer with him; he was alone. And he was unable to stop moving toward the door. Although he resisted with all his might, his hand was grabbing the knob, turning it.

And he knew what was behind that door. The Horrible Thing. It hadn't occurred in this house; this house was green, a strange house. And yet he knew it awaited him within. Pushing open the door, he sat up in bed, drenched with sweat, trembling.

After a few moments he swung his legs over the side of the bed and rubbed his eyes, feeling much calmer. Why was it so hard for him to deal with it in his dreams? Awake he had no such difficulties. He could picture the Horrible Thing. It was in the past. Long, long ago. He recalled hearing somewhere that Freud had called dreams the window into the unconscious. Did the nightmares mean there was something wrong with him? He pushed the thought away. There was obviously nothing wrong with him.

Getting off the bed, he went to the closet and studied his clothes, trying to decide what to wear. On the left were slacks, jeans, shirts, and sports coats. On the right were his work clothes. He selected jeans and a western shirt. Today was not a work day.

As he was closing the closet door, something caught his eye, and he paused to investigate. Sure enough the shoulder patch was coming off one of his khaki work shirts. Giving the patch a gentle tug, he felt a few threads give; it would have to be resewn by the uniform company. As if to teach the firm a lesson, he tossed his clothes on the bed, then grabbed the patch and ripped it off. He put it on the dresser so he'd see it, remember to take it and the shirt to the uniform place.

It was a pretty patch. A mountainous western landscape with brown letters around it. They spelled out: Deputy Sheriff, Ramsey County.

Having just returned from the small Denver college where he taught a course in comparative theology twice a week, Reverend Paul Maxwell stepped into his church's kitchen, his eyes scanning the sink, the stove, the oven. He glanced in the refrigerator, closed the door. Satisfied that everything here was okay, he turned to leave; then he remembered the things that had mysteriously appeared in the garbage can. He moved to the plastic container and lifted its lid. Inside was a fresh batch of fast-food wrappers and drink containers.

He reached into the can to sort through the leavings, then suddenly withdrew his hand, having realized how these things got here. The Boy Scouts had met here last night. The scoutmaster had a key to the back door. Although the boys weren't allowed in the part of the church in which services were held, they did have access to the kitchen.

There was certainly nothing improper about Boy Scouts' eating hamburgers. Except perhaps in the mind of a nutritionist, the minister thought with a chuckle. Putting the lid back on the can, he left the kitchen.

As he continued his inspection of the building, his thoughts turned to A. J. Sebastian. Despite all his prayers, at least part of him had given up on ever seeing the old man again. Later today he would check the caretaker's home once more, although he didn't expect to learn anything. Well, he thought, I have to try. If it turns out he is gone for good, I'm the only one in the world who'll notice his absence, the only one who'll care.

To Paul Maxwell, that seemed an awesome responsibility.

It was late afternoon when the Boogeyman parked his green car across the street from the building. An inconspicuous structure of white stucco, it had evidently been a home at one time, as had the other buildings in this block. Clearly the street had been rezoned. Front lawns had become parking lots; signs proclaimed the presence of a florist, a printer, a place that sold pots and picture frames. The homes had been small middle-class places, the dwellings of clerks and mechanics and factory workers. The Boogeyman waited.

He was glad he'd finally punished the Lopez family. Dealing with the woman sheriff had occupied his thoughts too long; it was time to get back to the Boogeyman's primary duties. The punishment of Melissa James was unstoppable; if he never set foot in the church again, if he died this instant, Sunday morning would come, and the children would die.

And now he was going to devote much more effort to punishing people like the Tuckers and Evanses and Lopezes. No longer content to wait until he stumbled across those who needed discipline, he was going to actively seek them out.

Across the street a station wagon pulled up. A blond woman got out and hurried inside, reappearing a moment later with a young boy in tow. The child was crying; the woman said something in a harsh tone. The Boogeyman looked away, no longer interested.

After the station wagon had gone, he let his eyes drift back to the white stucco building. Unlike the other former homes here, this one still had a front yard, which was surrounded by a low chain link fence. As he'd pulled up, he'd noticed a swing, slide, and monkey bars in the backyard, all the equipment idle. A small sign on the fence explained the building's purpose. In blue letters on a white background, it said:

ANNA LEE'S DAY-CARE CENTER

The Boogeyman continued to wait.

When Melissa arrived home that evening, Keith met her at the door. As soon as she was inside, she collapsed against him, just wanting to be held.

"I heard what happened," he said. "It was on the news."

She nodded against his chest, saying nothing. Images of bloody bodies swirled in her head. The Lopez family, the Evans family, the Tucker family. The faces of the victims changing randomly. She'd steeled herself for what she would see today; she'd been able to deal with it. The father outside, the mother and child in the bedroom, all three killed with a shotgun. She'd looked at the bodies, remained professional, detached.

But now as she stood here, clutching Keith, new faces joined those whirling in her brain. Some were ill defined, victims yet to come. But she also saw Billy and Sarah, their expressions filled with fear, their eyes pleading for help she was unable to give. Melissa closed her eyes tightly, but it was impossible to shut out images that came from within.

"Oh, Keith," she said. "What can I do?"

"You're doing everything it's humanly possible to do."

"No," she said, desperation creeping into her voice, "I can't be. Because if I am, then we're not going to find them in time."

Keith squeezed her more tightly, saying nothing. They stood there a few moments, Melissa's mind churning with her fears, frustrations, and feelings of inadequacy; then Keith said: "I didn't make any dinner tonight. I thought we might go out and get something. Maybe it will help get your mind off things."

"No, Keith. Please. Let's not. Something might happen, and I wouldn't be here to get the call."

"In that case," Keith said gently, "it'll have to be TV dinners or cube steaks thawed in the broiler."

"I'm really not very hungry."

"You can't quit eating."

She tried not to think about what—if anything—Billy and Sarah had been eating, for if she allowed herself to dwell on that, she'd be unable to face food of any kind. And Keith was right. Drained by sleepless nights and the constant anxiety, she'd been running on reserves of energy that would eventually have to give out. Not eating would only make things worse.

"I could pick up some carryout food," Keith offered.

"No," she said, "don't do that. Cube steaks will be fine." It all sounded the same to her. Food was food. She'd force herself to eat it, because she needed it. And she didn't want to be alone right now, even for the length of time it would take Keith to pick up some carryout food.

Releasing her, Keith took her coat and hung it in the closet. Accompanying him into the kitchen, Melissa said: "I can cook. You don't have to do all the work."

Gently he pushed her into a chair at the breakfast table. "You've got enough things to do. Let me take care of the little things for you."

The way Keith had come to her aid since the kidnapping was no little thing. Melissa wanted to tell him that, but the words went unspoken. Had she tried to explain how she felt, she would have broken into tears midway through the first sentence.

And then Keith's eyes found hers and held them. "Thanks for everything," she said and quickly looked away.

"I'm here to help, Melissa. If you need something—anything at all—just ask, okay?"

"Okay," she replied. And then, to change the subject, she said: "Uh, if you think of it, remind me to take that plastic handcuff strap with me in the morning. I meant to turn it in today, and I forgot."

"Sure," Keith said. Pausing to switch on the electric oven's broiler, he went to the refrigerator and got the frozen cube steaks, along with two containers of leftover vegetables.

Melissa's vision blurred with tears, and she held them back. Crying won't help the children, she reminded herself. You have to be strong. Stronger than you've ever been before.

18

The house was a small white home in a neighborhood of small white homes. Parked a few houses away on the same side of the street, the Boogeyman waited, watched. This was where the woman and girl had led him. They'd emerged from the day-care center, laughing, smiling, happy. And he'd known that they would have to be punished.

It was nearly nine o'clock; the neighborhood was dark, quiet, its residents carrying on their lives behind closed curtains, unaware of his presence. Having been here for nearly three hours, he'd seen the people who lived in this block return home, disappear into their houses. But except for the woman and girl, no one had entered the house he was watching.

The Boogeyman mulled over the possibilities. The woman's husband could have a job that took him out of town. Or he could work nights. Or this could be his day off. Or he could be out of work. Of course, it was also possible there was no husband. The mother could be divorced or one of those women who chose to have a child but not get married. Or maybe more than one child. The little girl might have brothers and sisters.

Too many possibilities and not enough information, he decided. Tomorrow he would have to learn more about the family. At the moment he didn't even know its name. Starting the car, he drove out of the neighborhood.

Deputy Jason Williams drove his cruiser along the four-lane street, his thoughts elsewhere. A tall dark-haired man in his late twenties, he was having marital problems. The difficulties were of his own making, he knew that, but his immediate concern was how to resolve things, not who was at fault.

Stopping at a red light, he forced himself to note the blue pickup that had pulled up beside him, and the gas station on the corner. He was on patrol, which meant he was supposed to be keeping an eye on things in Ramsey County—at least that part of it covered by patrol district 4-A. The light changed, and he stepped on the gas, gently easing the car up to about thirty miles an hour, five MPH below the limit. The blue pickup slowly pulled away from him.

Williams had been cheating on his wife. Three or four times a week he slept with different women. To him that's what sex was all about: finding new women to bed. But his wife, who stayed home and took care of their two kids while he was out screwing around, was not pleased with the arrangement. At the moment she and the kids were at her mother's house, and she was threatening to divorce him and hit him for both child support and alimony.

"If you don't stop leaving me and the kids alone all night," Wendy had warned, "one of these days you're going to come home and find us gone." Obviously she'd meant it.

He probably never should have gotten married in the first place. Oh, he didn't mind supporting a family. In fact it made him sort of proud, and he really enjoyed Jake and Walt, his two boys. The trouble was he couldn't stand having nothing to look forward to except work and watching TV and occasionally having dinner at the steak house or Wendy's folks' place.

The deputy sighed. He didn't like bowling or movies or any of the other things Wendy always wanted to do. Hell, he thought, you might as well admit it: The only thing you really like is chasing women.

Which did nothing to solve his problem. Exasperated, he kicked his speed up to about five miles an hour over the limit, slowly catching up with all the vehicles that had passed him so cautiously moments before. You're not supposed to speed, he reminded himself. You're supposed to set a good example. In driving, even if not in marriage.

He slowed; then the light ahead turned red, and he stopped. Absently he watched traffic on the cross street begin to move. A van and a station wagon pulled into the intersection, then a compact. A green sedan turned onto the thoroughfare, going in the same direction he was heading. A green Chevy. The killer who'd snatched the sheriff's children had used a green Chevy. Beside him on the seat, the license number was on his clipboard. There were many green Chevys around, but just to be on the safe side, he intended to catch this one and check its license number as soon as the light changed.

When it turned green, the yellow compact in front of him moved forward slowly. He honked, but the compact didn't go any faster. Realizing what was going on, the driver of the red Horizon beside him slowed, making room, and the deputy changed lanes, speeded up, passed the yellow compact, and sped after the green Chevy.

Williams wasn't using his emergency lights or siren, because he didn't want the driver of the green car to know he was there. The first set of taillights he caught turned out to be a pickup, the next a compact station wagon. He caught and passed a white car, a brown one, a black one. Where was the Chevy? Had he lost it? And then he spotted it, the next car ahead of him.

He realized the car could well hold nothing more sinister than a little old lady on her way home from a charity bake sale. Still, this had to be done right, so he quickly closed the gap between his cruiser and the green sedan, noted the license number, then immediately backed off, hoping the driver of the Chevy hadn't noticed him. Switching on the interior light, he glanced at the number on his clipboard and felt his pulse begin to quicken. The numbers were the same.

"Four-Adam to control," he said into the microphone, his voice filled with urgency.

"Go ahead, four-Adam," the male dispatcher said.

"I'm behind a green Chevy with a license number that matches item one on the hot sheet." He gave his location.

"Stand by," the dispatcher said. "Any unit in the vicinity of four-Adam?"

"Two-Charlie to control. I'm on Ridgeway, about three blocks away."

"Ten-four," the dispatcher said. "Back him up. All units, we're ten-three." Which meant emergency radio traffic only.

"Where are you now, two-Charlie?" Williams asked.

"I'm behind you, about two blocks back."

"Ten-four. There appears to be only one subject in the vehicle."

"Ten-four."

Glancing in his rearview mirror, Williams saw the other patrol car coming up behind him; it wasn't using emergency equipment, so as not to tip off the driver of the green Chevy.

"Ten-twenty, four-Adam," the dispatcher said.

Williams gave his present location.

"Any other units in the area?" control asked.

"Three-Adam's at Gilford and Plains."

"Ten-four, three-Adam. Head in the direction of four-Adam, in case you're needed. All units involved in the hot-sheet item-one matter, be advised that Lieutenant Collins is en route."

"I'm behind you," said Williams's backup. Glancing in the mirror, Williams saw the white patrol car, Brad Foster driving it.

"See if you can get ahead of him," Williams said. "Then I'll close the gap, and we'll take him."

"Ten-four." Brad Foster sped past him.

As Foster pulled parallel with the green Chevy, Williams increased his speed. But suddenly the green car's taillights came on, and it made an abrupt turn onto a side street, leaving Foster's patrol car on the thoroughfare.

"He's made us!" Williams shouted into the microphone. "Pulled a sharp right onto . . ." Whipping his cruiser around the same corner, Williams noted the street sign. "Onto Anderson Place, heading east. I'm in pursuit."

Williams switched on his emergency equipment. The siren screamed. Ahead, the green Chevy hung a left.

"South on Smithson," Williams yelled, sticking with the green car. It was about half a block ahead. The driver was good, but his sedan lacked the power of the patrol car's high-performance engine. The cars roared down a residential street, going sixty-five miles an hour. The green car was only a quarter of a block away now. It braked and turned to the left, then to the right, then left again into an alley.

Surprised, Williams performed the maneuvers awkwardly, pulling into the alley just in time to see the green car turn left at the other end. Grabbing the microphone, he explained as best he could where he was. Garbage cans, garages, and dark backyards flashed by, and then he was out of the alley, turning left, his eyes scanning the street for the taillights that weren't there.

"Shit," he said, the realization settling over him. "Oh, shit." Then into the microphone he said: "I've lost him."

The radio came to life, everyone wanting to know where everyone else was, the lieutenant giving orders, trying to at least trap the killer in the general area. I've lost him, Williams thought. The psycho that's killed three families and kidnapped the sheriff's kids.

Oh, God. How could I have lost him?

He was shaking so badly that he had to pull over to the side of the street. Resting his head on the steering wheel, he realized that if the Boogeyman killed again, if he harmed the sheriff's kids, it would be Jason Williams's fault. Maybe one of the other units will spot him, he thought.

But Williams knew it wouldn't happen. The Boogeyman was gone.

After driving without lights through a number of alleys, the Boogeyman switched them on and pulled onto a four-lane thoroughfare. Ten minutes later he was pulling the green sedan into the garagelike storage facility he rented. Quickly getting out of the car, he closed the metal overhead door.

It had been close. Too close. He hadn't been paying attention, and as a result he hadn't seen the patrol cars until there was one beside him and another coming up fast behind him. He'd looked over, instantly recognizing Brad Foster in the patrol car. Fortunately it was exceedingly unlikely that Foster had recognized him.

He'd known it would happen. Sooner or later a police officer would spot the green sedan, check the license number. He'd been foolish to continue using it this long. It was good fortune the deputies had tried to take him in an area he knew so well. Otherwise the green Chevy's smaller engine would have put him at a tremendous disadvantage.

The car's true license plates lay on the cement floor next to the wall. Picking them up, he studied them, trying to decide what to do. Finally he put the plates back in the same spot, having decided to leave the car here. Except for his neighbors, who paid little attention to him, no one knew he had the green Chevy, since he used it only for Boogeyman business. From now on, he decided, it would be best to steal a car whenever the Boogeyman's affairs needed attending to.

It was only a couple of miles to his house, not that bad a walk. If he stuck to back streets and alleys, he should have no trouble getting there unseen. Raising the door a few feet, he ducked under it, then closed and padlocked it. Hurrying across the asphalt in front of the storage facility, he reached the street, then cut across a vacant lot, heading for a residential area that began a block away. As he walked through the dry grass and weeds he felt burrs sticking to his jeans and socks.

What about the hostages? Would it be too risky now to continue visiting them each night? No, he decided, there was no reason to stop caring for them. He could use his other car for that; there was nothing suspicious about a single man who got off work at midnight—and sometimes later—being out in the middle of the night. And he really should do his best to make sure they didn't suffer any more than necessary, for it was the mother being punished, not the children.

About a block ahead of him, a car passed through an intersection, but it wasn't a patrol car. The Boogeyman crossed the street and headed into an alley.

Melissa hung up the wall-mounted phone, turning to face Keith, who was sitting at the kitchen table, watching her expectantly.

"They spotted the green car," she said, "the Boogeyman's car. It got away." Seeing the worry on Keith's face, Melissa realized she must look as dazed as she felt. She sat down, her eyes still on Keith's.

"What happened?" he asked.

"A patrol unit spotted a green car and checked the license. It was the right one. Two units tried to pull him over, and somehow he got away from them. That's all I know."

"Did they get a look at the driver?"

"One officer did, when he pulled alongside. There was one person in the car, a blond guy. It was him, Keith. And he got away."

"Melissa . . ."

She stood up. "Keith, I'm going down to the courthouse."

"Why? What's happening?"

She stared at him, trying to sort out her thoughts.

"Is there some kind of a search going on?" Keith asked, studying her face.

"A search? No, I don't think so."

"Then why are you going back to the office?"

"I . . . I don't know." She slowly lowered herself into a chair. "I guess there's no reason to go, is there?"

Melissa's eyes grew moist with tears that were ready to flow if only she'd let them. But she held them back. "I'm all right now. It was just a shock to learn that we were so close and then failed."

And what happens now? she wondered. He almost got caught tonight. Will that make him more cautious? Will he be even harder to find now—with only four-and-a-half days left? Four-and-a-half days until . . .

She cut the thought off, unwilling to complete it.

* * *

Sarah sat beside her brother on the bench, the blond man facing them across the wooden table. As he'd been doing, their captor had chained Billy to the table, leaving her free to move around. While she ate her hamburger, she tried to keep her eyes from drifting to the trash can. All day she'd been waiting for the police to arrive and begin searching for them, her greatest fear that their rescuers would be unable to find the place where they were held prisoner. But now that fear was giving way to the same doubts she'd had last night, doubts that the billfold would be found at all. Had she simply thrown it away by putting it in the garbage can? Would it be dumped into a garbage truck and be taken wherever trash went, never to be seen again?

There were probably numerous things in Billy's wallet that had his name on them, Sarah realized now. She could have saved some of them for future use instead of putting the billfold and all its contents into the garbage can. She looked at Billy, half expecting him to be glaring at her accusingly, but he merely glanced at her and resumed eating his hamburger.

"What time is it?" she asked the blond man just to break the awful silence.

"About three in the morning."

"Is this about when you always come?"

He studied her a moment, as if assessing her reasons for asking, then replied: "Yes, approximately."

The silence resumed, broken only by the sounds of chewing, sucking through straws. Sarah said: "Was it a nice day today? We can't tell, you know, except by the brightness of the light that shines into the church."

"Sorry about that," the man said. "But it can't be helped." He took a bite of his hamburger.

Sarah wanted to scream at the man: *Well, if you're so sorry about it, why don't you let us go?* But aware that doing so would be unwise, she said: "What was the day like?"

"Cloudy and cool."

Sarah finished her burger and fries in silence. When the meal was over, she quickly gathered up the cups and burger wrappers, stuffed everything into the bag in which it had come, and carried it to the trash. Lifting the can's plastic lid, she found everything just as she'd left it, the debris from yesterday's meal right on top, apparently undisturbed. Pushing a couple of burger wrappers aside, she exposed a corner of the wallet.

Uncertain what to do, she stood there, staring into the trash. Could she retrieve the wallet without getting caught? If she was going to try it, it had to be done quickly, before the man suspected anything was wrong. And then she heard movement, the rustle of clothing.

"Are we going back now?" Billy asked. He was warning her that the man was coming to investigate.

Quickly she dropped the trash she held into the can, covering the wallet. And then the man was beside her, looking into the plastic container. A terror-filled second passed; then Billy screamed, distracting him.

"I want to go home!" the boy yelled, standing by the table, tugging on his chain. "Why can't I go home?"

"Shut up!" the man snapped, taking a menacing step toward the boy.

Replacing the lid on the can, Sarah rushed to Billy, as if to calm him. "Billy, it's okay," she said, pushing him back down on the bench. "It'll be okay. Don't make the man mad."

She was proud of him. He'd apparently realized the wallet was still there, and when he'd seen that the man might be on the verge of reaching into the garbage can, he'd yelled, hoping to draw his attention. She'd been afraid to attempt using the moment to retrieve the billfold, but at least the man hadn't discovered it.

"Come on," their captor said. "It's time to go back."

To put the finishing touches on his performance, Billy sulked while the man unchained him from the table. And then, carrying the loose ends of their chains, Sarah and Billy were led toward the sliding panel that provided access to their prison. Sarah tried not to think about the wallet that was now buried even more deeply in the trash.

She felt like a slave in an old movie; the only thing missing was the beatings. What will happen to us? she wondered fearfully. She didn't believe what the man had said about a week. Although she had no idea what the man had in mind, it had occurred to her that she and Billy could identify him. But if he was going to . . . to kill them, then why hadn't he done it?

And then she knew the answer. Because he might need to prove they were alive. Sure, the man was just making up stuff when he said he wanted to punish their mother. He really wanted a ransom. And then, when he got it, when he didn't need them anymore, would he let them go?

Sarah started to cry because she knew the answer to that too. Of course he wouldn't let them go, not when they could identify him. I want to see my room again, she thought. I want to see the new movies. And my friends. And the new TV shows I haven't seen yet this season. And Mother. Oh, Mother, please find us. Please.

As the tears trickled silently down her cheeks, some part of Sarah that was still a little girl, that was totally incapable of dealing with all this, was crying:

"Mommmeee! Mommmeeeeeeeee!"

When Melissa left the house that morning, a TV camera crew was outside to get pictures of her as she walked to her white car with the gold star on its door. There were three of them—a man and two women—standing on the sidewalk, apparently not entering her property without permission.

"Anything new since he was spotted last night, Sheriff?" one of the women asked.

"Lieutenant Castle's in charge of the investigation," Melissa said, unlocking the car. "All statements will come from him."

The news people kept the camera trained on her as she backed out of the driveway and drove off. TV reporters had been at her house before, she knew, to shoot pictures of the scene of the kidnapping, but this was the first time she'd encountered them there. They were constantly at the courthouse, taking pictures of her whenever they had the chance, but they all knew that she had no comments to make, so they rarely asked her for any. Although Melissa hadn't seen any national newscasts in a while, she'd been told the story was on all three networks.

I'm a celebrity, she noted bitterly and then pushed the thought aside. It was unimportant.

At the courthouse, she checked her desk for messages, then removed the plastic handcuffs from her purse and put the bag in the usual drawer. Taking the plastic strap with her, she hurried into Castle's office, where she asked the lieutenant the same question the reporter had put to her: "Anything new?"

Castle looked up at her, the weariness on his face immediately apparent. "Nothing," he said. Then he slammed the desk with his fist. "Dammit, we almost had him last night." He sighed. "The officers didn't screw up, not really. Williams was alert enough to spot the car, and then he called for backup, exactly what he should have done. It was one of those things. It happens." Then, his eyes meeting Melissa's, he added: "I just wish it hadn't happened now, under these circumstances."

"We've got four days to find him again," Melissa said.

The lieutenant nodded, looking even more tired than he had a moment ago. His eyes shifted to the plastic strap in Melissa's hand. "What are you doing with that?" he asked.

"I found it in the den. One of the men must have dropped it." She laid it on his desk.

Castle frowned. "Your den?"

"Yes."

"And you don't know how it got there?"

"Well, I thought you or Goldman or Walczak . . ."

"Wait a minute." He got up and hurried out through the side door, the one that led to the office used by the other detectives. Uncertain what was happening, Melissa sat down to wait for the lieutenant's return. He reappeared about a minute later.

"I just talked to Walczak and Goldman. Neither of them had one of those in his possession the night of the kidnapping." He sat down behind his desk. "And neither did I."

"Then how did it . . ." And then she knew what Castle was thinking. "You mean the Boogeyman might have left it behind?"

"He could have used these to cuff his hostages."

"But why? They're only children."

"I've got a better question than that. Why did he use this particular device? These things are only used by law enforcement agencies. Nobody else would have any use for them. They're used for breaking up demonstrations and things like that, for when you've got to arrest a large group of people."

Uncertain what Castle was leading up to, Melissa remained silent and let him continue.

"Okay," he said, his eyes finding hers, "if this was left by the killer, it means he had access to it. The most likely place to get one of these is from a law enforcement agency. The Boogeyman could be a cop.''

"But . . .'' Melissa's thoughts swirled. There wasn't much to go on to reach such a conclusion, and yet the notion that it might be a cop had jarred something in Melissa's mind. She tried to find it, to bring it fully into her consciousness. And then she had it. ''I know a cop who hates me,'' she said. ''A lot.''

Frowning, Castle searched her face. ''You mean Nelson? I don't think he'd do—''

''He does hate me,'' Melissa said, interrupting. ''I fired him, remember? And he knows all the things not commonly known about the Boogeyman case. Such as the purple messages.''

''You'll never convince me that Nelson is the killer,'' Castle said.

''No, not the killer. Just the kidnapper.''

The lieutenant studied her a moment; then he said: ''You mean he set it up to look like the Boogeyman did it. For revenge.''

Melissa nodded. ''All he needed was a purple crayon, a pencil the same color, and a green car. He already had the blond hair.''

Again Castle was silent a moment before speaking. Finally he asked: ''Are you just tossing this in as an idea to kick around a little bit, or do you want to take some specific action?''

''For now let's get a picture of Nelson and show it to that neighbor of mine who saw the kidnapper. I doubt it will do much good, but we can decide what to do next after we've tried that.''

''Okay. We should be able to get a photo from his personnel file.''

The lieutenant started to rise, but Melissa held up her hand. ''There's one more thing I need to find out concerning last night. The officer who pulled alongside, did he get a good look at the driver of the green car?''

Castle slowly shook his head. ''All he could tell us was that it was a man with blond hair.''

''There's not much point in having him go through the mug files or try to work something up with an artist, I take it.''

''No.''

''Damn.''

"I know exactly how you feel," Castle said softly. "We had him cornered, all but caught, and got absolutely nothing out of it, not even so much as a useful scrap of information."

You don't know how I feel, Melissa thought. Your kids haven't been seized by some psycho. Either way, she realized, whether it was really the Boogeyman who'd taken her children or Nelson pretending to be the killer, Billy and Sarah were in the hands of a warped and very dangerous individual.

Castle stood up. "I'll get that picture."

19

"Yes?" Paul Maxwell said, taking in the man who'd just knocked on the rectory door. In his sixties, he was a squat fellow with thin gray hair, a day's growth of whiskers on his round face, and bright-blue eyes. He stood in the doorway, holding the tweedy cap he'd removed as soon as the minister had opened the door.

"Name's Wilbur Tyler," the man said. "Mr. Garvey suggested I look you up. Said you might need some help around the place."

"Help?" Reverend Maxwell replied, uncertain what this was all about. He presumed the Mr. Garvey the man referred to was Vincent Garvey, the scoutmaster.

"Yes, sir. I was the maintenance superintendent at an apartment house until I turned sixty-five a few months ago. Forced retirement, I think it's called. Anyway, Mr. Garvey knew I was looking for some work, and he suggested I check with you. Said you might need somebody temporarily, until your regular man got back."

The minister nodded. He recalled telling Garvey about A. J.'s disappearance. "Come in. We'll talk about it."

When they were seated—Tyler on the couch, Maxwell in a small easy chair—the minister said: "How much did Mr. Garvey tell you about the situation here?"

"Only that the man you had working for you had disappeared and that nobody seemed to know what had happened to him."

"You understand that if he returns—"

"He'll get his job back. That's fine with me. I'm not looking to take anybody's job."

Maxwell knew that the reason he hadn't tried to hire anyone was because doing so would have meant he'd given up on ever seeing A. J. Sebastian again. But now he had an out. Tyler was willing to work on a temporary basis, as someone filling in for the absent Sebastian. At least for the moment, the only thing he'd be forced to admit by hiring Tyler was that he needed some help around the place.

He said: "I hope you know the church can't pay very much."

"I've got Social Security, so I really don't need very much. Just enough to make up for the pension I would have gotten if I'd worked for a regular company instead of that outfit that owns that apartment building."

"Exactly what did you do there?"

"Oh, painted and fixed things mainly. Unstopped a lot of clogged drains and toilets."

"There isn't much to do here, you know. It wouldn't be much of a challenge."

Wilbur Tyler smiled, revealing stained teeth. "I've reached the age where I don't have much interest in being challenged. I just need to keep busy. And to make a few dollars, of course." Then, his blue eyes fixing on the minister's, he said: "I'm honest, I'm always on time, I'm good with my hands, and I need work."

Maxwell hesitated, then asked: "Uh, do you drink?"

"Every now and then I like a good belt. But on the job I'm always sober; you can count on it."

Ten minutes later Maxwell hired Tyler as A. J. Sebastian's temporary replacement. Tyler started work immediately.

Edgar Smithers, the man who'd glimpsed a man in a green car the night of the kidnapping, sat in an armchair, concentrating on the photo in his hand, while Melissa and Castle sat on the couch, watching him. Smithers's Early American living room was neat and antiseptically clean, not a speck of dust anywhere, not even so much as a magazine lying slightly askew on a table. Obviously not a house in which children live, Melissa decided, instantly regretting the thought.

"Hmmm," Smithers said without taking his eyes off the photo.

A woman wrapped in a pink bathrobe, a towel around her head, appeared from what had to be the bathroom and disappeared down the hallway, steam spilling out the door through which she'd emerged. Smithers didn't seem to notice.

Finally he lowered the photo, shifting his gaze to Melissa and Castle. "It could be him," he said.

"Could you be a little more definite?" Melissa prodded.

"Well . . ." Again he looked at the photo. "Well, I just can't say for sure. It might be him, and it might not. Like I told you before, it was dark, and I wasn't paying much attention. I'm absolutely sure it was a man, and I'm absolutely sure it was a green car, but that's about all I can say."

They thanked Smithers for his help and left. As they walked to the car, Melissa said: "Let's check with motor vehicles and see if by any chance Nelson has a green Chevrolet."

"Okay," Castle replied. "That's easily done."

"And I want to put a watch on Nelson."

"We'll have to get the men from patrol," he said doubtfully. "Captain Pruitt's stretched pretty thin now, with his people checking out the churches. He may not agree to it."

"I hadn't planned on making it optional," Melissa said flatly. They had reached the car, and she turned to face Castle, who was regarding her with an expression she was unable to interpret.

"We can't leave the county completely unprotected. There have to be some deputies to handle routine business."

"Then we'll put some people on overtime. I'm sure there are contingency funds in the budget, for emergencies. And this is an emergency."

The lieutenant nodded. "You're right about that."

"It's not just that it's my kids. It's an emergency because there's a madman on the loose who's killed eleven people, and we have no reason to think he might be tiring of it. The possibility that Nelson's involved may be a slim one, but I think we have to check it out. If the kidnapper and the killer aren't the same person, we need to know it.''

"You're the boss," he said. Melissa searched for some sarcasm in his tone but found none. And in his eyes had been . . . what? Approval? Respect? He'd looked at her, she realized suddenly, the way a teacher might look at a student who'd excelled on an examination.

Although it was a moment she should have enjoyed, she was unable to do so, for there were too many things to do. Too many things of life-and-death urgency. They climbed into the car.

Wilbur Tyler stood in the church, surveying the rows and rows of wooden pews he was going to have to polish. To do it properly, to really get in there and work the polish into the wood, would be an all-day job. Tomorrow or the next day, he decided. He should have at least one day to get acquainted with the place before undertaking a task like that.

His eyes taking in the rest of the room, he noticed the wooden panels that were recessed into the walls. These, too, would need to be polished, rubbed until the luster of the wood was no longer dimmed by years of neglect. The missing caretaker had done a mediocre job. Wilbur Tyler would do better.

As he turned to leave this part of the church, he wondered whether he could get to the walls before Sunday. No, he decided, that would probably have to wait until next week. He headed toward the kitchen.

Seventeen years he'd worked for the owner of that apartment building and no pension. He'd asked Mr. Bigsby about it, and Mr. Bigsby had just smiled sincerely and suggested that he consider setting up his own retirement plan. Trouble was those plans were for people who didn't need every cent they made just to survive. They were for the Bigsbys of the world, for the people who didn't need them.

Pushing all this from his mind, he wondered what Hattie would fix for dinner. He'd called her from the minister's place to let her know he got the job. She'd probably have something real special for dinner tonight, something to celebrate. Although her rheumatism kept her from working, she could still cook up a storm. She just had to make things that didn't require constant stirring, things that allowed her to sit down for a few minutes at a time.

In the kitchen he quickly looked the room over, deciding that everything here was in pretty good shape except for the floor, which had a lot of dead wax to be stripped off. His new job wouldn't be too bad once he got everything in order. Keeping things in shape was a lot easier than getting them that way. As soon as he had the chance, he'd get in here and work on the floor. For now he'd just see whether the trash can needed emptying.

Moving to the plastic container, he lifted the lid. It was about half-full, hamburger wrappers and the like if the stuff on top was any indication. Wilbur Tyler liked his trash cans empty, not half-full, so he carried this one out to the spot behind the church where he'd seen a number of large metal garbage cans. Lifting the lid off one, he dumped in the trash from the kitchen, then replaced the cover and headed back inside.

The cans, he noted, weren't chained, to prevent their being tipped over by dogs. He'd have to see to that when he had time.

The Boogeyman knocked on the door of the small white house. Dressed in slacks and a sports jacket, he carried a clipboard. Should anyone come to the door, he would explain that he was with the city directory and ask how many people were in the family, where they worked, what their names were. Though small, the houses in the neighborhood were well cared for, with yards that were tended, trim and siding that received a fresh coat of paint from time to time. Having satisfied himself that no one was home, he turned and walked casually away from the door, a person with perfectly legitimate business at the small white house.

Although he'd used his own car—with its own license plates—to come here, he'd parked it far enough away to be sure that no one would connect the auto with anything that happened later in the small white house. He still planned to steal a car whenever the Boogeyman was going to administer punishment, but for the sort of thing he'd just done, the risk of swiping a car was greater than the risk of using his own and parking it a few blocks away. Reaching the end of the block, he turned the corner.

The trip hadn't been wasted, for mounted next to the front door had been a mailbox with the name Cox on it. And now that he knew the name, he could most likely get the information he needed by phone, which was much safer than appearing in person.

Cox. He turned the name over in his mind, wondering how many Coxes lived in the little white house, how many would have to be punished.

Standing near the altar, Reverend Paul Maxwell and his new caretaker watched as the two deputies searched the church. Using mirrors attached to metal rods, they were walking along each row of pews, carefully checking beneath them. The sheriff's office had called about an hour ago, asking permission to search the building. On one side of the aisle was a dark-haired officer in his late twenties or early thirties. On the other side was a young woman, an absolutely stunning redhead.

"I may be old enough for forced retirement," Wilbur Tyler said, "but I'm not too old to appreciate a good-lookin' woman."

The minister nodded, saying nothing.

"You really think women should be cops?" Tyler asked.

"Sure. Why not?"

"What happens if she has to arrest somebody?"

"If she's been trained properly, there shouldn't be any problem."

"I suppose," Tyler said, obviously unconvinced. "You really think the killer might try something here on Sunday?"

"They're checking all the churches, anyplace people would congregate on a Sunday morning." He assumed the caretaker knew the details of the Boogeyman affair, since with all the media coverage it would be difficult not to.

"Sure hope they find that sucker," Tyler said.

"Me, too," Maxwell replied somberly. "Me, too."

"Hey!" Billy yelled suddenly. "Up here!" He was looking down through the grate.

"They can't hear you," Sarah said. "Who's there?"

"Help!" Billy screamed. "Help!"

Sarah crawled over beside him, and what she saw in the

church made her heart start beating faster. A woman dressed in a uniform. A sheriff's uniform! The woman was one of the officers who worked for her mom.

"Help!" Sarah yelled, and then they were both yelling, screaming at the top of their lungs. Below them the deputy moved slowly between the pews, doing something with a mirror on a long rod. She was looking for something, Sarah realized, maybe something to do with them. She screamed with renewed determination.

But the woman below never looked up, never even paused, and a moment later she was out of sight. Sarah stopped yelling, although Billy continued, his voice dropping in volume as he became more hoarse. The deputy, Sarah realized, was probably still nearby, probably within twenty or thirty feet of her. And yet the woman might as well be in Canada.

Billy was crying now, silently, because he had no more voice, tears rolling down his cheeks, dripping onto the floor in front of him. Dry-eyed, Sarah rolled over so that she faced away from him, wondering whether it was possible to cry so much you had no more tears left, to use them all up. She also wondered whether it was possible to just close your eyes and stop living.

Not bothering to analyze her motives for posing such a question, she lay on the wooden floor of their prison, staring off into the shadows, her mind too bogged down in misery to function. Behind her, Billy emitted hoarse sobs.

When the officers had finished their search, they joined the minister at the altar. Tyler had gone about his business.

"Find anything suspicious?" Maxwell asked.

"No, sir," the male officer said, "nothing at all." They'd checked the entire building—upstairs, the kitchen, all of it.

"Thank you for your cooperation," the woman said, smiling politely. She handed him a card that read: Marla Clark, Deputy Sheriff, Ramsey County. "If you can think of anything that might help us, we'd appreciate it if you'd call that number and ask for Lieutenant Castle."

Accepting the card, the minister said he would, and a moment later the deputies were gone. It was only then that he recalled the fast-food leavings that had appeared in his trash and wondered whether he should have told the officers about it. No, he decided. The deputies had checked the place over, finding nothing. What would they do, search it again because of a few burger wrappers?

As he was leaving the church, the minister detoured into the kitchen to check out the garbage can, finding that his new caretaker had emptied it. No matter. The Boy Scouts had most likely been responsible for the burger wrappers he found yesterday, and there was undoubtedly a simple explanation for those that had appeared in the trash on Monday.

He decided to tell Tyler to check the kitchen garbage can in the mornings and let him know should further fast-food debris appear.

Because Castle had spent most of the day coordinating things from the courthouse, Melissa had spent most of it in her office, trying to concentrate on the paperwork that kept arriving on her desk and piling up unattended to. She closed the file folder she'd been staring into, realizing she had absolutely no idea what it was about. She glanced at the clock; it was 3:45.

She stood up, intending to find Castle, and then she saw the deputy standing in her doorway. It was Bob Sanchez.

"Hi," he said, stepping into her office. "Any news?"

"No. Nothing you wouldn't have heard." She sat down again.

"If there's anything I can do . . . well, you know."

She nodded.

"I'd have checked with you sooner, but—"

"I know, I haven't been here. I spend as much time as I can in the field. It makes me feel like I'm doing something—even if I'm not."

"Hey, I've been hearing some good things about you."

"Oh?"

"The faction that was against you has cooled off. A lot of them are beginning to think that maybe you're okay."

"It's sympathy," Melissa said. "Because of what happened."

Sanchez shook his head. "Come on, we're cops. We have to deal with victims all the time. If we let ourselves feel sorry for them, we couldn't do the job. We'd fall apart. Victims who are also sheriffs get no special consideration—at least not in the sympathy department."

Melissa felt herself warming to the conversation. To Sanchez. "I appreciate what you're trying to do," she said, "but there's no way I could have won many of them over in the short time I've been here. Especially the die-hard woman-haters."

"Hell," Sanchez said, "*no one* is ever going to change them." He grinned. "By the way, I heard you were crawling around beneath a building with a flashlight."

"How'd you hear about that?" Melissa asked, surprised. "Castle and I were the only ones there."

"Word gets around."

"Don't be so damned cryptic."

Before Sanchez could respond, Castle stepped into the room. "Good afternoon, Lieutenant," the deputy said, rising. "I was just on my way out."

Castle waited until Sanchez was gone, then said: "According to motor vehicle records, the only car Nelson owns is a red Pontiac."

Melissa considered the information a moment. "Well, I don't suppose it changes anything."

"You ready to roll? I've got everything here pretty well under control now, and there are still some churches out there to be checked over."

"Okay," Melissa said, "but first let's talk about a couple of things."

Castle took a seat. "Fire away."

"What assurance do we have that the officers assigned to the surveillance of Nelson won't tip him off? Even if they don't do it directly, it seems likely that the whole department will know what's going on before long, and he still has buddies on the force."

Castle frowned. "Well, there are no absolute assurances. Pruitt's picking officers for the surveillance who weren't buddy-buddy with him, and he's ordering them to keep it to themselves. But I've got to warn you that there's no such thing as a secret in a police department. Tell the national secrets to a cop, and if there's a spy on the force, the other side will know them all within twenty-four hours."

"Okay," Melissa said, "the other thing. I realize that you have to be here a lot to coordinate things, but I really can't handle it. My mind's not on these damned papers.'' She waved at the file folders on her desk, the overflowing in-basket. ''It's on my children, and it's on the lunatic who's killing people. I need to be out in the field, doing something.''

''All right,'' the lieutenant said, ''I'll set it up so you can go out with another officer when I'm going to be tied up here.''

''Don't make it easy on me,'' she said, her eyes finding his. ''I need to know the officers who hate me just as much as I need to know the ones who are willing to give me a chance.''

He searched her face a moment, then nodded. ''You're the boss,'' he said.

It was dark when the white Ramsey County sheriff's unit rolled slowly through the closed gas station and stopped at a phone booth. Getting out of the car, the uniformed officer slipped into the booth, dropped some coins into the pay phone, and dialed.

''Hello,'' a woman's voice said on the other end of the line.

''Uh, is this Mrs. Cox?''

''Yes.''

''I'm calling for the city directory. . . .''

When he drove away from the phone booth a few minutes later, the Boogeyman had learned all he needed to know about the Cox family. Divorced, Lois Cox lived with her only child, a daughter.

20

As usual Billy and Sarah sat on one side of the table, their kidnapper on the other. The nightly menu varied only slightly, tonight's meal consisting of double-patty cheeseburgers, fries, Cokes. Sarah watched the blond man as he took a bite of his burger. He was reading the advertisement that had come in the bag with the food, a sheet with color pictures of various fast-food items. The man seemed relaxed, neither suspicious nor wary.

Which was exactly how Sarah had hoped he'd be, for tonight she was going to try to retrieve the wallet.

Her feelings of defeat had worn off. She'd realized that if they gave up it meant they were willing to be this man's prisoners, willing to be at his mercy. We have to keep trying, she thought, filling herself with determination. We have to.

Sarah stuffed some fries in her mouth, wondering whether it was apparent that they had a plan, whether the man could tell just by watching them. Her mother could, as could a teacher she'd had in fifth grade, Mrs. Ronley. Sometimes it seemed almost any grown-up could tell when you were involved in something adults disapproved of. It wasn't really like that, she knew; but when you were a kid, it seemed you always got caught, and Sarah did not want to think about what might happen if the man caught her tonight.

The plan was really pretty simple. Sarah would take the trash to the garbage can, and Billy would distract the kidnapper long enough for her to find the billfold. And she knew now where she would put it once they got it back. Every time the man took them back to their prison, they had to wait while he slid open the wooden square in the wall. They stood right next to the front row of pews. The only light would be the man's flashlight, and while he was busy, she could drop the wallet, ease it under the pew with her foot. Whoever cleaned the church would find it. Or maybe somebody sitting in the second row of pews.

The man was the last one to finish eating. He dropped the ad he'd been reading into the bag, then shoved it at Billy. "Pick all this stuff up and put it in the bag," he ordered.

Suddenly Sarah was worried. Would he tell Billy to take the bag this time? He wouldn't know where the wallet was. But then she recalled that Billy was chained to the table and she wasn't, making it pretty unlikely that he'd be the one to take the bag to the garbage can. Of course, even worse than using Billy, the man might decide to do it himself. Trying to look uninterested, Sarah waited.

"Give it to your sister," the man said as soon as Billy had

picked up all the trash on the table. Billy handed it to her, their eyes meeting for just an instant.

Both relieved and afraid, Sarah took the bag to the garbage can, her chain snaking along behind her on the floor.

As she reached for the lid, Billy said: "Is it okay if we talk, mister?"

"What do you want to talk about?"

"How about football?"

"Are you a fan?"

"Yeah. The Broncos."

At that point Sarah stopped hearing the conversation, for she'd just removed the cover from the garbage can. Stunned, she stared into the empty container. And then her heart sank. The wallet was gone. For good. Behind her Billy was doing his best to keep the blond man distracted. Sarah could hear the desperation in his voice. She dropped the bag into the can; it hit the bottom with a thump.

"Hey," the blond man said, "is that can empty?" He was squatting beside the table, unchaining Billy.

"Yes," Sarah replied, "it's empty." Billy was looking at her, unable to hide his dismay, but the man didn't notice.

"Then get that stuff out of there and bring it here," the man said.

She did so, offering the bag to him when she reached the table.

"Just put it down," he said.

"Why do you want your trash back?" Billy asked. No longer chained to the table, he was standing up now, as was their captor.

"Simple," the man answered. "Our trash just blends in with the rest of it when the can's full. But when there's nothing else in there, our stuff might be noticed." He smiled. "And we wouldn't want your presence here to become known, would we?"

Neither Billy nor Sarah answered.

It was about 3:45 A.M. when the Boogeyman parked his stolen station wagon on a residential street that paralleled the one on which Lois Cox lived. The neighborhood was dark, the only illumination coming from widely separated and fairly low-intensity streetlights. He'd picked this spot because should he run into difficulties at the Cox house, he'd be able to cut through the backyard, then through the abutting property to his car.

Because he'd picked the ignition lock, he was careful to move the switch only far enough to kill the engine without letting the tumblers reengage. When he returned to the car, it would be as if the keys had been left in the ignition, keys that were invisible to prying eyes. He'd found the station wagon parked on the street near a large apartment building. A short walk from his house. He'd taken the car before going to the church to feed his hostages, and he still had the bag containing the used napkins and other trash from their meal. It would have to be disposed of; it was the only thing in the car with his fingerprints on it. Adjusting his gloves, he climbed out of the car, then gently closed the door and slipped into the shadows.

He moved between two houses and into the backyard, his main concern that he didn't awaken a nearby sleeping dog—or worse, that one would be sleeping in the yard he was in. At the end of the property was a low chain link fence. He slipped over it into the Coxes' yard.

Despite the dark he was sure this was the right place. He'd counted the homes between the corner and the Cox house; then he'd counted them again along the street on which he'd left the car. There was nothing fancy about the way the neighborhood was laid out. The property lines extended straight through from street to street.

Again he found himself hoping there wasn't a Doberman in the yard with him, crouched in the shadows, waiting. In the quiet of the night, he could hear an occasional bark, but the sounds were distant, posing no threat.

Suddenly his legs hit something. He struggled for balance and lost it, falling on top of the thing that had tripped him. Uncertain how much noise he'd made, he lay motionless, listening. No dogs barked; no lights came on.

Something tubular was poking him in the stomach. A handlebar. His hands exploring the object, he determined he'd tripped over a tricycle. He pushed himself off of it, resolving to be more cautious as he moved through the dark yard.

And then his mind flashed back to his boyhood, when he'd had a tricycle of his own. His father had come home late, and there had been a crash as he pulled into the driveway. Awakened by the sound, the boy lay in bed listening, hearing his father swear, then throw something against the side of the house. A moment later there were more sounds. The door slamming. His father's raised voice blaming his mother for not making the boy keep his things out of the driveway. Then the blows, the sound of someone falling to the floor. In the morning the boy had found his flattened tricycle in the front yard. And his mother, her face puffed and discolored, had moved slowly, awkwardly, that morning.

Pushing the image away, the Boogeyman discovered he was at the back door of the house. It had two locks, both the variety you'd buy at the local hardware store. Taking the small case from his jacket pocket, he selected two picks and inserted them in the lock above the knob. It was a dead bolt, the kind law enforcement agencies were constantly urging homeowners to install. It took him about a minute to pick it. Then he started on the lock in the center of the knob. A few moments later he pocketed his picks and turned the knob. The door refused to open.

It had to be locked from the inside. A sliding bolt, or maybe more than one. The only way to get in through this door would be to break it down.

Stepping back, he studied the windows. Although he had a glass cutter and the other things he'd need to get in that way, this house had those small, high windows that were the fashion some years ago. They were too high for him to reach. He headed for the front of the house.

Reaching the corner of the building, he paused to scan the area. The houses were dark, the street deserted, the nearest streetlight half a block away. Stepping onto the concrete front porch, he moved to the door, deciding to try it first. Should this door, too, be bolted from within, there was always the front window. That was one thing about these houses with the little high windows in most of the rooms; they nearly always had a big picture window in front. He took out his picks.

*   *   *

Edwina Johnson had just gone to bed. A seventy-two-year-old widow, she was able to keep any hours that suited her, and it wasn't unusual for her to stay up until three or four in the morning, pursuing her passion: reading mysteries. She rarely watched television; her set was an ancient black and white with a wobbly picture. If it broke, whether she'd fix it was questionable, since doing so would use money that could be spent on books. Because she rarely parted with a volume, almost every interior wall of her small one-story house was lined with bookcases.

She was floating somewhere between sleep and wakefulness when she heard the noise. It sounded as if someone had bumped into something and fallen in the Coxes' yard. Fully awake now, she listened intently, hearing nothing. She decided to investigate.

Flipping the covers aside, she swung her legs over the edge of the bed, then rose slowly, cautiously. She didn't have rheumatism or anything like that, but when your legs were nearly three-quarters of a century old, it took them a moment or two to start working. Once she was sure of her balance, she moved to the window and looked out, her eyes scanning the Coxes' place, seeing nothing but shadows.

And then she realized that one of the shadows had just moved. She squinted, trying to see what was there, wishing she'd remembered her glasses. Could it be an animal, perhaps a stray dog? Could Mrs. Cox have gone out for something? No, that didn't make sense. If she was up, the house wouldn't be completely dark; there'd be lights on. And she'd have taken a flashlight.

Suddenly the shadow moved again. It came closer, and then it was between Edwina's house and the Coxes', and even without her glasses Edwina could tell it was a man. A prowler . . . or worse.

The man paused at the corner of the house, then stepped onto the front porch, out of her sight. Automatically grabbing her robe, Edwina got her glasses from the bedside table, then hurried into the kitchen and reached for the light switch, stopping herself just in time. She didn't want to let the man know that anyone in this house was awake. And she had no need for the light anyway; her wall phone was one of those with a lighted dial. Grabbing it, she dialed 911.

"Sheriff's office," a man said.

Edwina took a moment to compose herself, then gave her name and address and explained what she'd seen.

"Can you see the prowler at this time?" the man asked.

"No."

"And when you last saw him, he was on the front porch, is that correct?"

"Yes."

"All right, ma'am, I'll send an officer to check it out."

"Yes, thank you. Please hurry."

After hanging up, Edwina started back toward her bedroom to keep watch. Abruptly she stopped, turned around, and dashed back into the kitchen, grabbing the phone. The number, what was the number? She had to warn Lois Cox.

She dialed 555, then hesitated. Oh, what is it? she demanded of her memory. Then she dialed 9554, and the phone rang on the other end of the line. Oh, hurry, Lois, she thought. Hurry. And the receiver was picked up.

"Hello," a sleepy male voice said.

A man? Was Lois . . . entertaining someone? "Put Lois on. This is her neighbor. It's an emergency."

"Huh?"

"Put Lois on."

"Look, lady, there's nobody here named Lois, and it's four o'clock in the morning. Good-bye." The line went dead.

For one horrifying moment, she thought she was talking to the prowler, that he'd gotten inside and done something awful to Lois and her daughter. Calm down, she told herself. Calm down. Certain she'd remembered the number correctly, she dialed again, more carefully this time. The phone rang five times before it was answered.

"Hello." A woman's voice. Edwina was filled with relief.

"Lois?"

"Yes. What . . . who's this?"

"This is Edwina, next door. There's a prowler over at your place. I saw him. I called the sheriff."

"I . . . what? A prowler?"

"Are all your doors and windows locked, honey?"

"Yes. I always lock them."

"Now, listen to me, honey. The last time I saw him, he was

on the front porch. I don't know how long it's going to take the sheriff to get there, so I want you to turn on your porch light. If he's still there, that will scare him off. Will you do that?''

"Yes. Okay. I'll do it right now."

As soon as the connection was broken, Edwina hurried back to her bedroom and peered out the window. She saw lights come on inside the Cox house, then the porch light, bathing the front yard with that peculiar shade of yellow that wasn't supposed to attract bugs. Suddenly the man was there, dashing between the two houses and into the backyard. From reading detective novels, she knew how important it was to fix the image of the culprit in your mind, but all she saw as he rushed by her window was dark clothing and blond hair.

Looking toward the street, she saw that a sheriff's car had just arrived. It sped off, presumably to intercept the prowler. Now that she knew Lois Cox and her daughter were safe, Edwina was thrilled to have all this happening right outside her window. What fun! she thought. This was better than a detective novel.

Having finished picking the first lock, the Boogeyman went to work on the second. Working with his picks, he teased the tumblers into position and felt the cylinder turn. In a moment he would know whether this door, like the one in back, was bolted from within. He turned the cylinder as far as it would go and withdrew his tools. The door had one of those handles with a thumb-operated lever that controlled the bolt. He put his picks away, rubbed his hands together, and reached for the handle. The porch was flooded with light.

Startled, he jumped back from the door. Then he ran. As he rushed along the side of the house, he observed that lights were on inside. He'd been so busy working on the locks that he hadn't noticed. Behind him he heard a car engine. A powerful engine. Like the one in the patrol car he'd been driving a few hours ago. Had someone spotted him, called the sheriff's office? He didn't slow down to look.

He ran to the left of where he thought the tricycle should be, hoping he didn't trip over anything else. Ahead was the fence. He slowed, feeling for it with his hands, and crashed into it.

Hurling himself over it, he ran into the next yard, between two houses, and dashed for the waiting station wagon.

Suddenly lights came on, blinding him, and a voice said: "Freeze! Police!"

Deputy Harlan Kelso, who was patrolling district 2-B, was only a few blocks away when he got the prowler call. He headed for the address.

"Any unit that can provide backup?" the dispatcher said over the radio.

"One-Adam to control. I'm at Thornton and County Road Twelve."

"Ten-four, one-Adam. Two-Baker, be advised that one-Adam's about a mile from you."

"Ten-four," Kelso said. "I'm just about there."

A few moments later he was in the right block, driving slowly to give his backup a chance to catch up with him. Ahead he saw the lights come on in a house on his right, then the porch light. A man dashed from the porch and around the side of the house.

Kelso grabbed the microphone. "Two-Baker to control. The subject just ran around the side of the house. I'm going over to the next block and try to cut him off."

"Ten-four," the dispatcher said. "One-Adam, how far away are you?"

"Ten or twelve blocks."

"Ten-four."

Reaching the end of the block, Kelso turned right, then right again at the next intersection, switching off his lights. Peering into the darkness, he drove slowly, with one hand on the control for the car's spotlight.

"Two-Baker to control. I'm in the next block with my lights out. I got here pretty quick. I might have beat him."

Then he saw something moving just ahead and to the right. A man. Kelso switched on the spotlight, training it on the suspect. Quickly switching the microphone from the radio to the car's rooftop loudspeaker, he said: "Freeze! Police!" Flipping the switch in the other direction, he said: "Two-Baker to control. I got him. I'll be out of the unit."

Drawing his gun as he climbed out of the car, he approached

the suspect cautiously. The man was standing near a large tree with his back turned.

"Hands on your head," Kelso ordered.

The man complied. He was tall with blond hair.

"Turn around," Kelso commanded.

The man didn't move.

"Hey!" Kelso shouted. "Turn around. Now!"

Still the man didn't move.

"Come on," Kelso said. "We're going to see your face eventually. If you don't want to do it that way, we'll do it this way. Lie down and spread 'em."

The man didn't budge. Angry now, Kelso stepped up behind him and gave him a shove. "On the ground, sleaz-ball."

The man tilted forward, as if he was about to take a staggering step because of the shove Kelso had given him, and then he whirled, his hand grabbing the deputy's wrist, and suddenly the two of them were face-to-face, struggling for the gun. Kelso knew he had screwed up. In his twenties, he was maybe a little stouter than average, but he was no match for the blond man. Suddenly Kelso's opponent knocked the deputy's feet out from under him, and both men were on the ground. In the distance he heard a siren. Help was on the way. He held on to the gun with all his strength, but the blond man was slowly wresting it from his grasp. The siren grew louder. Hurry, Kelso thought. Hurry.

The blond man was on top of him now. As Kelso struggled to retain possession of his weapon, he looked into the face of his opponent, which was illuminated by the spotlight.

"Oh, Christ," he said, recognizing the face. "What are *you* doing here? Why—"

Kelso didn't complete the sentence because he'd just lost the gun, and a sound was ringing in his ears, a bang. And he felt pain, but he was uncertain what hurt. The pain was diminishing now, so it really didn't matter. He heard a car start up, tires squeal. Then there was just the siren. And the sound of his squad car idling. Suddenly a woman in a bathrobe was bending over him.

"Are you all right?" she asked.

He tried to answer but couldn't. Although the siren was closer now, it seemed very far away somehow. While his mind struggled to sort out these things, the woman's face blurred and then dimmed and then vanished altogether. For a moment the sound of the siren lingered somewhere in his brain, and then there was nothing.

21

Melissa and the four detectives sat roughly where they had at the previous meeting. Castle sat facing them, his back to the blackboard. It was 7:30 in the morning.

Melissa had gone to the scene, viewed what had happened to one of the officers under her command. Sickened by the sight, she'd tried to assess her responsibility in Kelso's death and found she was unable to do so. As the boss, she had to share in the blame; she knew that. But it was something she'd have to deal with later, when there was time.

"Who killed Deputy Kelso?" Castle asked. "Was it the Boogeyman? There are a lot of criminals out there with blond hair."

"That's not something we have to decide right now," Melissa said. "Until we learn otherwise, we have to work the cases as though they were unrelated."

Walczak, Hanson, Brown, and Goldman studied her silently. Castle said: "I agree. I don't think there's any other way to handle it."

Melissa could feel the tension in the room, see the strain on the taut, stony faces of the men around her. One of their own had been killed, and there was a score to be settled. But the desire for vengeance was only what bubbled on the surface. Below it and giving it impetus was the knowledge that what could happen to Kelso could happen to them.

When it became clear no one had anything to add, Castle went on. "The perpetrator was trying to get into the house of Lois

Cox, age twenty-seven, who lives there with her three-year-old daughter. She says she has no reason to think anyone would want to harm her, and her possessions don't amount to that much, not enough to attract a burglar who's pretty sophisticated at picking locks."

"Picking locks," Walczak said. "Seems to me that brings us back to the Boogeyman."

"I didn't say we should ignore the possibility that the Boogeyman killed Kelso," the lieutenant said. "I'm simply saying that we can't afford to assume that he did it. We have to approach it as a separate killing and see where it leads."

Hanson said: "This Cox woman is divorced. How about her ex-husband or maybe a lover she dumped or something like that?"

"The husband lives in Rapid City, South Dakota, now," Castle said. "I've got Rapid City PD trying to confirm that he wasn't out of town last night. In any case, he really doesn't fit the description. Mrs. Cox says he's about five ten, slender, and has light-brown hair. Also Cox says she has no steady boyfriends, just casual ones, and none of those is a tall, strapping guy with blond hair. As she put it, her taste runs more to chess players than football players."

The lieutenant cleared his throat. "Unfortunately, the only person who saw Kelso's killer was Cox's next-door neighbor, and the only description the neighbor could give was a tall, solidly built blond guy wearing dark clothes. The neighbor never got a look at his face."

"Nobody saw anything where the shooting took place?" Brown asked. He and Walczak hadn't been summoned to the scene to help with the investigation. Everyone else in the room had been there.

"No. The shot woke up some of the people in the neighborhood, but most of them got up too late to see anything. One couple saw a station wagon pull away, but neither of them got the license number."

"If it was the Boogeyman," Walczak said, "he's ditched his green Chevy."

"I'd have ditched it before now," Hanson said.

Castle rubbed his brow. "The Department of Motor Vehicles

sending us a list of the owners of green Chevy sedans the year and model of the one in Melanie's Bascom's photo. It will cover the metro area and all of Ramsey County. Also, the motor vehicle people are having their computer check driver's license information against the names of the owners, so we'll get a separate list of green Chevys owned by big blond guys.''

''Let's just hope the car's not stolen or registered to the guy's wife or brother or somebody like that,'' Goldman said.

Melissa could see that the killing of Deputy Kelso had made a bad situation even worse. It might have been the work of the Boogeyman and it might not, so they had to split their efforts, further tax their limited resources. Meanwhile, there were only three days left until a madman blew up her children.

The first thing Wilbur Tyler did after arriving at work that morning was to go into the church's kitchen and check the garbage can. It was one of those minor details, a task to be tended to before he became involved in other things and forgot to do it. He lifted the lid of the plastic container, finding it empty. Putting the cover back on, he went about his business. He'd report his findings to Reverend Maxwell when he saw him.

James Lawless steered his big white garbage truck along the narrow paved drive that took him to the rear of the church, where the garbage cans were located. It was a nice Thursday morning, sunny and kind of warm for November.

Swinging the truck around the corner of the building, he pulled up to the cans, set the brake, and climbed down from the cab, glancing around to see whether the Reverend Maxwell was about. Although Lawless didn't go to church, he liked Maxwell; the preacher always had a friendly word for him and sometimes a cup of coffee with some cookies.

This morning the reverend was nowhere to be seen, so Lawless grabbed the first of the four metal cans and emptied it into the back of the truck, keeping an eye on the stuff that came out. It was valuable sometimes. Soft-drink bottles that could be turned in for the deposit, stuff that could be repaired, things like that. Once he found a ten-dollar bill, which he assumed had come from the pocket of some discarded garment. In this can there was nothing but tin cans, milk cartons, and the like.

Forty-seven years old, Lawless was stocky and had a bit of a beer belly, which he truly acquired from drinking beer. It wasn't unusual for him to down a six-pack a night. Still, he wasn't too chubby, mainly because he got so much exercise on the job. As he liked to explain to his friends, lifting all those big metal cans kept him in shape, so he didn't get too fat from lifting all those little metal cans.

Having found nothing of interest in the first two garbage cans, he lifted the third up and tipped it into the back of the truck, shaking out its contents. As a lot of paper cups and fast-food stuff fell out, he thought he saw something, something dark, rectangular, but a bunch of papers came out, covering whatever he'd spotted.

Putting the can back, he shrugged. You kept the best watch on the stuff you could, and sometimes you were lucky. But one thing you didn't do was dig through the damned garbage once it was in the truck unless you were absolutely certain you'd seen something valuable. It was, well, a matter of dignity. You didn't have much on this job, but you did have a little.

He emptied the fourth can, finding one Coke bottle, then grabbed the lever that controlled the hydraulic packing mechanism. The motor revved as the newly acquired garbage was pushed tightly into the forward part of the compartment, joining the trash he'd picked up earlier.

A moment later he was on his way to the next stop.

B. B. McFarland sat in his office at the Ramsey County Sanitary Landfill reading a paperback he'd found in the dumping area. Actually that's what the so-called sanitary landfill was: a dump. And his office was an unpainted shack with a leaky roof. The paperback novel was boring, one of those ordinary life stories with no spies, no shootouts, and—worst of all—no sex. Tossing it aside, he decided he should have left it where he found it.

A skinny man, he was tall, with sunken cheeks, and he walked in a slouch. Some people called him Snake, which was okay with him. As far as B. B. was concerned, that was one of the biggest mistakes people made in life: letting things get to them. Shrugging things off made life much easier.

Hearing a truck engine, he stepped outside to see who was coming. A white garbage truck turned in through the gate, raising a cloud of dust as it made its way toward him. B. B. sniffed the air. The breeze was coming from the east, instead of blowing across the mounds of garbage as it usually did. But then he never noticed the smell anymore, not after working here for twelve years.

"Hi, B. B.," the driver said as the truck rolled to a stop. It was Jim Lawless, who drove for Colorado Refuse Removal. "Where ya want this stuff?"

"How about the front lawn at the White House?"

"Can't do it. Company's only licensed to operate in Ramsey County."

"In that case, you can put it right over there." He pointed at the spot he had in mind.

He watched to make sure the truck was headed for the right place, then went back inside and entered the arrival of one Colorado Refuse Removal truck in his log. The garbage collectors were charged for each load they dumped. B. B. had often wondered what he'd do if any of them offered him a bribe to forget to write down some of their trips here, but no one had ever approached him with such a proposal. Of course, if anyone was getting bribes, it would be someone down at the courthouse, some accountant who changed the entries made here at the dump.

Standing in the doorway, he watched Lawless dump his load. It was the last load that would fit in that spot. His eyes scanning the dump site, he tried to decide where to send the next truck. The dump was nothing more than a huge field in which a bulldozer was used to dig large pits into which refuse was dumped. When a pit was full, it was bulldozed over, and a new one was carved out. The trouble was, his bulldozer was in the county shop for repairs. If he didn't get it back soon, he'd have nowhere to put any more garbage. And the trucks would still come.

Oughta send 'em down to the courthouse and have 'em dump

right there, he thought. That'd get some action. Probably get me fired.

B. B. shrugged. There was nothing he could do about the situation, so there was no point in worrying about it. A few moments later he waved to Lawless as his truck rumbled out of the dump, stirring up more dust.

The Boogeyman sat at his kitchen table, his eyes fixed on the cup of cold coffee in front of him. He'd been awake since escaping from Kelso, afraid of the dreams he'd have. He didn't know whether the nightmares would involve the Horrible Thing or something else; he only knew the thought of dreaming terrified him.

It had all gone wrong last night. He'd very nearly been caught. Had Kelso not made the mistake of shoving him, he'd be in jail right now, where he would waste away, unable to fulfill his duties as the Boogeyman. He shuddered at the thought, for someone else would become the Boogeyman then; gone forever would be his chance to become a fully supernatural being.

And life as an ordinary mortal, the life he'd been forced to live for so many years, was unbearable.

He felt no remorse over killing Kelso, even though the man had been a fellow officer. Capture was unthinkable. It had to be avoided at all costs. And Kelso had been in the way.

He dismissed the matter from his thoughts. If one was to be the Boogeyman, one had to be willing to use people as necessary. To punish the woman sheriff, he planned not only to kill her children but to blow up everyone attending Sunday services at the church. Doing so would add to Melissa James's punishment, which was sufficient justification for the act.

He pushed the cup of cold coffee away from him. The time he'd been spotted in the car hadn't upset him nearly this much. Probably because he'd never come close to getting caught that night. He knew the area much better than Williams or Foster did, and he was a better driver than either of them. And unlike the Denver police force, which could concentrate a sizable number of units in an area very quickly, the Ramsey County Sheriff's Department had its officers spread out thinly and over a much larger area. It took time for them to converge.

That was what had saved him last night as well. Kelso had been forced to take him alone. Even so, the deputy had come close—oh, so close. Again the Boogeyman shuddered.

Forcing himself to think about something else, he considered what to do with his green car, which was still locked inside the storage facility. He could trade it in or sell it, he supposed. After mulling that over for a minute or so, he decided against it. By trading or selling the car, he would be associating himself with a late-model green Chevrolet sedan, information that would go into a computer, information that could be retrieved from the computer. Although the Department of Motor Vehicles had him listed as the owner of the car right now, it had him listed as the owner of a brown Chevy, its color before he'd had it painted.

And then he knew what he would do. He'd have the car painted brown again and sell it. No one would ever know it had been the infamous green car used by the Boogeyman. Suddenly feeling better, he chuckled. Things were going to be all right.

He'd been foolish to use the car as long as he had, he supposed. He knew some girl had taken a picture from which Castle had been able to learn the number of the stolen plate. And daily at briefings he and the other officers on his shift were reminded about the green car, the importance of spotting it. He'd continued using it, he supposed, because it was part of his trademark, like the purple crayon. It was a matter of style.

Getting up from the table, he dumped the cold coffee in the sink and refilled the cup from the coffeepot on the stove. As he stood there sipping the hot liquid, he wondered what he was going to do about Lois Cox and her daughter. He considered it unlikely that Castle would put a watch on the Cox house. Still, he might. And the lieutenant *had* ordered a watch on Sergeant Nelson's house, which might mean he had some reason to suspect a deputy. It would not be a good idea for him to be found anywhere near the Cox place.

And yet the Cox woman and her daughter had to be punished. Could he wait for the mother to pick up the girl at the day-care center, follow them, perhaps run them off the road? Possibly. But here too it was a matter of style. It simply wasn't the way the Boogeyman did things.

Perhaps the best thing to do would be to wait, to find some

others who needed punishing, then take care of the Coxes later, after the attention of the authorities had been diverted elsewhere. He chuckled. It always struck him as funny when he thought of the authorities like that. After all, he *was* the authorities.

He'd be glad to get to work today, so he could find out what was happening. The radio news had quoted Castle as saying it hadn't been determined yet whether the blond man who killed the deputy was the Boogeyman. But the reporters only knew what Castle told them, and Castle never revealed everything he knew.

I'm famous, he thought. I'm constantly on the front pages of the papers, on the local TV news, even on the national news. Then he laughed. Of course he was famous. Everybody had heard of the Boogeyman.

Melissa watched Roger Goldman as he drove his unmarked car along the two-lane road, passing homes and small businesses. The heavyset detective had said almost nothing since they left the courthouse, his opinion of her apparently unchanged since their first meeting. Melissa recalled the bodies of the Evans children on the kitchen floor. And she recalled the contemptuous look Goldman had given her.

Today Goldman was merely being aloof; he hadn't been openly hostile to her. But then who would pick on a mother whose children had been kidnapped by a crazed killer?

It was late afternoon. Melissa had spent the morning with Brown, checking out blond men who owned green Chevrolets. The list supplied by the Department of Motor Vehicles showed 175 sedans the right year, model, and color. Ten were registered to blond men in the right age group. So far they'd failed to turn up anyone who was unable to account for his time during all three of the mass killings they were certain were the work of the Boogeyman.

It was time-consuming work. The men had to be located; then alibis had to be checked, rechecked. The effort was further complicated by the fact that only two of the blond male green-Chevy owners lived in Ramsey County. The others lived in Denver or its suburbs.

It was possible that none of the ten would turn out to be

suspects. What then? There simply wasn't time to check out the remaining 165 green Chevrolets. And if the car came from outside the metro Denver–Ramsey County area, it wouldn't even be on the Department of Motor Vehicles list.

Goldman signaled his intention, then swung the car into the left lane and passed a slow-moving pickup loaded with bales of hay. They were headed for a church the department had been unable to get permission to enter until now. It was owned by a fanatical TV preacher with a small but loyal audience. The man had at first refused to permit officers on the premises, saying the police were an arm of an establishment riddled with atheists and communist sympathizers. Then today, for reasons of his own, Reverend Francis T. Underhill relented.

"Kelso had three kids," Goldman said unexpectedly.

Melissa nodded. She knew. And she was glad it had been Captain Pruitt and not she who'd had the job of informing Kelso's wife. "Is anyone taking up a collection?"

"Yeah. Patrol division's handling it."

"Who do I see?"

"Sergeant Hillman."

The conversation died as quickly as it had begun. Ahead was a modern brick church set well back from the street, with a paved parking area. Goldman pulled into the lot.

The complex consisted of two buildings, the church and a flat-roofed one-story brick structure to its right. Metal lettering on the building's side said Christian Communications Center. Beside it, aimed heavenward, was an enormous satellite dish.

Getting out of the car, they walked to the church, finding the massive wood doors locked. They were about to head for the other building when one of the big doors suddenly opened.

"Can I help you?" Tall and slender, the man was middle-aged and had immaculately groomed dark hair with a touch of gray around the temples. He wore an expensive-looking brown suit with a carefully folded handkerchief protruding from the breast pocket.

"I'm Sheriff James, and this is Detective Goldman," Melissa said, flashing her ID. Goldman, who'd been reaching for his own ID, glanced at her.

"Oh, yes, Mrs. James. I'm Reverend Underhill, and I'm sorry

to hear what happened to your children. I've prayed for them."
He frowned, cocking his head. "I'm surprised you're not at
home, waiting for word." The preacher smiled at her, then
shifted his eyes to Goldman. "I understand you'd like to look
the place over."

"Uh, yes, sir," Goldman replied. "If you've been following
the news, you probably know that—"

"Yes," Underhill said, interrupting. "This killer has threatened
to blow up his hostages and some other people, too, on Sunday
morning. So, naturally, you suspect a church."

"That's right. We'd like to look the place over, if you don't
mind."

"Yes, of course."

As the preacher ushered them inside, Melissa was surprised to
find that she was clearly in a TV studio. There were only a few
pews, positioned so they wouldn't interfere with the TV cameras,
at least four of which stood idle in the back of the room, near the
enclosed director's area. Above her head was a mass of studio
lights.

"We do Sunday services from here," Underhill said. "Perhaps
you'd like tickets."

"Tickets?" Goldman said.

"We have to do it that way, or more people would show up
than we have seats for."

"Is there anywhere in here someone could hide?" Melissa
asked.

"Not in here," Underhill said. "It's one big room. That's all
there is."

"No cellars or attics or anything like that?"

"No. Just the director's booth over there."

"What about nooks and crannies where someone might hide
something?"

"Ah, you mean explosives. The only place I can think of
would be in the booth, inside the cabinets that house the
equipment."

"How about under the altar?" Goldman asked.

Underhill frowned. "There might be a way under there. I'm
not sure."

"How much trouble would it be to look inside the equipment you were talking about?" Melissa asked.

"I can get an engineer to remove the covers. It's easily done."

After an engineer had shown them the insides of the equipment in the director's booth, Goldman examined the altar, finding no way to get beneath it. Then they inspected the rest of the building. From the car Goldman got a pair of mirrors with metal rods attached to them, and they checked the bottoms of the pews, discovering nothing suspicious. And then Melissa spotted the small metal door in the wall, partially obscured by a camera that had been parked in front of it.

"What's that?" she asked, pointing at it.

Underhill and Goldman joined her. "Ah," the preacher said. "That goes to the tunnel. Well, it's not really a tunnel. It's more of a crawl space. The cables run through there to the next building. There's just barely enough room for a man to crawl through."

Melissa and Goldman exchanged glances, both of them knowing it would have to be checked. Melissa tried to recall how far away the other building was. Seventy-five feet? A hundred?

With a sigh, Goldman gathered up the mirrors they'd been using and took them to the car, returning a moment later with a flashlight.

"I'll do it," Melissa said.

Surprised, Goldman studied her a moment; then he shook his head. "I'll take care of it. It's my job."

"Mine, too," Melissa said, taking the flashlight. "Besides, I'm a lot skinnier than you are."

Goldman looked at her uncertainly, saying nothing.

Melissa grabbed the small metal handle and opened the door. Lying on the floor, she shined the light into the opening. Ahead was a very narrow tunnel, the floor of which was covered with thick TV cables. It sloped downward, then leveled out. Melissa crawled forward. After she'd gone ten feet or so into the tunnel, she heard the preacher say:

"How could you let her go in there like that, a woman?"

"She's the boss."

"Well, she has no business being in there. She should be making a home. That's God's way."

"The most important part of *her* home has been kidnapped by a psycho," Goldman said, the irritation in his voice obvious. "If it was your kids, wouldn't you want to do what you could to help get them back?"

Melissa was unable to make out the preacher's response.

"You okay?" Goldman called.

"Fine," Melissa yelled.

"We'll meet you on the other side."

"Okay."

She crawled forward, the cables hurting her knees. The tunnel was made of concrete. Barely wide enough for her, it would have been a tight squeeze for Goldman. There were no shelves or anything like that where a bomb could be hidden. But then this was hardly the place for one. Blowing up the tunnel would disrupt Reverend Underhill's television equipment, and that was about all.

And then she realized that it could be an ideal place for hiding hostages, if only it could be entered secretly. Was this what it was like for Billy and Sarah? Were they imprisoned in a place like this? For a moment she felt dizzy, and the tunnel seemed to be closing in on her. She crawled faster, her slacks filthy, the cables chafing her knees through the cloth.

When, sore and a little frightened, she reached the other end, Goldman reached in through the opening, pulling her out and helping her stand. She was a mess. The preacher eyed her disdainfully.

The Christian Communications Center was larger than it had seemed from the outside. Among other things, it had its own studio and cameras and director's booth, along with satellite transmission equipment, offices, and storerooms. It took them over an hour to search it. They found nothing suspicious.

Grubby from all the dust in their prison and so many days without bathing, Sarah and Billy sat at the table and ate their roast beef sandwiches. Sarah had asked the blond man to let them wash in the rest room, but he'd refused. She figured he didn't want them dirtying up the place because that would make it pretty obvious that someone had been there.

Another thing she wanted was a toothbrush. Her mouth felt as though it were filled with something foul. Every time she took a bite of her sandwich, she was sure some of the putrid stuff came off on the food. The thought nearly made her retch.

She and Billy had discussed attempting to escape and concluded it was impossible. They couldn't break away and run while the man was moving them between their passageway-prison and the kitchen, because the man was undoubtedly faster than they were. And then there were the chains, which had to be held in one hand to prevent them from catching on something.

They'd even considered trying to overpower the man, perhaps hit him with something and knock him out, but that notion was quickly dropped. First, the man was much stronger than they were. Second, they had nothing with which to hit him. And third, if they hit him and failed to knock him unconscious . . .

When they finished eating, Sarah automatically gathered up the trash, but the man stopped her from taking it to the garbage can.

"I'll take it with me," he said. "The can's still empty."

It made no difference to Sarah. The garbage can no longer offered any hope. Nothing did.

22

When Melissa arrived at the courthouse the next morning, Castle gave her a verbal report that contained nothing encouraging. The effort to check out blond men who owned green Chevrolet sedans had so far failed to produce any suspects. The calls from people claiming to have seen her children had pretty much stopped. All that had come in had been checked out, and all had proved to be worthless. The searches of churches and other places where people might congregate on a Sunday morning were winding down, in both Ramsey County and the metro area. Absolutely nothing suspicious had been found.

They were still unable to say with certainty whether the blond man who'd picked the locks at Lois Cox's house was the Boogeyman. The effort to link Cox with the Boogeyman's victims was continuing, but so far it had turned up no connections. Neither friends nor family nor neighbors had any idea why anyone would want to harm Lois Cox or her daughter.

Nor had the watch on Sergeant Nelson turned up anything. The fired deputy had left the house only twice, both times to go to a nearby liquor store.

After spending most of the day with Walczak confirming the alibis of two blond Chevy owners, Melissa got back to the courthouse about midafternoon. Putting her purse in the bottom drawer of her desk, she dialed Castle's extension and asked the detective to come to her office.

"Anything new?" she asked when the lieutenant stepped through the doorway.

He shook his head. "Nothing."

"I want to pick up Nelson for questioning."

Castle looked doubtful. He remained standing. "We can't arrest him, you know. We don't have anything on him."

"Can we ask him to come in voluntarily?"

"Yeah. But if he says no, there's nothing we can do about it."

"Let's ask him."

"Okay."

"You're not going to try to talk me out of it?"

"No. I personally think you're barking up the wrong tree, but I've been wrong before. And let's face it. We only have a day and a half left. We're down to the point where we have to try everything." He searched her face a moment, apparently concerned about what impact his words might have had on her. Then he left, saying he'd send someone to get Nelson right away.

A day and a half. In less than two hours, people all over the metro area would be leaving the places where they worked, heading home for the weekend. It was Friday. TGIF. And she wondered whether Sarah and Billy would see another Friday, enjoy another weekend. Melissa pushed the thought aside; tormenting herself would not help the children.

Have I done the right thing? she asked herself. Or should I have just left Nelson alone? She was an amateur, she knew, trying to do the best she could without messing things up or making a fool of herself. The decision to send someone for Nelson had been made; what was done was done. She waited.

Forty-five minutes later Nelson stepped into her office, accompanied by Castle.

"Mr. Nelson," she said, "thank you for coming in." And then she realized her error in addressing him as mister. It was a pointed reminder that he was no longer *Sergeant* Nelson.

Dressed in jeans and a wrinkled shirt, the blond man glared at her with bloodshot eyes. "How come you're having me watched?" he demanded.

"Watched?" Melissa said, caught off guard.

"Let's not play around, all right? I know just about all the guys in the department. I saw them out there. I recognized them."

Melissa wondered how well the officers on surveillance had tried to conceal themselves. Politely she asked: "Would you mind telling me what you were doing last Saturday night?"

"That's not what I came here to talk about. You're harassing me. You've got a personal vendetta going against me. I want the harassment stopped, or you'll be hearing from my lawyer."

"You should know that surveillance is one of the things police officers do. It doesn't require a warrant, and it's not harassment as long as the officers don't make a nuisance of themselves."

"It's harassment if it's unjustified," he said angrily.

"If you'd tell me what you did Saturday night, we could clear all this up right away."

Bunching his fists, Nelson stood there for a moment glaring at her; then he said: "Go to hell."

With that, he turned and strode from the room.

Looking at Castle, who'd stood off to the side during the confrontation, Melissa said: "I'm not saying he's the kidnapper, but he certainly hates me enough to want revenge." She shuddered. No one had ever stared at her with such loathing before.

"You're right," Castle said. "Do you want to continue the watch on him?"

"Until Sunday morning." After which it wouldn't matter. After which nothing would matter, unless they got some leads and got them quickly.

Castle hesitated, as if wanting to say something reassuring but unsure of what; then he left the office.

Looking out his living room window that night, Reverend Paul Maxwell watched until the last car had pulled away from the church, indicating that the Women's Charitable Aid Society meeting was over. Unlike the Scouts, this group didn't have its own key, which meant he had to lock up the building after everyone had gone. Slipping on his jacket, he picked up his flashlight and headed for the church.

After locking all the doors except the one he planned to leave through, the minister decided to check over the entire building, just in case a forgotten cigarette was smoldering somewhere. He checked the rooms upstairs, then moved to the ground floor, making his last stop the kitchen.

Snapping on the light, he spotted the damp rag hung over the sink's spout. The Women's Charitable Aid Society had used the kitchen for something. Having made sure the oven and stove were off, he stopped at the plastic garbage container and lifted its lid. Inside were numerous paper plates, along with plastic forks and some Styrofoam cups. The ladies had had coffee and cake.

He switched off the light and left the building.

Melissa slept poorly that night, tossing and turning, sometimes feeling so cold that she clung to Keith, as if trying to suck every last breath of warmth from his body. Occasionally a car would go by, its lights brightening the curtain and seeping in around its edges. Dogs barked now and then. Once or twice a door slammed. Time passed.

Rolling away from Keith, she stared at the ceiling. Morning would come and with it the knowledge that she had only twenty-four hours to locate her children. One day. One. The number hung there, somewhere in the shadows above her head, taunting her.

Shivering, she rolled over and grabbed Keith. He slipped his arms around her. She could feel his body heat. And yet she was so cold.

As he drove home from work about one A.M., the Boogeyman passed within three blocks of the house in which Lois Cox and her daughter lived. Although he knew for sure now that the place wasn't under surveillance, the neighbors and the Cox woman herself would be especially alert for a while. Two weeks, he decided. He would visit the Coxes again in two weeks.

And tomorrow he would go to the shopping center, sit, wait. And watch the people with children.

Ten-year-old Danny Simms and his eleven-year-old pal Corky Coogan walked along the dry creek bed, killing time, because they had no money, no plans, and because Saturday morning was no time to be home with your parents, who'd usually find things for you to do if they noticed you hanging around.

It was sunny now, but Danny could see the clouds building near the top of the mountains. And vaguely he thought he could smell that sweet odor in the air that usually accompanied rain. But then maybe it was just his imagination.

A thin boy, Danny had blue eyes and dark hair. His friend was blond and about the same height, but stockier.

"You want to go over to Timmy's and shoot some baskets?" Corky asked with no real enthusiasm.

"Naw. Besides, Timmy's dad doesn't like me very much."

"How do you know?"

"I can just tell, that's all."

They walked on in silence, following the creek bed. There were no houses in this area, only grass and weeds and brush, most of it brown this time of year.

"My dad says we might go to Disneyland next summer," Corky said, breaking the silence.

"Oh," Danny replied, trying not to let his jealousy show. Timmy had been to Disneyland, and so had Jerry. And Chuck. Everybody but him had been, and the only place he ever got to go was up to Idaho to visit his aunt and uncle.

"I want to take the boat ride through the jungle."

"Oh, really," Danny said, trying to sound uninterested.

"And Futureland."

"There's the dump," Danny said, changing the subject. Surrounded by a rusty barbed wire fence, it lay off to their left, piles and piles of what people threw away.

"Let's go take a look around," Corky said eagerly.

"In the dump?"

"Sure. There's all kinds of neat stuff in there."

"Like what?"

"Me and Ricky found a gun in there once."

"Bull."

"We did. It was an old one, with some of the parts missing. It wouldn't shoot or anything."

"Then how come you never showed it to me?"

"Ricky's got it."

While talking, they'd left the shallow creek bed, and now they were headed for the dump. Though neither of them had actually said so, the decision to explore the place had been made. They slipped through the fence, their small frames fitting easily between the rusty strands of wire.

"Phew!" Danny said.

"You'll get used to it. Most of the stuff people throw away isn't the smelly kind of garbage. It's more like trash—you know, old papers and stuff. And junk."

A road of sorts curved through the site. On each side of it were huge pits, both of which were completely filled with refuse. At the far edge of the pits, small mountains of dirt were piled.

"They use that dirt to cover the garbage after the pits get filled up," Corky said. "They're really full today. There wasn't nearly this much stuff when me and Ricky were here."

They were on the roadway now, the pits on each side of them. Corky was right; you did get used to the smell.

"Come on," Corky said, heading for the pit on their right. "We can't do anything from up here." He slid down the bank. Danny hesitated, then followed.

Danny found a small statue of a man holding a golf club. At first he was going to keep it for the clubhouse he planned to build, but then he changed his mind and abandoned it. Corky found a bicycle wheel with a few bent spokes. He carried it with him for a while, then gave it up in favor of a fifty-five-miles-an-hour speed limit sign riddled with bullet holes.

"This would look neat in my room," he said.

Twenty minutes later, with Corky still hanging on to his speed limit sign, they reached the end of the pit. Danny picked up a piece of pipe and began poking through the trash. Corky picked up a board and began doing the same thing.

Danny was getting bored. Most of the stuff here was bottles and cartons and papers, stuff that was completely useless. Jabbing his pipe into a pile of liquor bottles, he saw something scurry out from under a nearby cardboard box and disappear under a refrigerator. A rat, he presumed.

"Hey," Corky yelled, "Look what I found." He was about twenty feet away, holding up a small object.

"What is it?"

"A wallet."

"Any money in it?"

"Naw. Nobody'd throw away a wallet with money in it."

"So, what do you want with it?"

"It's a pretty neat wallet. And it's in good condition." Carrying both the billfold and the bullet-riddled sign, he joined Danny.

"Let me see," Danny said, taking the brown wallet. First he checked the hidden compartment to make sure Corky hadn't overlooked any money that might have been concealed there; then he looked at the identification card. It stated that the wallet belonged to William James and gave an address and phone number. Flipping through the plastic card holders, he found more things—library and school identification cards, pictures—things that wouldn't ordinarily be thrown away.

"You know anybody named William James?" Danny said.

"You mean the guy who used to own the wallet? No, I never heard of him. But I think there was a president named William James."

Danny handed back the billfold. The name sure sounded familiar. Maybe Corky was right; it was the name of a president.

They crossed to the pit on the other side of the road. A few minutes later, Danny saw the name James again. In a headline on a discarded newspaper:

MELISSA JAMES WINS SHERIFF'S RACE

And then he knew where he'd heard of William James. The sheriff's two children had been kidnapped. The boy was named Billy. Sure, the story was on the radio all the time. And on the TV news every night. He'd even tried to imagine himself in Billy's situation, wondering what he would do.

Quickly he explained all this to Corky; then the two boys dashed for Danny's house, which was closest, leaving the speed limit sign in the dump.

Melissa and Castle were in the lieutenant's office when Walczak hurried in looking excited. "Some boys have found a wallet with the name William James in it," he said.

Twenty minutes later, Melissa and Castle were at a home in a middle-class subdivision that lay partially in the City of Denver and partially in Ramsey County. She recognized her son's wallet the moment she saw it, and a few moments later, accompanied by the two boys, they were on their way to the dump.

When they arrived, they found a chain across the entrance, a sign attached to it saying: Closed.

"Show us where you found it," Castle said.

The four of them stepped over the chain; then the boys led them to the edge of a dumping pit. "Right there," Corky Coogan said, pointing.

"Yeah," agreed Danny Simms, "right there."

"It was right on top," Corky added.

They checked the shack near the entrance, finding no one, then returned to the car. Reaching in through the window, Castle grabbed the microphone.

"Three-oh-one to control."

"Go ahead, three-oh-one."

"Walczak should be in the detectives' office. Tell him to drop whatever he's doing and find out whether there's usually somebody on duty out here at the dump."

"Ten-four."

"And send me a couple of patrol officers."

"Ten-four."

He laid the microphone on the front seat. To Melissa he said: "We're going to have to go through that garbage."

She nodded, trying her best to keep from her consciousness the image of two small bodies being unearthed from the garbage.

To the boys, who stood beside the car looking important, Castle said: "I'll see that you get home as soon as I can. In the meantime I'd appreciate it if you stayed here by the car. And if you should hear any radio calls for three-oh-one or four-ninety-nine, that's us, so let us know, okay?"

The boys nodded. In the distance, thunder rumbled. A storm was building to the west.

Castle got a small shovel from the trunk of the car; then he and Melissa climbed into the pit. "We're looking for anything else that might belong to your children or anything that might tell us where this trash came from."

They picked through cans and bottles, eggshells, coffee grounds, and old newspapers. Discovering an envelope with an address on it, Melissa pocketed it. A moment or two later, she found another and compared them.

"These two addresses are at least fifteen blocks apart," she said.

"I'm not surprised," Castle said, tossing aside a crushed cardboard carton. "A garbage truck probably dumped this here. In a lot of places that don't have city garbage collection, the private collectors get assigned specific areas of the community. But here you can hire any collector you want, so a truck will make one stop, then drive a few blocks and make another. Before it's picked up enough garbage to need dumping, it's covered a lot of territory."

"That doesn't help us much."

"No. And neither does the fact that this is Saturday. Except for us, county government has come to a complete stop. It's going to be hard to find anyone who knows anything about the dump."

"Uh, ma'am . . . sir . . ." Danny Simms was standing at the edge of the pit, looking down at them. "They want to talk to one of you on the radio."

"I'll be right there," Castle said, scrambling up the bank. When he returned a few moments later, he said: "We may have had some luck, finally. Walczak has located the guy who works here. He's on his way.''

Her thoughts swirling, Melissa wondered whether the discovery of the wallet could somehow be the break that would enable them to locate the children. It was about noon; less than twenty four hours remained until . . . until the Boogeyman carried out his threat. And it *was* the Boogeyman, she was fairly certain. She was continuing the watch on Nelson merely as a precaution. But then, with the lives of her children at stake, any precautions were justified.

Two uniformed deputies showed up and joined in the effort to sort through the garbage. And then a tall thin man wearing a battered hat appeared at the edge of the pit.

"Hey," he called, "what'd ya want to see me about?"

"Are you the guy who works here?" Melissa asked.

"Yes, ma'am. Name's B. B. McFarland."

Melissa and Castle climbed out of the pit and introduced themselves. "Can you tell who was the last person to dump in this spot?" Melissa asked.

The man studied them a moment. "Why? One of them fellers at the courthouse been takin' bribes to change the dump log?"

"No," Melissa said. "Nothing like that."

"We found something here, and we're trying to figure out where it came from," Castle explained.

"Hmmm," McFarland said, nudging his hat a little farther back on his head. "Oh, sure, I remember now. It was Jim Lawless. Drives for Colorado Refuse Removal."

"What day would that have been?" Castle asked.

"Ummm . . . let's see. Day before yesterday. Thursday."

Pulling a notebook from his pocket, Castle wrote the information down, getting the man to repeat the name of the driver and the firm for which he worked.

"You're lucky there's anything there for you to find," McFarland said. "Bulldozer's been in the shop all week. Otherwise that whole pit would have been covered over."

"Do you know where we can find this Lawless?" Melissa asked.

"Don't know where he lives. I suppose they'd know over at

Colorado Refuse, though. Office is somewhere on Omaha Drive, I think.''

Leaving the patrol officers to continue sifting through the garbage, Melissa and Castle radioed in to get Walczak working on locating Jim Lawless, then drove the boys home, and headed for the courthouse. As soon as they stepped into Castle's office, Walczak joined them.

"There's no answer at the garbage company,'' he said. "City directory shows no Jim Lawlesses who are garbage men. I've already called all the Jim, James, and J. Lawlesses in the phone book. Two didn't answer, and all the rest say they're not garbage collectors and don't know any garbage collectors. One got downright nasty about it.''

"Who's in there with you?'' Castle asked.

"Just me. Hanson and Brown are checking out the alibis of blond guys who own green Chevrolets. Goldman's in the city, working with Denver PD. I think they're going to check Stapleton today.''

"The three of us will be enough,'' Castle said. "Check unlisted numbers for James Lawless while the sheriff and I start calling garbage companies. The competitors ought to know who runs Colorado Refuse.''

Moving into the room that served as the office for all the detectives except Castle, each of them sat down at one of the metal desks. Melissa was at Brown's, Castle just to her right in Hanson's spot.

"I'll take *A* through *M*,'' Melissa said, grabbing a phone book.

"Okay,'' the lieutenant replied, flipping open his own phone book.

At the first two numbers Melissa tried, no one answered. She dialed the third.

"Hello,'' a boy said.

"Is this Shreve's garbage service?''

"Yes. Just a minute, I'll get my dad.''

A few moments passed; then a man was on the line. "Yes?''

"This is the sheriff's office calling. We're trying to find out who owns the Colorado Refuse Removal company.''

"Colorado Refuse? Oh, that's Rosemary Copeland. It's a

small outfit about the size of mine. Strictly a family affair. Her and her daughter and her daughter's husband do most of the driving. I think they got one guy working for them.''

"Jim Lawless?"

"That sounds right, but I can't remember for sure."

"Do you know the names of the daughter and her husband?"

"Uh, yeah . . . let me think here a moment. Okay, I've got it now. Ryan. Mike and Karen Ryan."

"Do you know where they live?"

"The Ryans? No. But Rosemary Copeland lives at the address it gives for the office in the phone book."

Melissa ended the conversation and turned to Castle, who was concluding his own phone conversation. As soon as he hung up, she said: "I've got it." She gave him the names.

Castle checked the white pages. "Here it is. Mike and Karen Ryan. Lists both names, so it's got to be the right Ryan." He dialed, waited about a minute, then hung up. "No answer."

Walczak, who was at the desk in front of Castle's, swiveled his chair so he faced Melissa and the lieutenant. "Phone company doesn't have any James, Jim, or J. Lawlesses we didn't already know about. And the two who didn't answer still don't answer."

"Let's check the neighbors," Melissa said.

"Good idea," Castle said. Turning to Walczak, he asked: "What did the city directory show for the two you can't get hold of?"

"One's not listed, and the other's an independent trucker. Of course, that doesn't mean much. Trucker's rig could have been repossessed, and he took the best job he could find. Sometimes these listings are out of date before they go to the printer."

"I'll take the garbage companies if you'll take the two James Lawlesses," Castle said to Melissa.

"Okay by me," Melissa replied, grabbing her coat and purse, which she'd put on the desk behind her.

Walczak held up a sheet of paper. "Here's the addresses."

It was starting to rain when Melissa reached the first address. It was a small stucco home in a semirural area, a place where the lots were big enough for people to have a horse or a cow or chickens and where no zoning ordinances prohibited them from doing so. Pulling into the gravel drive, she climbed out of her car and hurried across a small weed-filled yard to the front door, big cold raindrops hitting her head and shoulders. She knocked and waited.

The afternoon sky was darkening. Directly overhead, lightning ripped across the sky, followed almost immediately by a thunderclap that shook the earth. The rain started falling more heavily, hissing as it came down. Melissa had waited long enough; James Lawless was not home. She hurried back to her car.

Lightning flashed again, more distant this time, and then the thunder rumbled. Melissa backed out of the Lawless driveway and drove the two hundred feet or so to the driveway of the next house. It was about the same size as the Lawless place, two bedrooms probably, and had beige wood siding. A middle-aged woman answered the door.

"I'm from the sheriff's office," Melissa said, flashing her ID.

Before Melissa could say anything further, the woman pushed the door open, saying: "My goodness, come in out of the rain. You'll get soaked."

Melissa stepped into a small living room that was inexpensively but comfortably furnished. Although her coat had a few wet spots, she'd managed to avoid getting drenched. She sat on the couch.

"I'm looking for your neighbor," she said. "Mr. Lawless."

"Jim? What do you want with him? And would you like some coffee or maybe some hot chocolate to warm you up?" The woman was tall with dark hair and a ruddy complexion.

"No, thank you. What does Mr. Lawless do for a living?"

The woman sat down a foot or two from Melissa on the couch. "He's a trucker. Drives an eighteen-wheeler."

"Has he ever worked as a garbage collector to your knowledge?"

"Jim? No. He hauls produce between here and California. That's why he's not home. He's on the road. And when he's on the road"—she looked at Melissa conspiratorially—"Christine is never home either, if you know what I mean."

"I take it Christine's his wife."

"Oh, yes. Maybe I shouldn't be blurting all this out like this, but . . ."

Melissa didn't hear any more of what the woman had to say. It had suddenly dawned on her that she was sitting here listening to gossip while her children were in the hands of the Boogeyman. And then she realized what she'd been doing. The gossip had offered escape, the chance to do something routine and pointless, the chance to lose herself in the story of the unfaithful Christine and forget for a precious few moments the horror of the present reality.

The afternoon's almost gone, she told herself. Time's running out. She stood up.

"Thank you," she said, cutting the woman off in midsentence. "You've been very helpful." The woman stared at her, looking surprised, as if unable to believe anyone would walk out on such a juicy tale.

Outside it was raining lightly, the sky still dark, thunder grumbling distantly. Starting her car, she grabbed the microphone.

"Four–ninety-nine to three-oh-one."

"Go ahead, four–ninety-nine," Castle said.

"I'm ten-eight from the ten-twenty on Barcelona Lane. Subject is negative." She was uncertain at what point she'd mastered the jargon of police communications; lately, whenever she used the radio, the words and numbers were just there, as if she'd always known them.

"The garbage company was negative too. There was a fence with a house, garbage trucks, and a very unfriendly German shepherd inside. Nearest house was half a mile away, and the people there didn't know anything. I'm en route to the Ryans' address."

Fifteen minutes later, driving in a downpour now, Melissa was in another neighborhood of small homes, trying to read the house numbers through the water flowing down the car's windows. Finally she spotted the one she sought, number 4473, a brick house whose walls had been painted light green.

She hesitated, reluctant to step out into the torrents of cold water. But then she could not help her children by sitting in the car. She opened the door.

Splashing through the water that flowed over the surface of the street, she hurried to the front door, ringing the bell and knocking.

There was no roof over the stoop; within moments she was drenched.

When she was certain no one was going to answer, Melissa ran almost blindly through the rain to the house on the right, grateful to discover that it did have a covered porch. It was a small frame house, painted a reddish brown. The door was opened almost as soon as she knocked.

"Yes?" The man was about fifty, with gray hair cut in a flattop. He eyed her curiously, obviously having no intention of suggesting that she come in and drip all over his floor.

Pulling her ID from her purse, she held it up. "I'm from the sheriff's office, and I'd like to ask you a few questions about—"

"Hey," the man said as he snapped his fingers, "I recognize you from TV. You're the woman sheriff, the one who . . ." He let the words trail off.

"The one whose children were kidnapped," Melissa said. She shivered. The rain was freezing.

The man seemed to be fumbling for words. Before he could speak, she said: "Your neighbor, James Lawless, do you know where he works?"

The man frowned. "Uh . . . oh, gosh, I've heard the name of the outfit, but I just can't remember it."

"What does Mr. Lawless do?"

"He drives a garbage truck."

Bingo, Melissa thought. But then she tried to quell her excitement. This was a lead, nothing more. Finding Lawless might not put them the least bit closer to finding her children.

No, she thought, I can't let myself believe that. I have to hope.

"Do you have any idea when he'll be home?" Melissa asked.

He snorted. "No telling."

"Do you have any idea where we could locate him?"

"Well, since this is Saturday, you might try every bar in Denver."

"This is important. It's urgent we find him as quickly as possible."

The man looked apologetic. "My wife and I don't drink, so I really can't give you the names of any of the places he goes, because I'm not familiar with any of them. All I know is that him and some of his pals usually go bowling on Saturday afternoons, and then they go drinking and womanizing. He might show up about two in the morning, or he might sleep over somewhere. You never know for sure.''

"Who does?"

He thought for a moment, then said: "I really don't know. I don't know the names of any of his friends, and he lives alone.''

Melissa handed him a damp card. "If Lawless shows up, please call us immediately."

"Okay, sure. Has he done anything—I mean worse than he usually does?"

"He's not in any trouble at all with the law. But it's urgent that we talk to him." She fixed her eyes on the man's. "Very urgent."

He nodded. "Unless he gets back after we're asleep, I'll sure call you. Uh, does this have anything to do with the murders— and the kidnapping?"

To further stress the importance of locating Lawless, she said: "He might be able to help us with that investigation, yes."

The man's eyes widened. "How could Lawless know anything about that?"

Without answering the man's question, Melissa thanked him for his help and dashed through the rain to her car. Shivering, she started the engine and switched on the heater. The windows had steamed up, making it impossible for her to see out of the car. She found some damp tissues in her purse and used them to wipe the windshield. Catching a glimpse of herself in the rearview mirror, she saw that her hair was plastered to her head, water dripping from the ends of the matted strands. She didn't care.

"Four-Adam," the dispatcher said over the radio.

"Go ahead," an officer replied.

"Ten-forty-four at Hepburn and Tinker." A minor accident, no injuries.

"Ten-four. En route."

"Three-oh-one to four-ninety-nine," Castle's voice said.

Melissa grabbed the mike. "Go ahead, three-oh-one."

"Neighbors say the Ryans have gone to Wyoming for the weekend, and the Copeland woman has gone with them. No one knows how to reach them, and they won't be back until

287

tomorrow evening. Apparently no one else knows anything about the operation of the company except your guy.''

Melissa told him that she'd found the right Jim Lawless and what she'd learned about him. ''I'm going to check the other neighbors now.''

''Ten-four,'' Castle replied tiredly.

''Any . . . any word from the dump?''

''Ten-four. They've knocked off out there. They didn't find anything else.''

Thank God, she thought. At least she would no longer have to block from her mind the image of two little bodies being discovered in the garbage. Her children hadn't been murdered and then . . . and then thrown away.

Resting her head on the steering wheel, she took a few moments to gather her strength, to let the warmth from the heater penetrate her wet clothing. Then she finished wiping the windshield, shifted the heater control to defrost to keep the glass clear, and drove the thirty feet or so to the next house. When she got out of the car, she left both the engine and heater running.

23

The Boogeyman drove his patrol car behind the mounds of sand and stopped, switching off the headlights. This was a favorite spot of his for hiding and waiting for speeders. The sand was piled here each fall by the highway department in preparation for dealing with the winter's icy roads. It was about ten o'clock. The rain had quit an hour ago.

A car went by, its tires throwing up a mist from the still-wet highway. He watched its taillights recede, unconcerned that it was going well over the speed limit, for he had not stopped here to watch for speeders. Switching on the interior light, he pulled a

---

piece of paper from the pocket of his uniform shirt. On it was a license number.

Picking up the microphone, he said: "One-Adam to control."

"Go ahead, one-Adam."

"I need a registration check on Colorado plate 817-CLC."

"Ten-four. Stand by."

Pulling out his pen and notebook, he waited. The dispatcher communicated with other units. There was a minor accident on Rocky Mountain Boulevard, a prowler in a residential area, vandalism at a school. Earlier he'd heard the radio traffic concerning the dump, and the transmissions between Castle and Melissa James. They'd mentioned garbage trucks and the names, Ryan, Copeland, and Lawless. Though none of it meant anything to him, he was certain it was about him. He was concerned, but it was a concern born of being uninformed. Things were happening and he didn't know what things.

No matter, he decided. He knew enough to be certain they weren't even close to catching him. And he would learn what the detectives and the woman sheriff were up to soon enough. If the powers that be didn't fill him in at the next briefing, the department's ever-active grapevine would do it for them.

"Control to one-Adam."

"Go ahead."

"Be advised that 817-CLC is registered to Edward or Michelle Bookman, 9908 Webster."

"Ten-four." Putting down the mike, he finished writing the address in his notebook. Tomorrow the city directory would have to phone the Bookmans.

Slipping the notebook and pen back into his pocket, he switched on the headlights and pulled onto the highway. In only a few hours he would be feeding his hostages for the last time. He wondered what to feed them for their last meal. And then he had it. Something kids liked nearly as much as ice cream.

Pleased with himself for having thought of it, he began humming a tune, his index finger lightly tapping the wheel in time with the rhythm.

Melissa sat at one of the metal desks in the detectives' office. Castle, Walczak, Brown, and Hanson occupied the others. Brown was dozing, his chin resting on his chest. Hanson and Walczak were nearly asleep. Goldman was parked at James Lawless's house, waiting. It was 12:10 A.M.

Time had all but run out. The group of tired officers in the room had done all they could do. They'd run down every lead, acted on every hunch, dug into every scrap of information that came their way. The leads had been too few, the hunches off the mark, the information wholly inadequate. They had tried their best. And they had failed.

No, Melissa thought, I can't accept that. There's still time. We may still find Lawless, and something he can tell us may be all we need.

Somewhere deep inside she knew that wasn't very likely, that if they did find Lawless, the most they could hope for was a lead that had to be laboriously tracked down. But she refused to listen to that part of her, for to do so would mean she'd given up on ever seeing Billy and Sarah again.

There's still time, she thought. There's still time.

Although Lawless's other neighbors had corroborated what the man next door had said, none of them had known what places he frequented or who his friends were. Melissa and the tired men in the room with her had spent hours calling the lounges listed in the Denver yellow pages. At none of them had anyone known Jim Lawless, nor had Jim Lawless responded at any of the places he'd been paged.

All the blond Chevy owners had been checked out, and all had been rejected as suspects. With the help of the Denver police and other area law enforcement agencies, the places people congregated on Sunday mornings had been checked out—throughout the metro area and all of Ramsey County.

And now everything had stopped. Most of the county was asleep by now. The world went about its business, unconcerned about the problems of Melissa James.

Looking at Castle, who was sitting at the desk next to hers, Melissa said: "Do you plan to be up all night?"

He nodded.

"Then why don't we send the rest of these guys home so they can get some sleep. We're likely to need some people here in the morning who are at least halfway fresh."

"You're right. They're just sitting here accomplishing nothing. They might as well be in bed. We can always get them at home if we need them. And for backup, there's plenty of patrol units out there."

He stood up. "Hey, everybody, wake up." Walczak and Hanson looked up expectantly; Brown continued to doze. "The sheriff and I will stay here. The rest of you go home and sack out for a few hours."

The two awake detectives eyed him uncertainly, then exchanged glances.

"Go on," Castle said. "You're not doing any good here."

Walczak said: "I'm not sleepy, Lieutenant."

"That's not how you look to me."

"I'll be okay."

"Then go relieve Goldman at the Lawless house. He was walking in his sleep the last time I saw him."

Walczak nodded and left. Hanson woke Brown, and the two of them rose. "If there's anything we can do to help, we'll stay," Hanson said.

Castle shook his head. "Try to get here by seven. I don't know what's going to happen in the morning, but we better be ready for it."

As the two men left, Brown stopped and looked at Melissa as though he were about to say something. Then, apparently unable to find the right words, he said: "Good night, Sheriff." Turning to Castle, he added: "Good night, Lieutenant."

And then Melissa and Castle had the office to themselves. She stared across the room for a few moments, then let her eyes drop to her wrinkled slacks. She was a mess. Her clothes, which had dried on her body, were still damp in places, and her hair was a matted mass of tangles. She considered going to the women's room and combing it out, then dropped the idea. The state of her hair was unimportant.

Picking up the phone, she dialed her home number. Keith answered on the first ring.

"Hi," she said, "it's me."

"Hi. What's the latest?"

"Nothing's changed. We're still waiting for the garbage man, who still hasn't come home." This was the third time she'd called him tonight. Having nothing to do but wait and worry, he appreciated hearing from her, even when she had nothing new to report.

"Maybe he'll show up soon," Keith said.

It sounded so pointless: waiting for a garbage collector who might not come home and who would undoubtedly be bombed out of his mind if he did.

"Lieutenant Castle and I are going to be here all night," she said.

"Would it help to know someone out there loves you very much?"

Had Keith actually said he loved her before this? Her thoughts were so scrambled she was unable to remember. "It would help," she said.

"Well, someone does," he replied. "Very much."

"Thanks." A tear trickled down her cheek.

For the second night in a row, it was after one A.M. when the Boogeyman finally got off work. Just before shift change, he'd answered a call on an attempted break-in at a small sporting goods shop. Even though entry hadn't been gained, the owner had come down to make sure, and then there was the report to be filled out.

The streets were deserted as he walked toward the lot where all but high-ranking county employees left their cars. He stepped over a puddle in the sidewalk. The rain had left the air more humid than usual. The clean, fresh odor that always accompanied a storm was gone now, replaced by ordinary dampness.

In the parking lot he made his way around more puddles, then unlocked his car and slipped behind the wheel. Tired, he didn't feel like going home and changing out of his uniform before feeding his hostages. Besides, what did it matter if they saw him in uniform? They would certainly never tell anyone, because tomorrow morning they would be dead.

He needed to maintain recognition, of course, but he had everything he needed for that in the trunk. So all he had to do was stop by and pick up the special treat he'd planned for the children's last meal.

He started the engine.

THE BOOGEYMAN

*   *   *

Sitting by the window, with the lights out, Reverend Paul Maxwell watched the church. This morning—yesterday morning now—when Wilbur Tyler had checked the kitchen garbage can, he'd found Styrofoam burger containers and other fast-food leavings atop the paper plates left by the Women's Charitable Aid Society. Somehow overnight the burger containers had appeared in the garbage, which had been locked inside the building. Since he didn't believe in magic, there was only one logical explanation: Someone had put them there.

And yet that seemed impossible, for no one was hiding in the church, and no one had broken in. And the police had searched the place, finding nothing suspicious.

Feeling sleepy, the minister rubbed his eyes. If someone was somehow getting into the church at night, why was he doing it? Just to eat some fast food and leave? It made absolutely no sense. He'd again considered calling the sheriff's office and decided against it. What would he say, that he was reporting some hamburger containers in his garbage?

Yawning, he wondered whether this could be some kind of prank. The fast-food phantom or something like that. Unlikely, he decided. The stuff in the trash could have too easily gone unnoticed. A prankster would want to make sure his work was discovered.

Maxwell's mind wandered then, recalling an old theology professor of his, a woman he'd nearly married, his thoughts lazily flitting here and there through his memory, stopping wherever they wished. Abruptly, a falling sensation urgently imposed itself on his consciousness, and he woke just in time to keep himself from slipping off the chair.

Shaking his head to clear it, he peered through the window. The night was black, without moon or stars, and he saw nothing but shadows. The church was a big ill-defined patch of black. Realizing he was just going to fall asleep again if he stayed here, the minister decided to give up his vigil and go to bed. And then one of the shadows moved.

Peering into the darkness, he tried to determine whether his sleepy brain had simply imagined it. The shadows all seemed quite stationary at the moment. After watching a few more minutes and seeing nothing, he decided to go over and check out the church. After which he would go to bed, leaving the fast-food phantom—if there was such a thing—to fend for itself. Slipping on his jacket, he grabbed his flashlight.

He circled the church, finding no one on the grounds, the doors securely locked. At the side entrance to the part of the building in which services were held, the minister took out his keys and let himself in, flipping on the lights. As he closed the door behind him, something slowly registered on his senses. An odor. As if someone had walked through the room just moments ago carrying a steaming plate of spaghetti and meatballs.

Walczak stared gloomily at the dark house in which James Lawless lived. Parked across the street, he had so far managed to stay awake, although he was uncertain how much longer he was going to be able to hold out. At least he was in better shape than Goldman had been. And he simply couldn't bear going home, not with the sheriff's kids in jeopardy and with time running out. It was a matter of . . . well, dedication. You just didn't quit when the scuzz-bags had attacked a cop's family.

His wife would have her standard lecture ready: that he was supposed to be dedicated to her and the kids, too, not just the job. But then she didn't understand. When you worked in a life-and-death kind of job, it wasn't so easy to walk away from it just because you got a little time off now and then.

Shifting his thoughts to the new sheriff, he wondered how all this was affecting the way she was regarded within the department. It was hard to say, because all the people who were against her were keeping quiet right now. His own opinion was that she'd made tremendous progress in the short time she'd been in office. She seemed levelheaded and willing to listen and learn. She demanded respect when she thought she deserved it, but without losing sight of the fact that she was greener than the greenest rookie. And unlike her predecessor, she was honest.

He wouldn't be too thrilled with the prospect of having her for backup in a hairy situation, but it wasn't because she was a woman. He thought he'd trust Marla Clark in such a situation. The difference was Clark had been trained to handle it. Still, the sheriff and the officer on the street had different kinds of jobs. As a sheriff, Melissa James had possibilities.

He realized, too, that if the Boogeyman killed her kids, it could destroy her.

Walczak was instantly alert as headlights appeared at the end of the block. He watched anxiously as an old sedan rattled down the street. And then it stopped in front of Lawless's house, and a single figure climbed out.

As the car drove away, Walczak was hurrying across the street toward the solitary figure that had emerged from the sedan. The detective saw that it was a man who was moving unsteadily.

"Hey, you James Lawless?"

The man turned. "W-what ya want with him?"

"I'm Detective Walczak, Ramsey County Sheriff's Department. If you're James Lawless, we need your help."

"That's me," the man said drunkenly. He was in his mid or late forties, short, somewhat chubby. Walczak put his hands on Lawless's shoulders, steadying him.

"I need to know about your garbage route on Thursdays. Are there any places on your route where people might get together on Sunday mornings?"

"Why you wanna know that?"

"We found something at the dump, something that came from your truck."

"On top of the pile?"

Christ, Walczak thought, wanting to shake the man. "Look, it doesn't matter where it was in the pile, okay? I need to know—"

"Hey," Lawless said, making a feeble gesture with his hand, "it does, too, matter where it was in the pile."

"Okay okay It was right on top."

"That means it was from one of my first stops. See, it comes out of the truck the opposite way from . . . uh, from how it goes in."

"Okay, what were your first stops on Thursday?"

"Uh, let's see. I did a few houses in Mountain View Estates. Then . . . uh . . . then . . ."

"You went to Mountain View Estates, then where?"

"Oh, uh, let's see . . . the next stop's a church, then some more houses—"

"What church?"

Lawless grunted.

"Damn you," Walczak said, shaking the man, "don't you dare pass out on me now. What church?"

"I don't know the name."

"Where is it?"

"Can't remember. Wanna go sleep."

"Hey! No sleep until you tell me where the church is!"

"Okay. It's on Grover Valley Street. Nine-hundred block. You seen my car?"

Leaving Lawless to fend for himself, Walczak rushed to his car and grabbed the microphone.

Sarah had been stunned when she'd seen the blond man in a deputy sheriff's uniform. As she sat beside her brother at the kitchen table, with the man sitting across from them, she decided there were only two possibilities. Either he was really a deputy, or he was pretending to be one for some reason. She thought he was probably a real deputy, because he looked comfortable in the well-fitting uniform and because of what he'd said about doing this to punish her mother.

"If you're wondering why we haven't eaten yet," the man said, "it's because I brought you a surprise for dinner. It got cold on the way here, so it's in the oven, warming up." He smiled.

Sarah was fairly certain she knew what the surprise was because she could smell its aroma coming from the oven. She tried to keep her expression neutral. Although this man could keep her physically imprisoned here, her thoughts were her own, never to be shared with him.

"I think it's about ready," he said, getting up. He got a rag from under the sink and, using it as a potholder, removed a large pizza from the oven.

"There," he said, laying it on the table. "How does that look?"

Although it looked delicious, Sarah kept her expression blank. From the corner of her eye, she could see that Billy was doing the same.

"Dig in," the man said, taking a piece.

The children waited long enough to be sure they revealed no enthusiasm, then helped themselves. The pizza, Sarah discovered, was indeed delicious. Pepperoni with mushrooms.

Avoiding their captor's eyes, she studied his uniform, suddenly realizing that she could see part of his name tag. The man's jacket was unzipped partway, revealing about half the tag, but his tie covered the first couple of letters. In the exposed space, two letters were visible: an *N* and part of an *O*. Searching her memory for names with *NO* in them, she came up with Nolan, Jeno, Totino, Reno . . . and then she stopped because two of the names were brands of pizza and another was a city. Besides, none of them had the two letters in the middle. Afraid the man would catch her staring at the tag, Sarah looked away.

As she opened her mouth to take another bite of pizza, the door opened, and a man stepped into the room. He was husky, maybe thirty-five, with light-brown hair. Sarah stared at him, and the man stared back, equally confused.

"What's going on here?" he asked.

Instantly the blond man sprang up, grabbing the stranger, who found himself pushed back against the counter. But the stranger recovered, and both men were struggling for the advantage, neither able to attain it. Somewhere inside Sarah, a voice was telling her that she wasn't chained, that she should run, get help. But she was unable to take her eyes off the battle going on before her.

What can I do? Sarah wondered desperately. How can I help. Her eyes darted around the room, searching for some sort of weapon. A knife. Maybe she could find one in a drawer and . . . and what? She didn't know how to stab anyone; she didn't think she *could* stab anyone, even him.

Suddenly the stranger wrapped his arms around the blond man and carried him across the room, slamming him against the refrigerator.

"Run!" the stranger shouted, glancing at Sarah and Billy.

Sarah sprang up, then hesitated. Could she abandon Billy, who was chained to the table? Still grappling with each other, the two men crashed into the garbage can, overturning it.

"Run!" the stranger yelled. "Get help! Hurry!"

Billy pushed her. "Go on, Sarah! Go on!"

Sarah ran. Uncertain where she was going, she rushed from

the room, passing through a couple of doorways, her chain whipping along behind her, and suddenly she was in the church part of the building. From behind her came the sounds of the fight, heavy crashing sounds. She dashed down the aisle to the main entrance of the church, grabbed the knob and twisted it, pushing against the door with all her weight. It wouldn't open.

Billy screamed.

"I'll kill him," the blond man yelled. "If you're not back here by the time I count ten, your brother'll be dead." Again Billy screamed.

Sarah stood by the door, desperately trying to decide what to do. The man and Billy were still in the kitchen. She had time to figure out the locks on the door. She could be on her way. Free. Able to get help.

"One," the man called.

Trembling, Sarah stood there, having no idea what she should do. Then Billy screamed in pain again, and that settled it. She couldn't let the man hurt her brother.

"I'm coming!" she yelled.

Dragging her chain behind her, she returned to the kitchen, where she found the blond man standing next to the table with Billy, holding the boy's arm behind his back. Billy's eyes found hers; they were filled with confusion and hurt and fear. The man who'd tried to rescue them lay on the floor, apparently dead. Blood was smeared on the floor tiles near his head. The kidnapper had stepped in it, his soles leaving a zigzag pattern on the floor, like tire treads.

The blond man seemed unhurt. He unchained Billy from the table. "Let's go," he said. "Back upstairs."

As the children moved toward the secret entrance to their prison carrying their chains, tears were streaming down Billy's face. Sarah felt too thoroughly defeated to cry, too numb to work up any tears. And she wondered who the man had been, the stranger who'd died because he tried to rescue them.

And then Sarah did cry. She cried for the man whose lifeless form lay on the blood-smeared floor tiles in the kitchen.

24

Angry because of the way the girl had repaid his kindness, the Boogeyman handled the children roughly as he chained them to the pipe. Then, leaning over the girl, shining the flashlight in her face, he felt the urge to hurt her. Night after night he'd come here with food just so the children wouldn't suffer unnecessarily. And then, while he was battling with the big man who'd walked in on them, she'd betrayed him.

Slowly the urge to hurt her faded. The children would die in a few hours anyway. Beating the girl would serve no purpose. Abruptly he turned and made his way out of the crawl space. Climbing down the ladder, he slid open the wall panel, closed it behind him, and headed for the kitchen. He would have to put the man's body somewhere it wouldn't be found until after Sunday services, and then he'd have to straighten things up, wash the blood off the floor.

It had occurred to him that the man he'd slain might be the minister. If so, there would be no services. No matter, he decided. The children would die right on schedule. And their death was the most important part of the woman sheriff's punishment.

Stepping into the kitchen, he froze, his eyes scanning the room. The man was gone. His hand dropped to his service revolver, his first thought that the man might be waiting somewhere in the room, ready to jump him. But then he realized that there was nowhere in the kitchen to hide. The man was on his way to get help.

Should he try to catch him? The man had hit his head on the counter, hit it hard; he might not have gotten far. No, the Boogeyman decided. The most important thing was to be absolutely certain that Melissa James received her punishment. First

299

he would see to that; then he could search for the man. He raced toward the part of the church in which services were held.

Reaching the panel, he slid it open and hurriedly climbed the ladder. The children looked up, surprised, as he entered the crawl space and then stepped over them, quickly making his way to the cardboard box at the end of the passageway. Shining his flashlight into it, he reset the timer. It would go off in half an hour. This time when he stepped over the children, they had fear on their faces. They knew something was about to happen.

The Boogeyman hurried down the ladder. If the man who'd interfered had been unable to get far enough to summon help, he could still be dealt with. The timer could be reset for tomorrow morning. If the man had made it to the phone, the police would come, but they would not find the children. Not in time.

Dazed, Reverend Maxwell staggered away from the church, uncertain where he was heading. The children had been inside, the kidnapped children, held captive by a deputy sheriff. His mind reeled; none of it made sense.

The rectory. He had to get to the rectory, call for help. Which way was it? Was he going in the right direction? And then he realized he was walking into the vacant lot that abutted the church property.

The minister stopped, tried to get his bearings. To his left the church door opened, and a flashlight appeared.

Castle drove, the light atop his car bathing the tree trunks and buildings in flashes of red. Despite her mounting excitement, Melissa tried to keep her hopes in check. The church was one of the first stops on a garbage run, nothing more. The wallet hadn't necessarily been picked up there; they were merely guessing that it had. The place had already been checked and crossed off the list.

For backup, they had a patrol unit on the way. Walczak was still with Lawless, trying to pin him down concerning his other stops that Thursday morning, just in case the church proved to be a waste of time.

"There it is," Castle said. Ahead was a two-story brick church.

Melissa picked up the microphone. "Four–ninety-nine to two-Adam."

"Go ahead, four–ninety-nine." Marla Clark's voice.

"We're at the church. What's your ten-twenty?"

"Three blocks away."

Castle steered the car into a narrow drive, coming to a stop a moment later behind the church.

"We'll be out behind the building," Melissa said over the radio.

"Ten-four," Marla Clark answered.

"Look," Castle said. "The back door's wide open."

Melissa relayed that information to Marla Clark; then she and Castle climbed out of the car.

The Boogeyman ducked behind a tree when he saw the police car arrive. From his hiding place, he watched Lieutenant Castle and the woman sheriff hurry into the building. As soon as they were out of sight, he headed into the vacant land that lay between him and his car. It was time to get away from here as quickly as possible.

Although most of the ground here was firm, he stepped into a puddle, the muck at its bottom sucking at his shoe. He'd gotten no mud at all on his feet crossing this stretch of land earlier.

Ahead was the street on which his car was parked. He had to get to it quickly, before any more units arrived. It was obvious that the big man had made it to a phone. Every available deputy was probably on the way here to help rescue the sheriff's kids. Not that it would do them any good. In less than thirty minutes the children, along with anyone else in the church, would be dead.

And then, ahead of him, he saw a flashing red light. He would have to abandon the car. They might be waiting for him there. What to do? Which way to go? And then he had the answer. He began moving in another direction.

In the kitchen Melissa and Castle found blood on the floor, an overturned garbage can, a partially eaten pizza. Questions swirled in Melissa's brain. Who had been eating pizza? Who had been injured? Could her children have been here . . . or still be here?

Her hand on her service revolver, Marla Clark stepped into the kitchen. "What happened?" she asked, her eyes sweeping the room.

"We don't know," Melissa said. Briefly she told the deputy about the wallet and what the garbage man had said to Walczak.

"Stay here," the lieutenant told Melissa. "Deputy Clark and I are going to check the rest of the building." When Melissa started to protest being left behind, Castle silenced her with a wave of his hand. "We don't know what might be waiting for us. Clark and I are armed, and we've been trained to handle these situations."

Melissa nodded. He was right. And she could hardly argue that he wanted her to stay here because she was a woman.

After Castle and Clark left the room, Melissa found her eyes drawn to the table. Noting the number of partially eaten pizza slices, she concluded that three people had eaten here. And that their meal had been interrupted. She shifted her gaze to the blood on the floor. Someone had walked through it, someone whose shoes left a zigzag pattern on the floor.

What had happened here? Could the three people at the table have been Sarah, Billy, and the kidnapper? Whose blood was on the floor? Horrifying possibilities churned in her mind. She saw Billy and Sarah lying on the floor, bleeding, the feet of the madman as he trod through her children's blood. She shivered.

When Castle and Clark returned, they reported finding nothing unusual in the rest of the building. The lieutenant studied the scene in the kitchen, his eyes shifting from the table to the bloodstains. To Marla Clark, Melissa said:

"I thought you were on day shift."

"Captain Pruitt transferred me to graveyard. He said he'd kept me on days for a while as a refresher to my training, but now I have to start where everybody else does."

And then Melissa recalled that Pruitt had informed her of his intentions concerning Clark. "How do you like it?"

Marla smiled. "I'm flexible."

"As we pulled in," Melissa said, "I noticed a small house, which I presume is the rectory. Why don't you go pound on the door and see if anyone's there." After the deputy had gone, Melissa turned to Castle. "What do you think happened here?"

"Three people were eating pizza, and someone interrupted

them. One of the four got hurt. There's no telling how seriously. That amount of blood could indicate anything from a cut finger to a fatal bullet wound. How do you see it?''

''Pretty much the way you do.''

Melissa noticed that two more deputies had drifted in. One was a tall man with dark hair, the other a big blond fellow. It was one of the weaknesses in the way the department operated. Whenever anything significant happened, officers who hadn't been dispatched to the scene showed up anyway, leaving their own districts unprotected. It was something she meant to crack down on when . . . when this was over.

She made a mental note of their names. The dark-haired officer was McKay, and the name tag of the big blond man identified him as Manolis.

Marla Clark returned, saying no one answered the door at the rectory.

''So where's the minister?'' Melissa asked, looking at Castle. ''You suppose it could be his blood on the floor?''

Castle frowned. ''I don't know.'' Using his pen to open the doors, he began looking into the cabinets above the counter.

Another officer had shown up. Bob Sanchez. She acknowledged him with a nod of her head. He responded with a boyish grin.

Having finished with the cabinets, Castle moved to the refrigerator. ''Everything in here's been knocked over,'' he said. ''Someone must have given it a pretty good shove.'' Closing the refrigerator door, he turned to face the assembled officers and said: ''Okay, let's search the grounds.''

''What are we looking for?'' Manolis asked.

''Whatever we find. A wallet belonging to the sheriff's son was discovered at the dump. It's possible that this is where the truck picked it up. We don't know where the minister who presumably lives in the rectory is. We don't know what happened to this room, except that someone got hurt here and some people ate some pizza here.''

As the deputies filed out of the kitchen, Melissa found herself staring at the bloody tracks on the floor. Suddenly she realized that the footprint at which she was looking was outlined in mud, not blood. Shifting her eyes to a bloody footprint, she saw that the two were identical, both having the same zigzag pattern. Her mind churning furiously, she began putting things together.

"Hold it!" she yelled. "Everybody back in here."

The deputies returned, eyeing her curiously. Picking out the blond man, Melissa shifted her gaze to his shoes, which weren't muddy. It can't be, she thought. He's the only one who's blond. It has to be him.

"Let me see the bottom of your feet," she said, pointing at Manolis.

Looking thoroughly confused, the blond deputy complied. His soles were smooth, without treads of any kind. Castle stood beside her, obviously bewildered. Her eyes scanned the feet of the other officers, suddenly freezing on a muddy pair of shoes. Traveling up the deputy's body, they stopped on his face. She was looking at Bob Sanchez.

Stunned, she simply stared at him for a moment. Then she said: "Lift your foot, so I can see the bottom."

He obeyed, revealing the zigzag pattern. Still somewhat dazed, Melissa pointed to the bloody tracks on the floor. "They match," she said softly.

Sanchez looked at his foot, the bloody tracks, then his foot again. His eyes met hers; he seemed puzzled. "It's a very common shoe. I bought it at a large shopping mall."

Of course, she thought. How could I have suspected Bob Sanchez, of all people? She glanced at Castle; he was frowning.

"You . . . you don't suspect me of anything, do you?" Sanchez asked, his voice filled with amazement.

The room was silent a moment, the deputies exchanging uncertain glances; then Manolis said: "Bob, how'd you get here, anyway?"

"What do you mean?" Sanchez asked.

"You got off about an hour ago. I was at the courthouse when you left."

"I've got a monitor in my personal car. I was in the area, so I thought I'd stop to see whether I could help."

"You didn't have one when I rode with you," Melissa said.

Sanchez shook his head. "This is ridiculous. I just bought it. Bearcat scanner. Just what is it you suspect, anyway?"

Melissa knew that everything Sanchez said made sense. And

yet she thought she'd spotted something in his eyes—or maybe just a hint of something. What was it? Guilt? Fear?

"Look," he said, "I'm not your kidnapper. As a matter of fact, it happened while I was at work. I'm off on Mondays and Tuesdays."

"You traded that weekend," Manolis said. "Garon took your shifts on both Friday and Saturday, and you promised to work two days for him that he could add to his vacation."

On Friday, Melissa realized, Sanchez had been out with her. Had she mentioned that she'd be going out again the next night? Or when Sanchez had driven Linda Sue home, had the babysitter told him that she'd be working at the James house again the next evening?

Having noticed a spot on Sanchez's pants, Melissa moved closer to him. Was it blood?

"Hey, come on," Sanchez said. "This is ridiculous. I'm not the Boogeyman. I'm not even blond."

"No one here has accused you of being the Boogeyman," Castle said. "You brought up that idea."

Instantly Sanchez lunged at Melissa, grabbing her and spinning her around. Holding her from behind, he pressed his service revolver into the side of her neck. Her brain trying desperately to grasp the situation, she found herself staring at the startled faces of the other officers as she was being slowly dragged from the room.

"We're going outside," Sanchez said. "If anyone comes out after us, I'll kill her."

And then she was outside, Sanchez still holding her from behind, the two of them moving backward away from the church. The surface beneath her feet changed from asphalt to earth. She passed bushes and scrub brush.

It can't be, Melissa thought. It can't be. At the same time, another part of her mind knew this man was insane. And that he was about to kill her.

And where were Sarah and Billy? Dead, their bodies buried here in this lot, their bodies beneath her feet? She stepped on a piece of discarded wood.

"Bob," she said weakly. "Bob . . . ." But she had nothing to say, no plea that could possibly do any good.

Confused images tumbled through her mind. She saw Billy riding his first tricycle, Sarah opening a Christmas present. And then she saw herself responding to Sanchez's kisses, so close, so very close to going to bed with him. The realization was shattering. She had very nearly slept with the man who'd killed twelve people and kidnapped her children.

No one had emerged through the back door of the church. But there were other doors. Castle and the other deputies had to be coming for her. They wouldn't let him kill her.

Abruptly she was thrown off-balance, and Sanchez released her. Someone had grabbed him, she realized suddenly. Two figures were struggling in the darkness, struggling for control of the gun. Her thoughts scrambled, she simply stood there, watching the contest, uncertain what to do.

"Run," an unfamiliar man's voice gasped. "I can't hold him much longer. Run!"

Her mind cleared then, and she realized that her rescuer was losing the contest, that any second now Sanchez would shoot him. The men fell, one of them groaning. They wrestled for a moment; then one of the figures got to his feet, stepping back and leveling the gun. It was Sanchez. His back was to her. Melissa took two quick steps forward, bringing up her foot as hard as she could. It caught Sanchez squarely in the crotch. The breath shot out of him, and he shuddered. Then he turned.

Driven by some instinct she didn't know she had, Melissa kicked him again in the same place. He gasped, hesitated, then took a wobbly step toward her. She didn't see the gun; apparently he'd dropped it. As Melissa prepared to kick him again, a hand shot out and threw her to the ground. Sanchez took another step toward her.

Feeling around for a weapon, her hand touched a piece of wood. Grabbing it, she tried to judge its weight and length. It felt like a two-by-four, old and splintered, two or three feet long. Some part of her was screaming for her to yell, to tell the others where she was, but if she tried it, she doubted she'd have enough strength left to swing the board. Sanchez reached for her. She scrambled away, got to her feet, then turned and raised the board. Instantly Sanchez lunged at her, and she brought the board down on his head, nearly losing her grip on it when it made contact. Sanchez fell at her feet.

Suddenly she was surrounded by deputies with flashlights. "Are you okay?" someone asked.

"Yes," she said, but she realized she was shaking.

And then she saw the man who'd tried to rescue her, a big man with a gash on the side of his head. Marla Clark was bending over him.

"I'm Paul Maxwell," he said. "I'm the minister here. After I hit my head on the counter, I came out here, and . . . .and I think I fainted."

"Hey, look what I found in a bush back there," Manolis said, holding up a blond wig. Melissa stared at it. The Boogeyman was Bob Sanchez in a blond wig. Her brain was unwilling to accept it.

Suddenly her mind cleared. McKay was checking over Sanchez. Melissa joined him.

"How is he?" she asked.

"He'll live."

And then she saw Sanchez's eyes. Watching her. Hating her. She squatted down beside him. "Where are my children?"

"What time is it?"

"You answer my question, and I'll answer yours," she said with a calmness she didn't feel. She wanted to strike him, beat the truth out of him.

"Have it—" He winced in pain. "Have it your way. In about fifteen minutes, the dynamite will go off. Bye-bye, church; bye-bye, kids. Ka-boom!"

"Where in the church? Where are they?" She grabbed Sanchez by the collar.

"You won't find them." He laughed. "You have to be punished."

"Where are they?" she demanded.

Suddenly tears were running down Sanchez's cheeks. "Oh, why did you kill Mommy? Oh, why, why, why? Mommy was so good." Then he emitted a piercing shriek that became a low wail and finally trailed off. "Daddy's the Boogeyman. Daddy had to punish Mommy." Abruptly Sanchez curled into the fetal position. Melissa stared at him, horrified. He began sucking his thumb.

Castle took her by the arm and helped her to her feet. "He's not going to tell us anything," he said.

"Sarah and Billy are inside somewhere," Melissa said. "He's set some explosives to go off in fifteen minutes."

"I heard." He turned to the minister, who was standing now. "Do you have any idea where they could be?"

"No," Maxwell replied. "There's simply nowhere inside the church to hide anyone."

"Manolis," Castle said, "you and McKay take Sanchez in. Clark, you come with us. Reverend, we're going to need your help, if you're up to it."

"I'm a little shaky," he said, joining them, "but I think I'll be all right." They started for the church.

"Do you think the children are really in there?" Melissa asked. "Sanchez could have been lying."

"They're in there," the minister said. "I saw them."

"Where?" Melissa asked urgently.

"In the kitchen. They were eating pizza. They had chains attached to their legs."

Melissa shuddered. "Were they all right?"

"They hadn't been harmed, as far as I could tell."

"Okay," Castle said when they reached the rear entrance to the church. "I want to do this room by room. Look for trapdoors. Knock on the walls and see if any of them sound hollow."

"You might need a flashlight," Clark said to Melissa. She stepped over to the nearest patrol car, grabbed one, and handed it to Melissa.

"Wait," Maxwell said. "Uh, I think I've got a set of plans for the building somewhere."

"Go get them," Castle said.

"And hurry," Melissa added, hearing the desperation in her voice. "Sanchez said we have fifteen minutes, but I think he was just guessing. It might be less."

As they entered the church, Melissa fought to control her panic. Running frantically through the building wouldn't help Billy and Sarah. We'll find them in time, she told herself, forcing herself to believe it. We will; we will.

Castle went upstairs while Melissa and Clark checked the

ground floor. They started with the kitchen, knocking on the walls, opening all the cabinets.

Melissa's thoughts churned. That Bob Sanchez could be the Boogeyman was almost inconceivable. As was what had just happened in the vacant lot. The image of her kicking the man, then felling him with a board seemed unreal. Bob Sanchez in a blond wig. Madness.

These things continued to bob on the surface of her consciousness as they left the kitchen and moved into a room that contained the heating and air-conditioning equipment. Melissa's eyes scanned the ceiling, the floor. She tapped the wall as she moved through the room. Ducts rose from the green metal box that was the heater and air conditioner, fanning out at the ceiling like tracks from a roundhouse. For just an instant, Melissa wondered whether her children could be inside the ducts, bound and gagged, maybe even drugged. But then she realized that was impossible. There was no way to get into them without taking them apart, and they clearly hadn't been disturbed in years.

"Hey, where are you?" Reverend Maxwell called.

"In here," Melissa said.

Sticking his head into the room, the minister said: "I found the plans. Let's go into the kitchen, so I can roll them out on the table."

Melissa and Clark followed him into the kitchen. A moment later, Castle showed up. As they gathered around the table, Melissa checked her watch.

"We've got about eight minutes," she said.

Castle flipped through the blueprints until he found one that showed a floor plan. "There's nothing here," he said. "Nowhere anyone could be hidden."

"The building was changed," Maxwell said. "The church ran low on money partway through the project."

Castle nodded. He flipped over the blueprint he'd been studying, glanced at the next one, then flipped it over as well.

"Wait," Clark said. "What was that?"

"It just shows plumbing and stuff like that."

"Turn back to it," she insisted.

Castle did so, and she studied the blueprint, frowning. "Here," she said, tapping the paper with her finger. "What's this?"

"Oh, Jesus," Castle said, and then Melissa saw it too. The blueprint showed a number of pipes running through a crawl space between the first and second floors.

"But where's the entrance?" Clark asked.

Castle checked the next blueprint, then the next, and the next. "Nothing here shows an entrance."

"Exactly where is this crawl space?" Melissa asked.

"In here," Castle replied and led them into the church part of the building. He pointed to the vents above the pews. "It's there somewhere. Runs across the room, from wall to wall."

They all stared at the ceiling. Castle said: "Come on, Reverend. Let's check upstairs. You two see what you can find here."

"Four minutes," Melissa said as the two men headed for the stairs.

She and Clark moved to opposite sides of the room and began tapping the recessed wooden panels that made up the wall. None emitted what Melissa considered to be a hollow sound.

"Hey, come here!" Clark said excitedly. "This one moved."

Melissa quickly joined her.

"Push here," Clark said, indicating a panel near the floor.

Putting down her flashlight, Melissa did so; the panel moved in about a sixteenth of an inch or so. She pushed again, harder, but the panel moved no farther than it had the first time. Clark joined her, both of them pushing as hard as they could, and still the panel moved inward only about a sixteenth of an inch.

"Maybe it's just loose," Clark said. "Maybe there's nothing back there."

"Oh, God," Melissa said, glancing at her watch. "Two minutes."

Again both of them put their weight against the panel, and this time it did move, but not in the direction they were pushing it.

"It slides!" Melissa said excitedly. "It doesn't swing; it slides."

Putting both hands against the panel, she slid it to the side, revealing an opening. Grabbing her flashlight, she slipped through the opening, her heart beating furiously. She switched on the light. A metal ladder led upward. To the crawl space. To her children. Behind her, Marla Clark was calling for Castle.

Frantically Melissa climbed the ladder. Partway up she felt faint. Using sheer willpower, she forced the lightheadedness away. She had to save her children. Nothing else mattered.

At the top of the ladder was a small door. She pushed it open, shining her light down a narrow passageway. And into the eyes of Billy and Sarah.

"Oh, thank God," she said. "Oh, thank God you're all right."

"Mommy?" Billy asked hesitantly.

Melissa hurried to them.

"Mommy, Mommy, Mommy!" Billy squealed, reaching for her.

Melissa resisted the impulse to grab them and hug them. There was no more time left. She had to get them out of here. And then she saw the chains. Dropping to her knees, she grabbed one of the chains and began pulling on it. Billy and Sarah were screaming, crying. No, Melissa thought. Stop. This isn't doing any good. Shining her light down the passageway, she saw the box.

The box with the electric wire dropping into it.

Oh, God, she thought, there's no more time, no more time. Suddenly there was more light in the crawl space, and then someone was on top of her, climbing over her, and she saw Castle moving toward the end of the passageway toward the box. Shining his light into it, he reached inside. For what seemed like an eternity, he stayed there, fiddling with the box. Finally he leaned back against the side of the crawl space.

"I've turned it off," he said.

"You're sure it's off?" Melissa asked.

"I'm sure. It's sitting on top of one hell of a lot of dynamite, too."

Melissa hugged Sarah, then Billy, then both of them together. Words were unnecessary. Just sitting here hugging, touching, being safe and together, that was enough. It only vaguely registered when Castle said: "There were thirteen seconds left on the timer."

EPILOGUE

Melissa and Keith sat on the couch in the living room watching the TV set, more because it was on than because they had any real interest in the program. He slipped his arm around her, and she rested her head against his shoulder.

"It's so nice, being here like this," she said, "with Billy and Sarah in the den, all of us here together, safe."

Keith responded by giving her a squeeze. It was Friday evening, nearly a week since the early-morning rescue of Billy and Sarah. The children seemed to have suffered no lasting effects from their ordeal. This being the week of the Thanksgiving holiday, they hadn't returned to school yet; that would come on Monday. Their pictures had been on the front pages of both Denver dailies, and they'd been on television. Billy relished their celebrity status; Sarah hated it. Given their personalities, the reactions were predictable.

Yesterday Keith had joined Melissa and the children for an old-fashioned family Thanksgiving dinner, with turkey and all the rest. It had been absolutely wonderful, especially when she realized how close they'd come to never having seen this Thanksgiving at all. To say they had a great deal to be thankful for was an understatement. She pictured Keith carving the turkey, the children handing him their plates . . . and then she pushed the image away, for it brought tears to her eyes.

In the back of her mind, she was already planning to make the forthcoming Christmas the biggest and best the children had ever experienced. Don't spoil them, she cautioned herself. But then, for a while at least, they deserved to be spoiled.

Sarah came in from the den, carrying a sheet of paper. "Mom," she said a little hesitantly.

"What?"

"Can I ask you something?"

"Sure."

"Why do you think he did it?"

This was what she'd told them to do, to talk about their ordeal, to ask questions, to get everything out in the open. "He's insane," Melissa answered. "He's—"

"You mean he's a psycho."

"Yes. He's sick, mentally sick."

"I understand that. But didn't he have reasons?"

Melissa nodded. "He did, but they wouldn't make sense to us."

"What makes a person get like that?"

They'd learned so much about Sanchez in the past few days. They knew about the storage facility where he kept the repainted green car, about the time he'd spent working for a locksmith in Albuquerque, about his horrible childhood. And there were other things that although Melissa had been unaware of them had been common knowledge within the department. Things like the failure of Sanchez's marriage, the death of the only child it had produced.

And there were things that might never be known, such as whether Sanchez had anything to do with the disappearance of Reverend Maxwell's caretaker, an old man named A. J. Sebastian.

Addressing herself to her daughter's question, Melissa said: "A lot of things made him that way, honey. I guess the biggest thing happened when he was a boy. His father killed his mother, and he found the body."

Sarah made a face. "How awful," she said. The girl considered this information a moment, looking puzzled. "You mean . . . you mean what he did wasn't his fault?"

Melissa hesitated. "Uh, whether he knew what he was doing was wrong hasn't been decided. That'll take a while. First there has to be a hearing to determine whether he's competent to stand trial."

It was clear from the expression on Sarah's face that Melissa hadn't really answered the question, but the girl didn't press for a better explanation. She held up the sheet of paper in her hand. On it was written one word in pencil: SANCHEZ.

"That night when he came in uniform, I could see part of his name tag," Sarah said. "I saw the *N* and part of the *C*. I thought the *C* was an *O*, and I kept trying to think of names with *NO* in them." She shrugged. "We never did recognize him with the wig on."

"I'm not surprised, since you only saw him once."

Sarah nodded. She started toward the den, then abruptly turned, hurried over to Keith, and kissed him on the cheek. "Thanks for taking such good care of my mom," she said, smiling at him.

Before Keith could respond, she disappeared into the hallway that led to the den. To Melissa, he said: "Do you think I've been accepted?"

"It looks that way."

"When everything has settled down and life is back to normal, I'm going to ask you to marry me, you know."

"I . . ." Surprised, pleased, and a little confused, Melissa took a moment to sort out her thoughts. "You realize, I hope, that I'm going to continue to be a full-time sheriff, not a housewife." He started to speak, and she held up a hand to silence him. "If I get things going the way I'd like down there, I might even run for reelection."

He kissed her cheek. "Good. My mother always wanted me to marry a sheriff."

She laughed. And then, suddenly certain she was doing the right thing, she said: "Well, when all this is over and things are back to normal, I'll probably accept."

They explored each other's eyes, putting off for just a second the embrace, the happiness, the tears of joy that accompanied such moments. And then, abruptly, their mood was shattered by the voice of a little boy.

"Hey, Keith!"

Keith rolled his eyes. "What?"

"When are we going to see the Broncos play?"

"Beats me."

"But . . . you promised. Remember?"

"Did I really promise?"

"Yes."

"Oh. Well, in that case . . ." Pulling two tickets from his shirt pocket, he handed them to Billy, whose eyes had widened.

"Oh, wow! The Broncos! November twenty-ninth. When's that?"

"Day after tomorrow."

He began jumping in joy. Melissa exchanged knowing glances with Keith. Although they were technically engaged, they'd have to wait a while before telling the children. Sarah came in to see what all the commotion was about.

About the Author

A former TV reporter and news director, B. W. Battin lives in Minnesota with his wife, Sandy. When not writing, he enjoys cooking ethnic foods—especially those of New Mexico, where he lived for many years.